DISCARDED

P9-AAY-970

BITTER TRAIL

AND

BARBED WIRE

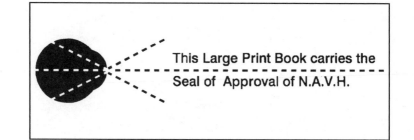

This Large Print Book carries the
Seal of Approval of N.A.V.H.

BITTER TRAIL

AND

BARBED WIRE

ELMER KELTON

THORNDIKE PRESS
A part of Gale, a Cengage Company

Farmington Hills, Mich • San Francisco • New York • Waterville, Maine
Meriden, Conn • Mason, Ohio • Chicago

LIBRARY OF CONGRESS CIP DATA ON FILE.
CATALOGUING IN PUBLICATION FOR THIS BOOK
IS AVAILABLE FROM THE LIBRARY OF CONGRESS

ISBN-13: 978-1-4328-5433-1 (hardcover)

Published in 2018 by arrangement with Macmillan Publishing Group, LLC/Tor/Forge

Printed in the United States of America
1 2 3 4 5 6 7 22 21 20 19 18

CONTENTS

■ ■ ■ ■

BITTER TRAIL

■ ■ ■ ■

1

The horse tracks appeared suddenly out of the chaparral, milled in brief disorder, then struck northward up the crooked wagon trail that snaked its dusty way through the mesquite and catclaw and prickly pear.

Coming upon the tracks, Frio Wheeler reined his horse to a quick stop. His hand dropped instinctively toward the stock of the saddlegun beneath his leg. He peered through narrowed eyes at the trail, which disappeared into the rippling late-summer heatwaves and hostile brush. He took off his flat-brimmed black hat to wipe dust-thickened perspiration onto his sleeve and turned to the Mexican who rode beside him.

"What do you make of it, Blas?"

Sombreroed Blas Talamantes turned in his big-horned Mexico saddle to look at the tracks as they led out of the mesquite. Sweat-soaked, his homemade cotton shirt clung to his back.

"Twelve, maybeso fifteen horses."

Frio Wheeler stepped from the saddle and squatted on the ground for a close look. He fingered the tracks. Not very old — an hour or two, maybe. Made since daylight, at least. "A few years ago, I'd've said Indians."

Blas Talamantes shook his head and pointed. "A piece of cigar, Frio, over there. Vaqueros, maybe?"

"Maybe cowboys. More likely renegades from across the Rio." Wheeler swung back onto his horse, took a grim look across the drought-stricken country, and brought the saddlegun up into his lap. "Best listen hard, Blas, and keep our eyes peeled. There's a war on."

This was the Rio Grande country of Texas in 1863, a small extension of the bloody conflict ablaze upon the battlefields of Virginia and Tennessee, upon the green rolling hills of Gettysburg. Here on the underbelly of the Confederacy lay the South's only open border, its only port free of the Union blockade. Along this thorn-studded trail to the Rio Grande, dust boiled high over trains of mule-drawn wagons and ox-drawn carts, carrying their heavy burden of Confederate cotton southward to be sold across the river in Mexico. Moving north, the same trains would carry war supplies for the Trans-Mississippi Department of the Confederacy — rifles, powder and bar lead, sulphur, mercury, and cloth.

At the end of this trail across the barren sands and the forbidding chaparral waited the twin cities of the Rio—Brownsville on the Texas bank, Matamoros on the Mexican. Once sleepy border towns, separated by the sluggish waters of the muddy Bravo, they had awakened to the rattle of sabers and the boom of cannon. They were swollen now and bustling with the international commerce of war. Gold coin clinked to the groan of wagon wheels, and tequila spilled in the streets.

Though this was a long way from Virginia, men rode with eyes open and their guns ready to use, for the hatreds of war had come to the Rio. By the hundreds, Texans with Union sympathies had fled southward across the river. Some had gone north by boat from Bagdad and other Mexican ports to join Lincoln's forces and wear the blue. Others remained in Mexico. Many of these waited impatiently in Matamoros, listening eagerly for war news, looking across the river with longing eyes at a homeland that now had become an enemy. Sometimes, in league with border bandits of either Anglo or Mexican blood, these men swam the river

11

at night to raid and burn in the name of the Union, then ride back to sanctuary across that narrow, muddy boundary. *Renegados,* the Confederate Texans called them, using the Mexican name. It was a time of indistinct loyalties and confused hatreds, when friends had become enemies and old enemies had somehow become friends — a mixed-up time when all the rules had been lost. . . .

Frio Wheeler touched big-roweled Mexican spurs to his sorrel's ribs and moved him into an easy trot. Wheeler sat upright in the saddle, shoulders squared with a pride born of his place and time. He was in his early thirties, though it would have been hard to guess his age from looking at him. He was a man seldom under roof. His skin was burned Mexican-brown from the scorching sun of Texas's ancient Camino Real, the Royal Road, and from wagon trails through the Wild Horse Desert and the chaparral. His brown hair, which needed a cutting, was beginning to show a glint of gray. Turkey tracks had bitten deep at the corners of his blue eyes, for he habitually squinted against the glare of the sun-drenched land.

Riding beside him, Blas Talamantes was the more spectacular. His high-peaked

Mexican sombrero was twice as wide as Wheeler's plain old black hat. His brown leather breeches were decorated with lacing laboriously sewn by a loving woman's nimble fingers. Wheeler had allowed his big spurs to darken with grime and tarnish, but Talamantes had kept his own polished to a bright silver. Both men rode with collars and sleeves buttoned against the sun.

There was much about them that was similar — size, build, and age. By a like token there was much that was different — their upbringing, their heritage of two cultures a world apart. To Wheeler, the first consideration always was to tend to the business at hand. To Blas, business was not unimportant, but a man should also seek out whatever beauty, love, and adventure the day might yield, for there might not be a tomorrow; and if there were no tomorrow, the business would have been of little import.

The two men had ridden together a long time now, and the things about them that were different had been put aside. Wheeler was *patrón,* and Talamantes was the man hired. But over and beyond that, they were *compadres,* so that it was not always apparent who was *patrón* and who was *empleado.*

Blas Talamantes had the better ears. "Frio,

13

I hear shooting."

Frio stopped and slowly turned his head, seeking the sound. It came to him on the hot breeze from uptrail.

"Renegados," he guessed, his mouth drawn tight. "They've hit some small outfit that's short of men."

"Maybe yours," said Blas.

They rode on with their rifles ready. The firing was nearer now, dropping down to a few sporadic shots and eventually stopping altogether. Presently they saw white smoke begin to spiral upward over the brush.

"Cotton smoke," Frio said. "I expect that's some CSA bales that'll never make it to Matamoros."

They heard hoofbeats drumming toward them. Frio jerked his head to one side, signaling Blas to pull out of the trail. "Two of us couldn't dent them much," he said, "but they could plow us under."

This was a hostile country where almost everything went armed for its own protection, whether it be plant life or animal. The thick mesquites and catclaws at trailside were white-flecked with cotton scraps that their tough thorns had ripped from bale-laden wagons. Frio and Blas sought a way through this brush and the thick growth of man-tall prickly pear. They dismounted, rifles in hand, and stood with fingers over their horses' nostrils. The sound of the hooves came louder, and Frio could glimpse a flash of movement.

Watching over a tall clump of pear, he saw the men pass by in a jog trot. He saw the black-clad Mexican in front, wearing a sombrero so wide that in the afternoon sun it cast a shadow to his waist. He saw the two Anglos who moved side by side, half a length behind the Mexican. Trailing these, a dozen more riders straggled along, all of them apparently Mexican. They led four strings of mules, these still wearing the harness with which they had drawn the cotton wagons. Trace chains rattled from the steady swing of their pace.

The men passed, but the gray dust still hovered a while behind them, drifting at last out into the heavy brush.

Frio Wheeler's eyes glowed with helpless anger. "My mules." He swung back into the saddle, Blas following suit. "Blas, did you see who was ridin' out in front?"

Blas nodded, his mouth grim. "Florencio Chapa! *Bandido muy malo,* with a heart like a grinder's stone." He paused, looking at the ground. "The gringos, you see who they are?"

Gringo could be a fighting word on the

15

border if used in the wrong tone. But there was no offense in the matter-of-fact way Blas said it.

Frio's jaw ridged with regret for what he had seen. He knew from Blas's eyes that the Mexican had known the men. "You mean Tom McCasland? Yes, I recognized him."

"He is your best friend, Frio. Or he *was*." The last came more like a question.

"War changes things, Blas."

"That other gringo, he is Bige Campsey. In the old days Tom McCasland would never ride with a man like Campsey."

Frio shook his head. "Like I said, war makes a man do lots of things. Come on, we best go see how bad the damage is."

They found five wagons strung out in the trail. The one in the lead, loaded with burning cotton bales, collapsed in a shower of sparks as Frio and Blas rode up. The other four wagons were being saved, though the Mexican teamsters were letting themselves be scorched to push burning bales out of the wagon beds and onto the ground. Without asking questions, Frio and Blas pitched in to help. They tossed their rawhide ropes over the tops of smoldering bales and spurred their horses out, dallying the ropes around their saddlehorns and pulling the bales down from the wagons.

The raiders had missed dumping some of the water barrels. A sandy-haired young Texan was running back and forth, dipping water and pitching it onto a wagon, dousing flames. With the bales out of the way, some of the Mexican freighting crew shoveled dirt over the fires, slowly snuffing them out.

Cotton smoke is a hard kind to take, and the choking smell of it clung awhile from the still-smouldering bales that lay about in scattered confusion. Cotton-bale fires were difficult to kill, but Frio thought most of these were under control. He had already given up on the sixteen bales in the collapsed lead wagon. A few others also were too far gone to save, for the stubborn fires would continue to eat away like cancer within the heart of the bales.

Without taking time for a close look, Frio decided four of the five wagons could be salvaged. Damage appeared to range from slight to rather bad, but none beyond repair. They were the big prairie-schooner kind of freight wagons with a twenty-four-foot bed, the hind wheels almost six feet tall, the front ones just short of five — solid-iron axles, the wagon tires six inches wide and an inch thick. Hell-and-high-water wagons, these were. In this dry country they saw mostly hell.

A Mexican teamster came leading ten mules out of an opening in the brush. The only team that had been saved, they still wore their harness. The mules danced wild-eyed, smelling the smoke. But the teamster was talking to them in fast-flowing Spanish that included some profanity, and they weren't going to give him much trouble.

Frio wiped grimy sweat onto his sleeve. He looked around for the sandy-haired boy. "What about it, Happy? Anybody hurt?"

Happy Jack Fleet had only recently come of age, and the excitement of the skirmish still played in his eyes. There was, indeed, a happy look on his smoke-smudged face. That the kid had actually enjoyed this fight came as a surprise to Frio, though on reflection he knew it shouldn't. From the beginning, Happy had struck Frio as the kind who would charge a bear with a slingshot and laugh as he did it. He wasn't old enough to have had the wildness stomped out of him.

Happy said, "They hit one man in the shoulder. Antonio Garza, on the lead wagon. Nobody killed."

Frio nodded, glad it hadn't been worse. "Guess it's foolish to ask what happened."

"They came on us all of a sudden." Happy's voice still carried a remnant of the

18

fight's intoxication. "Wasn't time for us to circle up, even if there'd been room to." He glanced at the pear and thorny brush that closed in tight alongside the trail. "All we could do was pile off and take to the pear. They had things pretty much to suit their-selves, except that we kept them dodgin' some. They set fire to the cotton and cut loose the teams, all but the last one. We had it too well covered."

Frio said, "I expect you did the best you could."

Happy's eyes laughed a little. "Them Mexicans of yours are teamsters, not sol-diers. They couldn't hit the side of a barn if they was locked up in it."

"I hired them to skin mules. Didn't figure on them havin' to fight."

"You may need to figure on it from now on."

They walked over to where the wounded man had been stretched out on the ground, a dirty blanket under him. The head team-ster, known as the *caporal,* was trying to slow the blood and get a look at the bullet hole. In Spanish he said, "Flaco, build a fire. We have to take the bullet out."

The wounded man groaned his dread, but he made no further protest. The Mexican people had a way of shrugging their shoulders and taking whatever misfortune fate chose to hand them, and there was usually enough of it to go around. The fire was built and the water put on to boil. When all was ready, the *caporal* turned to Frio.

"*Patrón,* you have the steadiest hands of any man I know. Will you do what has to be done?"

They had brought up all the tequila that was left on the train. It wasn't much, for the trip to Brownsville was nearly over. But the wounded man was so drunk by the time the operation began that he had little idea what was happening. He fainted shortly, and the job went with ease from there on. Done. Frio let the wound bleed a little to wash it clean and turned the rest of the task over to the *caporal.*

Happy Jack had watched without a comment. Now he turned away with Frio. "They're a hardy breed, these Mexicans. You can't kill one of them with a double-bitted ax. Small wonder there's so many of them."

To the people who were acquainted with him around here, the kid was simply Happy Jack, a cowboy and nothing more. He had come riding down one day from what in that time was known as West Texas — a little way beyond San Antonio. He bore a cowboy's quiet distrust of anyone who didn't ride a horse. With the rash pride of youth he felt he was a man sufficient unto himself.

"I guess you got a look at your ranch," he said to Frio.

Frio nodded. He had started these five loaded wagons south from San Antonio, then had left them in the rolling live-oak hills. He had ridden ahead at a fast pace to have time for a quick look over his ranch and still catch the wagons before they completed the more than two hundred miles to Brownsville and Matamoros.

Frio Wheeler had drifted down to this region several years ago from his home territory along the Frio River. He had found there was room here; room for a man to grow big if he started early enough and helped push an undeveloped land. Captain Richard King was doing it on his ranch along Santa Gertrudis Creek. Frio had seen no reason he couldn't do likewise in the brushland and the coastal prairies of the lower Rio Grande. He had brought cattle here and started to build. It had looked as if the future was unlimited. Then had come the war.

It wasn't that the South didn't need beef; it did, and desperately. But distance was one of the enemies here. It was one thing to haul cotton and other nonperishables overland a thousand miles and more. It was quite another to drive cattle. It had been tried and abandoned as an impractical job. South Texas cattle had slumped in value. Frio Wheeler had raised a stake and gone to freighting, for this way he could mark time and hang onto his part of the ranch while doing a job that might help bring a Confederate victory. It was a job fully as important as marching off to Virginia with a rifle over his shoulder. The war wouldn't last forever. The Yankees would soon realize they couldn't whip the South, and they would come to terms both sides could live with. Then maybe a man could go back to the business of growing, of sweating a civilization out of this region the early Mexicans had called the Desert of the Dead.

Frio managed to see the ranch only occasionally anymore, but Blas Talamantes had stayed there as his *caporal.* War had drawn away most of the manpower, and they were short-handed. But Blas at least was able to hold Frio's ranch together. He was getting most of the calves branded, something many ranchers weren't able to do. The herd was steadily building because there was so little market, so few sold. When this war was over there would be old steers in that brush with horns longer than a man's arm. Perhaps then, Frio thought, a hungry North might be in the market for beef. No matter what a man thought of Yankees in general, their money spent good.

Now Happy Jack stared regretfully at the burned-up cotton bales and the ruined wagon. "I wish we could have done more, Frio."

It hurt, but Frio had picked up from the Mexican people some of their ability to shrug and turn their backs upon misfortune. "It's spilt milk now. What worries me is gettin' the rest of this cotton to the river with just one team. We'll have to load one wagon and haul it in. We'll cache the other wagons and the rest of the cotton bales in the brush till I can get fresh teams back up here. I'll leave you here in charge, Happy."

Disappointment came to Happy's eyes. "You goin' across the river to Matamoros?"

Frio nodded. "I generally do."

"That's where you'll find the ones that done this. Them two gringos that was sidin' the bandits, I expect they've got a Union flag over their door. I'd like to go help you hunt them."

Frio shook his head. "Happy, they're fair game on this side of the river. Over there, they can't touch us and we can't touch them. We can't afford to get Mexico turned against us."

"Mexico ain't goin' to turn against us. She's makin' too much money out of the cotton trade."

"Happy, last year a Unionist by the name of Montgomery joined with some Matamoros bandits on a raid in Zapata County. They killed Isidro Vela, the chief justice. He was well thought of on this side of the river. Some time later a bunch of our boys crossed over the Rio at Bagdad, caught Montgomery, and hung him. Nobody denied that he had earned it, but it almost caused Mexico to close the border. Bad as he needed killin', it wasn't worth the cost.

"Sure, it hurts to stand on the riverbank and watch somebody like that runnin' around loose on the other side. But it works as much in our favor as it does theirs. More, maybe. The Yankees keep all our ports bottled up, but there's nothin' they can do about the trade that goes out of a Mexican port. Long as Mexico stays neutral, we all win. She ever changes, we lose."

Happy Jack pursed his lips. "Then you don't aim to start no fight with them?"

"No fight."

The young man pushed his hat back and leaned against a wagon wheel, disappointed.

"I reckon I'll stay here. I won't be missin' nothin'."

2

Through the ages, the Rio Grande had been as unpredictable as a woman. She had changed her mind dozens of times, altering her course and leaving deserted a multitude of old riverbeds that the Mexicans called *resacas*. Most of these had haired over with grass and weeds, though the drought of recent months had burned away much of the vegetation. Along the edges of some *resacas* stood the stately old palm trees that had caught the fancy of the first exploring Spaniards and had prompted them to name this the River of the Palms.

The Gulf breeze blew in welcome from the east, waving the palms and easing the heat that Frio Wheeler had borne across the sands and the heavy brush. It always pleased him to reach the first of these ancient riverbeds, for it meant Brownsville was close at hand. He and Blas Talamantes rode horseback several lengths ahead of the lone wagon with its load of smoke-blackened cotton. They passed near the old Resaca de la Palma battlefield where General Zachary Taylor and his troops had drawn some of the first blood in the Mexican War of 1846, just seventeen years ago. Lots of men who lived in Brownsville, and far more who lived across in Matamoros, had vivid memories of that fight. Frio had listened to many a bloody tale.

Far across the river stood the twin spires of the tall brick cathedral on the Mexican side. There was nothing so spectacular on the Texas bank. Brownsville was much newer than its Spanish-speaking sister, and somewhat smaller. There had been no town on this side when Taylor's troops had built the eight hundred yards of earthwork that was to become known as Fort Brown. Today Brownsville with its stone and lumber buildings still had a new look about it.

Town dogs came running out to meet and greet the riders, yapping at the heels of the horses and backing away only when Blas took down his rawhide rope. The dogs fell to one side and picked up the mules as the wagon drew close. The mules gave them less attention than they would give a mosquito.

"Blas," said Frio, "I'm goin' to lope on ahead and visit some folks. I'll see you directly down at the cottonyard."

Blas smiled thinly. "No hurry, we get there just fine." He paused, then added, "Someday maybe you better marry that girl."

Frio grinned and moved into an easy lope. He rubbed his face and found it still smooth, for he had shaved in camp that morning.

Brownsville was growing rapidly because of the war trade. Every time he came in from a trip, it seemed the town had edged a little farther out along the wagon road. People were coming in faster than houses could be built. Here and there he could see tents and Mexican-style *jacales,* thatched with reeds and broomcorn. Soon he was riding in the heart of the town, past the Miller Hotel, the new city market, the palebrick Stillman home, which had been the first permanent house in Brownsville. In the dirt streets he passed Confederate soldiers from the fort, whiling away off-duty time by making the rounds of the saloons. Mexican *dulce* vendors were attempting to sell them candies made of brown *piloncillo* sugar. The soldiers were not interested in candy, but they were plainly interested in a couple of the flashing-eyed girls who were trying to sell it.

Down beyond the brick quartermaster's

fence that stood between Fort Brown and the town, General Hamilton Bee wouldn't be thinking about girls. He would be nervously studying his dispatches, wondering when and if the Yankees might land troops at the Boca Chica and march the thirty miles inland across the sea meadows to capture Brownsville. Frio could well understand why Bee would be nervous, sitting here with just four companies of the Thirty-Third Texas Cavalry, a battery of light artillery and a scattered few militia companies that he didn't altogether trust, dispersed up and down the river for three hundred miles.

With this invaluable border cotton trade and thousands of pounds of war goods coming over each day at Brownsville, it was incomprehensible to Frio that the Confederate government would let it be jeopardized by lack of troops. But one of the biggest disappointments the Southern people had suffered was the slow realization that their new government in Richmond could blunder along as foolishly as the Washington government ever did. Sometimes he thought it would be a wonder if both sides didn't lose the war.

Meade McCasland's frame mercantile store fronted on Elizabeth Street, which the pioneer merchant Charles Stillman had named for his wife. The store had a tall false front with a dummy balcony that opened from nowhere and led the same way. Gray-haired Meade McCasland never had liked that feature, for to him it smacked of deception, and there was not an ounce of deception in his soul. From the day he had bought it, he had intended to cut the storefront down to size. But these were busy times, and he had more to worry about than an unwanted balcony.

Frio Wheeler reined through the wagon traffic toward the hitchrack in front of the store. He held up, to let a droopy-mustached old Mexican pass with a burro-drawn cart and forty gallons of muddy Rio water that he would sell for two dollars a load.

A little Mexican boy of about six came bouncing off the porch, running excitedly. "Mister Frio! Mister Frio!"

Frio stepped to the ground and scooped the boy up in his arms, whirling him once around and putting him down again. "*Como le va,* Chico?"

Dark skin accented the sparkle of the boy's white teeth in a smile that was so wide it must have hurt.

"*Muy bueno.* Much good. This time you stay a while, no?"

Frio tousled the kid's black hair. "This time I stay a while *no*! Got to work. How is Señor McCasland? And Miss Amelia?"

The boy shrugged. "They not sick. Señor McCasland, he is work pretty hard. *La señorita,* she is worry what for you don't come a little quicker."

Frio dug a coin out of his pocket. "Go buy you some dulce."

The boy took the coin and shouted his thanks over his shoulder as he trotted barefoot off down the street, looking for a vendor. Frio walked inside the frame building and paused to let his sun-accustomed eyes adjust themselves to the interior. It was hot in here. Frio had heard it said that this country had summer nine months out of the year and late spring the other three.

Meade McCasland was showing some newly arrived English cloth to a couple of women customers. Once a strong man, he was breaking now with the weight of years and personal sorrow upon his broad shoulders. He saw Frio, and he said in a quiet Southern voice, "You ladies just take your time and look all you want to. I'll be right here." He strode forward and gripped Frio's hand so tightly it almost hurt.

"Glad to see you back, Frio. Have a good trip?"

31

Frio smiled, warming inside, for there was not a man alive he liked better than Meade McCasland. What little Frio could remember of his own father was reflected in this man. "It wasn't dull," he said and let it go at that. "Things seem to be bustlin' around here."

McCasland nodded. "More and more people coming in. Bookkeeper down at Kennedy & Co. said he saw more than a hundred ships anchored off Bagdad a few days ago. Every flag in Europe. A couple of Union blockaders were patrolling up and down like a pair of cats waiting at a mousehole, but there was nothing they could do about neutral vessels unloading on Mexican soil."

A thought came to Frio, unbidden: *They could take over Brownsville easy enough. That would stop it.* He didn't speak the thought. He knew it had come to McCasland often enough anyway, and his friend had more troubles now than any two men ought to carry.

"You're lookin' well, Meade," he said, stretching the point a little. The old man didn't look good at all. "And Chico looks like you've been feedin' him all right."

Meade came close to smiling. "Chico never misses a meal." The boy's mother had worked for the McCaslands after her husband had been killed by *bandidos* on the Laredo road. When she had died of the fever and there had been no one else to care for the boy, Meade McCasland had taken the task upon his own shoulders.

Frio asked, "And Amelia? How's she?"

McCasland was plainly pleased that Frio asked. "She's back in the living quarters. She'd be up here now if she had any idea you had come in. I think she's been afraid you'd find some good-looking young lady in San Antonio."

Frio shook his head. "Never noticed they had any."

"They do. At least, they *did.* Never will forget the first time I was ever in San Antonio . . ." Meade looked away, remembering. "But never mind that, just go on back. She'll be tickled to see you."

Frio walked through the door that separated the store from the dwelling in the rear of the building. Hat in hand, he closed the door quietly behind him. Amelia McCasland stood with her slender back turned. She and a young Mexican housegirl were holding up some unrolled new cloth, and Amelia was talking about what a lovely dress it was going to make. The widening of the housegirl's eyes caused Amelia to turn.

33

"Frio!" she cried, almost dropped the cloth. He saw joy leap in her pretty face, then confusion as she glanced back at the Mexican girl.

"Señorita," the girl said discreetly, "I will go on and start work in the kitchen."

"Yes, Consuela, please do that."

Frio stepped closer to Amelia as the girl left the room. Amelia smiled. "Well, come ahead, I'll let you kiss me."

He leaned down to give her a quick, unsure kiss. She caught his arm. "Not like that," she said. "Like this!" She tiptoed up and put her hands at his back and pulled him close. Her lips were warm and eager as they met his. In a moment she let her heels touch the floor again. She leaned back, her hands tight on his arms. Eyes sparkling, she said, "That's more like it. You going to ask me this time to marry you?"

Frio didn't know whether he ought to smile or frown. It seemed easier to smile. "Hadn't figured on it."

"And why not? Maybe if you'd ask me, I'd say yes."

"It seems to me you're the one who's proposing. I always thought that was for the man to do."

"It is, but you won't do it." Mischief was shining in her eyes. "Do you think I'm too forward, Frio?"

"Well, you're not the most bashful girl I ever met."

"I can't afford to be. Traveling as much as you do, you might meet somebody else. I've got to get you first." She watched him, waiting. "But, if you won't ask me this time, I'll just have to wait till the next trip, I guess. Sooner or later you're going to ask me."

Serious, he said, "Amelia, I've told you before: these trails can be dangerous. It's one thing to leave a sweetheart behind. It's another to leave a wife. Besides, I'm travelin' all the time. What kind of married life would that be for either one of us?"

The sparkle slowly went out of her eyes, and she went serious too. She leaned her body against him again, the side of her face pressed against his shoulder. "You'd be home once in a while — for a day, for a night. Better to have even so little than to have nothing at all."

It always seemed to Frio that Amelia had to work a little at her brashness. It served a purpose: to keep the sadness beaten back. But always the sadness lurked there somewhere, for this had been a tragic house.

"Better we wait a while yet, Amelia. Wait and see what the war is goin' to do." There was something more, something besides the war. She had lived all of her life in town. He wasn't sure how well she would fit on the ranch, especially during the early years when life there would necessarily lean toward the primitive. Not for all the money in the world would he have said so, but he was afraid she might not be able to take it. "Let's wait, Amelia," he said again.

"Until next time," she answered and put the subject aside. She motioned Frio toward a red-upholstered settee. "You were longer this time than usual."

"Took a while to get the government cotton together. Matter of fact, I had to leave ten of my wagons in San Antonio, waitin' for a load. Private speculators have been goin' around over the country, buyin' up cotton to try and make money on it. Government's had a hard time gettin' what it needs for the war trade."

Anger flared in Amelia's blue eyes. "Looks like the government could stop these speculators."

Frio shook his head. "Politics. Hard to catch them, and some have so much influence in Austin and Richmond that nobody can touch them anyway. Conscript law says anybody freightin' nongovernment cotton loses his exemption, but they don't enforce it much. War seems to breed its own brand of snakes."

They fell into silence. Frio liked just to sit and look at her. Gradually, though, his gaze drifted to a big charcoal drawing, framed and hanging on the wall. A Mexican artist across the river had done it just before the war. The likenesses were as real as a photograph: Meade McCasland, his wife and his daughter Amelia in the center, sons Tom on the left, Bert on the right.

On first thought it seemed to Frio that the artist had been kind to Meade, making him look much younger, leaving out the deep lines that had creased his face. But on reflection he knew the likeness had been real enough at the time. Most of the facial lines and much of the gray had come upon Meade since the war had started. He had suffered enough grief to kill some men.

Tennessee-born, McCasland had drifted to Texas in the 1830s and had fought beside Sam Houston at San Jacinto, avenging friends who died in the Alamo. He had come to the Rio Grande a few years after the Mexican War. He had loved his country, this sad-eyed man, and in the Texas secession referendum had voted like Sam Houston to keep Texas in the Union. But when the final count showed a majority for secession, McCasland had wept silently inside, then swallowed his bitter disappointment and accepted the Confederacy. His was a Southern heritage, and he would not stand against his friends.

Meade had not foreseen the split that was to come within his own family. In the echo of the guns at Fort Sumter, the youngest son Bert had marched off in gray to fight with the South. Tom, the older, remained fiercely loyal to the Union, quarreling even with his father. With others, Tom had tried to organize a resistance against the Confederacy in Texas. Failing, the militant Knights of the Golden Circle hard on his heels, he had retreated unwillingly across the river to sanctuary within the stone walls of Matamoros.

Mrs. McCasland fell easy prey to the fever, for she had lost the will to live. Bert was dead at Glorieta alongside so many others of Sibley's Brigade, and Tom was in exile beyond the Rio Grande. Meade McCasland was left with only his daughter.

Meade hadn't seen Tom in almost two years, though they were hardly more than a mile apart. Amelia crossed the river to visit him occasionally, for Tom held no bitterness against her.

It was in Frio's mind to tell Amelia what had happened to him on the trail, so that she might try to persuade Tom to stay on the south side of the Rio. He said, "You been across lately to see Tom?"

"I was there a couple of days ago, but I couldn't find him. He's been . . . seeing a woman named Luisa Valdez. She was at his place. He was away on business, but he's well. She said we have nothing to worry about." *Nothing to worry about!* A sour taste came to Frio's mouth. He realized that nothing Amelia could say would sway Tom much. No need to tell her and Meade Mc-Casland that Tom's business had been north of the river, that it had been to ride with the *bandidos* of Florencio Chapa and attempt to destroy a wagon train.

Leaving, Frio found the happy Chico chewing candy on the front porch. The boy ran ahead and unhitched the sorrel for him.

Purely by chance, Frio overtook his wagon as he reined the horse away from the Mc-Casland store and down the treelined dirt street. Blas Talamantes eyed him with a little surprise.

"You don't stay very long."

"Afraid I might say somethin' that had no need of bein' said."

They slanted down toward the big government cottonyard at the bend of the river.

Beneath the dust of plodding hoofs and grinding wheels, he could see a thousand bales or more of CSA cotton. They were lined up awaiting sale and transshipment by rope ferry across to the Matamoros side, this to give them at least the cloak of legality and make them untouchable by the Yankee blockade ships. Across the river Frio could see one of the small shallow-draft steamers that belonged to M. Kennedy & Co. It was pulling in toward the Matamoros wharf, likely with a load of war goods freshly unloaded from some European ship anchored off Bagdad on the Mexican side of the river's mouth. The steamers had been signed over to Mexican owners and flew the eagle flag of Mexico, which was often referred to in joking disrespect as the Turkey Buzzard. But everyone knew this was only a wartime ruse, for the crews were the same as they had always been, and the original Texas owners still gave the orders.

Frio stopped the horse a moment to watch the boat and then let his gaze sweep downriver to where the Rio made another bend and was lost from sight. By land it was only thirty miles out to the gulf from Brownsville. By the river, with its leisurely snaketrack course, it was nearer sixty. The flow was lower than usual because of the months of drought, and the little steamships had to pick their way cautiously past the sandbars and snags.

Frio wished he had time to ride out to the Boca Chica and watch the activity. He liked to go to the gulf and stand with wet boots on the salty beach at the river's mouth, watching rollers wash in tirelessly upon the land. He liked to look out across the blue waters at the white sails of the trading ships that rocked at anchor and imagine he could hear whispers from across the sea, beckoning whispers from strange lands he hadn't seen and never would. It always called up a wanderlust within him, a haunting wanderlust he would never be able to satisfy. He had never been out of Texas, except into Mexico, and he knew he would never go.

"Frio!"

Someone called his name, and he cut his eyes back to the cottonyard. He saw a heavyset, middle-aged man walking hurriedly toward him, a battered old felt hat pulled down over his eyes, an account book under his arm. Cotton agent Hugh Plunkett glanced at the trailing cotton wagon, then back to Frio.

"You all right, Frio?" he demanded. "Been worried half to death!"

Frio frowned, puzzled. "You knew we had

trouble?"

Plunkett nodded vigorously, his gaze exploring up and down as if he were looking for bullet holes. "One of my Mexicans was over in Matamoros this mornin'. Saw some of Chapa's men come in with a big string of mules. They had your brand on them. I figured they'd killed you."

Frio's fist clenched. "Where'd they take the mules?"

"There's a sort of a wagonyard over there owned by Pablo Gutierrez, the fat one they call El Gordo."

Frio said, "I know him. Brother-in-law of Florencio Chapa, isn't he?"

Plunkett blinked. "Since you mention it, I believe he is."

Tightly Frio said, "It adds up. I bet you if I was to go over there, they'd sell me back my own mules."

"I wouldn't pay! I'd go and take my mules and kill the first man that opened his mouth!"

Frio glanced at the saddlegun on the sorrel and shook his head. "I admit it's a temptation. But we can't be raisin' any dust over in Mexico. I'll just have to swallow my medicine and act like it tastes good."

He told Hugh Plunkett about the raid and about losing some of the cotton.

Plunkett was sweating profusely, for a humid heat lay here along the river. "Frio, the cotton is the government's loss, but I'm afraid the wagon and the mules are yours. I wish there was somethin' I could do."

"There isn't, Hugh," Frio said regretfully. "Don't worry yourself."

Plunkett grunted angrily as a gust of hot wind slapped dust into his face from the passing of a high-wheeled Mexican ox-cart, loaded with cotton bales on their way down to the ferry. "Damn this river country anyway," he flared. The government had sent him here against his will, and he hadn't softened a bit. "We fought a war with the Mexicans once to take this country away from them. I say we ought to fight them again and make them take it back!"

Frio smiled and forgot his loss for a while. The cotton agent would probably still be griping when he got to Heaven, and nobody would think any more of it there than they did here. Frio handed Plunkett the manifests he had received with the cotton in San Antonio. Plunkett called up some of his help. They unloaded the bales from the lone wagon and checked them against the papers.

Frio said, "I'll go back and fetch in the rest of it soon as I get some mules to pull the wagons and a little lumber for patchin'."

Plunkett scowled. "You really goin' over there and buy back your mules?"

"I figure to try. They're good mules."

"I'd make somebody bleed for this."

"They will, Hugh." Frio's eyes narrowed. "Somebody is goin' to pay!"

As his empty wagon pulled out of the cotton-yard, Frio swung into the saddle and looked around for Blas. Hugh Plunkett snapped his fingers, remembering something. "By the way, Frio, there's been a man lookin' for you. I oughtn't to even tell you."

"Who is it?"

"Cotton trader, that loudmouth Trammell."

The name brought a grunt from Frio, and a frown of distaste. "I got no business with that profiteer."

"I figure he wants to try to hire your wagons away from the government. Don't you let him do it, Frio."

Frio shook his head. "I'd as soon hire to Florencio Chapa. At least he admits to bein' a bandit."

3

Frio and Blas led their horses off the Santa Cruz ferry on the Mexican side and looked southward across the Estrero del Bravo to where the heart of Matamoros lay. About them bustled the river trade, cotton being unloaded from the ferry and carted up to yards to await shipment on the steamers. Mexican laborers and cotton buyers of many nationalities walked around among the dust-grayed bales stacked haphazardly here on the bank. Men shouted at each other and at their mules and oxen. Dust lifted and was slow to settle, for it had been a long time since rain.

The Gutierrez wagonyard lay southwestward, on the river. Frio swung into the saddle and started riding along the bank, Blas with him stirrup to stirrup. They passed a group of Mexican women washing clothes in the slow-moving water at river's edge.

Frio wondered if the clothes would ever get clean.

A little farther, a group of girls bathed in the river, shouting and splashing. Some of them had few if any clothes on. Their wet brown skins gleamed in the sun.

"Now there," said Frio, "is a sight to gladden a man's heart."

Blas nodded and smiled and turned once to look back after they had passed the girls.

Matamoros! The formal Mexican name was much longer: *La Heroica y Invicta Ciudad de Matamoros*. The heroic and invincible. Named for a patriot priest who had died for Mexican freedom, this old border city had long known the smell of trouble, the sound and fury of war. Its time-stained walls were pocked with the marks of bullets and shells. Even now it was gripped by civil war, as was its sister city across the river, for the Indian patriot Juarez was locked in mortal combat with the imperialists and the French, who had proclaimed Maximilian emperor of all Mexico. Here in Matamoros seethed the same turmoil that had gripped the rest of the country, the Juarez Rojos opposing the Crinolinos, who supported Maximilian. At the moment the Crinolinos had control.

To most of the population there was

always a war in progress, or just finishing, or just about to begin. They took it as a matter of course, like the droughts and the floods and the pestilence. Life would still go on after the armies had marched away. Commerce continued as if there were no struggle. Coins changed hands and the city grew, even as generals sparred and hapless soldiers gasped out their lives on bloody sand.

The trading circles spared little thought to politics.

Frio and Blas rode past the rude *jacales* that housed the poor. Half-naked children played in the dirt streets, and disheveled women cooked on outdoor ovens and open fires, sharing the food with the flies. These were tiny houses, the cots folding up against the walls in daytime to give what little room was to be had. Rapidly as the city had grown, these people were lucky to have even this, for many others lived with no roof at all.

Frio saw a big corral, started with rock but finished crudely with brush. "That would be it," he said.

They rode around the outside of the fence, looking in the corral at a motley collection of bone-poor horses and droopy-headed burros. There was no feed in the

47

corral and only one tiny water trough, which now was half mud. Frio saw his mules, gaunted by the long, fast trip. They probably hadn't been fed at all, and they hadn't likely watered since they had been swum across the river. Anger stirred in him, but he curbed it. Here he would be doing the listening, not the talking.

He and Blas reined in at a low-built stone structure that was the Gutierrez headquarters. Several carts and sagging old wagons stood around in front of the building. An old *peón,* shoulders bent from a life of hard work, stepped out with his hat in his hand. He bowed from the waist. In Spanish he said, "How may I serve you, *patrón?*"

"I am looking for El G—" Frio caught himself. He had been about to say *El Gordo,* which in Spanish meant *the fat one* and was not usually a term of endearment. "I would like to speak to Señor Gutierrez."

The *peón* hesitated. Frio added, "It is on business. I would like to buy some mules from him."

"Then," said the old man, "if you will step inside, *mi jefe* will be most glad to see you." There was a nervousness about the old man, an undertone of fear. Likely as not that tattered old shirt covered whip scars on his bent back. Here a rich man like El

48

Gordo could virtually own a poor man, much as across the river a white man could own a black one.

The *peón* walked cautiously through a door and closed it quietly behind him. Frio could hear a voice in angry impatience, demanding what the old man wanted. In a moment El Gordo Gutierrez stepped through the door, his belly sagging, his mouth wide in a false smile. His eyes smiled too, in anticipation of profit. Gutierrez didn't seem even to see Blas Talamantes. He ignored him as a *hidalgo* might ignore another man's *peón* grubbing in the dirt. He bowed from the waist, which was something of an effort for him, and said to Frio, "My house is yours, señor. Tell me how I may serve you, and I shall be the happiest of men."

Frio sensed that Gutierrez knew him. He was glad the man didn't extend his hand, for he wasn't sure he could have brought himself to shake it. "I need to buy some mules. Thought maybe you had some for sale."

"Ahhh." Gutierrez rubbed his hands. "You are indeed a fortunate man, señor, for it happens I have just brought in a large group of mules from one of the best ranches in Mexico. I would be glad to show you." He motioned toward a back door, which would lead to the big corral. Frio stepped toward it, then stopped as he glanced into the room from which Gutierrez had come. Two men slouched at a table, a bottle sitting in front of them. Frio stiffened. One of them was the *bandido,* Florencio Chapa. Chapa sat watching him, amusement playing in his black eyes. His was a cruel face that could grin while his hands cut a man's throat.

The other man was, in his own way, even more dangerous than Chapa. This was General Juan Nepomuceno Cortina, the wily political opportunist whose brigandage had been carried out on such a high plane as to keep him in a position of power no matter which political party might be gaining the edge in Mexico. Born of aristocratic blood but hardly able to write his own name, he was the beloved "Cheno" Cortina to most of the Mexican people — Cheno the gringo-killer, the champion of Mexican rights against the encroachment of the Anglos. And if somehow Cortina seemed always to have gained more for himself than for his followers, that was of no matter. He was Cheno, and he deserved whatever good there was to be gained from life.

"This way, señor," Gutierrez said, holding the door open.

Frio stepped out into the sun, Blas following him. Frio glanced back over his shoulder, thinking he might again glimpse Cortina. This was the man who had taken a hundred followers across the river one early morning in 1859 and had captured Brownsville by storm, summarily executing five men — some of them Mexicans — who had earned his wrath. It took a Mexican general, Carvajal, to get Cortina out of Brownsville. It took the Texas Rangers under old Rip Ford to drive him back across the river. Even afterward, he kept crossing the Rio Grande to raid small *ranchos,* taking vengeance not only on Anglos but on the Mexicans who worked for them. He had been chased by the best of men, including even Robert E. Lee, who at the time had still been a lieutenant colonel in the U.S. Army.

Frio thought this red-bearded, gray-eyed highbinder probably was enjoying the war between the states, the thought of gringo killing gringo, with Cortina able to sit back and make money out of it through the cotton trade. Though he plied his banditry in higher and more sophisticated circles now, the love of it still burned in him, and he encouraged such savage *bandidos* as Chapa and the notorious Octaviano Zapata.

Gutierrez said, "You would like to meet Cheno? He's one good friend of mine."

Frio shook his head. "No, thank you. I'd rather just get on with our business." He knew he was rushing too much. Mexicans liked to take their time on a business transaction, to talk all around it as if it were not even there. But Frio didn't think he could stand to be in El Gordo's presence for very long. He wanted to rush it, to get it over with.

There was no mistake about their being his mules. He would have recognized them anywhere, even without the brands. If there had been any point in his demonstrating this, he could have popped a whip and shouted an order, and they would have moved into their places, ready to harness. The Mexican *caporal* had taught him that, to save time in breaking camp and getting the wagons out on the trail.

Smiling, Gutierrez said, "They are fine-looking mules. They would do a good job for your freight wagons."

That was the clincher. Frio knew for certain now that El Gordo was well aware of who he was. "I know they would," Frio remarked. "They're my mules."

"Your mules?" El Gordo put on an act of not understanding. "They are *my* mules. I bought them." His eyes smiled again. "But they can be your mules if you like. I would be glad to sell them."

I'll just bet you would, Frio thought, having to curb his anger again. "How much?"

The Mexican looked at the ground and rubbed his hands. "They are unusually good mules. Seldom does one see better. I would say they are worth a hundred dollars per head."

"Confederate?"

El Gordo violently shook his head. "Not Confederate money. Gold."

"I'll give you seventy-five, Confederate."

From there on it was simply a process of dickering and bargaining. El Gordo had set the original price at double what he expected to get. After a while they arrived at an agreement. Fifty dollars per head, payable in English paper. That much gold would take a wagon. The harness, some of it cut, would be thrown in free.

"Bueno," said El Gordo, "we shall drink on it."

They went back inside. Chapa and Cortina had gone. Gutierrez got two dry glasses and a bottle of tequila, deliberately ignoring Blas Talamantes. Frio handed his own glass to Blas and thus forced El Gordo to get a third one.

"To your health, señor," El Gordo said. "May we have more pleasant business together."

We're going to have a little more business, Frio thought darkly, *but you may not think it's so pleasant.*

He emptied the glass in one long swallow. It was harsh, leaving a deep track all the way down.

"Come on, Blas," he said. "We'll need to find some men and come after the mules. And I have to get the money for Señor Gutierrez."

They left the yard and rode toward the heart of the city. Frio looked once over his shoulder. "Blas," he said after some deliberation, "I guess you know a lot of people in this town."

They had just passed a nice-looking girl seated in the big window of one of the better homes, leaning against the wrought-iron grating. Blas glanced back at her and said, "*Sí,* Frio, but all that has changed. I am married now. María is all the woman I need."

"You misunderstand me, Blas. I was just wonderin' if you might know five or six jolly Mexican boys who might like to pull a good honest robbery."

Blas smiled broadly as comprehension

came. "*Sí,* Frio. I think maybeso."

"Do it, then. I'll go to the British consul and get the money. Then I'll wait in that little bar down from the consulate till you show up. Tell them I'll let them keep a hundred apiece if they do the job right."

Blas started to turn away, then stopped. Worry creased his face. "One thing, Frio. You never can tell. Maybe they run away and keep it all."

"A chance I'll take. I wouldn't be any worse off than I am now."

Here on the border, where the trade was heavy, gold was not hard to come by. For more than a year now Frio had insisted upon foreign currency or gold in payment for his government hauling. Stern realism dictated the measure. Even here on the border, people were trading two dollars of Confederate paper money for one in gold. From things he had heard in San Antonio he knew they were swapping as many as four to one in the Deep South. As long as the gold was available, he would take it. Everyone on the border did.

Because it would be easy for the Yankees to sail up to the Brazos Santiago or the Boca Chica one day and march in to capture Brownsville, he could not afford to keep his money in Texas. There was as yet no trust-worthy bank in Matamoros, but an English cotton buyer had helped Frio work out an arrangement with the British consul. Frio could keep a supply of floating cash at the consulate and could send the rest by draft to a bank in England.

English money was acceptable at face value in Matamoros because so much of it was used in buying cotton. Frio drew out two thousand dollars — the equivalent of it — for the forty mules. Carrying it in a small bag, he strolled down the street to the bar where he had said he would meet Blas. There he ordered a good Scotch whisky, which arrived there now aboard the trading ships, and hunted a place to sit down. He put his back to a solid wall. With all this money on his person, he didn't care to be slipped up on.

From here he could see the cosmopolitan parade of humanity that passed the door — cotton buyers and merchants from England and France, Belgium and Germany; sailors from vessels of many nations, delayed at the Boca Chica by repairs; Texans who had come to Mexico because of pro-Union feel-ings, or simply to escape the draft; Negro slaves who had fled from bondage. There were even federal observers sent here from

Washington to keep a futile watch over the border trade. They knew what was going on but were powerless to put even a small dent in it.

A man could sit in one spot here on the main streets of Matamoros for just a day, and half the world would pass before him.

In the main, it seemed to Frio, Matamoros was still a more solid-looking town than Brownsville. It was larger, had more fine homes, had most of the better eating and drinking places and the only real theater. One had to overlook the fringe of primitive *jacales* and tents and open-air campers who had swelled the city of late. One also had to overlook the many cheap cantinas and gambling places and rowdy sporting houses that had sprung up to accommodate the flush pockets of freighters and sailors and traders, Confederate soldiers and plain salt-sweat laborers.

Two men entered the bar and ordered drinks. One of them spotted Frio, spoke quickly to the other, then began walking in Frio's direction. He was a portly man with a florid face and eyes that somehow reminded Frio of a coyote's. The clothes he wore had been well tailored and bespoke easy money, but now they looked as if he might have slept in them.

"Hello, Frio Wheeler," he said loudly, as if he had found a long-lost friend. He walked up and slapped Frio's shoulder with a big soft hand. "Been hopin' I'd run into you someplace."

Frio's voice lacked enthusiasm. "Hello, Trammell." He didn't offer to shake.

Trammell hailed the other man with a broad sweep of his hand. "Guffey, come over here. I want you to meet the best cotton freighter on the whole Mexico trail."

Frio didn't stand up nor did he offer his hand to the tall, consumptive-looking Guffey. Trammell was telling him Guffey was a cotton buyer out of New York — strictly nonpolitical — but Frio only half listened. He already knew Guffey by sight and reputation. Trammell said in his big, loud voice, "How about havin' a drink with us, Frio?"

It graveled Frio a little, this careless use of his first name. In his view that was a privilege granted only to friends. He did not count Trammell as a friend. "I've already got a drink. Thanks anyway." He hoped this might discourage Trammell and that the man would go away. Instead, Trammell scraped a chair across the floor and seated himself uninvited. "Let's sit down here, Guffey. I got some business I want to talk over with Frio."

Frostily Frio said, "We got no business together."

"You don't know it, but we do."

A waiter brought a bottle and two glasses. Trammell poured a glass full and swallowed it down in two long gulps. His face twisted sourly, and he rasped a long "Ahhhh!" Across the table, the lank Guffey only sipped at the whiskey, his nose wrinkling as if he smelled something dead. Frio scowled, looking the two men over, sorely tempted to get up and walk out but realizing Blas wouldn't know where to hunt for him.

Here's a real pair for you, he thought. Trammell was a trader who had gotten fat buying cotton from poor farmers in East Texas and selling it to the Confederacy at high prices. It had been charged but never proven that he bribed government buyers to give him a premium. Now he had found there was even more cream to be skimmed by not dealing with the Confederacy at all, but by hauling his cotton to the border and selling it directly to the buyers from overseas. That way it wound up to his credit in European banks. None of it had to be traded for war goods.

As for Guffey, he was a Yankee cotton buyer. How he did it Frio could only guess, but Guffey actually was getting his hands on arms and ammunition that were being manufactured for the Union army. He was shipping them to Matamoros and trading them to the Confederate government in return for cotton, which he could sell at ruinous prices to fiber-hungry mills in the east.

The .36-caliber Navy Colt that Frio carried on his belt had been Union war goods that had come through Guffey's hands.

Trammell set his glass down with a hard thump. "Frio, how would you like to make yourself a big pile of money? Good gold money that spends anywhere you want to take it."

"I'm doin' all right."

"Join up with me, man, and you'll make more than you'll know how to spend. You could buy yourself the best ranch in Mexico and have all the pretty señoritas a man could ever want, a different one for every day."

Frio could feel color rising warm in his cheeks. His narrowed eyes fastened on his glass to avoid looking at Trammell. "That might be to your taste. It isn't to mine."

"Just a figure of speech is all. Hell, money's to everybody's taste. You can do anything you want to with it."

Frio said, "Bad money breeds only trouble, and yours is bad money. I don't want any part of it."

Trammell stared incredulously. "There's no such thing as bad money. All I want you to do is haul my cotton. You're a good freighter, and you've got fifteen good wagons."

"Fourteen," Frio corrected him. "Lost one."

"Haul for me and you can have thirty wagons before you know it. I'll pay you twice what the government does."

Frio shook his head. "Not interested."

Trammell argued, "Look, man, I got more than four thousand bales of cotton bought in East Texas. Bought cheap. They stand to make me a fortune if I can get them down to the border. I'll split the profit with you if you'll haul them. Now, what could be more fair than that?"

"Sell them to the government."

"Sell . . . Man, you're crazy! I'm offerin' you a chance to make a small fortune, and you sit here starin' at me like some dumb Mexican." The big man grabbed Frio's shoulder and shook it. "Think of all that cotton, Frio. Think what I've got tied up in it. Think of me!"

Frio's hating gaze cut him like a knife. "I

am thinkin' of you, Trammell, and the thought makes me a little bit sick. You take cotton the Confederacy needs and sell it for gold to line your own pockets. Now take your hand off of me before I shoot it off!"

Trammell jerked his hand away.

Frio turned to the Yankee. "And you, Guffey, you're just as bad. Sure, the Confederacy needs all the guns it can get. But I mortally hate a man who would steal from his own side and sell guns to the enemy, even when we're the enemy."

Trammell sputtered, "You got no call to talk to us like that, Frio. We come for a nice, friendly little business talk and you —"

"I didn't invite you," Frio said flatly. "But now I'm invitin' you to leave. In fact, I'm tellin' you to."

Trammell backed toward the door, shaking his fist. "You'll regret this, Wheeler. We'll meet again."

"As long as I can see you," Frio said, "I won't be worried."

Blas came, by and by. He simply stood in the doorway and nodded, and Frio knew everything had been arranged. Walking outside, he saw half a dozen Mexicans a-horseback, waiting. Blas said, "I hire these to help us put the mules across the river."

"And that other little job?"

Blas winked. "I have fix that also."

They rode out to Gutierrez's. Frio placed the money in the big man's greedy hands and watched gold-lust dance in the dark eyes. The Mexicans harnessed the mules, then strung them out along the river, headed for the ferry.

Riding off behind the mules, Frio and Blas passed a tall stone fence and found four young Mexicans sitting there on their horses, waiting. They made no sign of recognition, but Frio saw Blas give them a quick nod as he rode by. Frio looked back over his shoulder a minute later and saw them riding leisurely toward the wagonyard.

After taking his mules to the Texas side, Frio rode the ferry back to Matamoros and returned once more to the bar near the consulate. He hadn't been there long when Blas came, bringing the same bag in which Frio had taken the money to Gutierrez.

"Did they take out their share?" he asked, not wanting to open the bag here.

Blas nodded. "Funny thing. When they rob him they find he has more money there than you give him. They take their share from El Gordo's money. You will find yours here, all of it."

Frio smiled, then suddenly the smile fell

63

away. "El Gordo . . . I hope they didn't kill him."

Blas shook his head. "No, they don't kill him. One of the boys, he's make El Gordo saddle a horse, and he's take him for a long ride down the river. He's going to let El Gordo walk back."

Frio could picture Gutierrez wobbling along afoot, carrying his great bulk on legs unaccustomed to walking.

"He'll know who arranged it, of course."

Blas shrugged. "Of course, but what can he do? You know who is steal your mules, but what could *you* do?"

Frio laughed all the way back to the consulate.

4

Frio knew where Tom McCasland lived in Matamoros, but he had never gone there to look for him before. Now and again he and Tom would meet by accident somewhere in the city. They were always civil meetings, but inevitably the barrier of war and the conflict of loyalties stood like a stone wall between the two men. Such meetings only aroused in Frio a painful memory of things that used to be — the hunting and fishing they had done together, horses they had broken, cattle work with the two of them and Blas Talamantes as a happy team. With these memories always came a fear that when the war ended, that friendship would never again be the same. Always when he saw Tom, Frio felt an aching sense of loss. He avoided a meeting if he had the chance.

This time he felt he had to see Tom, had to try to talk sense.

Frio knocked at the door of the small

frame house. For a moment he thought there would be no answer, then he heard someone walking softly. The door opened just a little, and dark eyes peered out cautiously. A woman's eyes.

"Quién es?" she asked suspiciously.

Frio removed his hat. "I'm lookin' for Tom McCasland."

"He is not here. Go away." She closed the door.

Frio rapped again. The door opened once more, a little wider this time. She was a Mexican woman in her mid-twenties — not a beauty, perhaps, but more than passable — and she was angry. "Look," she said in English that was surprisingly good, "I tell you already, he is not home. He has ride for you already one time this week. Why you don't leave him alone?"

"You got me mixed up with somebody else, ma'am. I'm a friend of his. I just want to talk with him."

The door opened a little wider. "You come to talk war? I don't want for him to ride out anymore. Next time they kill him maybe."

"I don't want him to ride out anymore either. That's what I came to talk to him about."

The anger began to fade from her eyes. "You are not another of those from the

66

yanqui government, wanting him to do the dangerous things?"

Frio shook his head. "I'm from *el otro lado,* the other side of the river. Name's Frio Wheeler."

"Wheeler." She frowned, slowly testing the word on her tongue. "Yes, I have hear him speak that name. You are a friend."

"I used to be. I hope I still am."

The door swung open. "Tom is not here, Señor Wheeler. But come in. Maybe we should talk together."

The room was not cool, for she had kept the front door closed against intrusion from the foot traffic on the street. He felt some flow of air through open side windows and a back door. The room was simply furnished, nothing fancy. He saw curtains, though, and a bowl of cut flowers adding a splash of color. Tom wasn't living here by himself.

"I haven't met you before," Frio said.

She had a handsome figure, and from the lightness of her complexion he thought she might be pure Spanish. There was still pride in the people of the *sangre puro,* the unmixed blood. He sensed that she was a lady, or had been.

"I am Luisa Valdez."

She would have stopped there, but Frio

glanced at her hand and saw the rings. Then she went on, for his eyes were asking the question he was too polite to speak. "Yes, I am a married woman, or was. My husband is one time an officer for the Juaristas. The Crinolinos, they kill him. Tom McCasland, he is good friend of my husband and me. When my husband is die, I have no people anymore, no money. For a woman without these things, there is but one way to live in Matamoros. I would die first. So I am come to Tom, and he is give me a place to live." She paused. "I know what you think, but he is a good man."

Frio said, "I know that, ma'am, a good man." He twisted his hat. "You in love with him?"

She was slow to answer. Then, nodding, she replied, "Yes, I love him."

"You figurin' on marryin' him?"

She dropped her chin. "He has ask me, and I am tell him no. I love him, Señor Wheeler, but war has make me a widow one time. I do not want that it makes me a widow again. I tell Tom that when his war is over, when there is no more fight, then I marry him. Not before that. I do not want to be widow ever again."

"I wouldn't want you to be. I want to have Tom stay in Matamoros where he won't be gettin' hurt. You know where he's at right now?"

She shook her head. "He is tell me he has government business. He says he will be back tonight and take me to the *fandango.*"

Frio had heard something about the big dance while he was sitting in the bar waiting for Blas. "You think if I went to the *fandango* I'd get a chance to see him?"

"He will be there."

Frio said, "Then so will I."

He started to back toward the door. Luisa Valdez stared at him with eyes that seemed to weep for sadness. She shifted to Spanish because the words came easier to her that way. "Señor Wheeler, there is much I do not understand. Where is there reason in all this war? You and Tom, you are friends, but one of you is on one side and one is on the other. You are friends and yet you are enemies. Where is there reason in this?"

He answered her in English, for though he understood Spanish well enough, he could not always express himself as he wanted. It was common on the border to hear bilingual conversations, each party using the language that came easiest. "Well, Mrs. Valdez, it's this way. . . ." His voice trailed off, for he knew he couldn't explain it to her. He couldn't explain it to himself.

"War," she said gravely, "is a useless thing, a foolishness that men create for themselves. They fight wars like they would race horses or gamble with cards or put roosters in a pit. It is the woman who suffers, because she must live on alone when her man has died. The men fight, but it is the women who must cry the tears and live an empty life after the foolish game of the men is over. If it were left to the women, there would be no wars."

Frio tried to meet her accusing gaze but looked away. There was no arguing with her, because he could find no answer for what she had said.

"You are a soldier?" she asked him.

He shook his head. "No, I am a rancher and a freighter. I freight cotton to the river and haul merchandise north."

"You are not a soldier, but your wagons carry the goods that go to fight the war. Is there really a difference?"

"Not much," he admitted, "when you think about it. But it's somethin' somebody has to do, and it seems I'm the one. Our side didn't ask for this war, ma'am. It was somethin' they forced us to."

Her eyes seemed to pity him. "I suppose the other side feels the same way about it."

Frio dropped his gaze. "I hadn't done

much thinkin' on it thataway."

"It is how Tom feels. Strange, isn't it? Both of you feel the same way, yet you find yourselves on opposite sides, against each other. Perhaps both of you need to do some thinking. Perhaps each of you could see the other's viewpoint if you tried."

Uncomfortable, completely out of answers, Frio found himself edging again toward the door. This was no ordinary woman, he could see that. Luisa Valdez had a mind of her own, a strong one.

He said, "Tell Tom, will you, that I'll see him at the *fandango*. No, on second thought, don't tell him. He might not go."

"He will go," she promised. "I will see to it."

He stepped outside. He started to put his hat on and walk toward the sorrel, but he turned back to Luisa Valdez. "Hang on to him, Mrs. Valdez, and keep him out of trouble. I'd like to see you married to him. I'd like to have you for a friend."

Her lips turned upward with a thin semblance of a smile. "*Ojalá*. You are a good man too, I think. I would hope we can be friends."

The Matamoros *fandango* was more than a dance. It was a meeting place for friends who hadn't seen each other in a long time. It was a whole-family affair and a drinking bout and a gamblers' haven, all rolled into one. It wouldn't get started until nine o'clock, because darkness wouldn't come until after eight. The last of the diehards wouldn't leave before daylight had come again.

Frio went back on the ferry to the Brownsville side to bathe and shave and put on fresh clothes. He also took the opportunity to be sure his recovered mules had been given plenty of feed and fresh water. They had already taken on a good fill by the time he saw them. Tomorrow or the next day they would be ready for the trail.

He dropped by the McCasland place to visit a little more with Meade, and to see Amelia again. Amelia's eyes widened when he told her where he was going tonight. "The *fandango*? What do you want to go there for?"

"For one thing, they're fun. For another, I've got some business."

Her eyes narrowed. "What kind of business? What does she look like?"

Frio tried to keep his face serious. "Well, she stands about six-and-a-half feet tall, has one blue eye and one brown one. Get tired of one color, you just look at the other eye awhile."

"I'm green with jealousy." Excitement kindled in her face. "Frio, I've never been to a *fandango*. Take me with you."

"Amelia, a *fandango* across the river isn't like the dances you see over here. They're not what you're used to."

"That suits me fine," she said eagerly. "I've heard about them, but I've never had anyone to take me. I certainly couldn't go by myself. Now I've got somebody to go with, and I want to see one." Her eyes were aglow. She squeezed his hands. "Please, Frio."

"I'll level with you, Amelia. Main reason I'm goin' is to have a talk with Tom."

"I'd like to see him too."

"What we've got to talk about, you might not like."

Her eyes changed. She seemed to sense that something was not right. "You're friends, Frio. I hope you're not going to argue with him again about the war."

"Not the whole war, Amelia, just a little part of it."

"I still want to go."

He gave in grudgingly. "All right," he acceded, against his better judgment. "I'll be back about eight and get you. I'll borrow a rig."

73

Later he asked Blas Talamantes if he was going. Blas shook his head. María was at the ranch, Blas explained, and a dance wouldn't mean much without her. It had been only three days since Blas had left the ranch, but already he was homesick for his wife.

Amelia's face was aglow with adventure as Frio slowed the buggy horse to a walk in the heavy traffic around the Matamoros main plaza. The smell of flowers and the sound of music were in the air. Young couples strolled arm in arm along the fenced walkways that led inward toward the center circle of the plaza like spokes slanting to the hub of a wheel. Old men — and those not yet old but married long enough to enjoy getting away from their women — sat on benches beneath the trees to tell lies about their exploits in war and on the perilous trails.

Amelia looked up in the gathering darkness at the two tall spires of the huge cathedral that sat beside the American-looking customs house. "A beautiful thing, isn't it?" she said. "Even when they were hungry, they took from what little money they had and built a church."

"The soul," said Frio, quoting a Mexican priest he had heard, "may hunger more than the body."

Listening in the night, he could hear voices speaking many tongues — Spanish and English, naturally, but French and German as well, and others he could not identify. All these people, drawn from across the world to this unlikely place by the smell of money — and the money because of war.

His mind went back to the sorrow he had seen in the dark eyes of Luisa Valdez. "It's a soul-hungry time," he said.

Paper lanterns of many colors spread their light on the hundreds who were drawn to the gaiety of the *fandango.* By nine-thirty most of the crowd was there. Somewhere off to one side, boys were firing squibs and firecrackers, and frightened horses jerked at the reins that held them to a fence.

The little orchestra began to play. It was made up of an old fiddle, an ancient clarinet, and a drum, the latter nothing but a barrel with rawhide stretched across the top. There was a guitar and a trumpet. Leader was Don Sisto the fiddler, a stoop-shouldered old man with a gray mustache and fiercely proud eyes, and a leather outfit that must once have been something to see. Like its wearer, it had been too many miles down too many roads.

Her hand clasped on Frio's arm, Amelia McCasland walked about, fascinated by what she saw. Always there had been a quiet admiration and a soft spot in her heart for the Mexicans. Benches had been placed in such a manner as to form a large square. Dancers used the center area while spectators sat on the benches. Many of the Mexican women smoked, just as did their men. Amelia watched in wonder. Across the river it was not unusual for Texas women to dip snuff, but she had never seen them smoke. Well, almost never. Now and again she had seen an immigrant Southern woman — not of the gentry — smoke a corncob pipe.

Outside the benches, gambling tables and drinking booths had been set up. Frio didn't count them, but he guessed there must have been forty tables, most already occupied by games of monte. The players bent in intense concentration. Men, women, and even a goodly number of children stood around the outer fringes, watching the monte with as much eagerness as did the players themselves.

A sudden stir began at the entrance. Frio saw a bright-colored uniform and the proud bearing of the man who wore it. A worshipful retinue followed along with the officer. Even the monte players looked up, and many of the people began to cheer.

Amelia squeezed Frio's arm. "Is that who I think it is?"

He nodded. "It's Cortina — the Red Robber of the Rio Grande."

She said quickly, "Shh-h-h, don't talk that way. You're in his country now." She stared at the fabled Mexican officer. "So that's what he really looks like. He isn't nearly so big as I thought he was the other time I saw him."

Surprised, Frio asked, "When was that?"

"The time he took Brownsville four years ago. It was one morning before daylight. I heard horses running and people yelling. There were some shots. I ran to the window just as a Mexican loped by shouting, 'Viva Cheno Cortina! Death to the gringos!' Then came Cortina himself, riding at the head of a group. It was dark, so I couldn't see him clearly, but he looked seven feet tall there in the saddle. Dad pulled me away from the window then. He and Tom and Bert kept me hidden in the cellar until Cortina and his men all left town."

Frio noticed that the music had slowed. Don Sisto had turned to see what the excitement was about, and his face had tightened with sudden anger. Though most Mexicans revered Cortina, Don Sisto was one of that minority who hated him with passion. Once Cortina's raiders had picked up Don Sisto and his band on the Brownsville-Laredo road, thinking them to be Texas-Mexican government officials. They had carried the men to Cortina to see if he wanted them shot. "Damned musicians!" Cortina had shouted impatiently. "*Fandango* sharps! Turn them loose and get them out of here!"

The insult had given Don Sisto's pride a wound that would never heal. "He did not need to treat us as if we were dogs," he had said a hundred times. "The least he could have done was to shoot us like men!"

Cortina's eyes touched Frio for a moment, recognizing him. Then the border chieftain found himself a seat at a table, the worshiping retinue crowding around him. Don Sisto went back to his music.

Frio said to the girl, "If you've had enough, I'll take you home."

"Not on your life," she thrilled. "I wouldn't have missed this for all of Abe Lincoln's gold."

He had looked all around the place and hadn't seen any sign of Tom. "Amelia, I'm no great shakes as a dancer, but I'd be much obliged if you'd try one with me."

He found the girl light and graceful in his

arms. Though he was wooden and unpracticed at this, she seemed to follow along without a bobble, making him feel like a good dancer. They danced one tune, two tunes, three. Each one was faster than the one before it. When the last tune ended, Frio was puffing.

"I'm about caved in," he grinned, not really wanting to quit. He enjoyed having her in his arms. "Maybe we better set a spell."

Amelia didn't seem to have tired a bit. Her eyes aglow, she laughed, "Who was it said this would be too tough for me?"

He took her hand and led her back toward the benches. He stopped abruptly as he saw Tom McCasland standing there with Luisa Valdez. Tom's face was sober, but Frio could tell it wouldn't take much prompting to cause him to smile.

Tom stepped forward and kissed his sister. "Hello, Sis. Never dreamed I'd see you here."

Amelia looked him up and down critically, as if worried about his health. "Found out Frio was coming. You couldn't have driven me away with a club."

Hesitantly Tom extended his hand. "Hello, Frio."

"Howdy, Tom." Frio gripped his old

friend's hand, and for a moment they stood looking at one another, searching each other's eyes to see if the old friendship had survived the years. It had.

Tom said, "I believe you've both met Luisa."

Frio bowed from the waist. Amelia nodded her head but stared uncertainly at Mrs. Valdez. She was plainly at a loss as to how she should accept the woman. There could be no doubt in her mind about the relationship between Luisa Valdez and her brother. It was a relationship that would have brought censure across the river. Here it seemed to be taken as a matter of course. Recognizing that she was south of the river and that it was not her place to pass judgment, Amelia said courteously, "It's nice to see you again, Luisa."

And Luisa Valdez, undoubtedly reading everything that passed through Amelia's mind, replied with all the grace of one to the manor born. "And you, Amelia. You are most pretty tonight."

Tom said, "I see an empty table over yonder. I've brought some brandy."

They sat, and Tom poured brandy into four small glasses. The two men and Mrs. Valdez sipped theirs with pleasure. Amelia went slowly, tasting with caution. For a proper young woman on the Texas side of the river, not even brandy was lightly taken. She had sampled little of it in her life.

Amelia and Tom talked of personal things, about life in Brownsville, about their father and his store. Finally Tom looked back to Frio. "Luisa said you wanted to talk to me. I can make a fair guess what it's about."

Frio glanced at Amelia. "Might be better if we went off someplace, Tom, just us two."

"If it's about the war, there's no use startin'."

"Not the whole war, Tom, just your part in it."

Tom shrugged. "There's not much to tell. I'm workin' for the United States government through Leonard Pierce, the consul. I keep watch, make reports about the border situation, the river trade and such."

Frio's eyes narrowed. "Does that job include goin' across the river?"

Amelia stiffened in surprise. Luisa Valdez was staring down into her brandy, her face grave.

Tom said, "What do you mean by that?"

Frio glanced at Amelia and wondered if he ought to say it. But she would find out sooner or later. "Tom, I lost four teams of mules, a wagon, and some cotton. One of my men was wounded. Blas Talamantes and me, we were in the brush and saw the raiders as they came by."

Tom lowered his head, "And?"

"And I want to know why, Tom. What's the sense of it? With all the hundreds of wagons that come down the trail, what good would it do you to knock out five, or even ten or fifteen? It's like tryin' to empty the Gulf of Mexico with a bucket."

Tom put his hands together and thoughtfully pressed his thumbs against his chin. "I didn't know they were your wagons, Frio, till we got there and I saw your brand painted on them. It wouldn't have made any difference, though, it had to be done." His eyes asked for understanding. "Frio, I love Texas as much as you do. I don't want to kill anybody. The way I see it, you don't have to kill a man to stop him; you can scare him away. If we hit a few wagons here, a few there, we can scare a lot of teamsters. We can make them afraid to start down the trail. Get enough men scared and we can slow down the border trade. Might even stop it."

"When a man's fightin' for what he believes in, he can take a lot of scarin' and still go on. What if they don't stop, Tom?"

Tom's face pinched with regret. "Then I guess we'll have to kill."

Frio stared awhile at his old friend, knowing that at heart Tom was as sick of the war as he was himself. "Look at the caliber of men you're ridin' with, Tom. Florencio Chapa, a cutthroat. His own people are afraid of him. Even Cortina hates him, though he uses him. And Bige Campsey! Now, there's a renegade for you."

"War forces a man into some strange partnerships, Frio. We need Chapa, and he's available, so we use him."

"Maybe it's the other way around; maybe he's usin' you. He's a born murderer. I could name you a dozen helpless Mexican teamsters he's tortured to death on the old Laredo road. All you've done is give him a chance to kill and claim it's legal. He rides out now and carries an American flag with him. No flag means anything to Chapa; not the Mexican flag and surely not yours."

Tom said, "He didn't kill anybody on this raid. That's one reason I went along, to be sure he didn't kill anybody he didn't have to. As for Campsey, he's loyal to the Union and wants to fight. He came here because he couldn't accept the Confederacy."

Frio said sharply, "He couldn't accept the draft. He came here because he shot a conscript officer in cold blood."

He could tell by the surprise in Tom's face

that this was news to him. "This kind of business takes rough men, Frio."

Frio begged, "Quit this, Tom, while you still can. One day they'll catch you across the river and you won't get back."

Tom slowly shook his head. "I know what I have to do, Frio. I've argued with you before about the Union and the Confederacy, so I won't do that now. Each of us has his own loyalties, and nothin' we say to each other will change that. But I want you to think, Frio. One day soon the Union is goin' to send troops in here and close this border. Nothin' you can do will alter that. The trail's goin' to be dangerous from now on. I wish you'd go back to that ranch of yours and stay there. This war won't last much longer. I want you to be alive when it's over."

"What makes you think you're goin' to win?"

"You may not have gotten the news yet, Frio. Have you heard about Gettysburg?"

Frio shook his head. "Who is he?"

"It's not a man, it's a place, a town in Pennsylvania. They've just fought a big battle there, the worst of the war. No one knows how many men died. When it was over, Lee and his army fell back toward Virginia. The Union will win now. It's just a question of time." His eyes pleaded. "See, Frio? There's no use for you to risk your life anymore. Your cause is lost."

Shaken by Tom's news, Frio still could not accept it, *would* not accept it. "It can't be. We've hoped so long, struggled so hard. . . ." He looked up. "A man doesn't accept defeat while he still stands. He fights as long as the breath is still in him. Stop my wagons? No, sir! I'll patch them and try to buy more. I'll haul cotton south as long as there's anybody to buy it, and I'll haul war supplies north as long as there's anybody left to haul them to. Quit? Hell, man, I haven't even started yet!"

Tom's eyes went cold in disappointment. "You may die, Frio."

"It'll be in the service of Texas."

Tom said softly, "I'm in the service of Texas too. I'm servin' her the way it seems best to me."

He looked up at the sound of angry voices. Frio turned in his chair. He saw El Gordo Gutierrez limping painfully toward him, his face livid with rage, his hands a-tremble. Beside him stalked the black-clad *bandido,* Florencio Chapa.

"You are a thief!" El Gordo bawled at Frio, his finger pointing. "You have taken my mules and stolen my money!"

The sight of the fat man somehow broke Frio's somber mood. Incredibly, he wanted to laugh. El Gordo's clothes were brush-torn from the long walk the young robbers had given him. Sweat poured down his face, leaving trails in the dust that clung there. He looked angry enough to blow apart like a runaway steam boiler.

Innocently Frio said, "I don't know what you're talkin' about. I paid you for those mules."

"And stole back the money!" The fat man cursed wildly in the saltiest border Spanish. He accused Frio of hiring *bandidos* to steal the money that was rightfully El Gordo's and Chapa's.

Understanding came into Tom Mc-Casland's eyes. Quickly he moved the women away. The music had stopped. The people stared.

Florencio Chapa's dark hand dropped to his belt and came up swiftly. A knifeblade flashed. "Gringo!" he hissed. "You are a gringo thief. I will spill your blood like a rooster in the pit!"

Frio pushed away from the table, into the clear. He carried no gun, no knife. He crouched, waiting to try to avoid the bandit's vengeful rush. His lips went dry, for already he could almost feel the cold steel of the blade. Chapa would be too much for a man with bare hands.

Tom McCasland stepped in front of Chapa. "Florencio, he is a friend of mine. He is no thief."

"Out of the way! You are just another gringo now!"

"He has stolen no money. He has been with me." It was a lie, but for a moment Chapa hesitated. Tom went on, his voice holding even. "My government has given you money and guns to fight with. Do you want that to stop?"

It gave Chapa pause. His black eyes still seethed with anger, but reason seemed to be struggling for the upper hand.

"Forget it, Florencio," Tom said. "There will be other days, other rides across the river."

Chapa still hesitated. Then the man in the bright uniform stepped forward. No policeman would have dared interfere with Florencio Chapa, but this man had no fear of him. Juan Cortina said in swift, quiet Spanish, "Go, Florencio my friend. Do not spoil the people's *fandango.*"

Chapa glanced at Cortina, his eyes rebellious a moment, then acquiescing. He straightened. Not wanting to, he slowly shoved the knife back into the scabbard at his belt. His sharp eyes fastened again on Frio, and they spoke silently of death. At length he turned on his heel. "Come, brother-in-law," he spoke to El Gordo. "We leave this place."

"But the money. . . ."

"Come. I say we leave."

Chapa took three paces and stopped to turn once more toward Frio, his face deadly. "Gringo, I will see you again!"

It was a minute or two before Frio walked back toward Tom and the women. "Thanks, Tom," he said tightly. He looked at the ashen-faced Amelia McCasland. "I oughtn't to've brought you."

Tears glistened in her eyes. She didn't reply.

Tom said with admiration, "So you skinned them at their own game and got your money back."

"I didn't say that."

"You didn't have to." Concerned, Tom said, "Up to now you've just been another damned gringo to Chapa. From now on you'll be a prime target. You've made an enemy of him, Frio."

Frio said, "I never wanted him for a friend." He turned to the girl. "Amelia, I better take you home."

The music had started again. Slowly the

crowd drifted back to its dance, to its monte. Tom saw Cortina still watching him, and he nodded unspoken thanks to the man.

Amelia said shakenly, "Yes, Frio, take me home."

As Frio and Amelia walked away, Luisa Valdez moved up and put her arm in Tom's. She stared gravely after the departing couple. "He is a determined man, Tom. He will fight so long as there is breath in him."

Tom nodded soberly. "I reckon he will."

"If you meet him on the other side of the river, you will have to fight him."

"Luisa, I'm servin' my country. I do what has to be done."

"In the end, one of you may have to kill the other."

Tom drew his lips against his teeth and closed his eyes a moment. "As your people say, Fortune and Death come from above. What can a man do to change Fate?" He took her hand and squeezed tightly and felt the responding pressure of her fingers. "Come, Luisa, let's go home."

5

Frio Wheeler squinted back through the dust at his lumbering wagon train, moving along the brush-edged trail behind him, making poor time because heavy sand tugged stubbornly at the iron-rimmed wheels. The mules strained in harness, sweat shining against their brown hides. They needed a rest, but it was less than a mile now to the well. They could have a rest there, and water too, unless this well had gone dry like some of the others.

Fall had come, but still there had been no effective rain. Where normally his mules could find cured grass, there was only the sand. Along trailside, dust churned by thousands of wagon and cart wheels had settled on the brush with the appearance of a dirty snow. No rain had come to wash it away. Now it was November, and it seemed that half his cargo was Indian corn, carried along of necessity to feed the mules.

Through the dust he saw Happy Jack Fleet coming forward in a trot. Happy wasn't hurrying, so whatever he had on his mind must not be particularly important. Eyes on the trail ahead, Frio stopped and waited. Happy Jack reined up and let his horse blow. Frio smiled at the sight of the young man's eyes, staring from a dust-masked face like two small pools of water in the midst of a desert.

"Must be nice to be an owner," the cowboy said. "Get to ride up front in the clean air instead of back in the dusty drags."

Frio shrugged, still smiling. "But think of the responsibility. Anything happens to these wagons, the loss is all mine. You've got nothin' to lose but your life, and maybe that horse."

"I hadn't thought of it thataway," Happy Jack admitted, his eyes shining with humor. "Guess you do take all the risk." He reached in his pocket and brought out a Havana cigar, bought in Matamoros. He allowed himself just one a day so they would last the whole trip. He wouldn't smoke it. He would simply start chewing on it and eventually wear it away to a nub. "Some of them mules are might' near dried out. Reckon that next well has still got water in it?"

"It had better have," Frio said. "We've

about emptied our barrels."

They had counted on the last well they'd passed, for it had contained water when they were on their way north. Now, on the return trip to Brownsville, they had found it dry. They had rationed water from half-empty barrels in hopes that the next one, at least, would still yield. Most of the natural waterholes had dried up or had receded to small stinking bogs rimmed with parched remnants of rank weeds and with the skeletons of starved cattle and wild animals of the brush.

Frio said, "Better ease on back and take up the rear guard again. No better place for *renegados* to hit a train than just before it gets to water. Stock is dry and slow, and the men have got their minds on a drink."

Happy Jack nodded. "Hear of any new raids lately?"

"Army courier the other day told me renegades hit a couple of small wagon trains a little ways south of here. Killed three teamsters, made off with some rifles and war goods. That's why I'm not lettin' my wagons split up, ever again. As many as we are, we can give them a pretty good scrap."

He hadn't seen anything of Tom Mc-Casland since that night at the *fandango*. He had seen Florencio Chapa once, over his rifle sight. Chapa had made an exploratory probe against Frio's wagons but had retired quickly upon finding how much firepower Frio's men could mass against him. He had not tried again, although occasionally Frio felt eyes watching him from the brush.

Chapa hadn't forgotten him. He never would.

Frio slipped his saddlegun out of the boot and took a position in front of the train. Presently he reached the clearing that marked the well. He eased into it with the wariness of a deer edging into an open field to graze. He stopped a moment, spotted the two men at the well — only two — and decided the way was clear. He rode ahead, putting the rifle back into the boot.

A Mexican family had settled here originally, and the ruins of their brush *jacal* had stood until one day last winter when a freighter had accidentally burned the place trying to keep warm. The Mexicans' laboriously hand-dug well was still as good as the first day they had dropped a bucket into it and had drawn up fresh water. That it had a slight salt tang was of little importance. Most water in this country did.

Frio frowned as he recognized the big man at the well — the cotton trader Trammell, who had tried once to hire Frio's wagons. Frio didn't know the tall, heavy-shouldered man beside Trammell, but he thought he could recognize the type. This was one of the kind who always came in troubled times — a tough, a saloon brawler more than likely. He wore a pistol in his waistband and gripped a rifle in his huge, speckled hands. The two men stepped forward as Frio approached. Frio dismounted.

"Howdy, Trammell," he said, his voice flat. "Where did you come from?"

"There's lots of trails through the brush, Wheeler, but they all lead to water. I'm headin' to Matamoros, same as you."

The trader was dirty and unshaven from long days on the trail. He jerked his head toward his companion. "This here is Bouncer Bush. I reckon you've heard of him?"

Frio had, and the name simply confirmed his earlier opinion.

"I got wagons comin'," he said, turning to point his chin at the first of them moving into the clearing. "If you'll pardon me, I'll be drawin' up water for my mules."

Trammell shook his head. "No, you won't."

Frio stiffened. "And why not?"

"Because there's just so much water in that well, and it takes a right smart of time for it to seep more in again. I got some wagons comin' too. I claim first right to that water."

"Your wagons aren't here yet. Mine are."

"But *I'm* here, and so is Bouncer. We rode ahead to stake us a claim. Now you just circle up your wagons and wait, Wheeler. Maybe by noontime we'll be through here."

Frio said, "I got thirsty mules, and they're goin' to have water."

Bush swung the muzzle of his rifle around. Frio looked down its barrel and felt his stomach draw up. "Trammell, you got no right to do this. It's first come, first served on this trail."

"And I was the first come."

"But not with wagons."

"I got Bush here, and he's got a rifle. You got any law that'll countermand that sort of combination?" The cotton trader grinned with sarcasm. "You talked a mite rough to me one time, Wheeler. I been hopin' ever since that I'd get a chance to rub your nose in it a little."

Frio's cheeks blazed with anger. "I never said anything to you that wasn't the truth. This just goes to prove it."

A movement caught Frio's eye. At the edge of the clearing, behind Trammell and Bush, he saw Happy Jack Fleet swing down from his horse. Rifle in hand, the cowboy began moving cautiously forward, trying to make no sound. Frio decided to keep Trammell interested and prevent him from noticing Happy.

"How does it feel to be gettin' rich off other men's blood, Trammell?" Frio asked. "Do you ever wake up at night and think about the boys who are dead because the cotton money that was supposed to buy them guns and ammunition went into your pockets instead?"

Trammell flared. "If it wasn't me, it would be somebody else. It had just as well be me."

"You don't ever worry about those boys up there fightin' the war?"

"Sure I worry; I'm a good Southerner. But I'm a businessman too. This war can't last forever, so I'm goin' to make all I can while I can. If them boys are fated to die anyway, nothin' I do is goin' to hurt them or help them. It's all written down up yonder in a Big Book, everything that's goin' to happen to a man, the date and the place. I can't change a word of it. And if I don't take care of myself, nobody else is goin' to."

Frio said, "Reckon you know what they've got written down in that Big Book for you, Trammell? I hope it's somethin' strong enough to fit the crime."

Face darkening, the trader took an angry step forward, then realized he was about to step between Frio and the rifle. He jumped aside with more agility than Frio would have thought he had. "I got a good notion to let Bouncer take care of you, Wheeler. Lord knows you got it comin'."

Frio smiled. "You waited too long. Now I got a man behind you."

Trammell snickered, thinking it was a trick. Then Happy Jack thumbed back the hammer of his rifle with a click that could have been heard halfway across the clearing. Trammell and Bush whirled, their jaws slack with surprise.

Happy Jack grinned, the unlighted cigar in his mouth, tilted upward. "This look about right to you, Frio?"

Frio walked around to peer into Trammell's astonished face. "I'd say you might be aimin' just a shade high, Happy. Bear down to about the fourth button."

"That's a target I couldn't hardly miss."

Bush dropped his rifle. Frio picked it up and let the hammer down easy, then pitched it off to one side. He took the pistol from Bush's waistband and sent it sailing after the rifle. "Now I reckon you men can sit yourselves down and watch us water our mules."

They brought the wagons out into the clearing. Frio's Mexican teamsters began dividing the wagons into two sections and circling them, curving so that the wagon tongues pointed outward. They started unhitching the mules then. Some of the Mexicans came to help Frio and Happy haul up water out of the well and pour it into hollowed-out trees that served as troughs. It would be a slow process, watering all the teams this way. But time meant little to a mule.

Trammell sat glowering. His own train came into sight while Frio's teamsters were watering the last of Frio's mules and filling the barrels on their wagons. By that time the water in the well had declined almost to the limit of the bucket rope's reach. It would take a while to seep full enough again to water Trammell's stock.

"Well, Trammell," Frio said, "we'll hit the trail again directly and turn this over to you. A man ought to've just shot you a while ago and left you here. Try somethin' like that again and maybe I just will."

Contemptuously he turned his back on the cotton trader and swung onto his sorrel horse. He looked a moment at Trammell's wagons filing out of the chaparral. There must have been thirty of them. At up to sixteen bales per wagon, that was not much short of five hundred bales on the one train. No wonder Trammell had been concerned about establishing a claim on the water, even an invalid claim. This much cotton at the present eighty-cents-a-pound river market represented a fortune.

Frio signaled his Mexican *caporal.* "Let's head them out!" He took the lead and moved on down the trail, pointing south. Behind him Happy Jack sat his horse, watching the wagons move into place and singing a Confederate war song dedicated irreverently to Abraham Lincoln:

"You are a boss, a mighty hoss
A-snortin' in the stable;
A racer too, a kangaroo,
But whip us if you're able!"

Frio saw the dust first, then heard the sound of the horses. He drew the saddle-gun, raising it over his head in the signal that would stop the train behind him. He glanced backward and saw the teamsters getting their wagons ready. Two gun-carrying outriders moved up, one on either side of the train. At the rear, Happy Jack came spurring fast. He overtook the outriders and sent one back to cover the end of the train. He galloped his horse up and reined him in beside Frio.

"We fixin' to have company?" It was a needless question, for he could see the dust.

The first riders came into view. Frio stood in the stirrups, looking through a spyglass he had won from a ship's officer in a Matamoros monte game. "Soldiers, Happy."

"Ours?"

"Who else?"

"The way they've stripped the garrison at Fort Brown, it's been just like sendin' old Abe an engraved invitation."

"That's the way of war. The privates fight to win it, and the generals give it away."

Frio recognized the men as some of General Bee's command out of Fort Brown. The soldiers pulled their horses to a stop in front of Frio and Happy. One was a lieutenant.

Happy said, "Say, boys, the river's thataway," pointing in the direction from which the soldiers had come.

"So are the Yankees!" replied the lieutenant excitedly. "We've just abandoned the fort. The Yankees have landed at Brazos Santiago!"

Frio felt as if one of his mules had kicked him in the belly. This was news he had expected for months, yet he wasn't ready for it. He swallowed hard. "You sure about that, Lieutenant?"

"There's no question of it, sir. Last spy report we had was that there were nearly thirty transports. Rumor was that ten thousand troops were moving on Brownsville, with Texas renegades from across the river showing them the way."

Frio swore, watching the rest of the Confederate entourage moving up rapidly. His mind went quickly to Amelia McCasland, and Meade. "What about the civilians in Brownsville?"

"Most of the Anglos are getting across the river as quick as they can. When we left they had the ferries jammed with household goods. They were pushing and shoving, fighting for places on board. It was an awful mess."

Anger touched Frio. "And you just rode off and left them that way?"

"Some of us would have stayed and fought, but the general said no. The handful of troops we had left wouldn't have held the Yankees back long." He looked behind him. "You'd better move these wagons aside and leave the trail for the general. He'll probably burn them anyway."

"The hell he will!" Frio blurted.

He turned and signaled for the wagons to move off the road. The signal was unnecessary, for the lieutenant passed the word to every teamster as he rode by. Frio and Happy Jack sat their horses in the trail and waited.

At length the general came, riding on an ambulance. He was forty-one years old, General Hamilton Prioleau Bee, and looked much older. He had been a state legislator from Laredo before the war, and he was destined to become a hero in battle before the war was done. But this was not his heroic day. His face was red with excitement and pressure. His hands were unsteady.

"Whose train is this?" he asked quickly.

"Mine, sir," replied Frio.

The general peered at him with narrowed eyes. "Oh, yes, Wheeler, isn't it? You've already heard? The Yankees are coming."

"I heard."

"I have orders from General Magruder in Austin not to let a bale of cotton fall into enemy hands. We fired all the cotton that was left in Brownsville before we retreated. We'll have to burn yours."

Frio squared himself in the saddle, his mouth turning down at the corners. "Not my cotton. I had *my* orders too. They were to get this cotton to Matamoros. You're not goin' to burn it!"

Bee stiffened at the unexpected disobedience. He started to reply, then sputtered. Frio could see the man's experience in evacuating Brownsville had left him almost totally unstrung. Bee studied a moment, then said, "Very well, not all of the cotton then. Dump half of it and set it afire. Maybe with only half a load you can keep these wagons moving at a good pace northward. We'll rally at King's Ranch and work out a plan of action."

Frio shook his head. "I've already worked out mine. I'm hangin' onto this cotton. Burn the other trains if you can, but you're leavin' mine alone!"

Bee sputtered again. "I've given you an order, sir!"

"I'm not a soldier." Frio leaned forward in the saddle. His voice dropped almost to a whisper, but it had the sting of a whip. "If you fire this cotton, you'll have to kill me first!"

Bee's mouth dropped open, but no sound came. He glanced around him to see if he had the support of his troops. He did.

Frio said, "General, the South needs this cotton. One way or another, I'm goin' to try to get it across the river. But I promise you this: If it ever looks like it's fixin' to be captured, I'll set it afire myself."

The troops pressed in, ready to follow their general's orders even if it meant blasting Frio Wheeler out of the saddle. But General Bee finally shrugged. He was angry, yet he was impressed by the unyielding freighter who sat here and defied him in the face of impossible odds.

"Very well, Wheeler. On that promise, I'll leave you your wagons. God help you." He thought a moment, then added, "God help us all!"

A moment later he was gone in a cloud of dust, trailed by mounted troops and by some forty wagons and carts carrying what supplies he had been able to salvage before putting the fort and the cottonyard to the torch.

When they had gone, Frio sat his horse in the middle of the trail, watching the dust slowly settle. His shoulders sagged, for the weight of the news bore heavily upon him. He seethed with anxiety for the McCaslands. He wanted to forget about the wagons and rush into Brownsville to find out what had happened to Amelia and Meade. But he knew his first responsibility was here. With the world collapsing around him, he had to save this cotton, had to get it across the river for the Confederacy.

Still, a man couldn't just rush blindly ahead.

Happy Jack sat quietly awhile, waiting. Finally, impatient, he asked, "Well, what next, Frio? What're we goin' to do?"

Frio shook his head, not answering.

Happy said, "This sure does clabber the sweetmilk. I been lookin' ahead real hard to some fun in Matamoros. Last time I was there I found a place that had a real pretty little dancin' girl. I swear, Frio, she was barefooted clear up to her chin."

Frio growled, "Hush, Happy, and let me think." In a moment he said, "I'm sorry, I didn't go to be so ornery. It's just that. . . ." His face twisted, and he broke off. But a minute later he straightened in the saddle. "Let's get these wagons out into the chaparral, Happy. Get them plumb out of sight from the road. Later on, you come back with some of the men and brush out the tracks. We don't want anybody to find that cotton."

"And you, Frio? What're you goin' to do?"

"I'm goin' to Brownsville. I've got to scout around and see what's happened. If I'm not back here by this time tomorrow, fire the cotton and head north. You're on your own."

"Them Yankees will nail your hide to the fence." There was no levity in Happy's face now. "I'll go with you."

"No. You stay and see that the job is done right." He touched spurs to the sorrel and said, *"Adiós."*

A little later he turned once and saw white smoke rising from somewhere to the north. Trammell's wagon train, he knew. Bee had reached the well, and he hadn't listened to Trammell as he had listened to Frio.

There goes Trammell's fortune, Frio thought, and he had not a spark of sympathy for the trader.

6

The south wind brought him the stench of smoke long before he reached the town. Dusk closed in. Through it he could see flames lick upward and drop again. Some of Brownsville was still burning. On his way in he had met refugees running north. Most of them could give him little information. No, they hadn't seen the Yankees yet, but they were coming.

There were more than twenty thousand troops, one panic-stricken old woman told him, half shrieking. They had been taken out of the Eastern jails and insane asylums just for this job. Their officers had given them whisky to make them mad drunk, and now they were coming to slaughter the town.

Darkness caught him, and he knew he was lucky that it did. It would be a foolhardy stunt to ride into Brownsville in daylight, not knowing the whereabouts of the Union troops, not knowing the situation in the town. He could see a steady glow, probably from the cotton bales slowly burning away on the riverbank. Now and again, a fresh blaze sprang up. Occasionally he caught the sound of gunfire.

If the Yankees were there, someone had remained to show them resistance.

For the first time, a half-panicky thought struck him. What if it were not Yankees? What if the troops had not yet arrived? With the town wide open, defenseless, it would be like a magnet to all the motley border rabble from both sides of the river. It would give them an opportunity to pillage and burn with impunity, for there would be no law, no retribution.

A fresh anxiety welled up in him. If Amelia was still there. . . .

He spurred into a lope.

At the first *jacales* he met a Mexican coming out from the direction of town. The Mexican turned off the trail and started to run.

"Don't be afraid," Frio called to him in Spanish. "I won't hurt you."

The Mexican came up uncertainly, ready to run at the first sign of treachery. Frio asked, "Have the Yankee troops arrived in Brownsville yet?"

Sombrero in hand, the man replied, "No, señor, no *yanquis*. But there are many *bandidos*. It is dangerous to go into the town now."

"What of the people?"

"Many have gone across the river." His eyes rolled upward as he remembered. "Aiii, what a terrible sight, all the fires, all the people screaming. . . ."

He told Frio how General Bee had dropped his siege guns into the river, how he had set fire to the fort and the supplies he had not been able to move. Despairing of getting all the Confederate cotton across the river, Bee had ordered his men to set ablaze all of it that remained on the north bank. Finally Bee and his troops had started out hurriedly to overtake their wagon train and put the abandoned town far behind them.

The Mexican told of frightened townspeople struggling to get their most valuable possessions onto the ferries and flee across the river. There were so many that ferries and skiffs could not hope to carry them all. Desperate men paid exorbitant prices and still fought with fists and clubs to win places on the boats for themselves, their families, and their belongings. Household and store goods were piled high along the bank of the river. Fires from Fort Brown began to spread out into the town, setting the frame buildings ablaze. Finally the flames had touched a huge cache of gunpowder in the fort. The concussion knocked people to the ground, caved in the sides of nearby buildings, and hurled blazing debris high into the air. Some of it came down amid the piled goods awaiting the ferries, and the riverbank became a heartbreaking holocaust. Many a family lost everything they owned.

The Mexican trembled as he told of the things he had seen. "Some of the people stayed on this side of the river, and now the outlaws have come to steal what has not burned. Bad men, señor — Mexicans, gringos, men with no country. More people will die tonight."

A tingling played up and down Frio's back. He started to touch spurs to the sorrel. The Mexican said, "Do not go. It is not safe there."

"Is it safe anywhere?" Frio asked him. He put the sorrel into a lope. As he rode, he drew the saddlegun and gripped it in his right hand, ready. Moving down Elizabeth Street he came into the heavy dry smell of smoke. It pinched his nostrils, burned his eyes. He coughed, gasping for fresh air. A gust of clean wind came from the south, clearing his lungs.

The fires had not touched the upper end of the street. He could see looters at work in abandoned stores, frantically pulling goods down from the shelves, searching out the things they wanted. He heard someone challenge a pair of men who came out of a store, their arms loaded. The two dropped their loot and attacked the man who had spoken to them. They beat him to his knees with their gun barrels. Frio rode in and fired the rifle once in their direction. The two men broke into a run, disappearing down a dark alley. One of them paused a moment to snap off a wild shot that missed Frio by a considerable distance. The slug struck a brick building across the street and whined away. The beaten man staggered inside the store.

Keeping to the shadows, Frio put the sorrel into a long trot down the street toward the McCaslands'. As he rode, his anxiety swelled and grew. The farther he went, the brighter danced the flames ahead of him. Much of that part of town nearest the fort was either ablaze or already burned. The stench was heavy. His lungs ached from breathing the smoke.

Every few moments he heard a vagrant

shot, or two or three. Somewhere, here and there, people were defending their homes, their stores.

He reached the McCasland block. His smoke-burned eyes peered through the eerie firelight for the store with the high false front, the empty balcony that Meade McCasland had disliked so much. He saw it, and his heart leaped. It was ablaze. From out in the street, three men knelt and fired into the flames. Inside, someone fired back.

Frio shifted the rifle to his left hand, with the reins, and drew his six-shooter. He spurred the sorrel into a hard run and headed straight for the three men, firing as he rode. For a moment they held steady and returned his fire. Then one of them slumped. The other two grabbed him and pulled him into the darkness of an alley. Frio fired after them until he realized he was wasting his ammunition. He might need it before he was through here.

The sorrel was dancing wildly at sight of the flames. Frio jumped to the ground beside a dropped bundle of clothes he saw in the street. He picked a shirt from among the garments and tied it across the horse's eyes, blinding him.

"Amelia!" he called. "Meade!" Over the crackle of the flames he heard no response.

"Amelia!" he called again.

From inside the blazing store he heard her answer. "Frio! Frio!"

He moved the horse along the side of the building where the flames had not yet reached. He tied the blindfolded animal across the street and then tried the door. It was bolted from inside. On the ground he saw an empty wooden packing crate. Using this, he smashed a window and crawled inside. He found himself in the living quarters.

"Amelia!"

He heard her answer from up front, in the store. She was locked in. He twisted his body and struck the dividing door with his shoulder. The latch section splintered, and the door fell open. The blistering heat slapped him across the face.

He saw her framed amid the crackling flames. She was sobbing aloud as she tried vainly to pull a man's body across the floor ahead of the rapidly gaining fire. The boy Chico huddled in a corner, eyes wide in fear.

The fallen man was Meade McCasland, and Frio could tell he was hard hit. But there was no time to think of that. There might not even be time to get him out of the building before the blazing ceiling came crashing down upon them. Frio grabbed

Meade from behind and half lifted him up, dragging the old man's heels as he hurriedly started backing out.

"Get out, Amelia, Chico! Out the door, quick!"

Chico unfroze and bolted out the door Frio had smashed. Amelia hung back, her hands cupped almost at her mouth, her eyes swimming in tears.

Frio got Meade McCasland through the door. A moment later the ceiling caved in. Now the living quarters were beginning to burn. "We've got to get clear," Frio cried. "We've got to get to the street."

Amelia hurried ahead of him and unbolted the back door. The furnace heat seared Frio's lungs as he knelt and worked Meade's limp body up over his back so he could walk upright and carry the wounded man. Frio went out first, pistol in his hand. The girl and the little boy followed him. Across the street, where Frio had tied the sorrel, the flames had not yet reached. Bent over by Meade's weight, Frio struggled across and gently laid the man down on a porch. Then, in the crazy dancing light of the blaze, he knelt to examine Meade's wound. He found his hands sticky with the old man's blood. Frio tore open Meade's shirt.

Just then Meade gasped and went limp.

Frio lifted a wrist and felt for the pulse. There was none. Slowly, gently, he folded the old storekeeper's arms. He turned back to Amelia.

"I'm sorry," he said.

Her hands went over her face, and her shoulders trembled. Frio stood up and took her into his arms. The little boy knelt beside the old man and sobbed brokenly. Across the street the flames swept through the rest of the building. The roof seemed for a moment to buckle, then it went down with a roar that sent sparks high into the air. The sorrel danced in fear, for he could hear and smell even if he could not see.

From down the street, Frio heard a man's voice calling: "Dad! Amelia!" He heard a horse running, and he saw the figure break into sight. The man slid the horse to a stop and for a moment appeared on the verge of rushing into the blazing hull of McCasland's store.

"Dad!" he called again. "Amelia!"

Frio shouted, "Over here, Tom!"

Tom McCasland came running, leading the horse. He let the horse go, and it went to Frio's sorrel. Tom grabbed Amelia. "Amelia, are you all right?"

Then his gaze dropped to the floor of the porch. He choked, "Dad!" and knelt quickly.

He touched the hands and knew without having to ask. His body trembled as he slowly, lovingly moved his fingers over the quiet, still face. Finally he asked, "How did it happen?"

Frio said, "Looters. I just got here myself."

Amelia McCasland forced herself to speak. Her voice was thin. "Dad wouldn't leave. Said this was his home. Said he hadn't ever run in his life. He didn't think the Yankees would hurt us. He didn't count on this." She looked across the street at the death throes of the building that had been home. She cried a moment, then controlled herself. "With dark, the looters came. He tried to run them off with a rifle. They threw a lighted lantern through the window, then shot him as he tried to beat out the flames."

Tom choked. "If I had known . . . If I had had any idea . . . I was out at Brazos Santiago, where the troops were landing. I thought sure you-all would cross to Mata-moros before the trouble started."

Frio said, "Where are the Yankees at, Tom? Have they got here yet?"

Tom shook his head. "They'll get here, but it'll be a while. There's a storm out on the gulf. They're havin' a hard time gettin' the transports unloaded."

"How many troops?"

"Seven thousand seasick soldiers."

Frio took hold of the girl's arms. "Amelia, we've got to move. I'll take you anywhere you want to go, but we've got to get away from here. Some of those looters will be around again. They'd better not catch a woman out in the street."

She nodded woodenly and knelt to look at her father again. "What about Dad?"

Frio said, "I reckon we'll have to leave him to Tom."

Tom said, "Yes, Frio, I'll take care of Dad. But you're not goin' anyplace."

Frio turned quickly and found Tom Mc-Casland holding a pistol on him. "Tom, what is this?"

"I'm placin' you under arrest, Frio. I'm goin' to hold you till the Union troops get here."

Frio swayed. He would have expected almost anything but this. "Tom, we've been friends for so long. . . ."

"That's why I'm doin' it. Leave you free to ride up and down in the chaparral and somebody'll kill you sure. Because you *are* my friend, Frio, I want to see you live. I want to put you away in some safe Union prison camp till this war is over. I want to see you stay alive to marry my sister and be the father of her children."

Frio's voice held an edge of steel. "Do this, Tom, and you'll never be my friend again."

"I've got no choice. I want you to live, even if you hate me for it. Now ease that pistol out of the holster and drop it."

"You wouldn't really kill me."

"But I'd wound you. I'd cripple you if it meant keepin' you alive. Drop the pistol, Frio."

Frio dropped the pistol. It clattered on the porch. Amelia McCasland stared at it a moment. Then she picked it up. She swung it around to point at her brother.

"Now, Tom, you drop yours."

"Sis!"

"Drop it, I said."

Stubbornly Tom held his ground. "What're you doin' this for, Sis? I'm only tryin' to help you and Frio."

"Whatever Frio wants, that's what I want. If he wants to be free . . . if he wants to keep fighting . . . then that's what I want for him. Drop the gun."

"You're my sister. You wouldn't kill me."

"Like you told Frio, I'd wound you. I'd cripple you if I had to."

Her voice was rock steady. She meant it, and Tom knew she did. He shifted the pistol around in his hand and gave it to Frio butt first. "You're makin' a mistake, Frio. This was a way out for you if you'd just taken it."

Frio said, "The war's not over yet, Tom. As long as it's still on, I'll do my part as I see it." He jerked his head toward the two horses. "I reckon we'll have to take your horse."

Grudgingly Tom said, "Help yourself. There's nothin' I can do."

Frio and Amelia moved toward the horses. Amelia wore a housedress with long skirts that were going to make it difficult for her to ride astride. "Can you manage?" he asked her.

She nodded. "I'll have to."

He gave her a footlift onto Tom's horse and looked away as she pulled the skirts up. When she was in the saddle, he turned to his sorrel. He pulled away the blindfold and mounted. "Come along, Chico," he said to the little boy and swung him up behind the saddle. Chico's arms went around Frio's waist, taking a death grip.

Amelia had a last look at the gutted store and at her father lying on the porch, his one remaining son standing with shoulders slumped in sorrow. Tightly she said, "Take me out of here, Frio."

They moved away from the flames, away

from the terror that was Brownsville on this, the blackest of its nights.

7

Water was always the first consideration of those adventuresome men who turned to cattle-raising in antebellum Texas. They could find grass almost anywhere — free grass — but water was often a rare commodity. The early Mexican rancheros in lower Texas settled wherever they located living water, or where they could dig shallow wells and find a dependable supply. If grass ran out, cattle could still survive for a time on dried mesquite beans and the many kinds of brush. If water played out, death was as certain as a change in the moon.

Frio Wheeler and Tom McCasland had bought their land from crusty old Salcido Mendoza, who had fought against Zachary Taylor in the Mexican War. Media Mejico — half Mexico — the natives called the region between the Nueces and the Rio Grande. Mendoza could see to his disgust that it was inevitably becoming gringo country. He didn't want to live here anymore and be forced to rub shoulders with contentious, pale-eyed adventurers from the north, not when he could move south of the Rio and find land that would remain forever *puro Mejicano.*

A warm feeling always came to Frio when he rode out of the brush and gazed upon this headquarters, scattered without plan or form below the never-failing spring. The improvements weren't much to look at, but they belonged to him: Mendoza's old rock house that was Frio's living quarters — the few times he was ever able to sleep there anymore; the smaller stone house in which Blas and María Talamantes lived; the shady brush arbors, the several brush *jacales* that Mendoza had built for his help, all of them empty now because war had left the ranch without labor; the far-flung brush corrals, built — like everything else here — of materials that the land itself had yielded up.

When Frio and Tom had come to their last violent quarrel over the war and had broken their partnership, they had split their holdings down the middle. They had drawn for high card, and Frio had won this headquarters.

Frio had had little time for sleep since the burning of Brownsville. Shoulders sagging in weariness, his face grimy and bearded, he turned in the saddle and looked back at his jolting wagons, trailing along far behind him. The mules were dry and tired but still straining against the harness. Dust hit the rear wagons. Amelia McCasland rode on the one in the lead, beside a leather-skinned teamster. She sat hunched, numb from grief, near exhaustion. Her face seemed to have thinned. The weather had turned cold, and blue fingers held a blanket around her shoulders.

As the wagons came up even with him, Frio said, "We're here, Amelia."

She straightened. A little of the dullness left her eyes. She looked a long time and said, "It's the prettiest sight I ever saw."

She had visited here many times when Frio and Tom had been partners. Those had been warm and glowing days, a time for youthful dreams, for songs and happy laughter. Seemed there was precious little chance for happiness anymore.

Down the creek, longhorn cattle caught sight of the wagons emerging from the brush. They hoisted their tails and clattered off into the thickets, leaving only dust to show where they had been. These *cimarrones* were outlaw cattle that had lost domesticity in the centuries since their ancestors had escaped from Coronado and others of the early Spaniards. Of all colors and fleet as deer, they had reverted to a primal state almost as wild as the wolves and the panthers. It took fast horses to overtake them, strong men to bring them to hand. Frio had gloried in that kind of work during his free years before the war. Many a time he had camped around a waterhole with Blas and Tom McCasland, waiting to catch these wild cattle as they came up to drink. It was an adventure that lifted men's spirits, though it broke their bones and tore their hides.

Blas Talamantes left the ranch outbuildings and rose toward the wagons, a rifle ready across his lap. Recognizing Frio, he spurred into a lope.

"Frio," he said in astonishment, looking at the wagons. "What for you come here with the cotton?"

"Had to go someplace. The Yankees took Brownsville."

Blas slumped in the saddle, regret in his eyes. He saw Amelia McCasland on the lead wagon, and his gaze cut back to Frio with a question. Frio said, "They killed her father and burned his place. I couldn't leave her there."

"*Así es la suerte,*" Blas murmured, accepting tragedy as a fact of life. "Bad luck. María has our house warm. We take her there."

Frio nodded tiredly. "Fine. We got a boy with us, too."

The boy Chico sat huddled on the second wagon, bundled in a blanket. Nothing showed but his eyes and his nose.

"If he is a boy," said Blas, "he will be hungry. María will fix something."

They led the wagons down to the house and into the open gate of one of the big brush corrals. While the teamsters and Happy Jack Fleet began unhitching the mules, Frio helped Amelia down from the wagon. She shivered from the chill and rewrapped the blanket around her. Blas Talamantes reached up for the boy and carried him in his arms, talking softly to him in Spanish.

María Talamantes stood in the open door of her stone house, watching with wide and puzzled eyes. *"Entre,"* she spoke to Frio and the girl.

Frio said, "María, this is Amelia. She'll be here awhile."

María bowed. She was a tiny woman, not more than five feet tall. *"Mucho gusto de verle."* Blas gently set the boy down upon the hard-packed dirt floor. Chico's blanket dropped, and his bewildered, cold-purpled

125

face lifted toward María. He seemed about ready to cry, for tragedy and change had come too rapidly for him to grasp. María exclaimed, *"Pobrecito,"* and knelt to feel his stiffened hands. "Poor boy. Come to the fire. We will get you something warm to eat *muy pronto.*"

Amelia and the little boy warmed themselves by the open fireplace, where blackened pots were hanging to heat over the crackling flames. "We have beans and chili," María said. "I will fix coffee too. It is good weather for hot food."

The bright-eyed little woman got busy putting coffee on to boil, setting bowls on the small table. She was a good cook, if a man's taste ran toward Mexican foods, and Frio's did. He had often thought the best thing that had happened to this place was Blas's marrying her and bringing her here from Matamoros. Since María's arrival, Frio had never had to eat his own cooking when he was at the ranch.

Frio noticed the telltale swelling of her stomach. He glanced at Blas. "You didn't tell me. Which is it goin' to be, a boy or a girl?"

Blas smiled with pride. "A boy, for sure. All the Talamantes children were boys."

"Ojalá," Frio said. "For you, I hope so."

María did not slow down until she had all the food on the table, and she sat then only because Amelia insisted upon it. Mexican women took pregnancy as a natural condition and did not coddle themselves because of it. A young married woman was usually in one stage or another of pregnancy.

Frio ate silently. Finished, he said to María and Blas, "The señorita will be here awhile, she and the boy. They've had a bad run of luck." Briefly he told what had happened. He watched Amelia's face tighten and feared she might cry. But she remained dry eyed. It came to him then that she was probably tougher than he had given her credit for.

María stared gravely at the girl, her black eyes soft with sympathy. "Have no worry, Frio. We will take good care of her."

Later Frio walked over to his own house, carrying with him coals from María's fire. He put them into his cold fireplace and with his big Bowie knife began to peel shavings from dry wood to work up a blaze. Presently he had a good fire going.

Hearing someone enter, he turned. Amelia pushed the door shut behind her and stood with the blanket draped over her shoulders. She said nothing.

Frio remarked, "Coaxin' up a fire to take

the chill off the place. You can have this house, Amelia, for as long as you want it."

She slid the blanket off her shoulders and dropped it onto a chair. "What will you do?"

"Go on with the wagons, try to get them across the river somehow."

"When will you be back?"

He shrugged. "*Quién sabe?* War like it is, who can tell?"

Her hair was in pleasant disorder about her cold-flushed face, and he could see beauty there, even with the tragedy in her eyes. She moved closer. "Don't leave too soon. Your men need rest. *You* need rest."

"The war won't stand still."

She put her arms around him and leaned her head against his chest. "I don't want you to leave me, Frio, not yet. I want you to stay here with me, just a little while." Her arms tightened. "Just stay and hold me, and don't let go."

Standing with arms tight about her, he buried his face in her sweet-smelling hair. He held her silently and listened to the crackling of the fire.

Frio loped well ahead of the wagons and reined the sorrel down toward the river. He pulled in at a mud-plastered *jacal* a hundred yards back from the bank. An old Mexican stuck his head distrustfully around the side of the hut. Slowly recognizing Frio beneath the dust and the whiskers, he stepped out into the open, smiling broadly. He hunched his shoulders, which were covered by a faded old serape so worn that it looked as if rats had been chewing away the edges.

"My friend the Frio," he said, pleased. "A good name for this kind of weather, for it is a little *frio,* a little cold."

"Qué tal?" Stepping to the ground, Frio took the old man's hand. In Spanish he said, "Good to see you, Don Andres. It has been too long. One does not have time these days to visit friends."

The gray-bearded man shook his head. "Too much of the war. It seems there is always time for war, but never enough time for one's friends. Come inside. Perhaps I can find something fit for a friend to drink."

The old man lived alone in the hut, for his wife was buried in a tiny picket-fenced enclosure a little way upriver. Most of his children had scattered to the winds, only a couple of them still living nearby. The tiny house was a boar's nest. A bright-feathered gamecock sat with all the pride of ownership on the edge of the old man's unmade cot, secured by a leather thong tied to its leg. Don Andres patted the fighting rooster

129

as he walked by.

"It could be worse, Frio," he said. "We could be like the rooster and have only enemies."

From a shelf Don Andres took a clay jug and handed it to Frio. "The first drink is for my good friend."

Frio took a swallow and choked. He passed the jug back to the old man. "If that is what you give your friends, what do you give your enemies?"

"I have no enemies. Living far out here on the river, I cannot afford them." He took a long drink and shook his head. "The pulque is not as good as it used to be. Nothing is as good as it used to be. The young ones, they have lost the touch." He drank three long swallows and wiped his mouth with the gnarled knuckles of his left hand. "I am glad that I am old and am not much longer for this world. All grace and beauty has left it. And all the good pulque."

He sat down at a tiny table and beckoned for Frio to take one of the rickety rawhide chairs. He set the jug on the table between them. "Did you come to visit an old man, or is it war business that brings you here?"

"I must admit, old friend, that I am here of necessity. You know that the Yankee troops have taken Brownsville?"

The *viejo* nodded gravely. "Do not let it concern you, Frio. In my life I have seen many armies come across this land. Always they go again. One has only to wait and be patient."

"I have all my wagons with me, Don Andres. I have no time for patience."

The old man thoughtfully rubbed his bearded chin. "The young ones never do. How can I help?"

"For one thing, I need information. Have you seen any bluecoat troops come this way?"

Don Andres nodded. "A *yanqui* patrol came yesterday. It was on its way upriver."

Frio frowned. "You have no idea how long it might be before it passes this way again?"

"I asked no questions. I thought if they wished me to know anything, they would tell me without my having to ask. And they told me nothing."

Frio clenched his fist, helplessness rousing an anger in him. "They might not come back for days, or they might be here in an hour."

"If I had even dreamed you would wish to know. . . ."

Frio waved his hand, dismissing the subject. "Do you still run your ferry?"

Don Andres nodded. "*Sí*. It is old and

broken down like myself. But, blessed be God, it is still there, and somehow it still finds its way across the river." His eyebrows went up. "You would cross your wagons on Andres's little ferry?"

"I have no choice. Either I cross them here or I have to take them all the way upriver to Laredo, perhaps even to Eagle Pass. I am too close to the river for that now. The Yankees would find me."

"Perhaps they may find you anyway. It will take a long time to cross your wagons with my little wreck of a ferry."

"It's the only one there is. We'll rush it."

Old Don Andres took another long swallow from the jug. "Once I was young and always in a hurry. But I finally learned that one does not rush the river, Frio. If one takes it on its own terms and at its own pace, he lives to be an old man like me. If he does not, then he dies, and the river goes on without him."

He extended the jug to Frio, but Frio shook his head, too preoccupied to care about a drink. Don Andres placed the jug back on its shelf and stretched himself. "But we shall see how much we can hurry it. Who wants to live forever?"

Blas had come along to help. Frio sent him

downriver to look for any sign of patrols. He sent Happy Jack upriver to hunt the Yankee troops that had been here yesterday.

"Now, boys," he told both of them, "some people claim that any Rebel can whip a dozen Yankees, but I'm afraid they've stretched things a mite. Don't mix it with them none. Just try to slip away without bein' seen and get back here as fast as you can run."

Happy Jack had winked at Blas. "Bet you if the truth was known, a Rebel couldn't whip more than *half* a dozen of them."

Frio had eyed Happy Jack narrowly, not sure but what the young hellion would spark a fight if he thought he had half a chance. "Mind me now, Happy. You get yourself back here if you see any Yankees. And try not to bring them with you."

When the pair had gone their separate ways, Frio signaled the wagons out of the brush and down toward the river. Usually he was happy to leave the closeness of the chaparral and break out into the open. This time he felt somehow naked and helpless without the mesquite and the "wait-a-minute" catclaw to help hide his cargo of cotton.

He rode on down to the river, where Don Andres waited at the ferry with a pair of his grandsons who were to help. Frio swung down for a critical look at the ancient conveyance. It was one of the old-fashioned kind that used the river's own current for its motive power. A heavy rope strung across the river kept the ferry from being carried away. Frio frowned. Like the *viejo* had said, the ferry had been here a long time. Too long, perhaps. The old lumber had twisted and rotted. Here and there Frio could see holes almost big enough for a man to stick his foot through. But people didn't use the ferry much anymore. Don Andres didn't earn enough from it to justify fixing it up. It kept him in beans and chili and pulque. When he was gone, the ferry probably would go too.

"Not very big, is it, Don Andres?"

The old man shook his head. "When I was a young man and built it, it was for burros, and sometimes for oxcarts. We had nothing bigger in those days. We had never seen anything like your gringo wagons."

Through the years the ferry had been used largely by smugglers, moving goods into Mexico without having to pay a duty such as was required in Matamoros or the other legal crossing points. By rights, the Mexican government should have burned this ferry years ago. But when, every so often, the customs officers came around, Don Andres made it a point always to have some coin hidden away so he could pay them their *mordida*. "Little bite," the word meant in English. It was an unwritten law on the Mexican side of the river, a courtesy payment for services rendered, or for action withheld. The Americans would have called it a bribe, but then, the *yanquis* were notorious for being too blunt. *Mordida* was a much better-sounding word.

Frio stepped off the ferry's length, his mouth going grim. It would hold one loaded wagon at a time. It wouldn't take a team of mules. For one thing, it wasn't big enough. For another, some of them might break their legs stepping through the holes. No, they would have to swim the mules. Low as the river was, there wouldn't be a great deal of swimming to it.

Don Andres was plainly chagrined over the shortcomings of his equipment. He shrugged and said apologetically, "A poor man has only a poor man's ways."

Frio replied, "We'll make the best of it." He signaled for the *caporal* to bring along the first wagon. The heavy brake dragged in shrill protest against the rear wheels as the wagon started down the incline. Frio climbed the bank to look for any sign of

135

Blas or Happy Jack. He didn't expect to see either one and hoped he wouldn't. If they came back this soon, it could only mean trouble.

They weren't in sight. He returned to the water's edge, where the ferry bobbed gently up and down at its mooring.

"We'll put the team across first," he said to Don Andres and the *caporal.* "Then it can pull each wagon off the ferry and up the other bank."

A couple of teamsters took off most of their clothes and pitched them onto the first wagon, where they would stay dry. Then, shivering with cold, they moved the mule team out into the water and splashed across the river.

Frio and the other teamsters put shoulders to the first wagon and grunted and pushed it onto the ferry, tongue first. Panting hard, Frio stepped back onto the dry ground and waved his hat.

"Take it across, Don Andres."

Frio stood and watched while he tried to regain his breath. The river wasn't particularly wide at this point; the main reason the old ferryman had picked this place to set up long years ago. But right now it seemed to Frio that it must be half a mile to the Mexican side. Old Don Andres and his two young grandsons used long poles to shove the ferry out into the stream. Carefully they quartered it around so that the current began to catch the conveyance and carry it along.

Impatience gnawed at Frio as he watched the ferry's snail-paced movement across the brown Rio. The great weight of the wagon and cargo was almost too much for the ancient conveyance. It pushed the platform so far down that water lapped up over the side. A little imbalance might tip it.

The *caporal* brought down another wagon and moved it into position. Across the river, the two naked and cold teamsters had the mule team waiting when the ferry reached the far side. The first thing they did was put on the dry clothes it had brought along. Then they hitched onto the wagon and pulled it up the south bank, hauling it well out of the way. As the ferry returned, the teamsters unhitched the mules and brought them back to the small mooring for a second wagon.

So it went, one wagon at a time, at an eternally slow pace. Over and over, Frio counted the wagons as each one reached the far bank — three, four, five, six, seven. And still seven on this side, waiting to cross.

He heard a running horse. A Mexican

teamster called him and pointed upriver. Frio swung onto his sorrel and moved up the bank. He saw Happy Jack spurring hell-for-leather, horse beginning to lather.

Happy slid to a stop. Arm outstretched, he jabbed a finger toward the northwest. "That bluecoat patrol the old man told you about — it's on its way!"

8

Frio's stomach drew into a knot. "How far off is it?"

"Five, maybe six miles upriver when I left them. They're just walkin' their horses like they're not too anxious to get back to the fort and go to work."

"Did they see you?"

"If they had, they'd be right behind me. I was careful." His brow furrowed in concern, Happy counted the wagons that still waited on the north bank. "We ain't got time to cross that way, Frio. Them Yankees, they'll be here before you can finish."

Frio frowned, indecisively rubbing the back of his neck. "How many men would you say there were?"

"Twenty-five, maybe thirty." His eyes narrowed. "You ain't about to try and stand them off, are you? Most of these teamsters can't shoot for sour apples. They're no match for them troops."

"No, Happy. I was just thinkin' how we might decoy the federals away for a while, you and me."

"Just us two, and all them Yanks?" Happy Jack stared incredulously. But slowly his mouth began to lift at the corners, and he shrugged. "You're crazy, but I reckon that makes you a match for me. Let's go."

First Frio rode down to speak to the *caporal.* "Unhitch all these teams but one and get some of the boys to swim them across, now. Just leave one team to pull the wagons up to the ferry. When you get the last wagon loaded, swim that team across too. If you see the Yankees comin', set fire to any wagons that are still left on this side. Then get the hell across that river!"

"Sí, patrón," the *caporal* said. Before Frio and Happy Jack had ridden away, he was already carrying out the order.

Without talking, Frio and Happy reined their horses northwestward and moved them into an easy lope. They followed the river trail, where Happy had seen the patrol. When they had ridden what Frio estimated to be two and a half or three miles, he pulled northward into the brush. He slowed to a walk and slipped his saddlegun out of the boot.

They heard the patrol before they saw it.

The troopers' voices carried sharply through the cold. Frio stood in his stirrups, listening. He turned to Happy. "Ready?"

Happy's lips were drawn tight, and he seemed to be giving the matter some serious second thought. "It's sure an awful lot of Yankees, even for two of us. But I don't aim to let no owner get ahead of me."

"We'll keep our distance," Frio said. "I'm countin' on these Yankees bein' new to the brush country. I expect they'll be mighty cautious. All we need to do is keep them confused long enough to get those wagons across."

Happy admitted, "I'm confused already."

"It's like this: We'll split up a ways, make them think there's several of us. Shoot in their direction once with your rifle, move a little bit and give them a pistol shot or two. I'll do the same. We'll keep movin', that's the main thing. We'll keep drawin' them north, away from the river. And we don't ever want them to get a look at us. Keep them thinkin' we're a bunch."

Happy nodded, dubious but willing. "*Bueno,* you shoot first, when you think it's time. I'll make them think old Rip Ford has brought his whole army back to the Rio Grande."

Frio estimated that he was a hundred and

fifty yards north of the trail. Through one half-clear spot in the brush he would be able to glimpse the patrol as it passed. Cold though he was, he felt his hands sweaty against the gunstock. Finally he caught a flash of movement. He raised the rifle to his shoulder and gently brought up the muzzle. He squeezed the trigger, felt the rifle jar against him. His horse jumped, startled, but not before Frio saw a trooper's horse go down.

Frio spurred thirty yards, stopped, and fired again in the direction of the patrol. He heard Happy open up, firing twice, then moving and firing again. Men shouted, and horses began to strike the brush. Frio caught Happy's eye and waved him northward. They spurred away from the river a little farther, then stopped to fire another round of shots.

In confusion, the Yankee patrol commenced a blind, wild shooting into the brush. Frio could hear slugs whine by, snapping against the thin trunks of the winter-dormant mesquites and the catclaw.

Frio and Happy retreated northward again, pulling a little to the west, drawing the patrol away from the river crossing. Only occasionally could Frio catch a glimpse of Union movement. Mostly he had to go by sound. As he had hoped, the federals were proceeding slowly and with caution. This thick South Texas *bosque* was alien to them. Frio and Happy would fire several times, moving between shots, then pull back. The patrol continued to take the bait.

At last Frio signaled Happy to him. "I think we've done what we figured on. We'll go yonderway a little more, then try to sneak east and get back to the ferry while these soldiers are still huntin' around out here."

They rode north a mile. Then, certain they were out of sight and hearing, Frio reined east and spurred into a lope. Happy Jack kept close to him, picking his way through the brush. Happy was grinning in relief.

"It was fun," he said, "but I'm sure glad it's over. Way them Yankees poured lead into that brush, sounded like a bunch of bees. I was afraid somebody might get stung."

They reached the river crossing as the last wagon was pushed onto the bobbing ferry. Frio could see dust on the trail to the north. Whoever was leading that patrol wasn't as slow-witted as Frio had hoped. To the remaining teamsters, Frio said, "You-all get on the ferry and ride across with the wagon. Happy and me, we'll swim the team."

They stripped off their clothes and pitched them onto the ferry. The ferry slid away from the muddy bank. Frio held a moment, watching the dust, trembling from cold.

"Well, Happy," he said, "if we don't want to be shakin' hands with the Yankees, we better take us a swim."

He took up the long lines and led the last team down the bank. Happy brought up the rear, shouting and urging the mules off into the river. Quickly the bottom fell away from beneath the sorrel's feet, and he was swimming. Frio slipped out of the saddle, the cold water almost taking his breath away as it came up over his bare skin. Behind him, Happy went into the water and yelped a little like a coyote. Frio kept hold of the saddlehorn and let the horse carry him along. Behind him splashed the mules. And behind them trailed Happy, holding onto his horse's tail.

The ferry moved slowly along ahead of them, its pace barely enough that the two horsemen and the mule team did not catch up. Finally the ferry drew against its south-side mooring, bumping hard. Frio waded up onto dry land, still holding the reins. The teamsters who already had crossed were waiting to grab onto the mules as they drifted out.

Happy dragged himself ashore and turned to look back, trembling with cold.

"We got company over yonder, Frio."

One of the teamsters came running, bringing Frio his dry clothes from the wagon. Shivering, Frio pulled them on while he looked. The Union patrol had stopped at water's edge and stood looking across the river at the quarry it had just missed. One man, afoot, moved in quick, angry strides. Frio guessed him to be the officer in charge. The officer pointed. Half a dozen troopers rode over and cut Don Andres's ferry rope.

Shaking his rough old fist, Don Andres cursed in a manner that he had taken a lifetime to perfect. Some of Frio's teamsters quickly moved to tie the old man's ferry so it would not drift off downriver.

Happy Jack observed, "Sore losers, ain't they?"

Don Andres fumed. "In all the wars that have come across this land, no one has ever seen fit to cut my rope."

Frio said, "Don't worry, Don Andres. The Confederacy owes you a new one. I'll see that you get it."

The last wagon was drawn up into line with the others. The teamsters had built a large fire, and Frio and Happy Jack went to it to warm themselves. Both were nearly purple from cold.

Well satisfied, Frio said, "Amigos, you've

put in a good day's work. We'll camp here and rest. We'll head on down the river toward Matamoros in the mornin'. Nobody's apt to bother us anymore now."

Happy Jack said, "How about them Yankees yonder?"

"They won't cross into Mexico. It was sanctuary to the Yankees and the *renegados* when the Confederacy held the other side. Now it's sanctuary to us."

"They'll follow along with us all the way to Matamoros."

"Let them. They'll learn a lot about handlin' a string of wagons."

"Blas is still over there someplace."

"He'll be all right. When he sees we've made it, he'll slip back to the ranch."

Happy Jack stared awhile at the Yankees, eyes wide in wonderment. These were the first he had ever seen in uniform.

"They don't look no whole lot different from us, do they?"

Frio said in surprise, "Were they supposed to?"

Happy shrugged. "I don't know. Guess I thought they was supposed to have horns and a tail, or somethin'. Outside of the blue coats, they look like us. You couldn't hardly tell no difference."

Frio shook his head. "I don't suppose you could."

Happy Jack held his hands out over the fire and warmed himself, his face creased in thought. "Frio, you reckon we killed any of them with that shootin' we done?"

"We kept a long ways off, and we didn't get much chance to aim. I'd say the chance was mighty small."

Relief came into the cowboy's eyes. "I'm glad. I never killed nobody in my life."

The road followed the river all the way to Matamoros, though it was straighter, sometimes edging southward to avoid duplicating the river's needless bends. As Frio had expected, the patrol followed along all the way. Every time the road came close to water's edge, he could look northward and see the riders on the far side, watching.

As the train entered the western edge of Matamoros, innumerable lanky dogs came bounding forth as a reception committee. Mexican people began to line the streets. Frio could hear people shouting:

"Los algodones vienen!" The cotton men are coming!

Men, women, and children came hurrying to watch this first wagon train with its load of heavy bales. Frio could see in the faces of the adults a considerable measure of relief, even joy. These people had no stake in the gringo war, no particular enthusiasm for either North or South. Many of them actually looked upon the gringo as being akin to the plague, whether he be from Texas or New York. But they had a large stake in the border cotton trade, the hectic commerce the Civil War had brought to Matamoros. Union stoppage of the border trade had threatened ruin to the overgrown Mexican city.

A Matamoros merchant who was a friend of Frio's came trotting out to walk beside Frio's horse and look back down the dusty street at the strung-out wagons. "Then it is not true, Frio, that the *yanqui* troops have stopped the *algodones?*"

Frio shook his head. "Not true, amigo. They've slowed us down, but they won't stop us."

The merchant smiled. "*Bueno.* It had looked like a hungry winter."

Someone shouted, *"Vivan los algodones!"* Others of the crowd took it up, and cheers preceded the wagons down the long, winding street.

Passing a municipal building, Frio glanced up at the second-story iron-grilled balcony, where two men stood looking down upon the wagons. One was a U.S. Army colonel in full dress uniform, evidently here in his finest for a state visit to the powers of Matamoros. Beside him, resplendent in plumes and braid, was the erect figure of Juan Nepomuceno Cortina. Frio could see the Union officer's face flare with wrath and frustration. A half smile crossed the visage of Juan Cortina, for the Mexican could see an ironic humor in this development.

Frio suppressed an urge to give the officer a mock salute. Behind him, Happy Jack had no inhibitions.

"Hey there, Yank," Happy yelled at the colonel, "come on down and I'll let you buy me a drink!"

Frio could see the officer speaking angrily to Cortina and Cortina shrugging as if to say, "What can I do?"

At last Frio reached the riverbank cottonyard the Confederacy had maintained on the Mexican side, opposite Brownsville. He glanced across the muddy waters at the Texas city that now was closed to him. He could still see the charred remains of cotton bales and household goods on the far bank. There was no sign of the riverboats. The Santa Cruz ferry was crossing empty, except for a couple of passengers.

Portly old Hugh Plunkett came hurrying

across the nearly empty cottonyard to meet him. "Frio!" he shouted in surprise. "For God's sake, it's Frio!"

Hands outstretched, he reached up and grasped Frio's shoulders and shook the freighter for joy. The cotton agent's eyes glistened with tears as he looked at the wagons trailing in. "Well, I'll swun," he said wonderingly, over and over. "I'll swun." He walked out past the first wagon and stopped, watching the others come in. "How many did you get across with, Frio?"

"All I had. Fourteen."

Plunkett kept shaking his head. "I'll swun. I don't know how you done it. Thought the cotton trade was done for."

"They've crippled us, Hugh, but we're a long way from dead. Before you know it, we'll be bringin' cotton into Matamoros just as heavy as we ever did."

He told the cotton agent how they had done it. "Of course," he said, "nobody else will be able to use Don Andres's old ferry. The Yankees will keep a watch on it. But the Rio Grande is a mighty long river. They can't watch it all the way to Laredo. The cotton trains that are on the road now can swing west and cross way up yonder, beyond the Yankee patrols. It'll add a lot to the trip down from San Antonio — well nigh double it, I expect. But the cotton will come through — that's the main thing."

Plunkett nodded, his eyes glistening as he stared in triumph at the bales Frio had brought in. "Mexican customs officials will be put out about it," he said, "you crossin' where there wasn't a customs house. But a little *mordida* in the right place ought to fix that."

Frio looked across the river again, pointing his chin toward Brownsville. "How're things over there, Hugh?"

"Not good. A lot of people were burned out, or lost most of what they owned tryin' to get across the river. And it wasn't necessary. That's what makes it hurt so much, it wasn't necessary." His mood shifted from joy to momentary anger. "General Bee was in too much of a hurry about gettin' out of Brownsville. He listened to rumors, not to facts. Way it turned out, it was the third day after he left before the first Yankee troops got to town. Seemed there was a storm at the Boca Chica, and the soldiers had a hard time gettin' off of the boats. Bee could have brought all the refugees over here and ferried every single bale of cotton to boot. He could have hauled out every last bit of Confederate army supplies and not had to burn a single thing.

"But he got hold of bad information, and he panicked over it. Things would've been different if we'd had Rip Ford here."

Plunkett lighted a cigar, his face sober. "A lot of the Brownsville people have gone back home now to see what they've got left. They've decided the Yankees aren't goin' to shoot them. Them as go home are made to take an oath of allegiance to the Union. It don't mean much, though. I've taken an oath a dozen times to quit drinkin', and I ain't done it yet." He frowned. "One more thing. How do you stand with Juan Cortina?"

"I don't stand one way or the other. I only know him to see him."

"He's the top *tamali* around here now. While all the excitement was goin' on across the river, Cortina turned things upside down on this side. He shot General Cobos and has taken charge of Matamoros."

Frio's eyes narrowed. "He's no friend of the Confederacy. He might stop the border trade where the Yankees couldn't."

"I doubt that. It would mean too much loss to Matamoros. Cortina likes money even more than he hates Texans. He's on kissin' terms with the Yankees, but I expect he'll let the border trade go right ahead as long as there's profit in it. Just the same, he'll bear watchin'.''

The ferry pulled up. Frio's gaze was drawn to the two passengers. One was a Union officer, a major. The other was Tom McCasland. They walked slowly up to the cottonyard. The officer's face twisted with displeasure as he regarded the wagons. Tom McCasland's face showed only sadness.

Tom held out his hand. "Frio."

Quietly Frio said, "Tom," and shook hands.

Tom said, "Major Quayle, meet Frio Wheeler."

The major gave no sign that he intended to shake hands, and Frio didn't press the issue by putting out his own. Quayle said, "Is he the one who brought in the wagons?"

Tom nodded. To Frio he said, "Patrol sent a man ahead, said a wagon train had gotten across at Don Andres's ferry. I figured right then it would be you, Frio. You're the only man I know with guts enough to try a stunt like that, and luck enough to get away with it."

Hugh Plunkett grinned at the open anger in the major's face. "Looks like you soldier boys got seasick for nothin', don't it, Major?"

Major Quayle said crisply, "One wagon train doesn't mean anything. We were still a little disorganized. But this will be the last one, you can be assured of that. We'll patrol the river so that not even a hawk can get across it without our permission."

Frio squatted and leaned against a wagon wheel. With his finger he traced a rough map of lower Texas in the dust. "Major, you may know your maps, but you don't know the Rio Grande. You've got no idea what a long river she is till you wear blisters across your rump ridin' it. How much of it do you really think you can control? Up to Reynosa, maybe. Rio Grande City if you're real lucky. It's brush country, mister, plenty wild if you don't know its ways.

"No matter how far west you go, we'll go a little farther. You stop us here, we'll go to Rio Grande City. Stop us there and we'll go to Laredo to cross. We'll go as far as Eagle Pass if we have to. The point is, you won't stop our wagons. Do the damndest you know how, but we'll still keep them comin'."

The major's face colored, and his eyes snapped. "You secesh! You don't know when you're whipped!" He turned and stalked away. He went fifty feet, stopped, and turned back. "Are you coming, McCasland? We're going to talk to Cortina."

Tom nodded. "I'll be there in a minute." He looked at Frio again. "How's Amelia?"

"Tired out, last time I saw her, and still grievin' some. But she's in a safe place, and she'll be all right."

Tom said, "You're really goin' to keep the wagons comin', are you?"

"Just as sure as you're standin' there."

"Then there wasn't any use for the Union troops to come in, was there? Dad and all those others, they died for nothin'."

Somberly Frio replied, "It looks that way."

Tom's face clouded. "I warn you, Frio, we don't intend to leave it like that. One way or another, we intend to stop you!"

For a moment they stared into each other's eyes, neither man yielding. Frio said, "We won't be stopped. Don't try, Tom. I don't want to have to bury you!"

9

In the following weeks it gradually dawned upon Union General Dana in partially repaired Fort Brown that the federal occupation of Brownsville suffered serious shortcomings, that the "sealed-up" border had some bad holes in it. Slowly at first, then more and more frequently, Confederate wagon trains were appearing on the south bank of the river, hauling their heavy loads of cotton into the market at Matamoros, the teamsters gleefully thumbing their noses at the bluecoat troops north of the Rio.

That damnable Frio Wheeler had been only the first of them. Others, caught midway down from San Antonio by the sudden Union offensive, had simply been diverted upriver to points such as Rio Grande City. There they came under the protection of a bold troop of Texas-Mexican militia commanded by one Colonel Santos

Benavides, whose watchful eyes stayed on the trains until they crossed over the river to safe ground. With Wheeler's lead to guide them, the *algodones* then followed the Mexican trail on down to Matamoros. True enough, the detour added many long miles to the haul from San Antonio. But the presence of the Yankees proved of little more than nuisance value. Within weeks the movement of cotton into Matamoros and the northward flow of imported war supplies was almost as large as it had ever been.

Once Dana sent a steamer upriver in hopes of cutting off some of the wagon crossings. But the drought still held, and the river was so shallow that sand bars stopped the vessel before it got as far as Roma.

He sent mounted troops to capture Rio Grande City, but they were unable even to reach there. Always they encountered the wily Benavides, his guerillalike troop of ranch-trained vaqueros darting in and out of the brush, striking with the swiftness of a rattlesnake and retreating into the chaparral so quickly that the federals hardly knew what had hit them. Pursuit was useless, for the Union cavalrymen knew little about the border country. If they strayed far from the river they might starve, for drought had left most of the waterholes dry. Benavides and his men knew the trails, knew the location of every single waterhole that still remained on the Wild Horse Desert.

Of course there were appeals to General Juan Cortina, who held control of Matamoros. Cortina had the power to cut off the cotton trade with a word, a single action. He professed his friendship for the Union, entertained Union officers in his quarters, and in turn was treated most cordially by Dana and his staff. The Mexican general even gave the Union officers full use of three Kennedy & Co. steamboats that had been registered under Mexican names and employed by the Confederacy. But he did not cut off the cotton trade. Though he hated Texans, he knew that so long as Matamoros prospered, he prospered. When it suffered, he would suffer. Without the border trade, Matamoros would sicken unto death.

This, then, was the situation in which Dana found himself. He held what was supposed to have been the key city, yet the enemy was outflanking him at points beyond his reach. He had several thousand troops at his command, while the Confederacy had at best only a few home guard units scattered along the entire stretch of the Mexican border. He could not send troops across into Mexico. The same restrictions that once had stopped the Confederacy now conspired to stop Dana. Nor could he touch the neutral vessels that flaunted the Union blockade by clustering around the mouth of the Rio Grande in full sight of federal gunboats. Even as it was, the Lincoln government had its hands full, trying to keep England and France from swinging the full weight of their support behind the Confederacy. An angry incident at the Boca Chica might be all that was needed to touch off an international crisis, to turn Europe against the United States.

To make it worse, spy reports indicated that the Texas Colonel Rip Ford was mustering troops in the San Antonio area, planning to come down and wrest the border away from the Union again. To be sure, Ford wouldn't be able to amass men in numbers equal to those of the federals — at least, Dana doubted it. But if they were all of the same caliber as those hard-riding Mexicans under Benavides, it wouldn't take as many.

The Union general, visiting the Matamoros side of the river, watched Frio Wheeler come into town with his second wagon train of cotton since the federal occupation. The man had thirty wagons with him this time. He was a wheelhorse, this blocky-built, dusty-faced, bewhiskered Texan. He had led the way, and others were following. Frio Wheeler was regarded by the Texans as a leader in the border trade, a man to follow, a man to imitate.

Well, the general thought grimly, to kill a snake you cut off its head!

And shortly afterward, Union Major Luther Quayle found himself seated at a dirty little table in a dark and odorous Matamoros cantina, staring across a flickering candle into the evil face of Florencio Chapa. . . .

Frio coughed as the south wind whipped up dust from the edge of the trail. He could imagine how much worse it must be in the drags, where Happy Jack Fleet was not so happy, bringing up the rear of Frio's train along the Mexican side of the river.

It seemed to Frio that this drought would never end. It conspired to make a difficult situation almost impossible — compounded the misery that already was bad enough, bringing these groaning wagons and these thirsting mules the long way around on a trail woefully short of feed. All winter he had watched Mexican teamsters on the oxcart trains, burning the thorns from prickly pear and feeding the pear to their oxen. But mules wouldn't eat prickly pear, with or without the thorns. So all winter Frio had had to devote space to maize and corn, space that would better have gone to cotton.

The river had receded to shoals in many places. Once he saw the steamer *Mustang* snagged on a sand bar. The Union officer in charge of troops aboard paced back and forth, swearing. The ship's crew was making signs of trying to free the little ship, but Frio knew their hearts weren't in it. Their loyalty remained with the Kennedy & Co. leadership and the Confederacy. They were doing only what they had to do for the Union, and taking their own sweet time about even that.

From the rear of the train, Happy Jack Fleet yelled at the troops, "Why don't you Yanks get off and push?"

What the soldiers yelled back at him was unintelligible, but its general meaning was plain enough.

The train's entry into Matamoros attracted much less attention than had the first one, only days after the Union had taken Brownsville. Frio understood this; Texas wagons were arriving in Matamoros almost every day now. They were becoming commonplace. Yet he was aware of one thing: People were looking upon him personally with an interest they had never shown before. He was the one who had first beaten the Yankees, the one who had shown the others the way. Suddenly he was no longer "Frio" as much as he was "Mr. Wheeler."

Coming up in the world, he thought, finding it somehow a little humorous. He hadn't sought this new importance, and he didn't take it very seriously.

He led the wagons into the Confederate cottonyard and shook hands with Hugh Plunkett. Plunkett grunted. "Brought me some more work, is all you done. Don't a man ever get any rest?"

"I haul it, you sell it. This war ever gets over with, maybe we can both rest."

Frio saw a young Union lieutenant in dusty blue leaning against a gatepost. Plunkett explained: "They got a man over here all the time now, not doin' a thing but watchin' what we do, countin' how much cotton we get, how much stuff we ship in and out. It don't do them any good to know — just makes them mad. Looks to me like they'd be happier just to stay ignorant."

Frio grinned. "You got anything around here to take the chill off a man? We used up

162

our whole medicine supply on sick teamsters."

"Got some Scotch I swapped off of an
English cotton buyer. It's in the shack
yonder." He pointed toward a small frame
building he was using as an office.

Frio walked up to the lieutenant. "Yank,
we're fixin' to have us a drink. How about
takin' one with us?"

The federal's face was blue from cold, and
his eyes lighted at the prospect. Then he
shook his head. "I don't drink with the
enemy."

Frio said, "We're south of the river.
There's no such thing here as enemies."

The officer glanced across the river as if
he thought someone might be watching him
from the other side. He hung back a moment, then nodded assent. "If you don't tell
them, I won't. It can get almighty chilly here
even if it is so far south."

In the shack Hugh Plunkett fetched out
the bottle. There were no such refinements
as glasses. They simply passed the bottle
around. Frio watched warmth touch the
young officer, putting a healthy color back
into his pinched, blue face. He sat and
pondered the foolishness, the contradictions
of this war. If he and the officer were to
meet on the other side of the river, they

would try their best to kill each other. Here they sat together without enmity, taking the edge off their chill by drinking out of the same bottle.

Frio guessed this might be the deadliest war of its kind in history, with the friendliest enemies.

"Where you from, lieutenant?"

"Illinois. We have a farm back there — my folks do, I mean."

Frio nodded. "My folks did some farmin' too, once, and raised stock. I've sort of got away from the plow, but I still raise cattle."

"We have milk stock," the lieutenant said. "Good-blooded cattle."

"Mine are just plain native cows," said Frio. "You couldn't get a bucket of milk out of a dozen of them."

The lieutenant was plainly homesick. And now the conversation had opened a way for him to begin talking about his home. He seemed oblivious to Frio — asked him questions and then went right on talking without giving time for an answer. He talked of the green fields of Illinois, his eyes going soft and blurry, and for a little while the war was forgotten. Frio just sat back and listened, seeing in his mind's eye the land the young officer described, knowing he would never get to go there and see it for himself.

For a while, then, they were friends, and there was no war, no North or South.

At length the lieutenant squared his shoulders and handed the bottle back to Hugh Plunkett. "I guess I had better go. I have to count those bales."

Frio said, "I'll save you the trouble. There are thirty wagons, four hundred and eighty bales."

The officer stared quizzically. "That's military information. Why are you willing to tell me about it?"

"You'd get it anyway. Thought I'd save you the work."

The lieutenant smiled. "This is a crazy war."

When the Yankee was gone, Hugh offered Frio the bottle again. Frio declined. "We better be unloadin' those wagons."

Plunkett put away the bottle and turned, worry in his eyes. "Frio, I don't know how you done it, but you've made yourself some good friends among these Mexicans. Do you remember an old fiddler, one they call Don Sisto?"

"I know him. I've done him a favor or two."

"He was over here. Said I better tell you Florencio Chapa's been seen around town. Rumor among the Mexicans is that he aims to kill you."

"He's tried before."

"Maybe this time he figures on doin' the job right. Was I you, Frio, I'd keep some good men around me, and I wouldn't sleep sound till I saw them shovelin' dirt in Chapa's face."

To the single men of the wagon train, Matamoros afforded a chance to relax from the grinding toil of the trails, to jam into crowded cantinas, get drunk on raw liquor, seek the warm excitement of some willing señorita. Those men who had homes here or in Brownsville could spend a couple or three nights with their wives and children. The Mexican teamsters passed with comparative freedom back and forth across the river, for to the Yankees one brown face looked like another. To Anglos like Frio and Happy Jack, however, the river was a barrier they dared not cross. They could only stand on the south bank and gaze across at the lamplight of Brownsville, sadly remembering the time when they had not been in exile.

Frio intended to spend a couple or three days in Matamoros before starting the long return trip upriver. The mules needed rest. They needed green feed, too, but they couldn't get it. Frio wished he could loose-herd them on grass a few days and let them fill their bellies. There was no chance. The long drought had left little grass. And the Mexicans with their own herds of cattle, their countless burros and scrubby horses, had kept the land so overstocked that it would be a long time before there was feed enough again.

So, in lieu of pasture grazing, he turned his mules loose in a big brush-fence corral, for which he had paid the owner a small rental. He fed them all they wanted of hay, which he bought from a few Mexicans who irrigated small fields out of the river. He circled the empty wagons outside the corral and set up his camp.

He remembered what Hugh Plunkett had told him about Chapa, but he had never felt unsafe in Matamoros. He thought it unfair to make a bunch of the young men forgo the city's pleasure and stay for his protection. He let all of them go except a small guard of three, who would remain around camp, mostly to prevent pilfering. These three would be chosen each night by the men themselves, cutting cards. The married men with families here were exempt. Besides the three young men, a couple of the older ones elected to remain in camp. Both had families in San Antonio and considered themselves too far along in years to work up a fever over the flashing eyes and pinched-in waists of the dark-haired señoritas. They were content to buy a bottle and stay with the wagons.

Like these men, Frio felt little urge to try the night life. The pressures of being wagon boss had worn him out. He only wanted to rest. Besides, there was Amelia.

He got a chuckle, watching Happy Jack. Happy was shaved, bathed, his hair plastered down with grease and smelling to heaven of something they had sprinkled on his new clothes down at the barber shop. He stood in the firelight, admiring the cut of his coat and trousers.

"You sure you don't want to come along, Frio? Margarita has got a sister, and she's . . . Well, you've got to see it to appreciate it. You never saw anything like her."

Frio smiled. "I probably have. I've been around longer than you."

"You're lettin' yourself go to seed, is what you're doin'. Man, you just got one life. You better live it."

"Maybe you best take care of Margarita *and* her sister."

The young man laughed. "I haven't got *that* much life about me."

Happy walked out of the firelight and disappeared in the direction of the city. Slowly the rest of the men scattered too. Soon only Frio and the two *viejos* were left, and the three unlucky young ones who were to guard the wagons. Frio let the fire burn down almost to coals, so that it still put out heat but shed little light. He was wary enough not to make an easy target of himself.

He sat and stared into the coals, watching their kaleidoscopic change of colors as the heat built and waned. Listening to the night sounds of the Mexican city, he let his mind trail back to other times — to Brownsville and Matamoros as they had been before the war, to Amelia and Tom and Meade McCasland, to the ranch he and Tom had so hopefully started. He considered his own sacrifices and knew they were small compared to those made by so many others. Many men of his acquaintance had already given their lives for the South. He, at least, was still alive, still had his ranch and his cattle. And he had Amelia. When this war was over he would have something to go home to. From what he knew of the campaign in Virginia, thousands of men would have no home left.

He sat there remembering, and lost track

of time. He was aware of the two older men turning up their bottle and dropping it on the ground empty. They weaved unsteadily toward their blankets. A guard came up and spoke to Frio and poured himself a cup of coffee from the pot at the edge of the coals.

They heard someone approaching. The guard straightened, gun in hand. He said in Spanish, "Some of the boys coming back, probably. The foolish ones do not know how to take their time and make a night last." He called out, *"Quién viva?"* Who goes there?

A Mexican voice responded from beyond the ragged edge of firelight. "Señor Wheeler? I seek the Señor Wheeler."

Frio arose and drew his six-shooter, keeping well back in darkness. "Come ahead, with your hands away from your sides. Stop by the fire."

In the dim glow of the embers he could see that this was a stranger with a wide sombrero, open leather huaraches and the loose cotton clothing of the *peón.* "I have come with a message for the Señor Wheeler," the man said, taking his hat in his hands. He shivered from cold.

"Are you by yourself?" Frio asked suspiciously.

"*Sí,* señor."

The guard went to look. In a moment he

was back. "He is alone, *patrón.*"

Frio said, "What is it you want of me?"

"You have a young friend, a gringo with hair the color of sand?"

Frio stiffened. Happy Jack! "What about him?"

"He is in trouble, señor. There has been a fight, a bad fight, and he is hurt. He needs your help."

Alarm raced in Frio. But there was also doubt. "Who sent you?"

"A friend of the boy. A woman."

That added up, Frio thought. Still, there was an off chance this could be a lie, a ruse. "Where is Happy now?"

"He is in the woman's house. He asked for you. It is possible he dies, señor."

Frio could not hesitate long, even though a lingering doubt persisted. To the guard he said, "Felix, I had better go with him."

He could tell that the guard, too, had his doubts. "I will go with you, *patrón.* The other two can guard the wagons. They have the *viejos* for help."

"Thanks, Felix," Frio said gratefully. "Happy might need both of us."

They paused only long enough to let the other two guards know where they were going. They trailed out into the darkness afoot, following the man who had brought the message. Frio kept the six-shooter in his hand, ready. Felix did likewise. It occurred to Frio belatedly that Felix was one of the poorest marksmen in the crew. He hoped the teamster never had to use that gun.

The Mexican led them through narrow alleys, down dark streets. Dogs picked them up and trotted alongside, barking and making false runs at them. Candlelight flickered inside tiny brush *jacales,* leaking though cracks in the walls and doors.

"How much farther is it?" Frio asked. "If I had known it was this far, I'd have brought a horse."

"Not far now, señor," the man said and kept walking.

Frio didn't like the neighborhood. Dark doorways frowned upon the narrow dirt streets, doorways big enough to hide waiting men in their deep shadows. He kept to the center of the street.

He wondered at even the reckless Happy Jack coming into a section like this.

At last the Mexican pointed. "This is the place." He reached for a latch and swung the wooden door inward. "*Pasen,* señores."

Frio gripped the six-shooter a little tighter, peered a brief moment into the Mexican's face, then stepped through the open door toward the guttering light of a small candle.

Too late he sensed that the thing was all wrong. Too late he saw the dark shapes step away from the wall. He spun, bringing the pistol around. Someone shoved him from behind, and he went stumbling across the dirt floor. Heavy bodies landed on top of him almost the moment his shoulder struck earth. A boot stomped his wrist. Rough hands tore the pistol from his fingers, taking some of the hide with it.

He heard a dull thud as a sombreroed man clubbed Felix from behind with the butt of a rifle. Felix went to his knees. The rifle barrel swung savagely and struck Felix across the back of the head. The teamster went down like an empty sack. His blood made a dark stain on the dirt floor.

A harsh voice said in Spanish, "You hit him too hard, Florencio. He is dead."

Florencio Chapa shrugged and snarled, "It is a just punishment for any Mexican who carries a gun for a gringo. Be sure he is dead before you drag him away. If there is any doubt, shoot him behind the ear."

"There is no doubt, *mi jefe.*"

"Then drag him out of here. Leave him somewhere for the dogs."

In anger Frio tried to arise, tried to reach Chapa. Strong hands restrained him. Chapa waited until Frio's face was turned up to his own, the eyes flashing hatred. Then he kicked. Frio twisted away, but the heavy boot caught him on the side of the head.

"So you came for your friend," Chapa gloated. "Like a rabbit to the wolf's den, you came."

Held tightly, Frio could do nothing but watch as a couple of the men dragged Felix's body out into the darkness. The door closed behind them. Eyes glazing from the pain of the blow he had received, Frio blinked hard. Helpless anger surged through him. He knew he had to curb that anger, had to keep his head. Rage was a luxury he could not afford now.

He looked at the men standing around the wall. There were four of them besides Chapa, and besides the two men who held him down. One was the gringo renegade, Bige Campsey.

Campsey smiled crookedly. "I been listenin' to you rebs talk for two years. Thought I'd enjoy listenin' to one of you scream awhile."

Frio had often wondered why Chapa, hating gringos so passionately, allowed Campsey to ride with him almost as a partner. Perhaps it was that he sensed in Campsey a kindred spirit, a senseless sadism that transcended any national barriers.

Chapa said, "Stand him up!" The two men pulled Frio to his feet. Chapa smiled. It was a cold, cruel smile, the *bandido's* eyes like those of a snake. "You owe me two thousand dollars, Frio Wheeler. I am going to collect in blood!" He laughed harshly. "You gringos are stupid, the *yanqui* army as stupid as the rest of you. They could do nothing about you, so tonight they gave me money to get rid of you. Fools! I was about to do it for nothing."

Frio said in disbelief, "They paid you?"

Chapa nodded. "A very funny joke, *sí?*"

His fist darted. Frio tried to turn away but could not. Fire flashed before his eyes as the blow struck him full in the face. He tasted blood.

Chapa ordered crisply, "Off with his coat and shirt. Tie his hands." They tore the clothing from him, down to the waist. He struggled against them, but they stamped the breath out of him and then tied his hands with rawhide so tightly that he knew the circulation would be badly impaired. They stood him with his stomach to the wall, stretching his hands overhead and tying them by the rawhide thong to the rafter above him.

Chapa had a whip. He flipped away the coils and snapped the end of it. "You are a mule driver, amigo. You know how to use a whip on mules. Now see how it feels to you!"

Frio shrank against the wall as the lash cut into his back. He wanted to cry out but managed to control himself.

"Scream if you want to," said Chapa. "No one will hear you — no one who cares." He struck again. The lash was like fire. Frio's knees sagged.

Chapa said, "You will think you are going to die. You will wish you *could* die. But I do not intend to let you go too soon. You are going to die slowly, gringo. You are going to die a two-thousand-dollar death."

Chapa quit talking and used his strength in swinging the whip. Each time, Frio thought he would scream, thought he could not stand one more. Cold sweat stood on his face. Teeth clamped, fists knotted, he cringed against the wall each time he heard the cruel hiss of the lash starting to move.

He was no more than half conscious when they cut him down. He fell heavily to the dirt floor. They threw cold water into his face.

"Bring him outside," said Chapa. "We will see how well he drags."

On his hands and knees, Frio watched, while Chapa mounted a splendid horse in

176

the dim starlight — a stolen horse, without doubt. Chapa took down a rawhide rope from the big horn of his Mexican saddle and pitched the loop end out to Bige Campsey. Campsey put it around Frio's arms and jerked up the slack. Dallying the reata around the horn, Chapa touched wicked spurs to his horse. Frio was jerked forward onto his stomach. He felt himself dragging in the street, blunt rocks bruising him, tearing his skin.

The dragging stopped for a moment. Chapa came back in a lope, the big horse barely missing Frio. The *bandido* hit the end of the rope and jerked Frio around backward, dragging him again. Sixty or seventy feet and he stopped once more.

Head pounding, his body ablaze with pain, Frio knew he couldn't last much longer. Another drag or two and he would be unconscious, or nearly so. If he was to fight back, he had to do it now. He pushed to his hands and knees as Chapa turned the horse around for another run. Frio's hands were still bound, but his fingers closed over the rawhide rope and went tight.

Chapa spurred and came running. Frio waited, his heart pounding desperately. When Chapa was almost upon him, Frio arose on wobbly legs and flipped the slack in the rope. He saw it go around the horse's forefeet. He turned his body into the rope, hands behind him, binding the rope across his hip. He saw Chapa desperately claw a pistol from its holster and at the same time try to rein the running horse to a stop.

The Mexican was too late. The horse was running full tilt when his feet tangled in the reata. The rope came suddenly tight, and the jar of it sent Frio to his knees again. But he had done what he had hoped. The horse went down threshing, on top of Chapa. The barrel of the pistol drove deep into the dirt. Frio pushed to his feet and ran unsteadily. He was aware of Chapa's men shouting and surging toward him. But he was much closer to Chapa than they were.

On his side, his legs pinned under the still struggling horse, Chapa swung the pistol around. He held it in both hands, near his face. He aimed it point-blank, and Frio felt the heart drop out of him. Chapa squeezed the trigger.

The gunbarrel was jammed full of dirt, and the pistol exploded with a blinding flash. Chapa screamed in agony, clasping both bleeding hands across his face. Blood flowed out between the broken fingers.

The horse was struggling to his feet. With the little strength still in him, Frio swung into the saddle. The *bandidos* came running, Bige Campsey in the lead. Frio drummed his heels against the horse's ribs and hoped the animal didn't step on the long reata that trailed from Frio's wrists. Frightened, the horse broke into a run. He faltered a little, for the fall had hurt him. Frio kicked him again to keep him running. The bandits ran along behind, afoot. Frio bent low in the saddle, knowing they would shoot at him but hoping the darkness would protect him until he could get around the rock buildings down the street.

He heard the slugs whine by his head. For a moment he thought he was going to get away clean.

Then the bullet struck him in the back, deep in the shoulder. He reeled in the saddle, almost fell to the ground. His fingers grabbed desperately for the big horn of Chapa's saddle. They closed around it, and he managed to catch himself.

Moments later he realized dully that he was in the clear. The bullet was like a heavy, glowing coal in his shoulder. He felt his blood running down his bare back. It took all the determination he could muster to hold himself in the saddle. But somewhere yonder, somewhere ahead of him in the night, lay his wagon camp. He clenched his teeth in agony and swore to himself that he would stay alive until he found his wagons.

10

Tom McCasland rapped his knuckles gently against the wooden door. A voice answered, "Come in." Tom pushed the door open and saw Major Luther Quayle seated behind a table that served as a desk. Quayle stood up in pleased surprise.

"You didn't waste any time getting here."

"Came as soon as I got the word," Tom replied. He strode across and shook hands. The major reached behind some rolled maps on a shelf and brought out a bottle. He gripped a pair of small glasses between his thumb and two fingers. He poured the glasses full and handed one to Tom.

"This," he said, "is the only thing that makes life endurable in this godforsaken assignment."

Tom said, "You didn't call me over here to drink."

"No, but a drink might help. You'll need another one or two before I'm through."

"You must have a tough job for me this time."

Quayle only frowned, not making an answer. He sat on the corner of the table, his eyebrows knitted, and he studied Tom McCasland with a keen eye. Tom flinched, uncomfortable under the penetrating gaze.

"McCasland, you have a good reputation with us. When we came, you told us you would do anything for the Union. Up to now you've done everything we asked of you and never held back for a moment." He scowled down at his near-empty glass. "Now I'm afraid we're about to put you to the supreme test. Before I tell you what it is, I'll say this: We didn't want to ask you. We've tried alternatives, to no avail."

Tom said, "I'm a soldier, of sorts. I won't turn away from danger."

Quayle poured himself another drink. Tom waved the major away when he reached for Tom's glass. Quayle took a long swallow, obviously dreading what he was to say. "It's not so much the danger that concerns us."

He set the glass down and turned away from Tom. "McCasland, you're a longtime friend of this Frio Wheeler, aren't you?"

"From a long way back. We used to be partners."

"You know he's been a thorn in our side.

You know he's a kingpin in the border trade."

"I know all that."

"Did you know he was badly wounded in Matamoros a couple of nights ago?"

Tom sat up straight. "No! How bad?"

"Bad. But for us, not bad enough. He's still alive."

Tom breathed out a sigh of relief. Quayle turned to frown at him. "I can understand your feelings, McCasland. He's your friend. But at the same time, he's our enemy. It would have been better for us if he had died."

"How did it happen?"

"That bandit Chapa." Quayle pushed away from the table. "You won't like this, McCasland, but I think you'll understand why we tried it. We paid Chapa to kill him." When Tom's eyes widened in quick anger, Quayle explained, "Wheeler stays out of our reach. So long as he's across the river, not a hand can be raised against him — by us. But by a Mexican, that's another matter. Through our intelligence work we found out that there was bad blood between Wheeler and this Chapa. We thought that with a little extra incentive, Chapa would take care of the matter for us, and our hands would have been clean." He paused. "They would have *looked* clean, anyway. Hell, everybody knows war is a dirty business.

"What we didn't count on was Chapa's method. We assumed he would do the job the way we would, the quickest way possible to get it over with. But no, he wanted to do it by torture. He wanted Wheeler to die a slow death."

Quayle glanced at Tom again and looked quickly away from the steady, cold gaze he encountered. "If we'd known he was going to do it like that, we wouldn't have gone to him at all. We don't sanction torture, McCasland. Be that as it may, Chapa became so eager in his work that he got careless. Somehow Wheeler tripped Chapa's horse and made it fall on him. Wheeler dragged himself onto the horse and got away.

"Not completely away, though. That" — his nose wrinkled with disgust — "that *patriot* Campsey was there, and he wounded Wheeler as your friend rode off. Best we can tell from our intelligence reports, it was a rather bad wound, somewhere in the shoulder. Wheeler lost a lot of blood, but he got back to his camp. His men brought a Mexican doctor and saved him from bleeding to death. They took him across the river in a boat, in the night, and put him on a wagon right under our noses. They hauled him to his ranch." He scowled. "If all the secesh were that hard to kill, we never could win this war."

Tom said, "I heard his wagons moved out with a load of supplies this mornin', bound upriver. I thought he was with them. . . ."

Quayle shook his head. "He has a young fellow working for him — Fleet, I think the name is. *He* took the wagons. You can bet that if we don't find a way to stop Wheeler he'll be back with that train as soon as he has the strength to ride."

The officer poured Tom's glass full. "Better drink that, McCasland, before I tell you the rest."

Tom sipped suspiciously.

Quayle said, "This occupation of Brownsville has been a severe disappointment to us, as you surely know. We thought all we had to do was take the town and we would stop the Confederate border trade. It didn't work that way. All we've done is inconvenience them. The trade goes on while we stand here helplessly and watch.

"The key to it is the wagon trains. They stay pretty well out of our reach. Our troops don't know this country, and they can't do much by themselves. That's why we've hired all the border renegades we can find to help us, to guide our patrols to the striking points and back again. We do all we can to disrupt those trails. But the wagons keep coming. The reason is the influence of a few key men. Captain Richard King is one. Your friend Wheeler is another. King isn't my problem; someone else has that assignment. But Wheeler *is* my problem. I won't have a moment's peace until that man is dead."

Tom took the rest of the drink and stared again at the floor. "I don't know why you called on me. You know I can't help you."

"Wrong, McCasland, you *can.* The question is, will you?" The major walked around the table and stood directly in front of Tom. "We are reasonably certain that Wheeler is at his ranch right now, wounded. He's vulnerable. We doubt strongly that he has a guard that would give us any real trouble. Our only problem is to get there. We didn't want to ask your help on this, McCasland. We've tried for most of two days to find someone who would guide us to Wheeler's ranch. But the Mexicans who know the way are loyal to him or afraid of the others who are. We can't find one who will take us. You're our only hope."

Tom stood up, angry. He placed the glass on the table and strode stiffly across the room to peer out the window. "Major, what kind of a Judas do you take me for? Send

186

me out on any decent kind of a job — I've never turned you down yet. But to do a thing like this. . . ." He shook his head violently. "Court-martial me if you want to, I won't do it."

Quayle said sympathetically, "I expected you to be angry. But I also thought that when you considered it, you'd see why we had to ask you. Sure, I know he's your friend. That's what makes this war so monstrous, McCasland — we're fighting men who were our friends, even our blood kin." A sadness came into his eyes. "I had a cousin when I grew up. He was more than kin, he was the best friend I had. But when the war started we went separate ways. I chose the blue and he chose the gray. I saw him after Shiloh, dead. For all I know, my own bullet could have killed him.

"This is my point: Every day that the war goes on means more men dead on the battlefields. Every day by which we can shorten this war means that many men saved. Now, I'm not claiming that this border trade is the major factor keeping the Confederacy alive; it isn't. But it is *one* of the factors. If we can stop it, the Confederacy dies sooner — by days, maybe weeks, perhaps even months. No one can say how many lives would be saved. Thousands, maybe. Your friend is one of the keys. If we kill him, we can save men who otherwise would have died."

Quayle placed his hand on Tom's shoulder. "Think, McCasland. Think with your head, not with your heart. Is your friendship with this one man worth the lives of thousands? Would you stand by and see them die because you lacked the strength to kill one man?"

Tom swallowed. He stared out the window a long time. "God, Major, you make it hard."

"No one ever claimed war was easy."

"Whichever way I go, I'll regret it to the day I die."

"Our side didn't start this war."

Tom shook his head. "Who did? I guess when it's over we'll find that none of us was completely guilty, and none of us innocent."

"It's your decision to make, McCasland."

Tom rubbed his hand across his face. Misery dulled his voice. "I'd rather be dead than make it."

Luisa Valdez stood in the doorway that led to the tiny candlelit bedroom and stared with narrowed, worried eyes at Tom McCasland. Tom sat slumped in a chair, gripping a bottle of whisky at the neck. His eyes had long since gone glazed. Luisa walked over slowly and took the bottle.

"Tom, don't you think you've had enough?"

Shaking his head, he pulled the bottle out of her grasp. She took a step backward, raising her hand and touching a forefinger to the corner of her eye, wiping away a stray tear.

"Tom, I've never seen you like this. You've never been a hard drinker. What's wrong?"

Tom made no sign he had heard her. His eyes stared blankly off into the distance.

Luisa moved in again and placed her hand against his cheek. "Is it something I have done, something I have said? I didn't know I had done anything to displease you. I didn't mean to."

The sadness in her voice seemed to move him. He looked up at her and shook his head. "No, Luisa, it isn't you. You could never do anything to displease me."

She leaned down and kissed him on the forehead. "Then it can't be anything so bad that you want to drink yourself to sleep. Come on, Tom, let's go to bed. You'll feel better tomorrow."

He shook his head. "Once I do what I have to, I doubt if I'll ever sleep again, unless I drink myself to it."

Alarm showed in her eyes. "What have they asked you to do this time, Tom? Is it something dangerous again?"

"Dangerous? No, not especially. Not for me, anyway."

"Then don't let it trouble you so." She kissed him again. "Forget it for now. We'll go to bed."

He studied her with a brooding gaze. "You may not feel that way about me after tomorrow. You may have nothing but contempt for me."

Luisa stiffened. "Tom, what sort of job have they given you?"

Tom's head tilted over. He stared at the floor a minute, then took another long drink. "They're sending me to kill Frio Wheeler."

Luisa gasped. "Tom, you can't!"

"I never would have thought I could. But they've shown me that it has to be done. I'm the one who must do it."

Hands over her face, Luisa walked slowly to the bedroom door and turned. "But why?"

"Because his death could shorten the war. Maybe not much, but even a few days would save a great many men. One man's life against all those others. When you look at it that way, you see why it has to be done."

"Not just one man's life, Tom. He's your friend. When you destroy him, you'll also destroy yourself."

"All right, *two* men. What are we worth, two of us against all those who might be saved?"

"What of your sister, Tom? She's in love with him. Maybe you don't realize it, but I saw it that night at the *fandango.* You'll break her heart."

"She's young."

"She'll hate you."

Angrily he shouted, "For God's sake, Luisa, don't you think I know that? Don't you think I've run it through my brain a thousand times already? Why do you think I've been nursing this bottle all night? Maybe if I drink enough I can blot all these things out of my mind. Maybe if I'm drunk enough I can do what I have to without my conscience dragging me back. Maybe if I stay drunk afterward I won't have to listen to my conscience at all."

Luisa dropped down upon a chair and began to sob. Presently the empty bottle fell clattering to the floor. Looking up, she found that Tom had slumped over, asleep. Slowly she pushed to her feet, stooping to pick up the fallen bottle. She stared a while at the sleeping man and blinked back tears.

Finally, making up her mind, she wrapped a heavy woolen shawl around her shoulders and went out into the chilly night.

She started up the dark street, walking hurriedly. A pair of Union soldiers stepped in front of her before she reached the main plaza. She brushed past them, ignoring their remarks, thinking that it was hard to tell much difference between Confederate soldier and Yankee when they came across the river to Matamoros. Or Mexican soldiers, either, for that matter. Their wants were simple and predictable.

She was uncertain which house was the one she sought. She chose one and nervously rapped on the wooden door. She saw a light flicker as someone brought flame to a candle from banked coals in the fireplace. The door opened partway and a man's head showed against the dim light. His eyes widened at the sight of the slender woman standing there.

"Hello," he said. "You sure you got the right house?"

"I am looking for the Señor Plunkett."

He stammered. "W . . . well, I'm him, but I sure didn't send for you."

"I must talk with you. It is most urgent, about Señor Wheeler."

Plunkett said, "Give me a minute to get

some pants on, then come on in."

He was buttoning his shirt when she entered the room. He modestly turned away until he had the last button done, all the way to the collar. "Now, what's this about Frio?"

"You must send someone to warn him. They are going to his place to kill him."

Plunkett's mouth dropped open. "Who?"

"The *yanqui* soldiers. Tom McCasland is going to take them."

"McCasland?" Incredulous, Plunkett said, "But he's Frio's friend." He stared at her, not knowing whether to believe her or not. Recognition slowly came to him. "I know you. You're Señora Valdez. I've seen you with McCasland." His eyes narrowed. "Tom McCasland's your man. Why would you come and tell me this?"

The tears started again, and she turned half away. "To save Tom. They tell him he must do it for his country. But if he helps them to kill his friend, Tom will die too, inside. I would save him that."

"He ever finds out you came and told me, you're liable to lose him."

"At least I will know he is not eating his own heart away, remembering that he killed his best friend. Better to lose him and know he is alive than to have him and know that the spirit in him is dead."

Plunkett nodded slowly, his eyes grave. "You're a brave woman, Señora Valdez. You made the right choice. I know a man who can make the ride. He'll leave before daylight."

She turned toward the door, her shoulders slumped. "Thank you, Señor Plunkett."

He let her get halfway through the door before he said, "I promise you one thing: Nobody will ever find out from me how I knew about this."

She said, "Thank you, señor. But Tom will know anyway. He will guess."

She disappeared into the night.

11

The rough rock walls were without ornamentation of any kind — not a picture, not a crucifix. In his first hours here, Frio had lain with a blazing fever and stared with glazed eyes at the dark door of death, which had loomed wide and open in the gloom just beyond the foot of the bed. Later, fever subsiding but the bedclothes still sticking to his body, he had studied those bare walls until he knew every crack, every little squeeze of mortar. In their rough shape and from the shadows that lay across them he could make out vague pictures of faces and mountains and horses and cattle.

Most of the fever was gone now, though a lingering weakness continued to hold him down. He was tired of lying here this way when there was so much that needed to be done. Experimentally he swung his legs off the cot and let his bare feet touch the earthen floor. His head swirled. He had to hold it in his hands. The wound began to throb afresh.

Cooking in the other room, Amelia Mc-Casland heard him move. She dropped a stirring spoon into an iron pot and came to see about him. Frio pulled the blanket up to cover himself.

"Frio," she scolded, "you lie back and be still. You'll break that wound open again."

His head was swimming so much that it was hard to keep his eyes on her. "Just wanted to see how I'd feel sittin' up. I can't stay in bed forever."

"You'll stay there awhile longer if you want to live. Now lie down!"

Grudgingly he pulled his feet up and stretched out again. It was true he felt much better this way. He doubted he could get to the front door afoot. He had lost a lot of blood.

"I've got to be up and out with my wagons."

"Happy Jack can take care of the wagons for one trip, at least."

Frio's face twisted. A glowing anger had remained banked inside him since the night Florencio Chapa had so coldly killed Felix and had put the whip to Frio. "Just takin' care of them isn't enough. I want those wagons to roll far and fast. I want to show the Yankees how much war goods I can haul. I want to show them I'm a long way from bein' dead — that they wasted the blood money they paid Chapa."

Amelia said, "You're hating too hard, Frio. Hate is a cruel master." She sat on the edge of the cot, put her warm hand gently to his face, and tried to force a smile. "Try to put the hatred away. Be glad you can lie back and rest. Be glad you can spend some time here with me."

He reached up and took her hand. "You know people are goin' to talk, you stayin' in the same house with me."

"The condition you're in, what could happen?" She wrinkled her nose. "It'll take more than talk to hurt me anymore. Anyway, I'll let you make an honest woman of me anytime you want to."

He tightened his grip on her hand. "Someday, Amelia, when I can, I'll take you with me down to Matamoros. We'll be married there."

She leaned down and kissed him. "I'm only sorry it took a bullet in the back to make you say that."

Someone knocked at the front door. Blas Talamantes and his wife came into the house. María carried a tin bucket of milk. Blas strode directly into the bedroom, taking off his big sombrero. "Ah, Frio, you feel a little better, no?"

Frio nodded. "Some. How is everything goin'?"

Blas shrugged. "*Bueno*. The cattle are thin, but mostly they still live. Maybeso it rains in the spring."

Standing in the doorway, María held up the bucket. "*Madama,* I have bring milk for the *patrón.* It will help to make him well."

Frio grimaced. "Milk!"

María said, "You need it. You must drink it for strong."

Frio argued. "You need it worse than I do, María. You're drinkin' it for two." The tiny woman was showing her pregnancy more every day.

Blas placed his strong arm around his wife's thin shoulder. "I burn prickly pear for the milk cow. Pear makes for plenty milk. We get enough for María and for you, too, don't you worry."

María's fingers went up to touch Blas's hand, and she leaned her head down so that her cheek rested against the man's arm. She said, "So long as I have Blas, I have no need for anything else."

Blas smiled down at her. In the moment of silence, Frio heard a running horse. Blas heard it too, for he turned his head to listen.

The boy Chico burst through the door. Bundled in a coat twice too large for him, he had been playing outdoors.

He said excitedly, "Somebody is come!"

Through the open door they heard a man outside shouting, "Blas! Blas Talamantes!" It was a Mexican voice.

Blas stepped to the door and hailed the man. "*Aquí,* Natividad. Slow down a little. You live much longer."

Natividad de la Cruz stepped hurriedly up onto the little porch. "There is no time to slow down. The *yangui* soldiers, they are not far behind me. Where is the Frio?"

Blas's smile was wiped away in a second. "Frio is here, in bed. We cannot move him."

"The *yanquis* will do more than move him!"

Natividad, about the same age as Blas, was a one-time vaquero who worked for Hugh Plunkett in the cottonyard. Once Frio had brought medicine all the way from San Antonio for Natividad's sick wife. She had died anyway, but the man's gratitude had never changed. Natividad brushed past Blas and hurried to the bedroom.

"Mr. Frio, you get away from here quick! The *yanquis,* they come for to kill you!"

The color left Amelia's face. Frio demanded, "How do you know?"

"Señor Plunkett, he say for me to ride like the wind. My horse he is go lame, and the soldiers they pass me while I am finding another. I spur him hard and go around them, but they follow close. You got very little time."

Frio sat up shakily and put his feet on the floor again. Amelia protested, "Frio, you can't go, not in your condition. Let them arrest you. What can they do?"

Natividad said, "Pardon me, señorita, but Señor Plunkett he say they don't come to arrest him, they come for to kill him!"

Amelia cried, "You can't ride a horse, Frio. You'll tear that wound open and bleed to death!"

"I can't just lie here!"

Blas had listened gravely. Now, voice urgent, he said, "I fix. Miss Amelia, you and María and Natividad, you take Frio out into the thick brush. Go as far as you can. Wipe out your tracks behind you. I take Natividad's horse and lead the *yanquis* away."

He dropped his sombrero on the floor and took one of Frio's hats from a peg on the wall. He slipped off his Mexican coat and put on one of Frio's.

Frio shook his head. "Too risky. I won't let you do it."

Blas said sternly, "You can't stop me.

Hurry up now, all of you. *Ándele!*"

Natividad helped Frio pull on a pair of pants and get boots on his feet. Frio tried to stand alone but swayed and nearly fell. Natividad caught and steadied him, pulling Frio's good arm around his shoulder to give him support. He flung a blanket over Frio's back to keep him warm when they went out into the chill of the open air.

Tearful, María clutched at her husband. "Blas, Blas, don't do it!"

"Don't worry, *querida*. It is pretty soon dark. They will think I am Frio. I let them follow, but I don't let them get close."

María cried, "Blas, they will kill you!"

He threw his arms around her and crushed her to him. He kissed her, then pushed her away. "Go now. No *yanqui* soldier can kill me, not when I have a son on the way that I have not even seen."

Blas hurried out to see about Natividad's horse. Frio said, "Amelia, bring the rifle!" She got it. With Natividad to help her, she brought Frio out into the fading afternoon. The chill cut him at first like the sharp edge of a knife, María hurried along behind, carrying several warm blankets over one arm. She clutched Chico's hand and dragged the boy in a run. She paused a moment to look back at her husband, who stood beside the

201

horse, awaiting first sight of the Union soldiers.

"Blas," she called brokenly, "go with God!"

He blew his wife a kiss and watched her until she and the others disappeared south into the brush. Blas turned then and kept his gaze on the Brownsville trail. A cold sweat broke across his face. It wasn't long, perhaps ten minutes, when he saw the first bluecoat push warily out of the brush. Shortly he could see forty or fifty troopers. Their officer gave a signal. The soldiers spurred into a run toward the house.

Blas waited only long enough to cross himself. Then he swung into the saddle and broke north, putting Natividad's tiring horse into a lope. Blas purposely hunched over in the saddle, the way a wounded man would. It stood to reason they knew Frio was wounded, else why would they have come?

Looking over his shoulder, he saw that they were following him as hard as they could run.

Blas gritted his teeth and tore into the brush.

Tom McCasland had ridden in torture all day. The whisky he had drunk last night still burned in his belly like a bank of coals, and his head throbbed as if someone were crushing his skull with a sledge. He had no recollection of going to bed. The last he remembered, he had still been sitting up in a chair. He hadn't awakened until the impatient Major Quayle had sent someone this morning to find out why he hadn't reported when he was supposed to. The major had ridden beside him in angry silence all day. Because of Tom, the patrol had been delayed more than an hour beyond its scheduled starting time. Twice they had to stop and allow Tom to be sick. Small wonder Quayle was disgusted with him.

Well, Tom thought, what had they expected, asking him to do a job like this? They couldn't expect a man to help kill his best friend and do it cold sober.

For a while last night the liquor had at least numbed the edge of his guilt. Now nothing was left but the dregs of the whisky, and the guilt was with him again, riding upon his shoulders with the weight of stone. It shrieked in his ear like some querulous old beggar-woman at the city plaza, berating a passerby for dropping no coin in her outstretched hand.

When the war was over, he would have to leave this part of the country; he knew that.

He realized he would be regarded from now on as a Judas. He could never hope to make people understand. His friends would turn away, loathing him. And his sister. . . . He shook his head sadly at the thought of her. When Frio died, Amelia would reject Tom with a hatred that probably would last the rest of her life.

Yet, he knew what his duty was, and he would do it. But at what a cost!

Perhaps when the war was over he would change his name. Maybe he would go west to California, for that was a new and growing land. Or even down into Mexico. He knew the Mexican people well, and by now he spoke their language almost as they did. He could start fresh.

Or could he? Did a man ever really start fresh? No matter where he went, no matter if he changed his surroundings, his clothes, even his language, he would take his memories with him. He would take with him the cancerous guilt that eroded his soul. Not even the love of a woman like Luisa Valdez would be enough to offset that.

Luisa! He remembered the shock in her face last night when he had told her what he was going to do. She could not have been more shaken if he had struck her with his fist. He had half expected her to turn her back on him and call him a betrayer. Yet, this morning she had seemed strangely calm. She hadn't tried to argue with him. That was one thing about most Mexican women: They believed it was the man's place to make the decisions. Right or wrong, they followed him.

"It's getting late," Major Quayle said. It was the first time he had spoken to Tom in a couple of hours. "How much farther?"

"We're almost there. We'll break out of this brush in a minute and into the clearing where the houses are."

The major turned to the sergeant. "Get the men closed up. Tell them to have their carbines ready. We'll go in running. We'll give them no time to set up a defense."

Tom said bitterly, "Who? A wounded man, a couple of women, maybe one or two Mexicans? Remember what I told you, Major: My sister is there. I don't want her hurt."

"We'll get this over with in a hurry. She won't be hurt."

Won't be hurt! The major's words struck Tom like some sardonic joke. Killing Frio was the worst hurt they could do her.

They rode out into the open. Tom's sight was blurred, for last night's drinking had left its mark. But he saw the horse in front of the rock house. He made out a man standing behind the mount. He made out Frio's black hat.

Quayle said, "That him?"

Tom swallowed and looked down. "It's him."

Quayle waved his arm and shouted, "Charge!"

In an instant the troopers were in a gallop. The first rush left Tom behind. He had no wish to be up front. He had no wish to be here at all. He let the soldiers take over. Sick at heart, he watched the fugitive swing into the saddle and spur northward toward the heavy brush.

"Run, Frio!" he found himself whispering. "For God's sake, run!"

Tom touched spurs to his horse then and tried to catch up with Quayle, but already he was too far behind. The troopers hit the brush. The heavy limbs lashed at them, the thorns clutched and tore. But the soldiers had seen their quarry. They spurred through the brush like Mexican vaqueros born to the chaparral. They started a ragged pattern of shooting, but it was of no real avail. There was no chance for accuracy from horseback at a speed like this, through a thorny tangle of brush that grabbed at a man and tried to pull him out of the saddle.

For a mile or more they ran. The horses were beginning to labor. But the fugitive's mount was slowing more. In despair Tom watched the soldiers making a slow but steady gain. Of a sudden now he wished that by some miracle he could place himself on that horse up yonder, that he could take the soldiers' bullets instead of Frio.

To hell with the major! To hell with the Union! He wished he could call back the day, could have another chance at the decision he had made. Tears burned his eyes and trailed down his cheeks.

"Run, Frio! For God's sake, run!"

The soldiers shouted in excitement. Blinking hard, Tom saw that the quarry's horse had gone down. It lay kicking on the ground. In the brush the fugitive began to run afoot, limping as if the fall had hurt his leg. It occurred to Tom that Frio was making a pretty good account of himself for a man who had been wounded so badly.

Quayle signaled, splitting his riders, sending half of them around one side, half around the other. They would ring Frio and then close in on him. In a few minutes he would be a dead man.

Tom knew the situation was out of his hands now. Nothing he could do would help Frio. He stopped his horse and sat slumped in the saddle, the tears streaming. He wished God would see fit to strike him dead. Oblivion now would be a blessing.

Eyes closed, he could hear the soldiers threshing through the brush. They shouted to one another. Above them all he could hear the loud commands of Major Quayle. Finally came the exultant yells of the men as they cornered their prey.

A volley of shots echoed through the chaparral.

"Frio!" Tom cried. "Oh, God!" He touched spurs to the horse and put him into a run. The choking veil of gunsmoke still clung in the thick brush. Tom spurred past the soldiers toward the still figure he could see lying broken on the ground. He slid his horse to a stop and was off running.

The body lay facedown, torn half apart by the troopers' bullets. Major Quayle rode up and stepped out of the saddle as Tom gently started to turn the body over.

Tom looked into the dirt-covered face and felt his heart bob.

Major Quayle suddenly began to curse. "That's not Wheeler!"

Tom slowly shook his head, his chin dropping. He folded Blas Talamantes's hands carefully and wiped dirt from the Mexican's face. Tears burned in Tom's eyes.

"No, Major," he said tightly, "it's not Frio Wheeler. You've killed the wrong man!"

Frio's wounds burned as if a hot branding iron had been shoved against his shoulder. From its stickiness, he knew it was bleeding afresh. They had carried him here into the thickest of the brush, for he had little strength to support himself. He had leaned heavily upon Amelia and Natividad. María had followed along with Chico. The little woman had a broken-off catclaw limb and was walking backward, scratching out their tracks as she went.

Frio groaned despite himself, for the wound was blindingly painful.

Amelia said, "This is far enough. He'll die if we keep this up." While Natividad held Frio on his feet, Amelia found a thick clump of shoulder-high prickly pear, growing so tightly that at first glance there seemed no way into it. But she found a way and beckoned. "In here. If we'll all huddle in here, they may not find us."

Pear thorns dug into their legs like tiny needles of fire, but there was no time to worry about that now. They moved into the heavy clump. María came last, dragging the catclaw limb to brush away the sign of their passing. It wouldn't fool a good tracker, but it might be overlooked by the Yankees.

"Wrap Frio in this blanket," Amelia said to Natividad. She had taken command with all the firmness of a soldier. "We may have to lie here a long time, and he's going to be cold." They laid him out in a narrow spot between the prickly pears, one edge of the blanket beneath him. Amelia stayed on her feet and watched until the others had bundled themselves and were lying flat upon the ground. Then she crawled under the blanket beside Frio. She found him trembling from cold. She pulled her body against him and drew the blanket up tightly, hoping her own warmth would protect him. With that wound, pneumonia could come easily.

"It's going to be all right, Frio," she whispered.

Presently they heard a far-off volley of shots. María screamed, "Blas! Blas!"

Then came a deadly silence. They could do nothing except lie there and listen to the little woman alternately sobbing and praying. Amelia buried her face against Frio's chest and let her own tears flow.

Much later they heard men and horses approaching slowly. Chico whimpered. María's voice spoke quietly, steady now with resignation, "Easy, little one. Easy, so they do not hear."

The soldiers had fanned out in the brush and were combing it slowly, knowing the man they sought must be hiding there. Amelia turned and lay quietly, her breath ragged in fear. She knew the cold presence of death. At ground level was a small opening through the pear plants, and she could see a Union soldier moving in her direction. His gaze moved carefully back and forth. She held her breath, certain he was going to spot her. She wanted to pull the blanket back over her face but was afraid the movement would catch his eye. A scream rose in her throat. She clamped her teeth together.

The soldier rode close, peering over into this heavy growth of pear. Amelia's fingers closed on the rifle. If that trooper saw them, she would shoot him, even though she knew it would bring the others on the run. They wouldn't kill Frio without a fight; not without killing her too!

The soldier saw nothing. He pulled away. Amelia let her breath out slowly and loosened her hold on the rifle. Her heart seemed to race.

The line had passed. Unless they came this way again, Frio was safe.

She saw another movement then. Another rider was coming, one not in uniform. This man trailed along behind the soldiers, not taking part in the search. Amelia squinted, trying to make out his face.

He moved closer, and recognition came with a shock.

"Tom!" she cried out. Immediately she wanted to bite off her tongue. Tom Mc-Casland reined up. He had heard. His gaze searched through the prickly pear, and their eyes met.

She lay paralyzed in fear, watching her brother, sure he was going to call back the soldiers.

Then Tom tore his eyes away from her. He dropped his chin and rode on.

With dusk came the smoke, drifting slowly southward from the direction of the house. Frio sat up weakly. "They're burnin' us out," he said. A great sadness came over him. He knew Blas was dead.

María stood up, weeping quietly. Frio wished he could go to her.

"María," he said bitterly. "I promise you this: I promise you they'll pay!"

12

For a long time they waited there in the
darkness, blankets wrapped tightly around
them for warmth. The stars stood out with
a piercing brightness in the winter sky. Natividad de la Cruz pushed to his feet, speaking sharply under his breath when his leg
brushed against the hostile spines of a
prickly pear. "I think, Mr. Frio, the *yanquis*
have gone. If you like, I will go see."

Frio nodded painfully. "I doubt they've
left us anything to go back to. But go look."

The moon came up while Natividad was
gone. Its silver light made the bushes stand
out in bold relief. At least, thought Frio,
they wouldn't have to stumble along in
darkness, pierced by thorns at every wrong
step.

He shivered inside the blanket. Amelia
McCasland leaned to him, her body pleasantly warm. Another time it might have
been different, but her presence brought

him little comfort now. Pain pulsed in his shoulder, almost enough to make him cry out. It was as if the bullet were still lodged there with its white heat. Frio knew he would have a fever later. His mind dwelled on Blas Talamantes. He wondered where the Mexican was, wondered if death had come swiftly and with mercy, or if Blas had lain and suffered as Frio suffered now.

Presently they heard brush snapping. Natividad was calling softly. He knew the direction but not the exact place.

Amelia answered, "Here, Natividad."

The Mexican moved cautiously into the big clump of pear, avoiding its thorns. He gazed down gravely at Frio. "Mr. Frio, the *yanqui* soldiers have gone. We can go back to the house if you like." He paused and said, "But, as you say, there is no house."

Amelia looked at Frio, tears in her eyes. Then, squaring her shoulders, she said, "We will go back, Natividad, to whatever is left."

Natividad blinked, not following her reasoning. He shrugged and said, "Of course, señorita. Here, I will help you."

Gently he helped Frio to his feet. The wounded man closed his eyes tightly a moment, shaking his head. His brain seemed to swim aimlessly, and he cringed against a sharp shaft of pain. With Natividad's support, Frio made his way out of the pear.

It took them longer to get back to the clearing than it had taken to reach the pear in the first place. For one thing, there was not the pressure of pursuit. Secondly, there was the dread of seeing what lay in wait for them. Amelia took the lead. María trailed, holding onto Chico's hand. The little woman moved with her head down, but she did not let her grief blind her. She held to the boy, keeping him from walking into thorns, catching him when he stumbled.

Amelia stopped at the edge of the clearing. Frio heard her gasp, "Oh, Frio, oh no!"

Frio blinked, trying to clear the glaze from his eyes. In the moonlight he could see the bare rock walls and the glow from inside them. Though the walls would not burn, they probably were badly cracked from the heat of the blazing roof. The smaller house that Blas and María had used was gone, too, part of one wall caved in, flames still licking hungrily at the wooden beams. The troopers had set fire even to the brush *jacales* that old Salcido Mendoza had built long ago for his vaqueros and their families. The Yankees had not left a thing standing above ground except the corrals and the rock walls.

Anger surged again in Frio Wheeler, a

helpless anger that hurt all the more because all he could do was stand here and look. He couldn't even stand were it not for Natividad holding him up.

"We could as well have stayed in the brush," Frio gritted. "We'll have to sleep in the open anyway."

Natividad eased Frio to the ground. Frio sat with his fist balled as tight as he could make it. So many things he could think of now, things they should have done. They should have taken more blankets with them, for the ones they had would not be enough to shield them from the night's cold. They should have taken some food, too, for everything in the houses had been burned. And guns . . . there had been a couple more guns in the bigger house. Chances were the soldiers had found those and confiscated them if they had made any search before they put the place to the torch. Burn them or steal them, it didn't matter much now; the guns were gone. All Frio had was the one rifle.

Natividad gingerly dragged some of the slow-burning wood out of the two houses, careful lest he sear his hands. He piled it together, then fetched wood from Blas Talamantes's woodpile. Presently he had a fire started between the ruins of the two houses.

He said, "We need this tonight, I think."

María had been silent. Now, she asked, "What of Blas?"

Frio said, "Not much anybody can do for him now. Natividad will go look for him in the mornin'."

They spread their blankets near the fire so they would have its warmth through the night. Natividad brought up enough wood to last until day, piling it where he could reach it as it was needed. Chico was the first to drop off in fitful sleep. Before long he was moaning, caught in the clutch of some nightmare.

Sitting close beside Frio, Amelia said, "He was like that for a while after we first came here. Then he got over it. I guess today has brought the scare back to him."

"Poor button," Frio replied. "He must think his saints are almighty angry with him."

María Talamantes leaned over the boy, shaking him a little to try to stir him out of the dream. In Spanish she said, "It's all right, Chico. It's all right." She sat on the ground and took the boy in her arms, folding him to her bosom and rocking her body gently back and forth. Somehow in comforting the boy she seemed to find solace for herself.

Natividad got up and brought his blanket. He put it over the little woman and the boy. He said simply, "With this fire, the blanket is too warm for me." He sat nearer the blaze and gradually dozed off to sleep, his chin dropping to his chest.

For Frio there was little sleep. The fever grew. He sweated awhile, then chilled. His half-numbed mind slipped off into swirling dreams of violence and movement, to short flights of fancy — some angry, some happy, some frightening, some sad. The faces of Blas Talamantes and Tom McCasland and Florencio Chapa kept coming to him, again and again. He could see his wagons and feel the cold, muddy water of the Rio Grande. He imagined he could hear the guns in far-off Virginia and see the men there low on ammunition, short of guns, waiting for his wagons to bring these things across the river from Mexico. Half-awake, he peered with glazed eyes into the crackling coals of Natividad's fire and saw Brownsville aflame. He could hear the screams of Amelia McCasland, trapped inside the blazing store with her dying father. Another moment he would be back with Tom McCasland in the pleasant years before the war, riding across this ranch, putting their brand on the unclaimed cattle they found. There was no reason to the images he saw, no logical sequence.

He lay until dawn, dozing a little, then half awakening, never a moment free from the torment of his stiffened shoulder. Amelia slept fitfully beside him. With daylight it seemed to him that his fever was gone, and he could see clearly. He watched the sunrise. He saw Natividad reach out to put more wood on the fire, then stand up and stretch himself, his breath making a small patch of fog in the sharp morning air.

Quietly, trying not to awaken the others, the Mexican said to Frio, "There is no food. The boy will be hungry."

They all would be, but it would hurt the boy most of all.

As if in answer, Blas Talamantes's milk cow bawled beside the corral gate. Natividad carefully walked over and opened the gate so she could go in. The cow smelled her way suspiciously up to the ashes of what had been the small brush shed where Blas had been accustomed to milking her. She stood there dumbly and bawled.

Natividad kicked around the ashes of Blas and María's house and found a few blackened pots and pans. He also found a tin bucket. He carried them out to the creek, kneeling to scour the black from them with sand, then washing them clean with water. He held the bucket up to the rising sun to check it for holes. There weren't any. Next he found what was left of a pitchfork, half of the wooden handle burned away. He walked out to the nearest prickly pear and broke off all the spiny pads he could carry. He speared these, several at a time, on the tines of the pitchfork and held them over the fire, burning the thorns away. Done with that, he carried the fire-cleaned pear to the cow and fed it to her. While she chewed, he knelt and milked her.

Returning, he held the bucket up proudly for the awakening women to see. Amelia and Maria went to the charred remains of the houses and poked around for salvage. They found little. There was no food except the bucket of milk.

Frio said, "Natividad, we are afoot. They must have run off the horses. Can you shoot?"

Natividad shrugged. "Not the best. But maybeso I find us some kind of game."

Frio shook his head. "Not likely, not close to the house. I was thinkin' you might find a cow someplace around, or a steer. Take the rifle and shoot one. We'll have beef anyway. That's a start."

Taking the rifle and the few cartridges,

Natividad disappeared into the brush. After a long time they heard two shots. The Mexican returned, his shoulders bent under the weight of a quarter of beef. He said apologetically, "He was not a fat steer, but in the dry time one cannot choose. . . ."

Frio said, "You did fine."

"I will go back and bring more of the beef before the wild hogs find it."

Amelia sand-scoured an iron skillet she had rescued from the ashes. Using tallow from the fresh-killed beef, she soon had beef frying over the coals. By the time Natividad came back with another quarter, Amelia had steak cooked and ready to eat.

Frio drank a little of the warm milk, but he left most of it for María and the boy. What he wanted most was hot coffee. Texans here on the border had been comparatively fortunate in respect to coffee and some of the other imported goods. While the rest of the Confederacy was forced to do without, South Texans continued getting many of these things in limited amounts out of Mexico. But now there would be no coffee for Frio. It had gone up in flames.

Later, a couple of the loose horses came drifting in, for this was home. The Mexican penned them.

"Natividad," Frio said, "I'd be much

obliged if you would go out and find Blas. Bring him in so we can bury him decently. Then I'd like you to ride to Matamoros. and tell Hugh Plunkett what happened. You ought to be able to smuggle some supplies across the river on pack mules or burros and bring them here."

"*Sí,* I can do that. But it is not good to leave you here this way. You cannot defend yourself."

Frio shrugged painfully. "What choice do we have? You just hurry. Tell Hugh Plunkett we need help here. He'll find a way to send it."

The Mexican fashioned a hackamore out of some rawhide rope he found. Mounting bareback, he rode off and was gone an hour. When he came back, he was walking, leading the horse. Frio looked away, not wanting to watch. He knew that bundle across the horse's back had to be Blas. María Talamantes arose, crossed herself, and went slowly out to meet Natividad. Then she walked back, moving along dry eyed beside her husband's body.

They wrapped Blas in one of the blankets and buried him in a shallow grave. They placed rocks over him so the wolves would not dig him up. María would not want to leave him here forever. Someday, when she could, she would want to move him to consecrated ground.

There was not even a Bible to read from, for that too had burned. Frio stood on weak legs beside the pile of rocks and recited from memory what he could. María prayed almost inaudibly. When they were done, Natividad de la Cruz mounted the horse bareback and started toward Brownsville.

Frio saw the horseman approaching and thought at first it might be Natividad, coming back for some reason. Frio's sight was still none too good. Soon, though, he could tell it was not Natividad. He pushed painfully to his feet and supported himself against one of the fractured rock walls. "Amelia," he said evenly, "the rifle!"

She quickly handed it to him. With his left arm stiff, he didn't know how he was going to handle it if the need came.

Amelia peered toward the rider and turned back worriedly to Frio. "If it's the Yankees again, you've got to get out of here."

"Where? I've got no strength to run, even if I wanted to. I ran last night. I'm not ever goin' to run again!"

María came to stand with Amelia and Frio by the smoke-blackened wall. The boy Chico clung to María's skirt. Frio tried in vain to make out some detail about the rider. All he got was a blur. "What does he look like?"

Amelia's mouth dropped open. "It looks like . . ." Her chin came down, and her mouth hardened. "It looks like Tom."

Anger struck Frio. His grip tightened on the rifle. "Reckon he's brought the Yankees with him again?"

Amelia's voice was strained. "I don't see any sign of them." She glanced at Frio's rifle. "Frio, don't do anything in anger. Don't do anything you may regret."

Frio said tightly, "The only thing I regret is that I went through all those years callin' him friend."

Amelia blinked and stopped her tears before they really got started. Gravely she watched Tom McCasland ride in. Tom reined up thirty feet from the ruined house. He started to swing his leg over the saddle.

Frio said sharply, "Stay right where you're at! You're not gettin' off!"

Tom caught himself half out of the saddle. He stopped that way and let his eyes drift over the boy, the two women, and the wounded man who swayed there. Finally he said, "I'm gettin' down. Shoot me if you want to."

Frio raised the rifle, but he found he could

not bring his left arm across. If he fired, he would have to do it one-handed. The recoil would probably tear the rifle from his weak grasp.

Frio said, "You got no business here. Get back on that horse."

Tom replied, "Believe me, it took me a long time, workin' up the courage to come back. I'm not leavin' now."

"You got your Yankee friends hidden yonder, someplace in the brush?"

Tom shook his head. "Slipped away from them in the dark. They won't be back, not for a while. They rode half the night, afraid the fires would attract Santos Benavides and his Mexican militia."

Amelia said bitterly, "Why didn't you just keep riding with your Yankees, Tom? There's nobody here who wants you!"

Tom flinched. He stared at her, hurt in his eyes. "I'm still your brother, Amelia."

She shook her head. Her voice was like ice. "I had a brother once. His name was Bert, and he died at Glorieta. There is no other!"

Tom McCasland flexed his hands and looked down at his feet. "I guess I knew how it would be. But I had to come back anyway. I had to try and make you understand how it was . . . why I did it."

She said, "I guess I know why. You've turned Yankee. You've betrayed your family, your friends. . . ."

Tom pointed out, "I could have called them back last night, but I didn't."

Frio put in, "It was too late by then to undo the damage. Blas was already dead."

Tom's gaze went to the slight figure of María Talamantes, and he winced as if in pain. María stared at him with a level, burning gaze. If she had had a rifle in her hands, she probably would have shot him.

"Frio, I had to do it. The Confederacy is losin', there's no doubt about that. The question is, how long will it hold on? This border trade helps keep the war goin'. With you gone, the trade would be badly crippled. They made me see that it was your life against the thousands who might be saved if the war was cut a little shorter. It was a bitter choice, but I had to do it." Tom clenched his fists and said, "Now I've told you why I came. If you want to use that rifle, just go ahead."

Frio's hand tightened, but the rifle didn't fire. He asked, "How come you changed your mind last night? Why didn't you call the troops back?"

Tom shook his head. "I can't rightly say. Lost my nerve, I guess. All of a sudden those thousands of men didn't seem real to me. But *you* were real, Frio. You were my friend."

Frio's voice was harsh. "Friend? All these years Blas Talamantes was the best friend I had, and I didn't have sense enough to see it till he died to save me." He raised the muzzle of the rifle. "Now get back on that horse, Tom. If Amelia wasn't here — if she wasn't your sister — I'd kill you where you stand. As it is, I'll let you go." His eyes narrowed. "But one day we'll meet and she won't be there. When that day comes, Tom, I'm goin' to kill you!"

The gray look of defeat was in Tom's face. He swung onto the horse. To María he said, "I'm sorry. I wish it had been me instead of Blas."

He glanced once more in despair at Frio and Amelia. Then he turned the horse around and rode away.

13

With a raw north wind lashing against the endgates, the groaning wagons toiled through deep sand, mules straining against the harness. On the wagons, teamsters with serapes pulled up around their ears cracked whips and shouted at the mules to pull harder.

Down from the point of the wagon train came the rider, tall and gaunt, black whiskers grayed by trail dust, eyes steeled against the constant company of raw hurt. He rode with his left arm hanging stiff at his side, his heavy coat bulky with the thickness of a bandage wrapped around his shoulder. He paused at every wagon, his face dark as a storm cloud.

"Keep 'em movin'! Don't let 'em hold back on you! We got to make the well before dark!"

He rode hunched, for every step the horse took drove a thin shaft of pain through Frio

Wheeler's shoulder. But he never held back. He had worn out two horses already today, moving up and down this line like some grim, avenging demon, roaring orders, driving, threatening. His face had thinned. Dark hollows had dug in under his eyes. And the eyes themselves had something burning in them that made a man instinctively step aside. No one had seen him smile in weeks now. He had always been a firm man when it came to the wagons, but now he had gone beyond firmness. Not a man on the train was immune from the sharp lash of his angry voice.

He had been like this ever since he had caught up to his wagons on their way down from San Antonio, Happy Jack Fleet in charge. Frio had been a changed man. A couple of the more superstitious among his Mexican teamsters had speculated aloud if perhaps Satan himself had cast a spell upon *el patrón*. Perhaps the real Frio had died, and *El Diablo* had placed some malevolent spirit in his body to walk among men and do evil.

The Devil himself could not have driven the men much harder than Frio was doing. He had taken his last shipment of cotton by way of Rio Grande City and down to Matamoros in a day and a half less than any other freighter on the road. He had made the return trip with a cargo of English rifles, bar lead, powder, and mercury in two days less than anyone else. Now, this trip, it looked as if he was determined to shave time even from his own record.

"Patrón," one of the teamsters argued, "this team, she is get very tired."

"They'll pull if you crack that whip!"

Frio finally reached the rear wagon, his throat raw from dust and shouting. Happy Jack rode there, his solemn, appraising eyes mirroring his quiet disapproval.

Frio ignored the cowboy's unspoken but obvious opinion. "Damn it, Happy, can't you keep these rear wagons pushed up? Way this train is all strung out, we'll be the middle of next summer gettin' to Matamoros."

Happy met Frio's hard gaze without giving any ground. "Way we're goin' we won't get there at all. You're fixin' to have a bunch of dead mules on your hands. Maybe some dead *mulateros* too."

"The faster we move, the more trips we can make. We're doin' it for the Confederacy."

Happy's mouth turned down. "A mule, he don't know nothin' about war. He only knows when he's wore out. You can't talk much patriotism to a mule."

"They'll get their rest."

"When? That's what you said the last trip, but they didn't get any."

Frio snapped. "If you don't like the way I run these wagons, why don't you just leave?"

Happy's eyes reflected a quick anger, which he just as quickly shoved aside. "Because I know it's that shoulder that makes you so damn mean, and I keep rememberin' how you come to get that bullet in you. You thought I was in trouble, and you went to get me out."

Frio wished he hadn't spoken so sharply. If it weren't for this shoulder. . . . "I'd have done it for any man on the train."

"The point is, you did it for *me.* So I reckon I'll stay on till you kill me. But you're apt to kill yourself first, the pace you're keepin'." He frowned. "You ought to've listened to that doctor in San Antonio. He said you needed to be on your back instead of in the saddle. That shoulder still hurts you somethin' fierce, don't it?"

Frio didn't look him in the eye. "I hadn't noticed."

"You're a liar. You was more dead than alive when you caught up to us and took over the train. You ain't much better even yet. You're so bad poisoned that if a rattlesnake was to bite you, he'd die."

Frio lifted his right hand and gripped his left shoulder, his face twisting. "I know I been ridin' all of you pretty hard. Had a lot on my mind."

"You can't win the war all by yourself."

Frio lowered his hand, the fist knotted. "But I want them to know I'm still alive. I want them to know that they not only didn't stop me, they made me work harder than I ever worked before. I want them to stand there by the river and count those cotton bales and curse the day they sent that patrol out to kill me."

"That's how you're takin' your revenge, puttin' more bales across the river?"

Frio's clenched teeth gleamed white against the black of his whiskers as he stared south. "For now, Happy. For now."

Riding at the head of the line, Frio kept his sharp gaze sweeping along the fringe of brush, watching for anything that didn't belong — any movement, any patch of color. He didn't believe for a moment that the Yankees had given up on killing him. Way up front this way, he would make a prime target for any sharpshooter lurking out yonder. From the bushwhacker's viewpoint, though, it would be a risky proposition. Even though he could bring Frio down with an easy shot, the train's outriders and Happy Jack would go into immediate pursuit. Anyone who fired on Frio would be committing suicide.

Frio figured it would take a deep loyalty to the Union, a deep hatred for him personally, or a big offer of money to persuade a man to take that kind of assignment.

Happy Jack's quiet protest had forced Frio to recognize something he hadn't wanted to see. The mules *were* wearing out, and the teamsters weren't much better off. He *had* been driving them too hard. He knew his anger and hatred had given him a desperate strength and a dogged determination he couldn't expect the other men to share.

It was almost dark when he sighted the well he had been aiming for. He saw three men standing beside it, holding horses. His right hand tightened on the saddle-gun that lay across his lap, but he kept riding. From a distance he could tell that all three were Mexicans. Close in, he recognized one as a militiaman he had seen in Rio Grande City. The others would be too. Their old clothes had worn ragged, and the men looked hungry. The Confederacy had been woefully slow in paying its militia, especially down here on the river, so far from the seat of government.

With typical Mexican exaggerated deference toward an Anglo, the ranking one of the three stepped forward, sombrero in hand. "Señor Wheeler, we have wait for you. I am Pablo Lujan. These are Aparicio Jiminez and Lupe Martín."

Frio brought himself stiffly down from the saddle, his face contorted until the shock of movement was past. He extended his hand. "I know you, Pablo. You're with Colonel Benavides, aren't you?"

"*Sí,* we make a little patrol, these vaqueros and me. Long time ago we hunt stray cattle. Now we hunt stray *yanquis.* You see any?"

Frio shook his head. "It's been as peaceful as the inside of the Matamoros church, all the way down from San Antonio. You got trouble on this end?"

Pablo Lujan, nodding gravely, swept one hand in the direction of the brush. "There is sign. The *yanquis,* they have soldiers somewhere in the *bosque.* Some soldiers that are soldiers and some that are *not* soldiers."

"Irregulars?"

"*Sí,* that is the word. They put a blue uniform on some of the *renegados* and call them soldiers. But they are still only *renegados.* They know how to find water, which the *yanqui* does not. They know where to look for the wagon trains, which the *yanqui* does not."

Frio frowned, "It's nothin' new for the Yankees to hire outlaws and call them legal. They've done it right along."

Lujan shrugged. "In their place, señor, would we not do the same? Even in Colonel Benavides's company there are some among us who could never be priests."

Frio's mouth went aslant as he caught the humor in the Mexican's eyes. Frio didn't laugh, but he felt better for this encounter at the waterhole. He had always admired the simple, unquestioning logic of the Mexicans. They were a straightforward people in many ways, philosophically accepting life's many contradictions. He liked their logic even when he couldn't accept it for himself.

"What other news do you hear on the border?" Frio asked.

"We hear the Rip Ford is come pretty soon from San Antonio with many men to drive the *yanquis* back into the sea. Do you think this is true?"

Frio nodded. "I haven't seen him. I've only heard the rumors. But I expect it's true."

"We hear he has ten thousand men."

Frio shook his head. "*One* thousand would be more like it. Texas couldn't even feed ten thousand." It was always a mystery to him how rumors could magnify so much in war. They grew faster than a bunch of cottontail rabbits. Just such wild rumors as this had scared the Confederate General Bee into leaving Brownsville so precipitously.

But maybe this time rumor could play against the Yankees. If they had heard the same ten-thousand-man report as these Mexican militiamen, they were probably getting nervous now in Fort Brown. And Rip Ford was a shrewd soldier. Maybe he had fostered the rumor himself.

Frio said to Lujan, "Keep tellin' everybody it's ten thousand. Old Rip may have the battle won before it starts."

He looked back at his wagons, which were circling for a night's camp near the well. "Pablo, we'd be tickled if you boys would stay and eat with us tonight."

Lujan smiled. "What for do you think we wait here, Señor Wheeler? The militiaman must live off the land, and in this dry time the land is very poor. Sometimes, when God blesses us, we can eat with the wagons."

It was well after dark when the mules had been watered and fed and the teamsters could settle down for supper. Frio had no appetite and took little food into his plate. He picked around on it, not eating half. Mostly he drank coffee, black and steaming.

Happy Jack's appetite had suffered none. He finished a second helping of beef and beans and set his tin plate down on the bare ground beside him. He watched Frio sipping strong black coffee. "Frio," he said, "you're not goin' to get any weller till you start eatin' again. You don't eat nothin', just drink coffee and smoke cigarettes. You don't get half a night's sleep, either. You just pace around camp in the dark like a bobcat in a box."

"Shoulder like this, a man can't sleep much. As for food, who can eat much at such a time?"

Happy said, "I can." He pointed his chin toward the three Mexican militiamen, who were scraping up all the leavings, letting nothing go to waste. "Don't seem like dark times has hurt their appetite much, either. Them poor boys was hungry."

Frio grimaced, watching the three. "It's a long way to Austin, and a longer way yet to Richmond. Easy for the government to forget a handful of men down here on the border. But if it wasn't for Benavides and his militia, the Yankees would have the Rio Grande plumb to Laredo and Eagle Pass. There wouldn't be any border trade."

Happy nodded. "They're poor devils with their bellies half empty and the pants hangin' off of their seats. But we owe them a lot."

They sat awhile in silence. Frio stared into the dwindling fire, his mind wandering aimlessly down a dozen different trails. Happy brooded, chewing his lip. Frio began to notice, for it wasn't like Happy to worry much.

"You got somethin' on your mind, Happy?"

Happy shrugged. "Been worryin'. Guess I caught that from you, like some contagious sickness. Probably just foolishness anyway." His eyes met Frio's a minute. "Did you notice anything unusual today?"

"How do you mean?"

"I don't know. Didn't really see nothin', just kind of felt it. Had the feelin' somebody was out in that brush watchin' us. Trailin' along."

"How come you didn't tell me?"

"Because like I said, I didn't see nothin'. Just a feelin', a foolish notion, maybe. Way you been lately, you'd make anybody a little jumpy." Happy waited for some reply and didn't get it. "You haven't said anything, Frio. You think I'm just lettin' my imagination run wild?"

Frio shook his head and came as near smiling as he had in weeks. "No, Happy. I just think you're finally gettin' some idea of what a man has to suffer through when he's an owner."

It was a chilly night, the stars icy crystals sparkling against a black sky. Frio huddled by the fire, gazing into the coals, remembering. It seemed he was doing a lot of that lately during the long nights when he was unable to sleep, and when he was too tired or in too much pain to stalk around camp worrying the guards. He thought back on how he had left Amelia McCasland at the ranch.

He hadn't wanted to do it. When Natividad de la Cruz had returned with a wagonload of contraband supplies and a couple of men Hugh Plunkett had sent, Frio had tried to talk Amelia into taking María and Chico back to either Brownsville or Matamoros.

"There's nothin' left out here for you now," he had said, pointing to the charred ruins. "Not even a roof over your heads."

"We've got help," Amelia had answered. "We can put up a brush *jacal*. It'll be enough to keep us warm and dry."

"You've got no guarantee the Yankees won't come back and try again. Anything we build, they'll burn down."

"Then we'll build another, and another. You said you were through running, Frio. So am I. I've made up my mind: Right here is where I'm going to stay."

Frio had known enough stubborn people to recognize the signs. He knew there was no point in arguing with her. So he had the three Mexicans put up a pair of rude brush huts, one for the two women and the boy, the other for Natividad. De la Cruz was to stay and do what he could to keep the ranch together. That wouldn't be much, Frio had feared, for you didn't find many men like Blas Talamantes. Still, Natividad would try, and he would be some protection for the women. Maybe when this war was over there would still be enough of the cattle left so that Frio could start fresh and rebuild.

As soon as he could stay on a horse, Frio had told Amelia he was going to rejoin the wagon train. She had nodded in resignation and made no protest, for she knew something of stubborn people too.

She said, "You told me that the next time you went to Matamoros you would take me along. You said you wanted to marry me."

Frio had not tried to look into her eyes. "I

did, and I meant it. But things have changed now, Amelia. When Tom led the Yankees out here and shot Blas, that altered everything. One day I'll have to kill him. You might not want to be married to me then."

Amelia had said tightly, "Do you really have that much hate in you, Frio?"

Frio had reached up to touch his bad shoulder and said, "I reckon I do."

"Go then," Amelia told him. "Do whatever you have to. When it's over, I'll still be here."

The fire had burned low. One of the teamsters brought an armload of dead brush and dropped it near the glowing coals. "*Con permiso, patrón,* I will build up the fire."

Frio pushed himself to his feet and backed away a step. "Go ahead."

The Mexican began to lay wood on the smoldering fire. Flames started to build, licking around the dry mesquite and catclaw limbs. The dancing light brightened, framing Frio and the teamster against the darkness.

Frio saw a flash from out in the brush and at almost the same instant felt an angry tug at the sleeve of his coat. Unprepared, he staggered backward in surprise. His foot caught on the little pile of wood, and he fell just as the rifle crashed again. Later he knew that this fall had saved his life, for the bullet thumped into the sideboard of a wagon behind him. The fall jarred the wounded shoulder, and a paralyzing agony gripped him.

But if Frio was caught unprepared, Happy Jack and the Benavides militiamen were not. Almost as soon as Frio went down, he heard four more guns open up, aimed at the last flash from the darkness. The ambusher fired a third time, and the camp rifles roared again.

Out in the brush a man screamed. Still lying on his side, the shoulder throbbing, Frio heard a crackling of dry limbs in the darkness. Guns in hand, Happy and the three militiamen sprinted out toward the bushwhacker, half a dozen teamsters close behind them. Frio heard one of the militiamen cry out sharply in Spanish, "Do not touch that gun!"

The reply was a weak cry for mercy. Presently the militiamen came back into the firelight, carrying a wounded man. Frio had regained his feet, although he was shaking a little from surprise and pain. They laid the wounded man down by the fire. Happy returned, still looking off into the darkness. "Far as I can tell, he was by himself."

The ambusher was Mexican, and he was

dying. Frio could not remember ever having seen the hombre before. In Spanish he asked, "What did you do this for? Did the *yanquis* pay you?"

The Mexican's teeth grated in agony. He shook his head. "Not the *yanquis* . . . Florencio Chapa. He said he would pay . . ." The man cried out in pain. Shock covered his face with cold sweat. He would be dead in a minute. "Chapa said he would give me . . . much silver . . . to kill the man Wheeler . . . for the terrible thing he has done to Chapa."

"For what I did to *him*?" Frio said sharply.

"You have not seen him," came the weak reply. "Few have seen him since . . ." The man groaned as the pain grew more intense. "It is a terrible sight . . . a terrible sight. . . ." The voice trailed, and he was gone.

Happy Jack stood solemnly staring down on the ambusher he had helped to kill. At last he looked up at Frio. "Appears you've got more enemies than the law allows. I'm still glad I'm not an owner!"

14

Spring. Drought still clung stubbornly to the land. The brush leafed out green, for this was desert growth that had survived similar droughts periodically for thousands of years and had met Nature's strict law of selectivity. The plants that couldn't survive had died out in times so remote as to be beyond the memory of man.

Except for those scattered spots that had been fortunate in receiving the small spotted showers so characteristic of Texas droughts, there was no grass. It would appear to have died out. But Frio knew from past experience that it was merely dormant, waiting for rain to bring it springing fresh and green from bare ground.

The drought worked severe hardship on Frio and the other freighters who moved their wagons ever so slowly along the twisting trails from San Antonio to the Rio Grande and then down to Matamoros. They still had to carry feed for the mules, and this took up space that otherwise could have been devoted to cargo. In that respect the Mexican outfits with their ox teams and high-wheeled *carretas* had an advantage. They would make the oxen live largely off prickly pear, the thorns burned away. But the mule teams were still the fastest. Frio figured what he lost in carrying capacity he made up for in time.

There was a consolation. If the drought was hard on these men who rode the long trails for the Confederacy, it was far harder on the bluecoats who ventured out on horseback from the rebuilt gates of Fort Brown. Even with the Texas Unionists they had enlisted, the federals had not overcome the disadvantage of being strangers to the land. After all these months, they were still tied largely to the river. They could not stray farther from it than the water supplies they carried would allow. Moreover, the near-dry Rio Grande prevented them from making effective tactical use of the steamers. Had the river been flowing full, the big boats, bristling with Yankee guns, might have penetrated upriver past Reynosa and Rio Grande City to Mier, that bloody-historied town with a name still black as sin in the remembering eyes of Texas.

Frio rode straight in the saddle again. The pain was gone, and only a trace of stiffness remained in his left shoulder. He could use the arm for almost anything except heavy lifting. He had plenty of men to do that for him. Though still spare from constant riding, he no longer had that gaunt look that he had carried so long. He seldom smiled, but he was no longer a terror to the men who rode alongside him. They could talk with him man to man, and he would stop to listen. He knew when the teams were tired and needed rest. He still made good time on the trail, but he didn't kill men and mules to do it.

Leaving San Antonio on this trip, Frio had heard news that did more for his spirit than any amount of medicine: At last Rip Ford was about to head south. This forceful Confederate officer would have a good command with him — tough soldiers, expert horsemen. No one knew exactly when Ford was going to start or what route he would take. That was being kept secret. That he was going to move, though, was no secret. Ford wanted the federals to know it. He wanted the new General Herron in Fort Brown to sit and brood over it, as Confederate officers had brooded about the Union's coming.

Ford's campaign would be waged with nerves as much as with guns.

Here on the wheel-rutted trails of the *algodones,* stray units of bold federal soldiers had been fighting their own war of nerves. With them rode attached irregulars — mostly *renegados* — to strike sporadically at the wagon trains. The raids were scattered and completely unpredictable. Usually the riders set fire to as many wagons as they could, then faded back into the chaparral. This they had learned from their enemy Benavides. If they met determined opposition, they most often melted away and saved their strength to use against some weaker train.

Two abortive attempts had been made against Frio's wagons. Both times the Yankees had drawn back quickly, recognizing that Frio's train was too big for them, his men too ready to fight. Frio had drilled his men like soldiers in the art of defense.

He would have admitted that these federals showed good sense. They knew when to strike and when to run.

Today something was wrong. He had smelled it from the beginning, and a vague uneasiness had plagued him all day. This morning he had met a pair of Texas-

Mexican militiamen on the trail. They had told him Benavides had gone upriver to head off a detail of bluecoats who somehow had penetrated beyond Rio Grande City and were a threat to the western trails. Later in the day Frio had spied a horseman sitting far off in the distance, watching the train across a clearing in the brush. He had sent one of his outriders to investigate, but the man had faded away before the outrider came close to him.

A Union spy, Frio had been sure. Somewhere out here there must be a Union striking force, or there would have been no need for a spy. He had deployed the outriders and had ordered Happy Jack to fall well behind and watch for any sign of attack from the rear. This way the train probably could be warned in time to circle up for a fight.

At the midday rest, Happy Jack had ridden in unhappily, looking back over his shoulder. "Frio, I seen a man a while ago. He was just a-sittin' there on his horse, watchin' me from a couple or three hundred yards. I turned to ride in his direction and he just sort of melted. He was there one minute, then gone the next, hidden in all that brush."

Frio had handed the young man a cup of

coffee and watched him take it as eagerly as if it had been whisky. "Did he have a uniform on?"

Happy Jack shook his head. "No, his clothes was Mexican, and so was the riggin'. Kind of a fancy outfit, seemed like at the distance." He looked up, his eyes solemn. "Frio, I never did get close enough to be sure, but just by the way he sat there, the way he looked, I'd swear and be damned that it was Florencio Chapa!"

A chill passed through Frio. He touched the nearly healed shoulder with his hand. "Chapa wouldn't be out here by his lonesome."

Happy Jack frowned and flipped the dregs out of the cup. "No sir, he wouldn't. I'll bet you a pretty that he's got him some *bandidos* waitin' out yonder. Or he's spyin' for a bunch of Yankees and hopin' to see them kill you too dead to skin."

The chill came again. Something strange had developed about Chapa. From talk Frio had heard last time he was in Matamoros, nobody ever saw the *bandido* anymore. Oh, he seemed to be around, all right; he left his tracks. But he was keeping himself out of sight. What business he had in town, he sent someone else to do, sometimes the gringo

Campsey, sometimes his own Mexican lieutenants.

There was trembling talk of a masked Chapa, riding through the dark streets of Matamoros at night, evil as a black wolf and hiding his face from the world. Some of the Mexican people were sure Chapa had been revealed as an incarnation of the devil, that his presence had become a curse upon the land where he walked, that if he took off his boots his feet would leave a cloven track and nothing would ever grow there again.

Frio had never counted himself a superstitious man, but when a man lived among people who were prone to superstition, some of it was bound to rub off on him. Sometimes he could almost feel the presence of Chapa. It was an eerie sensation, a malevolent presence that made the hair stiffen on the back of his neck.

"Well," he said to Happy, "if it *was* Chapa, I expect we'll hear from him soon enough. We're coverin' mostly open country this afternoon. I'll string the wagons out two abreast and keep them closed up."

Happy Jack quietly ate his dinner, his eyes on Frio most of the time. Finished, he put away his plate and said with a gravity that was rare in him: "Frio, you're an owner, and it ain't my place to be tellin' you what

250

to do. But I'd give you a little advice: Let me ride out front and you stay up close to these wagons. If it is Chapa, and he gets you cut off from the bunch, he'll take you like a hawk takes a pullet. Won't be enough left of you to even hold a funeral."

Frio placed his hand on Happy Jack's shoulder. "Thanks, Happy. But I never ask anybody to do anything for me that I wouldn't do myself. I'll take the point same as I always do." Happy's eyes showed the young man's worry. Frio added: "I promise you this, I'll see everything that moves. I won't miss even a jackrabbit."

Frio took the point when the wagons strung out again. Gradually the brush thinned and the country opened up. Seeing less chance of being cut off unawares, he began gradually easing farther and farther out in front, the saddlegun across his lap, ready to use.

Moving along at the wagons' pace, he let himself think of Amelia McCasland, riding the ranges herself now like any cowboy, supervising Natividad de la Cruz and a couple of other vaqueros Frio had managed to find across the river. María Talamantes, her time no longer far away, was doing most of the woman work around the place. Amelia was busy a-horseback, seeing that

251

Frio's brand was burned on every un-claimed, unmarked animal she came across. There were a lot of them, for the hard winter had caused untold thousands of cattle to drift southward across the Wild Horse Desert from drought-stricken ranges above. Many had died of starvation, but a great number had somehow survived, gaunt and shaggy specimens of brute endurance that had survived by eating prickly pear — thorns and all. They were scattered from the Nueces to the Rio Grande, waiting to be claimed by whoever had the fastest horses and the longest ropes.

They hadn't married yet, she and Frio. There hadn't been time. But whenever Amelia spoke, it was always we or us, and Frio liked the sound of it. "We're going to come out of this thing standing on both feet, Frio," she had told him the last time he had seen her. "Nobody but God will ever know who all those cattle belong to, and He will give them to the one who claims them. They're going to be ours, as many of them as the vaqueros and I can brand."

A couple of times Yankee patrols had stopped at the ranch, hoping to catch Frio there. On both occasions they had started to burn the new brush *jacales,* but Amelia's stubborn defiance had stopped them cold.

Frio remembered wondering, a long time ago, if she was strong enough to be a rancher's wife in this backward country. The thought was ridiculous to him now. Amelia McCasland had a will of iron.

Frio saw the one man first. Stopping his horse, he reached into his saddlebag for the spyglass he always carried. It wasn't enough to bring the man up sharply. Frio couldn't recognize him. But that chill played up and down his back. Instinct told him this was Chapa. Lowering the spyglass and looking around, he saw dust farther to the right. He focused the glass on that and made out riders, coming up from the south. Sunlight touched something metal. A saber, likely.

Frio reined the horse around and put the spurs to him. Running hard, he drew his pistol and fired it twice, into the air. He waved his hat in a circular motion over his head. The teamsters in the lead saw him. They were already circling the wagons when he got there.

The Mexicans cracked their whips, shouted excitedly at the mules as they moved into their allotted places and drew the wagons up close for a defense. Jumping down, they freed the mules from the wagons but left them in harness. A narrow space remained between the last two wagons so the outriders could come through. Shouting, moving in a hurry and stirring lots of dust, the teamsters tumbled cotton bales down from the wagons and dragged them into line to serve as a breastworks.

Happy Jack was the last man into the circle, bringing up the rear. He jumped to the ground, saddle-gun in hand, and turned his horse loose in the middle. Three men dragged a cotton bale into place to plug the gap. Happy had seen the dust of the approaching riders.

"Yankees?" he demanded of Frio.

"I didn't ask to see their papers."

Happy glanced over the preparations that had been made in a matter of minutes. He whistled his approval. "Say, Frio, if this here war lasts another three years, them *mulateros* are goin' to learn."

"They've learned a right smart already. It'll be a tough outfit that whips this bunch now."

Happy's grin faded as he watched the dust. "Them yonder may be just the outfit that can do it. Jehosophat, how many are they?"

Frio's mouth went dry. The dust was still too thick to allow him any sort of count. A hundred cavrymen, at least. Maybe twice that many.

Seeing they had no surprise, the federals moved up boldly. They could tell the wagon train was prepared for a fight. Frio watched the commanding officer raise his hand and stop the men two hundred yards away. For a minute or two there was movement back and forth in front of the formation, a huddle of half a dozen riders. Presently one man moved out alone, approaching the wagon train. He held up a rifle with a large white handkerchief tied to the barrel.

Frio saw a couple of his teamsters leveling on the man. "It's a flag of truce," he called. "Don't anybody shoot."

He stepped between two wagons and watched the horseman approach in a leisurely walk. Frio squinted, wishing he had the glass with him so he could make the man out. He could tell the rider was a civilian, not in uniform.

Suddenly Frio spat. "I might've known it. That's Tom McCasland!"

Frio waited until Tom neared the circle of wagons, then he moved out into view, the saddlegun in his hand. Tom stopped his horse ten feet away and looked down at him, a light breeze picking up the white flag and waving it. The breeze carried a strong smell of dust.

"Howdy," he said evenly.

"Tom." Frio's voice was hostile.

"Been a while since I saw you last, Frio. How's the shoulder?"

"Good enough that I don't have to crawl through the brush anymore when the Yankees come."

"Mind if I get down?"

"Do what suits you."

Tom swung to the ground and stretched his legs. "Sure tired," he said. "Been a long ride."

"You could've saved it. You're not goin' to get anything here."

Tom allowed himself a long, silent look at the circle of wagons, and at the teamsters who knelt purposefully behind the downed cotton bales, each one with a rifle in his hands. Tom said, "I'll admit I didn't expect to find you'd been drillin' these men in military defense. I thought you were only freightin'."

"Everybody has got to be a soldier of sorts these days."

Tom's eyes were solemn as they cut back to Frio. "Of sorts, but that's all. Those men out yonder" — he pointed his thumb toward the Yankee troopers — "they're *real* soldiers, trained for this kind of thing. Frio, we came to stop your wagon train."

Frio's mouth was grim, but he made no answer.

Tom said, "We *will* stop you, Frio. How we do it is up to you." He swept his hand toward the soldiers. "We've got upward of two hundred and fifty men yonder. All well armed and well mounted. How many men have you got in here? Fifty at the outside. We've got you outnumbered by five to one." He cast a critical eye at the teamsters he could see peering over the bales. "And I'd say we've got you outgunned too, man for man. My experience is that most Mexican teamsters can't shoot."

Frio said tightly, "You can find out mighty quick."

"Give up, Frio. It'd be better all around. In any case, we're not leavin' here till we've taken these wagons. Give up now and there won't be any blood spilled. Not by your men and not by those out yonder."

Frio frowned, one eye almost shut. "Sayin' I agreed, what would you do to my men?"

"Nobody would get hurt. Those from Mexico would be sent home on parole. The others — you included — would simply be detained until the war is over. Way it's goin', that shouldn't be too long anymore."

"And the wagons?"

"We'll have to burn them." He watched

Frio's face. "I'm sorry about this, Frio. I know you've got a lot of money tied up in this outfit. That's somethin' we can't help. You can see for yourself, we have to burn them."

Anger began to churn in Frio. "What does Florencio Chapa get out of it?"

Tom's eyes widened in surprise. "Chapa? He's got nothin' to do with it."

Derisively Frio said, "Don't tell me you've gotten too much religion to ride with Chapa anymore."

"The Union washed its hands of Chapa when he tried to torture you. The government doesn't countenance that sort of thing, even in war."

Frio pointed to a figure sitting on a horse, far off at the edge of the chaparral. "Then what's he doin' there?"

Tom turned quickly, mouth open in surprise. "That can't be Chapa!"

"It is. We been seein' him off and on all day."

In disbelief Tom said, "But we haven't seen him since . . ." He broke off, understanding suddenly coming into his face. "We hired some Mexican scouts who offered to spy out your wagon train for us. We had no idea Chapa was behind them."

Frio snorted. "You expect me to believe

that, Tom, after all you've done? Promisin' nothin' would happen to us if we give ourselves up to you. . . . I'll bet you got a deal with Chapa to turn us over to him for his help. *Me,* anyway."

"No, Frio, I swear we don't!"

"Then what's he doin', hangin' around out there like a buzzard?"

Tom shook his head, completely at a loss. "He hates you, Frio. Maybe he just wants to watch us destroy you."

Frio stared hard at Tom McCasland, his eyes narrowed. He found himself wanting to believe Tom. It didn't seem likely that Tom was renegade enough to turn him over to Chapa. Not on purpose. But maybe Chapa had some idea for getting his hands on Frio anyway. . . .

Frio saw a movement off to the north, out of Tom's range of view. A rider was coming fast, pushing his horse as hard as it could go.

Tom said, "The major gave me ten minutes to talk with you, Frio. Time's playin' out."

Frio's eyes were still on the horseman. For some reason he felt a fresh surge of hope. He would play for time — all the time he could delay. "You won't get away with this, Tom. For all you know, Santos Benavides may be comin' right now. Those Yankees of yours are no match for him."

Tom shook his head. "No luck, Frio. We sent a small force to lure Benavides west. He won't be around to help you."

Still unseen by Tom, and unheard because of the rattle of harness and chain and the movement of the mules inside the circle, the horseman rode straight toward the Union column. Frio watched the man slide to a stop in front of the federals. Pandemonium struck among the blue-clad troopers. The half dozen men at the head of the column milled indecisively, looking north.

Frio glanced north and saw a column of dust rising, uptrail.

The federals began turning their horses around. In a moment they were in retreat, moving south. One Union officer remained momentarily, waving his hat at Tom and shouting. But Tom's back was turned to him, and the officer's voice, along with the sound of retreat, was lost in the noise closer at hand.

Frio watched without expression until he saw the officer give up and pull away, afraid to come any nearer for the time he would lose.

Tom said, "Time's up, Frio. What's it goin' to be?"

A harsh smile broke across Frio's face. "Maybe you better take a look behind you. Then you tell *me*."

Tom turned. The color left him momentarily as he saw that he had been abandoned. He turned back and found that Frio had raised the muzzle of the saddle-gun. It was pointed at Tom's chest. Frio said triumphantly, "There's a cloud of dust in the north yonder. Maybe that's what made those good friends of yours ride off and dump you in our lap."

Tom saw the dust. Disbelief was in his eyes. "It can't be Benavides. The spies told us. . . ."

Frio said, "The spies were wrong. Unless . . ." The idea hit him suddenly, and he felt an elation he hadn't known in months. "Rip Ford!" he exclaimed. "Bound to be! Rip Ford and his column, comin' south to retake the border!"

Tom still held the rifle in one hand, the white handkerchief tied to the barrel. The weapon was empty, but it would have done him no good now if it had been loaded. He dropped it. Shrugging, he said with a fatalism he had learned from the Mexicans, "So now we've swapped places, Frio. 'While ago I was givin' you my terms. Now you can give me yours."

Frio nodded grimly. "That time after they shot Blas, I told you I'd kill you one day."

Tom swallowed. "I remember. So now's your chance. Do it and get it over with." He squared his shoulders.

Frio studied him awhile, his hands tight on the rifle. "With you just standin' there helpless? That may be the Yankee way of doin'. It's not mine."

"You want to give me a gun and us two shoot it out?"

"I'd rather do it that way than this."

Tom shook his head. "I raised my hand against you once, Frio. I won't do it again, not this way."

Frio lowered the muzzle a little. "Then I reckon we'll just have to hold you and turn you over to the Confederacy."

Tom nodded soberly. "They'll kill me for you, and your hands will stay clean, is that it? You know they'll hang me."

Frio hadn't had time to consider that. The thought shook him. "Don't you think you've earned it?"

"By your lights, I suppose I have."

"Not by yours?"

"I did my duty as I saw it. It was bitter sometimes, but I did my duty the way you did yours. I don't want to hang, Frio. That's no fit way for a man to die."

Frio just stared at him, uncertain what to do.

Tom glanced toward the approaching dust. "Frio, if you want me dead, then for God's sake be man enough to shoot me! Don't leave me to hang!"

Frio still stood there trying to decide, his mouth dry and bitter. Once he might have squeezed the trigger without a qualm. Now, holding the power of death in his hand, he could not move. What he had taken for hatred against Tom he knew now had been a deep hurt, and a vengeful anger. Here, in the face of this mortal test, anger drained away. His hands trembled. His stomach suddenly went cold with the realization of what he might have done.

He stared into the anxious face of Tom McCasland and tried to find there the look of an enemy. Instead, despite all that had come between them, he saw only the face of an old friend.

He lowered the saddlegun. "You came under a flag of truce, Tom. I'll honor that. Now get on your horse and clear out of here, fast."

Tom's eyes were wide, as if he was afraid he hadn't heard right.

Frio said simply, "Damn it, man, I said get on that horse and ride!" He glanced toward the dust. He could almost make out the individual riders. "Don't go south after them Yankees. Ford's men'll catch you. Go west into the brush. Drop south later and swim the Rio."

Tom swung into the saddle. His horse sensed the excitement and began to prance, wanting to run. Tom held the reins up tight. "What are you doin' this for, Frio?"

Frio shouted, "How the hell do I know?" He reached down and picked up Tom's empty rifle with the handkerchief tied to it. He pitched it to him. *"Ándele!"*

Tom skirted the circled wagons and moved into a lope, heading toward the nearest brush. That was to the west. Frio stood slump shouldered and watched him disappear.

Happy Jack Fleet moved up beside Frio to watch the dust-veiled horsemen coming out of the north. "Frio, you done the right thing."

Frio shook his head. "I don't know, Happy. I swear, I just don't know."

The vanguard of the Texas column rode up in a lope, dust an impenetrable fog behind it. Only the two officers at the head of the group wore what could be recognized as a Confederate uniform. The rest of the men

264

wore civilian clothes or a mixture of civilian with uniform — whatever they had been able to scratch up for themselves. This outfit didn't stand on ceremony.

Pulling his horse to a stop, one of the officers took a quick glance at the circled wagons. His face fell on Frio. "You had trouble?"

Frio pointed his chin south, toward the thinning dust left by the retreating Union troops. "We came almighty close to it. Yankees. They went yonder."

The officer said, "We'll catch them, don't you worry!" He shouted an order and spurred his horse. The company fell in behind him, shouting in a blood-thirsty eagerness. This would be their first contact with the enemy, if they could catch up. It would be a real horse race.

The Texas troops galloped away, their dust sweeping across the circled wagons and setting some of the teamsters to coughing. Happy Jack grinned. "If they overtake them Yankees, there'll sure be some whittlin' done."

The second body of riders trailed just a little way behind. Leading them was an officer in a dust-gray uniform, sitting straight and proud in the saddle. He reined in at the wagons, his crow-tracked eyes sweeping the circle, taking in the defense preparations in one quick glance that told him all he really needed to know. Colonel Rip Ford asked, "Whose wagons?"

Frio stepped forward. "Mine, Colonel. Frio Wheeler."

The colonel stared, recognition coming into his eyes. He was a medium-tall man, this Rip Ford, with hair and short beard now mostly gray. He was still a year short of fifty, but the gray made him look older than he actually was, and some people with about as many years had grown accustomed to calling him "old" Rip Ford. Indeed, this man had lived more in those forty-nine years than many people could in ten lifetimes. Doctor, Ranger, legislator, trailblazer, newspaperman, soldier — he had been all of these things and still was. Often ignored by the higher-ups in government and military, made subordinate to men whose talents were far less than his own, Ford nevertheless had become something of a legend in his own lifetime among the people of Southern Texas. Some looked upon him almost as a latter-day Sam Houston. They believed Rip Ford could do anything he put his mind to, and they would remember him long after many of those who outranked him were forgotten.

"Frio Wheeler," Ford said in a quiet voice, beginning to smile. He extended his hand. "With all this dust in my eyes, and those whiskers on your face. . . ."

He came out of the saddle with a slow, stiff motion, for the ride had been long, and he was plainly weary. "Yankees try to take you?"

"They told us to give up our guns and our wagons. I never had a chance to answer them. They saw your dust and hightailed it south."

Still smiling, Ford said, "What was your answer going to be, or do I need to ask?"

The good nature of the officer eased Frio's coiled tension. "I was fixin' to say we wouldn't give up our guns, but they were welcome to what was in them."

Happy Jack had been eyeing the colonel with a youthful awe. He spoke up confidently, "We could've whipped twice as many, Colonel, and never broke a sweat."

Ford slumped wearily upon a wagon tongue and glanced southward. "We'll have to go in a minute. If Captain Adams catches up and engages them, he'll need help." He peered at Frio with strong interest. "I've kept up with you, Frio Wheeler. I wish I had you in my command. But you're doing us more good where you are than you could in a uniform."

"I'd be right proud if I could ride with you, Colonel. I'd sure like to be there when you go back into Brownsville."

"Maybe that won't be long, Frio. I'm going to nibble at the fringes first, giving Herron trouble at his outposts, cutting off his patrols. I'll scatter my forces so he'll never know whether I have six hundred men or six thousand. I'll grind him down until he'll be glad to shake the dust of Brownsville from his feet."

Frio said again, "I'd like to be there when that happens."

The colonel stood up, bone tired and hating to leave. "Maybe you can, Frio. Maybe you can." He remounted his horse. "Good luck. And keep the wagons moving."

The teamsters waved their sombreros and cheered while Ford's long column passed by, moving into a lope, setting the choking dust aswirl. A warm elation rose in Frio. These men of Ford's were the hope of Southern Texas. Not a praying man, Frio nonetheless lowered his head and whispered, hoping God would hear.

Out in the edge of the chaparral, grim eyes observed from beneath a broad black sombrero. They had seen the whole thing — the

Union approach and retreat. They had widened with surprised interest as Tom Mc-Casland rode free and disappeared into the west. Now they watched in hatred as Frio Wheeler led his wagons once more out upon the trail.

The man wore a black neckerchief over his face. He had allowed it to slip a little. Before turning back into the mesquite where a couple of his men waited, Florencio Chapa pulled the dusty neckerchief back up to cover all but his eyes. No one must ever see his face again. No one, perhaps, but Frio Wheeler. And that would be the last thing Wheeler ever saw on this earth!

Rip Ford was tightening the noose. Beneath a hot summer sun, his scattered men slowly approached the city of Brownsville from the north and the west. Not once since he had ridden down in April had all his troops ever come together at one time. Not once had Union intelligence been able to get even a fair approximation of Ford's strength. It seemed that everywhere the Union general Herron turned, the Texans were waiting for him. Herron had withdrawn his outposts one by one under Ford's unrelenting pressure, until now he had only Brownsville, and the thirty miles that stretched eastward toward the sea. He had five thousand federal troops at Fort Brown, or deployed eastward along the narrow-gauge railroad he had been building to carry supplies upriver from Brazos Santiago. For all Herron knew, Ford had that many men or more out in the dense *bosques,* awaiting only the order to move in and kill.

Now, so sick with fever that they had to help him into the saddle, Rip Ford stood his horse on the edge of one of the dried old riverbed *resacas.* Overhead, tall palm trees arched in the wind, their cupped fronds appearing almost black against the sky. Before him lay a scattering of Mexican *jacales.* Beyond these, in shimmering summer heat, stood a town waiting for deliverance.

"Brownsville." Ford tested the word fondly on his tongue and turned to Frio Wheeler, who sat on a sorrel horse beside him. "How long since you've seen it from the Texas side, Frio?"

"Been close to nine months now, Colonel."

"Perhaps it won't be long until you can ride down its streets again." Ford's voice was weak. His face was flushed and drawn from the siege of fever. But he had refused to allow anyone else to take over his command. For months now he had been preparing for the recapture of Brownsville. He had no intention of being on his back when the Texas troops moved into that town and raised their flag.

"Where do you suppose your wagons are, Frio?"

"I expect they ought to be at my ranch by now, sir. When we left San Antonio, folks were all excited about you whippin' the Yanks at Rancho Las Rucias. I figured that by the time my wagons got here, we could cross over at old Don Andres's ferry and save the miles we'd have to cover to Rio Grande City. With luck, I thought you might even have taken Brownsville."

"So you rode on ahead of the wagons to see how we fared?"

"Yes, sir. The wagons are in good hands. Happy Jack Fleet, the young fellow you saw with me a while back, he was to take them to the ranch and wait."

Ford smiled thinly, and the smile was quickly gone. The colonel was suffering. "I appreciate your confidence. I only wish I *had* taken Brownsville already."

"You will, Colonel. It's like a ripe apple, ready to fall into your hands. And I want to have a part with you in the takin' of it."

Ford gazed with sadness at what he could see of the town. "It's been a good town to me, Frio. I've had some happy days there."

"Too bad you weren't in charge of Fort Brown when the Yankees first came. Things might've turned out different."

Ford shook his head. "Nobody could have stood off that many federals with the few

272

troops the Confederacy had here. True, there are some things I'd've done differently. But the outcome would've been the same. Besides, *if* is the most futile word in the language. There ought to be a law against the use of it, at least in the past tense."

One of Ford's captains rode over and handed the colonel a long spyglass. "They've spotted us, sir. Yonder come some Union cavalry to give us a closer look."

Ford focused the instrument and held it a minute, scanning the dry landscape for sign of any other movement. He lowered the glass and nodded. "Good. There's a long *resaca* just ahead of them. As they move up out of it, tell the men to commence firing."

The captain argued, "Colonel, that's too long a range. We won't kill many Yankees thataway."

Ford shook his head. "I don't intend to. I never took pleasure in the death of any man, Captain, Yankee or what. If we can immobilize them or push them back without having to kill them, so much the better. There's been way too much killing in this war even as it is."

The colonel painfully started to swing out of the saddle. Frio and a couple of nearby officers were quick to step down and help him. Frio took the colonel's arm and could feel the heat of the fever, even through the sleeve. Ford thanked them when he was on his feet. An enlisted man in a Mexican sombrero stood by to take the reins and hold the horse for him.

Ford said quietly to those around him: "Looking through the glass a few minutes ago, I saw the Union flag waving on its pole down at the fort. Gave me a bad feeling, really, knowing I was about to fire on it again. I always loved that flag." He glanced at Frio. "Did you know that during the time Texas was a republic I was in its Congress? Back in 1844, I was the man who introduced a resolution in the House proposing that Texas accept annexation into the United States." The sadness showed again in his face. "Ironic, isn't it? Now, after twenty years, I find myself fighting to keep Texas out of the United States."

He looked down, and Frio thought he could see tears in the colonel's eyes. Or maybe it was the fever. "There are some good men down there in that fort, beneath that flag. Some of them are friends of mine. It's a sad, sad thing to be forced to go to war against your friends."

He glanced up at Frio, and Frio nodded slowly.

The colonel added, "Any man can kill an enemy, if duty calls on him to do it. But it takes a strong man to be able to kill a friend."

A chill went through Frio.

The captain spoke up. "They've come to the riverbed, Colonel. Shall I give the boys the word to fire?"

Ford nodded regretfully. "Cut 'em loose."

Frio had his hands full just holding onto the sorrel horse when the firing started. The mount had not been around guns like most of the soldiers' horses had. The first volley was so deafening it brought a sharp pressure of pain against Frio's eardrums. Powder smoke began rising gray and thick from a couple of hundred positions along a scattered line. Through the drift of smoke, Frio could see a half dozen Union horses down. The Yankees had spread out suddenly but were still riding, coming head-on.

From this point the Texans spent no more volleys. There was a constant rattle of uneven fire as individual soldiers chose their targets and squeezed their triggers. The range was still long. Many of the bullets picked up dust from the parched ground in front of the federals. Now and again a horse would fall, or a man. The federals swept into another old riverbed. A few seconds later

Frio expected to see them come up on this side, but they didn't. It occurred to him after a moment that they had taken cover in the bottom of the *resaca,* safe from the angry bullets of rebel guns. In a minute or two firing commenced over the rim of the old bed. The Union soldiers had dismounted and were answering fire with fire.

"A long-taw proposition," the captain said. "Neither side can do much like this."

Union bullets snarled harmlessly overhead, or dropped uselessly into the dust. Ford put up with it for a while. His men were firing only now and again as they saw a target. With them, ammunition was still too precious to waste. The federals were spending a lot more of it with no more results.

Presently Ford said, "Captain, let me see that glass again." He brought it to his eye and studied what part of the town was open to view. He nodded in satisfaction as he lowered the telescope. "It's about as I had expected. A Union relief column is on its way. Now is the time to give them a jolt." He pointed westward. "Is B Company deployed over yonder where I wanted them?"

The captain nodded. "Yes, sir."

"Good," replied Ford. "If you-all will

276

kindly help me onto my horse. . . ."

He swayed toward the mount. Frio and the others quickly went to his support. They helped him into the saddle. He looked down at Frio. "How about you, Frio? Want a closer look at Brownsville?"

Frio smiled. "Yep, Colonel, I sure do." He swung onto the sorrel.

To the captain, Ford said, "I'm going to take B Company and flank that *resaca*. I think when the Yanks see us coming they'll fog out of there in a hurry. As they do, you bring this company down. They'll be caught two ways. It's my hunch they'll stampede back toward the fort, and they'll carry that relief column with them."

The captain nodded, pleased. "I expect you'll spoil General Herron's supper, Colonel."

Ford replied, "Those Yankees have spoiled many a one of mine."

Too sick to be riding, but driven by his stern determination, Colonel Rip Ford led the way to where B Company waited in reserve. Frio had to spur to keep up with him. They reached the waiting men, who sat patiently smoking and telling yarns in the shadows of their horses.

The colonel said simply, "Boys, are you ready to go out there amongst them?" He turned his horse and started toward the *re-saca,* trusting the men to follow after him. They did.

The range was still at least three hundred yards when the colonel said, "Into the skirmish line, boys, and let's hear you yell."

The men fanned out in a long, ragged line. At Ford's order, they moved into a gallop. The shrill yell started at the center and rippled up and down the line like a shock wave. It was a savage, exultant thing that made hair stand on the back of Frio's neck. He found himself swept along with it. He yelled too. Saddlegun in his hand, he stayed near the colonel. There was little target, for the federals were down in the safety of the old riverbed. But at Ford's order his men began firing anyway.

Moving up a rise, Frio saw alarm strike the dismounted Yankees with the force of a bombshell. They ran for their horses, swinging into their saddles. The officers were moving as fast as their men. Those who could not catch their horses, or who had lost them, swung up behind other men. The Yankees spurred over the rim of the riverbed. For a moment it looked as if they would retreat eastward. But over in that direction, another group of Ford's horsemen popped up as if by magic. And now the captain came from the center of the line with all his men.

The bluecoats had only one way to flee, and that was south. They ran headlong, maintaining no formation. Theirs was a panicked flight, every man for himself, for only God knew how many of those screeching Texans were pouring out of the brush behind them.

In pursuit, Ford's companies joined on the ends and made a solid line, moving forward at a gallop, sweeping down into the sandy old riverbeds and out again on the far side, dodging their horses around the palm trees. The Texans kept up a desultory fire that was aimed more at frightening than at a kill. It was hard to shoot straight from the back of a running horse anyway. The man who claimed he could would probably lie about other things too.

The fleeing federals overran the relief column without slowing down. For a moment the second group of bluecoats seemed about to come forward and give fight. But they changed their minds, turned their horses about, and went running with the others, running for the cover they could find behind the lumber and stone walls of the town. To Frio it was much like a stampeding herd of cattle, sweeping up another herd in its path.

Ford was falling behind, for in his condition he had a hard time just staying in the saddle. He shouted for a cease-fire and pullback, and somehow some of the officers heard him through the din of hoofs and yelling men and roaring guns. Gradually the Texans pulled their horses to a stop almost within the edge of the town itself. They obeyed the colonel's orders grudgingly, for they had gotten a small, sweet taste of victory, and it was hard now to spit out the apple.

Forming again at the point from which the charge had begun, some of the officers voiced the same disapproval as their men.

Ford, who looked deathly tired now but nonetheless pleased, simply shook his head and lowered himself into the shade of a palm.

"You did fine, boys. Now we just let Herron stew over this thing for a while. Then we'll see what happens."

Night came, and Ford dispatched three men as spies to enter the town. Wearing old Mexican clothes, they could pass unnoticed wherever they wanted to go. Much later the three came back. Frio could read victory in the square thrust of their shoulders, their broad grins as they approached the colonel's small fire.

"Colonel," one of them said cheerily, without a salute, "it's just like you figured. Herron's loadin' up and pullin' out. They say he's retreatin' down the river — givin' up the town for good."

The colonel nodded and stared a long time into the coals. At first Frio thought Ford was simply lost in thought. Then he saw the colonel's lips move ever so slightly, and he caught a fragment of a whispered prayer. At last Ford looked up, his fevered eyes proud as his gaze moved from one to another of the men who stood in the circle of firelight. "Well, boys, we've done it. We've put him on the run with a force not a quarter the size of his, and we've shed precious little blood in doing it."

An officer said with emotion, "Texas will never forget this day, Colonel."

Ford shook his head. "I'm afraid you're wrong; they *will* forget what we've done here today. But their forgetting it won't alter the fact that it was done. History doesn't change just because somebody fails to get credit."

He turned to Frio. "How would you like to be the first man to bring cotton wagons into Brownsville after the Union occupation?"

Frio felt a quick glow. "I'd be tickled, Colonel."

"Well, then you go on to that ranch of yours and fetch them. By the time you get back, I think you'll find Brownsville ready and waiting for you."

16

As a schoolboy, Frio had studied about the glory of ancient Rome, and his imagination had soared grandly as he had pictured the march of the victorious Roman legions along the Appian Way. These things came back to his mind now as he made his own much smaller and probably dustier triumphal entry into Brownsville at the head of a long line of cotton wagons.

It was just three months short of a year since the dark and terrible night Frio had ridden out of burning Brownsville, taking Amelia and Chico with him. On the surface, the town didn't seem to have changed much, except those sections that had been touched by the great fire. Some of the damaged buildings had been reconstructed. Others still lay as they had fallen, their charred shells like blackened skeletons, a scar upon the land.

Townspeople — Anglo and Mexican alike

— stood in the street and cheered as the wagons rolled into view, the dust rising in a heavy fog behind them. Along Elizabeth Street, Frio could see Confederate and Texas flags flying from makeshift flagpoles and draped from second-story windows — flags wisely stored away these many long months of Union occupation.

Frio rode the sorrel horse that was his favorite. Amelia McCasland sat on the first wagon, face aglow as she entered the town that had so long been home. Chico rode on top of the cotton bales, waving with pride at the youngsters who watched him enviously. There was a touch of brag about him in the way he threw out his chest. This was the biggest day in the boy's life.

Rip Ford's Texas troops stood scattered up and down the street, being congratulated by the townsmen because they had made it possible for this wagon train to come into Brownsville. Other trains were bound to follow within days. All up and down the winding trails, riders were telling teamsters that Brownsville was open again, that they could cut south and quit the much longer routes that led to Laredo and Rio Grande City.

Two Mexican boys raced along afoot in front of the wagons, crying excitedly, *"Los algodones!"* The cotton men! Women waved handkerchiefs, and men shouted for joy.

Frio reined over and waited for the first wagon to pull up even with him so that he might ride beside Amelia. He wished they could have brought María along to see this show. But they had decided that the baby, born in April, was still too young to make the trip and breathe the thick dust of the wagon train. So María had remained at the ranch with the infant son she had named Blas. Natividad de la Cruz was there, along with a pair of vaqueros, to watch out for her. A widower himself, Natividad had taken an increasingly protective attitude toward María. Someday, when her grief had faded and the proprieties had been observed, Natividad would present his own case.

Ahead of the wagon train was the site of the McCasland store. Frio watched Amelia closely, worried about her reaction when she would see whatever was left of the place. He needn't have worried. She looked, and a momentary sadness came into her eyes, but there were no tears. Someone had cleaned off the lot. All the charred lumber had been removed. Only the smoke-blackened foundation rocks remained.

Amelia spoke softly, "I guess Tom must have seen to it that the place was cleared.

I'm glad he did."

It was the first time Frio had heard her speak her brother's name in months. Even when he had told her about Tom leading the Union patrol to try capturing the wagon train and about Frio's letting Tom escape into the brush, she had listened without a word of comment.

Frio said, "I expect Tom went back across the river when the Union troops left town."

Amelia nodded soberly. "He couldn't stay here."

They rode on down to the old cottonyard on the riverbank. As in other times, Hugh Plunkett stood there waiting, his face solemn but proud. He stepped to one side and waved the lead wagon on by. "Just take her down to the far end yonder," he yelled. He reached out with his big hand as Frio rode up. Frio leaned down to shake with him. "Just like it used to be, ain't it, Frio? Happy days have come again."

"Happy?" Frio said evenly. "Long as that infernal war is still on, I don't expect there'll be any happy days." He looked out across the big, empty yard. "One thing isn't like it was. No cotton here."

"There'll be aplenty of it, though," Plunkett said. "Your train is just the start. Before long there'll be so much cotton here a man can't hardly count it all." He nodded briskly. "Yes, sir, we'll show them Yankees."

Frio saw a movement at Hugh Plunkett's little frame-shed, where the cotton agent kept his papers. A woman stood there. Plunkett turned to follow Frio's gaze.

Frio squinted. "That's Mrs. Valdez, isn't it?"

Plunkett nodded, his mouth turning down sadly. "She's been waitin' to see you, Frio. She's got somethin' to tell you." Hugh rubbed the back of his neck and looked away a moment. "Before you go talk to her, Frio, there's somethin' you ought to know. I ain't never told you because I promised her I wouldn't. But now I think you ought to know what you owe to her. She's the one came that night and told me the Yankees were goin' out to kill you. Wasn't for her, you'd be dead right now."

Frio and Amelia looked at each other in surprise. Frio reached up to help Amelia down from the wagon before it went all the way to the end of the yard for unloading. Chico clambered down by himself, jumping the large part of the way and springing nimbly to his feet after going down on hands and knees.

Hugh said, "Now you better go talk to Mrs. Valdez."

Luisa Valdez's face was tense, and her hands were clasped together across her breasts. Frio saw the corner of a white handkerchief between two of her fingers. She had been crying. He took off his hat. Amelia went directly to the woman and took her hands.

"Luisa," Amelia said, "you have no idea how much we owe you."

Luisa Valdez shook her head. "You owe me nothing." She dropped her chin. But Frio already had seen the tears in her dark eyes. She said, "This is a great day for you."

Frio replied, "But not for you, it seems. What's the matter, Mrs. Valdez?"

Head still down, she said tightly, "They sent me to tell you about Tom."

Frio frowned. "What about him? Who sent you?"

"Florencio Chapa. Or rather, his men. They have Tom. They say they will kill him unless . . ."

Amelia stiffened. "Unless what? What do they want?"

"They want for Señor Wheeler to go and set him free. Florencio Chapa says you owe him two thousand dollars. He says he will wait at the Gutierrez place, the muleyard at the edge of Matamoros. He has Tom there. He says if you do not bring him the money, he will kill Tom."

Frio clenched his fists. "What makes him think I would do anything to help Tom Mc-Casland?"

"Chapa was in the chaparral the day you let Tom go before Colonel Ford could capture him. Chapa says you are still Tom's friend. He says you will pay. He says you must come today and by yourself."

Amelia's face had gone white. She turned away, hands over her eyes. Watching her, Frio said, "I thought you didn't care anymore about what happened to Tom."

Amelia shook her head. "It's easy to say things in anger. But he's still my brother. Nothing has ever changed that."

Frio put his hands on her shoulders. "And you still love him."

"That doesn't ever stop. I wanted it to, but I couldn't help it. You can't go back on blood." She paused. "I never told you, Frio, because I didn't know how, and I've never let Natividad tell you. But while we were branding cattle for you, we were putting Tom's brand on some too."

Frio blinked in surprise. He looked back into the bleak face of Luisa Valdez. He said, "You saved my life."

Luisa Valdez slowly shook her head. "I will not ask you to save Tom's in return. I think

Chapa cares little about the money. I think he only wants to get you there so he can kill you. Then perhaps he will kill Tom anyway. Chapa likes to see blood. It is like a sickness with him. So I do not ask you to go."

"But you're hopin' I will."

She didn't reply. She didn't have to, for he could see the answer in her face, in the way her hand gripped the tiny crucifix that hung from her neck.

Turning to Amelia, he said, "What do you want me to do?"

She threw her arms around him and buried her face against his chest. "I don't know, Frio. I just don't know."

The boy, Chico, stood nearby, frightened a little because the women were crying and he did not understand what was the matter.

Amelia cried, "Frio, I couldn't bear to lose you."

He stroked her hair. "If I stay here and do nothin', they'll kill Tom. So it comes down to kind of a contest, doesn't it? Which one is the most important, Tom or me?"

"Frio, how could I make a choice like that?"

"You don't have to. I'll go."

Her eyes were wide. "Chapa will try to kill you."

"I don't figure on makin' it easy for him."

"I'm not asking you to go, Frio. Don't go just for me."

Frio shook his head. "It's for all of you, I guess. You, because I love you. Mrs. Valdez, because I owe her my life. Tom because . . . because whatever he did, he thought he was right. Because for a long time he was my friend. And maybe because I keep rememberin' somethin' Rip Ford said to me. He said, 'Any man can kill an enemy, if duty calls on him to do it. But it takes a strong man to be able to kill a friend.' I guess Tom is a stronger man than I am. I had a chance to kill him, and I couldn't make myself do it."

He told Hugh Plunkett, Happy Jack, and the others what he was going to do. As expected, Happy put up an argument.

"You don't owe him nothin', Frio. If you ever did, you settled it that day you let him get away from Rip Ford."

Frio resolutely shook his head. "I'm goin'. I have to. And you men are all stayin' on this side of the river. I'm afraid if you try to interfere, they'll kill Tom."

"Chapa won't give you a chance!" Happy argued.

"He will if he wants that money."

Frio rode across on the ferry. It took him awhile at the British consulate to get the cash together. When he had it, he put it in a set of saddlebags and started upriver on the sorrel, toward the wagonyard. As always, he saw the washerwomen rinsing clothes in the Rio, though drought had caused the river to recede so much that they had to go far out into what was normally the riverbed to reach the water. Naked children splashed and played.

Riding, watching, Frio remembered with a tug of sadness the day he and Blas Talamantes had come this way together, headed for the Gutierrez place. Nervous now, Frio saw the brush corral of the Gutierrez wagon and muleyard ahead of him, and beyond that the portion of stone fence and the rock building.

Movement to his left brought him to a sudden stop. In an instant he had the saddlegun up and ready.

Happy Jack loped his horse out from between two brush *jacales.* Behind him lumbered a pair of the cotton wagons, both full of Frio's teamsters. The wagons bristled with guns.

Angrily Frio said, "Happy, what do you mean by this? I told you to stay on the other side of the river."

Happy was defiant. "So we disobeyed you. Fire us!"

Frio glared at them, but his anger couldn't hold. Gratitude swelled within him, despite his impatience. "Look," he said, "I know you want to help, and I wish you could. But Chapa said for me to come by myself. If you-all show up he's liable to panic and shoot Tom in cold blood."

Happy replied, "For all you know, he already has. And it's a cinch he aims to kill you too if he can. We want to see he don't get the chance."

Frio braced his hands on the saddle horn and leaned forward on stiff arms, letting his gaze roam across the eager Mexican *mulateros* who had come with Happy. He knew he might need their help. He wished he could figure a way to use them. But he said, "No, boys, you-all stay back out of the way. You're liable to be more of a liability than an asset."

Happy was plainly of a mind to argue, but finally he shrugged. "All right, Frio, play the game your way. But we'll be here. First sign of a double cross, we'll be on top of Chapa like a hawk on a rabbit."

Frio nodded. "Thanks, Happy. Thanks to all of you. Now, you must let me handle it."

Riding ahead, he kept his eyes on the rock building. There was no sign of life, and the wooden door was closed, but he could feel eyes watching him through the two open windows that faced to the front. A chill played up and down his back. He tightened his muscles, half expecting a bullet to knock him out of the saddle. His breath was short as he stopped the sorrel horse and stepped down carefully from the saddle. He unfastened the saddlebags and draped them across his left arm, holding the saddlegun in his right. Standing beside the stone fence, a hundred feet from the door, he called.

"Chapa! Chapa, you in there?"

He heard movement inside. He still had that chilling feeling that eyes were watching every move he made.

A voice answered from behind the rock wall. Frio thought he saw a man behind one of the windows. "Gringo, did you bring the money?"

Frio raised his left arm a little. "I brought it. Got it right here."

"Bring it."

Frio shook his head. "No. I came for Tom McCasland. You turn him loose out here and you get the money."

"Bring the money here and you will have your friend."

"And give you a chance to shoot me down at the door? No, I came to trade with you, not commit suicide."

"You have no choice. Bring the money."

"You just come on out here and get it."

Silence. Then a Spanish command was shouted out a side window. Chapa's voice said, "Gringo, you are a fool. I have men outside. They will take you *and* the money!"

Frio glanced to his right. Three men hurried toward him from behind another building. At his left, he saw two men rise up from where they had crouched behind the brush fence.

Trapped! he thought, in sudden desperation.

Two shots barked. The Chapa men stopped abruptly. Happy Jack and the teamsters rushed out from their hiding place, guns ready. The Chapa men hesitated, knowing they were caught in the open, that they couldn't get away. They dropped their guns. At a command from Happy Jack, they walked out with their hands up.

Relief washed over Frio. If it hadn't been for Happy. . . .

He shouted at Chapa, "I have men too. They've come to see that you give me an honest deal. Now show me Tom Mc-Casland."

"He is here. I do not lie to you."

"I don't believe you. I think you've already killed him. Before you get this money you've got to bring him out here and show me he's still alive."

There was a minute or two of quiet, as Chapa and those with him inside the building talked it over. Finally the door opened. Tom McCasland stepped out into sunlight, his hands tied behind him. With him came the renegade Bige Campsey. Frio narrowed his eyes. Tom was disheveled, and a big splotch of dried blood showed on the side of his head.

Campsey said loudly, "All right, Wheeler, here's your friend. Come get him and bring the money."

Frio stood undecided. He liked this rock fence in front of him for protection. Once he stepped beyond it, he was an easy target.

Campsey said, "Come on, Wheeler! We ain't goin' to wait all day!"

Frio felt his mouth go dry. He gripped the saddlegun so tightly that his hands cramped. But he looked at Tom, and he decided there was no choice but to take the risk. He moved toward the open gate.

Tom saw what Frio was about to do. "No, Frio!" he shouted.

Campsey turned to strike Tom. Tom bumped his body against the renegade. Caught off balance, Campsey staggered. Tom ran toward Frio, moving awkwardly because his hands were bound at his back.

"It's a trap, Frio!" he shouted. "They're goin' to kill you!"

Campsey raised his pistol. Before Frio could bring the saddlegun into line, the pistol barked. Tom stumbled and went down. Frio's rifle blazed. Campsey was slammed back against the wooden door. He staggered two steps out from the building, trying to bring the pistol up again. Then he fell forward on his face and lay still.

Frio shouted, "Tom!" And started to go on out. Guns flamed from the windows. Bullets flattened against the stone fence, forcing Frio back. But he had time to see Tom lying on the ground, motionless.

From behind Frio came the sound of other guns. His men had seen Tom go down, and they figured there no longer was anything to lose, no reason to stand back. They came running, Happy Jack out in front. They fired as they ran. At least twenty men joined Frio at the rock fence. Others circled around to the sides. They poured a murderous fire into, or at, the open windows. Powder smoke clung thick and choking. Inside that stone building the ricochets must be pure hell.

Happy Jack said triumphantly to Frio, "See there, I told you Chapa wouldn't tote fair. He's got no respect for an owner."

Frio raised his hand. The gunfire eased off. He took a long look across the fence. Tom had crawled a few feet, but now he lay still again.

"Chapa," Frio called, "you haven't got a chance anymore. Come on out of there with your hands up."

He heard angry argument from inside the building. The door opened. Half a dozen *bandidos* came out with hands over their heads. Some of them bled from wounds inflicted by the ricochets. A fat man crawled on his hands and knees, sobbing in terror, begging for mercy. This was El Gordo Gutierrez.

Frio waited, but there was no sign of the man he wanted.

"Chapa! No use you stayin' in there. Come on out!"

A voice cursed in violent Spanish, and a gun flashed in a window. A slug whined off the rock fence, sending stone chips flying.

"Gringo!" Chapa shouted. "Do you hear me?"

"I hear you."

"Your friend, he still lives. But I can kill him from here."

Dismayed, Frio realized the outlaw was right. Frio could see that Tom was breathing. He knew the *bandido* could fire on Tom from the darkness behind the window or the open door.

"If you kill him, you'll never get out of there alive!" Frio answered.

"Every man has to die sometime. He likes to take his enemies with him."

Frio swallowed, knowing he was helpless. It was hard to get any leverage against a man who was unafraid of death. "All right, Chapa, what do you want?"

"I want you, gringo! We finish this fight, the two of us. Nobody else."

Dread crept over Frio. He looked around him, desperately clutching for some idea. But none came. Tom would die for certain if Frio didn't act. "All right, Chapa. We both step out into the open. It'll be just us two, no more."

"Agreed. Come ahead."

Frio moved toward the open gate. Happy Jack stepped forward as if to stop him. Resolutely, Frio shook his head. "I'm goin' to do it, Happy. Chapa and me, we've had this a-buildin' for a long time. Stay out of it."

He walked into the open, the saddlegun in his right hand, hanging free at his side. He saw a movement inside the building and steeled himself, half expecting treachery.

But Chapa was true to his word. He appeared in the doorway. For just a moment the bandit's eyes touched the dead Bige Campsey. Then they lifted back to Frio.

Chapa's face was covered by a black neckerchief, all but his eyes. He stood one pace out from the door, those evil eyes narrowed with hatred. Dry-lipped, Frio moved toward him slowly, watching for the first indication of movement. Chapa gripped a pistol in his left hand, his arm hanging at his side. The right hand, which should have held the pistol, was shriveled and misshapen, like a claw. It was useless. Frio realized this must have happened to Chapa the night the pistol had exploded in his hand, near his face. That was the reason for the mask. The face must have suffered like the hand did.

Frio kept walking, closing the distance between the two of them. He was aware that Tom had raised himself up on one elbow. Tom was calling weakly for him not to go through with this. But Frio went on.

Chapa said in a raw, lashing Spanish, "You have come far enough, gringo. Before you die, I want you to see what you have done to me."

Black eyes burning, Chapa slowly raised the clawlike hand to the mask over his face.

Frio swallowed, not wanting to see, but he was held by some strange compulsion.

The hand ripped the neckerchief away. Frio gasped aloud, not ready for the hideous thing that had been a face. "Look, gringo," Chapa hissed, "see what you have done to me! See why I am going to kill you!" The face was a mass of angry red scar tissue from the cruel burn of the powder. The nose was half gone. The vicious mouth had healed back crookedly after white-hot metal had torn the lips.

Chapa said, "It makes your stomach sick, *verdad*? Think of how it must feel to own such a face and have to hide it behind a mask because children scream at the sight of it, and women turn away. For months I have wanted to die. But even more, I have wanted you to die. I have told myself that if I could see you dead, I would walk into the fires of hell content."

Chapa's eyes smoldered with the hatred that had eaten at him like a cancer. "My left hand is slow with the pistol. I know you will kill me, and I am ready. But before I die, I will also kill *you*. We will go to hell together."

Frio saw the *bandido*'s hand start up with the pistol. "Die, gringo!" Instantly Frio dropped to one knee, swinging the saddle-gun around. Without waiting to raise the stock to his shoulder, he squeezed the trigger. The rifle leaped.

Chapa stepped back under the impact. The pistol blazed. The bullet snarled over Frio's head. Chapa buckled, bending forward from the waist. His eyes were on Frio to the last. He tried with all the ebbing strength that was in him to raise the pistol again. He never could.

"Gringo!" he hissed. "Gringo *apestoso!*"

Even after death came, Chapa lay there on one shoulder, his glazed eyes still open, his pitifully butchered face scowling the bitter hatred that he had carried into death.

Tom McCasland lay pale and still in his little Matamoros house. Luisa Valdez sat in a chair at the head of the bed, silently watching him, a glow of contentment about her. Tom was hit low in the shoulder. The doctor had said he would live, though he might be months in recovering. Those were months in which he wouldn't be riding out — months during which she would not be spending the dark, lonely nights wondering if he would come back alive. For these months, at least, she would have him.

Frio Wheeler stood frowning down at Tom. "One thing you can say about that Bige Campsey, he was a consistent shot. He hit you in the same place he hit me."

Lying on his side, Tom looked up at Frio. "I never expected you to come help me. You didn't owe me anything. Why did you do it?"

Frio looked first at Luisa, then at Amelia, who stood beside him, her hand on his arm. "The women, for one thing. And, I reckon, for us. We were friends a long time before we were enemies, Tom. When it came right down to the taw line, I couldn't forget that."

Tom said gravely, "You know that as soon as I can get up from here and ride again, I'll be fightin' you the same as before."

Frio nodded, his face sober. "I know. I'll likely be fightin' you too. We've each fought this war accordin' to our own lights and done all we could for the side we were loyal to. Whichever way it goes, we've given our best. We've got nothin' to be ashamed of, either of us. Maybe someday, when the war is finished, we can find a way to be friends again."

Tom said, "It's liable to be hard. There's been a lot come between us."

"But it'll be worth the tryin'. Even if the South wins, nobody believes the country can stay divided. We'll have to find a way to stop bein' enemies and be friends again. The North and the South — you and me.

It had just as well start with you and me."

Tom said, "I'd like to try."

Frio nodded. "We'll do it, Tom. Now Amelia and me, we're goin' back to the other side of the river. It's where we belong now. Get yourself plenty of rest." He glanced at Luisa. "I know you won't lack for good care."

Amelia bent and kissed Tom on the cheek. "We'll see you again, Tom, when this thing is over."

Frio was at the door when Tom called him. "Frio, you goin' to marry my sister?"

Frio nodded again, and a faint smile came to his face. "Never was any doubt about it."

Arm in arm, Frio Wheeler and Amelia walked down the dusty street of Matamoros toward the river. Ahead of them, far across on the Texas side of the Rio Grande, the Stars and Bars of the Confederacy caught the wind and billowed out atop the tall flagpole in Fort Brown. How long it was destined to stay there, no man could say. All Frio knew for certain was that for however long it lasted, it was a proud sight to see. . . .

And in the end. . . .

The last battle of the Civil War was fought at Palmito Hill, some twelve miles downriver from Brownsville, May 13, 1865.

After retreating from Brownsville, the federal forces had taken an ineffective holding position at Brazos Santiago, where they then remained through the rest of the war. Some of the Union officers plotted quietly with the Mexican border chieftain Cortina, whose political position had been made precarious by French imperialist victories over the poorly armed patriots of Benito Juarez. Cortina was to capture Brownsville with his own troops in return for a commission as a brigadier general in the United States Army. The stand-firm leadership of Colonel Rip Ford brought these plans to naught.

Finally, in March, the Texan and Union

forces signed a truce, agreeing that further bloodshed along the Rio Grande would serve no useful purpose in the far larger war rapidly reaching its climax in the Deep South.

When news came early in May of General Lee's surrender at Appomattox, about two thousand bales of Confederate cotton remained on the riverbank in Brownsville. Northern cotton speculators in Matamoros, eager to get their hands on the cotton, persuaded the Union general that he should proceed to take it in the name of the Union even though such a move would violate the truce.

Under Colonel T. H. Barrett, sixteen hundred Union troops moved upriver toward Brownsville. News of Lee's surrender had thinned Rip Ford's Texas forces, but he was still able to muster about three hundred men, including the intrepid Benavides. He marched downriver and met the federals at Palmito Hill. Incredibly, his three hundred determined riders not only defeated the Union force but actually chased it seven miles before Ford called a halt.

"Boys," said that gallant man, "we have done finely. We will let well enough alone and retire."

This was his quiet benediction to four

tragic, needless years of conflict.

It was ironic that even though the Confederacy already had lost the war, it won its final battle in a futile blaze of glory on a desolate, sandy stretch of coastal wasteland fifteen hundred miles from Richmond.

■ ■ ■ ■

BARBED WIRE

■ ■ ■ ■

1

It was a sorry way for a cowboy to make a living, Doug Monahan thought disgustedly. Bending his back over a rocky posthole, he plunged the heavy iron crowbar downward, hearing its angry ring and feeling the violent jar of it bruising the stubborn rock bottom. He rubbed sweat from his forehead onto his sleeve and straightened his sore back, pausing to rest a moment and look around.

Across the broad sweep of the gray-grass valley, up the brush-dotted hill and down again on the gentle far slope, new cedar posts stood erect like a long row of silent soldiers. And stretched taut down the length of the line, four strands of red barbed wire gleamed brightly in the late-winter Texas sun.

Doug Monahan had the look of the cowboy about him, the easy, rolling gait, the slack yet somehow right way of wearing his clothes that stamped him as a man of the saddle. But he wasn't riding now, and he hadn't for quite a spell. Sweat darkened his hickory shirt under the arms and down the back, the spots rimmed with white salt and caked with dirt. The knees of his denim pants were worn through and frazzled out. His brush-scarred boots were run over at the heels from a long time of working afoot.

He gripped the crowbar with big, leather-gloved hands, lifting it and driving it down into the narrow posthole. Each strike chipped off rock and caliche. Sulfurous sparks flew angrily against his dusty boots. The rocky ground was fighting him every foot of the way.

At length he went down on his knees with a bent can to scoop dirt and chipped rock out of the hole. Wiping sweat from his stubbled face, he stood up and stretched. His gritty hands pressed against the small of his back, trying to ease the ache that was there. His gaze drifted in satisfaction back down the fenceline, where two other men also were digging postholes. Past them, a dozen cedar posts leaned at crazy angles in unfilled holes an even rod apart. Beyond these stretched the unfinished fence, stout heart-cedar posts hauled up from the river and tamped solid in holes nearly three feet deep.

And on them, the heavy No. 9 wire gleamed with its bright red coat of factory-dipped paint and its wickedly sharp barbs.

The pleasant tang of mesquite smoke drifted to him on the crisp breeze. Monahan looked down toward his chuckwagon. By the sun, which with retreating winter still stood a little to the south, it was almost noon. Paco Sanchez would have dinner ready directly.

Monahan frowned a little, watching his wagon. Gordon Finch sat there with three of his men, sipping coffee. Sat there like a lazy pot hound.

He had a right to, Monahan supposed, for after all, this was Finch's ranch. But nothing ever graveled Monahan quite so much as to have someone sitting around idly on his fat haunches and watching him work.

The easy breeze carried with it a sharp breath from the Panhandle to the north. Monahan shivered as the chill touched him. He picked up the crowbar and began chipping again. Hard muscles swelled tight within the rolled-up sleeves as the bar battered its way downward.

This was a real comedown for Monahan. Once he'd had a ranch of his own down in the South Texas brush country, and there had been a time when he might have been too proud to do this kind of work. But a long, hard drought can make a man do things he never thought he would.

Doug Monahan was young yet, with a glint of red in his hair and whiskers to go with the Irish name. He had blue eyes that could laugh easily, or could strike quick sparks, like the strong iron bar that bruised its way into the resisting earth.

Finishing the hole, measuring it by a ring he had painted thirty inches up on the bar, he walked to a small stack of cedar posts. He picked one and dropped it into the hole. He stood it straight, sighting across its axe-hewn top to hard-set posts which stretched out of view up over the hill. He glanced the other way, where stakes driven in a string-straight line marked the one-rod intervals for more postholes, as far as his eyes could see.

He watched rangy Longhorn cattle plod along in single file down a hoof-worn rut that had had its beginning with the buffalo. Headed for water, they followed an ancient trail that tomorrow would be blocked for-ever by these shining red strands of wire.

"Company coming yonder, Doug."

Stub Bailey was pointing to four riders who topped the hill and came down in an easy trot, following the new fence. Stub was a short, thickset happy-eyed man Doug had picked up over in Twin Wells and as good a hand as he had ever run across.

Monahan's glance touched the rifle that leaned against the pile of new-cut posts. He hesitated, then moved toward it.

"Reckon it's that trouble Finch hinted about?" Bailey frowned.

"I hope not."

"It's Finch's worry, ain't it?" Bailey asked. "That's what he come for."

Monahan grunted. His own idea was that Finch had come out to feed his men — and himself — at someone else's wagon.

He slipped off the work-stiffened gloves that were worn almost black. Shoving them into a hip pocket, he picked up the rifle and moved unhurriedly toward the wagon.

"May not be trouble atall," he said. "And I sure don't want Finch starting any."

Monahan was sure of only one thing about Gordon Finch, that he didn't like him. He wasn't even sure why. Maybe it wasn't for Monahan to ask questions or pass any judgment. After all, this wasn't his land. He had come here a stranger and contracted to build a fence for Finch — nothing more.

Finch had spotted the riders by the time Monahan reached the wagon. He stood up lazily, squinting, trying to see clearer. He

315

kept sipping the coffee. Monahan suspected he had laced it from a bottle in his coat pocket.

"Couple of my boys," Finch said in a gravelly voice that had a perpetual belligerence about it. He had a way of always sounding angry. "Bringing somebody in."

Finch's shoulders were a little stooped, and a soft paunch was beginning to push out over his belt. He had the florid face of the man who drinks too much and doesn't work enough to stay healthy. He could talk loud and make strong promises, as he had when Monahan agreed to take the fencing job. So far, he hadn't so much as paid for wire and posts, though he knew Monahan was working on a shoestring. He hadn't even furnished grub to the fencing crew.

He had come here yesterday, telling of a rumor that there might be trouble at the fencing camp. Not everybody liked this barbed wire.

"You just go right on putting up fence," Finch had said. "We're here to protect you."

Finch's men had done some scouting around, but all Finch himself had done so far was protect the chuckwagon.

Monahan saw worry in old Paco Sanchez's black eyes. Paco dropped a hot Dutch oven lid back over browning biscuits and wiped his dark, rheumatic hands on a flour-sack apron. His troubled gaze dwelt on the approaching riders.

"Go on with the cooking, Paco," Monahan said quietly. "Stick close to the wagon."

The aging Mexican nodded and eased toward the chuckbox. His eyes, bright as black buttons, flicked from Monahan's rifle to the four riders, then back again. Paco had lived many a long year within gunshot distance of the Rio Grande. He had seen much of violence. Now he was gentled by age, old and weary and dreading.

Monahan sometimes wished he could have left Paco in South Texas, for the old man deserved an easier life than this in his declining years. But nothing had remained to leave him with. The Bar M ranch was lost, and the cattle with it.

Stub Bailey eased and shook his head. "Won't be no trouble out of them two, Doug. That's just old man Noah Wheeler."

"Who's Noah Wheeler?"

Finch growled an answer before Bailey could reply. "A grubby old nester that got hold of four good sections of land that ought to be in somebody's ranch. Raises hay and sells it to some of them two-bit cowmen. He's got chickens, ducks, even some hogs. Rest of the nesters around here

317

went and settled along Oak Crick, but not him. He had to go out and grab ahold of good rangeland. Somebody ought to've run him back with the rest of the dirt farmers a long time ago."

Monahan glanced at Stub Bailey. Stub had been around Twin Wells long enough to know a little about most people here, and Monahan could tell that Bailey disagreed with Finch.

He could see that the old farmer was eyeing the red wire closely as he rode in. Noah Wheeler was a blocky man, solid as a rock fence. He sat his horse firmly, without the cowboy's easy, even lazy way of riding. His battered black hat fit squarely, its brim flat for shade and not for show. He wore a plain woolen coat, frayed with signs of hard work and long use. His heavy mustache, once brown, was now salted with gray.

The rider beside him was a girl. Long skirts all but covered the sidesaddle she rode. She was slender, the man's coat she wore fitting her rather like a collapsed tent. She seemed dwarfed by a wide-brimmed cowboy hat, evidently lined with paper to keep it on tight.

"Morning, Noah," Bailey said pleasantly. "How's the world serving you?"

Wheeler smiled, a pleasant, eye-crinkling

smile that held nothing back. "I can't complain about the world, but I sure wish this rheumatism would leave me alone."

Finch glared at the pair. His questioning eyes cut to one of the riders who flanked the old man and the girl.

"Found 'em comin' down the fence," the rider told him. "Noah said he was just lookin' for a way through, and I don't expect he meant any harm. But you said bring anybody we found, so we brung him."

If for no better reason than the contempt he saw in Finch's face, Monahan felt an instinctive liking for the farmer. It rubbed him against the grain when Finch said, "All right, Wheeler, move along."

Firmly Monahan said, "This is my camp. I'll say who goes." He told Wheeler, "Sorry to've bothered you. We been expecting a little trouble. You-all light and rest yourselves. Paco's got chuck about ready."

Wheeler's eyes lighted, and he forced down a smile as Finch sharply turned away. He stepped down from his old high-horned saddle and stamped his heavy boots, trying to restore the circulation in his cold feet. "Thank you, friend. We got food in the saddlebags. We didn't expect to run into anybody."

"Hot meal's a sight better," Monahan

319

replied. He moved toward the girl, hands outstretched, and lifted her down from the saddle. For just a second their eyes met. She gave him a quick smile, then shyly looked away. By her blue eyes, he took her to be Wheeler's daughter. Wheeler confirmed it.

"My name's Noah Wheeler. This is my daughter, Trudy."

Wheeler's giant hand was rough as dried leather and crushing-strong. He had spent his life at hard work.

Monahan bowed toward the girl in the old cowboy manner. She took off her big hat. He saw a fine-featured face, almost a pretty face, and honey-colored hair done up in long braids tied at the back of her neck. Again there was that shy smile. Country girl, right enough.

By way of conversation, Monahan said, "If I'd known we were fixing to have such company, I'd've cleaned up a little. I imagine I look like a prairie dog."

The girl made no reply, only smiled again. Wheeler said, "A working man ought never to apologize for his looks." He eyed the camp curiously. "We been hunting a few head of our stock. We try to keep them at home, but there's always some of these long-legged Texas cattle coming in and leading them off."

He studied the stacks of cedar posts that had been brought in by wagon. He bent over the red spools of barbed wire. He stooped stiffly and picked up a short curl of wire that had been snipped from a spool. He fingered it as if afraid it might bite.

"Bobwire," he said wonderingly. "Heard a right smart about it, but this is the first I ever seen." He touched a thumb to one of the barbs. "Sharp. These things could really rip up an animal."

"They learn in a hurry," Monahan told him. "You can't hardly get one to hit it a second time."

Wheeler smiled indulgently. "You look like a man who'd know horses. Pretty intelligent, a horse is. But about a few things he hasn't got the sense of a jackrabbit. If there's anything in ten miles that'll hurt him, he'll find it. Especially if he's the best horse you got."

He shook his head and dropped the wire. "The stuff's all right, I guess . . . just hate to think what it'd do to a horse."

Monahan washed his face and hands in a basin of cold water. He dug coffee cups out of the chuckbox and poured them full. He handed one to the girl and felt pleasure at her half-concealed smile. She hadn't yet said a word.

He watched for and caught the pleasant surprise in the girl's blue eyes as she first tasted the coffee. Paco Sanchez had the Mexican way of boiling sugar right in with the coffee. It was sweeter that way than if you just spooned sugar into the cup and stirred it.

Monahan handed a second cup to Wheeler and poured one for himself. "Most people think that way about barbed wire, the first time they see it. I did, too. But it isn't like that. I'll admit, it might cut a few at first, but you'd be surprised how fast they learn. They're using a lot of it down in South Texas. It's the answer for the stock men, Mr. Wheeler. Especially a fellow like you, farming and running cattle both. Country's too dry to grow hedges, and it'd bust the back end out of a bank to build a wood fence around a big pasture. But barbed wire is cheap. Most anybody can afford it. A couple of the farmers over on Oak Creek are interested. Soon's I finish this job, I'm going to do a little fencing there."

Wheeler shrugged, deep in thought. "Maybe you're right, but lots of people don't like bobwire. I've heard some bad things."

Monahan frowned into his coffee. "They just don't know. Anything new like this, it takes time."

Paco Sanchez walked up with pothook in hand. He lifted the coal-covered lid off the biscuits and set it down with a clatter, leaning it against the edge of the Dutch oven. In another oven, hanging on a hook suspended from the crossbar over the fire, steaks sizzled in deep grease. Paco poked at them with a long fork. Satisfied, he took the pothook and hoisted them away from the heat.

" *'Stá listo,* Doug."

Doug bowed and motioned the girl toward the chuckbox. Paco Sanchez stood beaming as she filled her plate from his ovens. Paco's skin was like fine brown leather, with just a trace of a shine across his high cheekbones, at the upper edge of his coarse gray whiskers. He had come up from the ranchos south of the Rio Grande, way yonder ago, up to the South Texas brush. For more years than Paco could count, he had worked as a vaquero, a brushpopper, his tough skin seared by the sun, scarred by clawing thorns. He had worked cattle for Monahan's father, and he had helped bring up Doug Monahan, had taught him the way of the vaquero.

Now crushed bones and his many years were piling up on him. The old Mexican was finishing out his time over the cook-fires. No pensioner, Paco. He wanted only to work — to stay with the Monahans. The aging chuckbox with a Bar M burned deeply into each side was all that was left to show for the ranch. And Doug was the only Monahan.

Eating, Doug found himself watching the girl. These farmer girls were taught to be wary of strangers. Especially a stranger who looked like a cowboy. She and her father ate silently and hungrily. Monahan could tell they had had a long ride. He felt a touch of pity for the girl. Pretty thing, she was, like a wild flower growing up in the middle of nowhere. A girl like this was meant to be seen.

Noah Wheeler pushed to his feet. He took his daughter's empty plate and cup and dropped them into the wreck pan along with his own. "Fine dinner," he said to Paco. "We sure did enjoy it."

"*Grácias,*" smiled Paco, warming to the compliment. "The camp is yours."

Wheeler turned to Monahan. "We'd best get along if we're going to find our cattle. No telling where those Longhorns have led them to."

He looked once again at the barbed wire fence which was edging slowly out across the range. "Going to be a big change. Always been open country. How far do you figure on going with it?"

Monahan replied, "I've contracted to build it all the way around Gordon Finch's range."

Wheeler's thick eyebrows lifted a little. "Finch's range?" He gave the rancher a sharp, questioning glance. "You got more ambition than I thought you had, Mr. Finch."

Finch's eyes flashed anger.

Wheeler walked to his horse and swung heavily into the old saddle. Monahan gave the girl a boost up. She smiled at him, and in a quiet voice she spoke the first words he had heard from her. "Thank you, Mr. Monahan. Maybe someday we can return the favor."

He watched them ride away, his eyes mostly on the girl.

Firing up a fresh cigar, Finch muttered contemptuously, "About time they left. They got the smell of hogs about them."

Flaring, Monahan turned to answer him, then thought better of it. He hadn't been paid yet. But someday someone was going to make Finch eat that cigar, raw, and maybe with the fire still on it.

Monahan knew it was trouble, as soon as he saw the horsemen. He was using a shovel handle to tamp fresh dirt tightly while Stub Bailey held a post straight. Looking up, Bailey stiffened.

"Uh-oh. Look yonder coming."

Doug let the shovel rest against his broad shoulder. He rubbed a sleeve across his forehead and blinked at the burn of sweat that worked into his eyes.

"*That* ain't Noah Wheeler," Bailey said with tightness in his voice. He suddenly looked as if he needed a drink. "Must be thirty–forty of 'em."

Monahan squinted. Fifteen or twenty, more like it; but that was enough. The riders were moving along the fenceline. As they moved, men stepped down from their saddles, stopping to snip the wire.

"They mean business, looks like," said Bailey. "Cuttin' it between every post."

Down at the chuckwagon, Gordon Finch stood frozen, watching and not making a move. Anger sweeping him like a sudden blaze in dry grass, Monahan dropped the shovel, grabbed his rifle and sprinted down to the wagon.

"Finch," he exploded, "where's that protection? You've sat around here filling your belly and getting in the way! Now what're you going to do?"

Finch's face had paled. "My men," he rasped helplessly, pointing. "They've rounded up all my men and got them along. There ain't a thing I *can* do."

Monahan's small fencing crew gathered and stood tensely beside the wagon, where Paco Sanchez's cookfire had burned down to a few glowing coals which he was keeping alive for supper.

"You want us to fight, Doug?" asked Stub Bailey, spinning the cylinder of a six-shooter.

"Put it up," Doug said. "We don't have a chance, and there's no use getting somebody killed." He set down his rifle and stood there waiting.

2

The riders came on leisurely, knowing they had the upper hand. They didn't leave behind them a single piece of wire more than twenty feet long.

"We're in for it," Bailey muttered. "That's the old he-coon hisself in the lead yonder, ridin' the gray horse. Captain Andrew Rinehart. He don't answer to nobody, not even to God."

A chill worked down Doug Monahan's back. He knew that this was going to be nasty. But this was Finch's land. He ought to have the right to do what he wanted to with it. . . .

The horsemen crowded in close, forming a semicircle around the small fencing crew. Some of the horses fidgeted, slinging their heads. Gordon Finch held back, sliding behind the chuckbox.

The captain edged forward on his big gray, as fine a horse as a man would ever see. Captain Andrew Rinehart was a man of strong will and fierce pride. He was an aging cowman with a clipped gray beard and piercing eyes that stabbed from under heavy gray brows. Despite the weight of years, his back was rigid. Not a young cowboy with him sat straighter in the saddle.

He was one of those real old patriarchs, Monahan knew, one of the kind who had whipped and carved this state into being. You still found a few like him down in South Texas. Monahan knew the breed, for his father had been one. Most of them were gone now.

Those commanding eyes searched the fencing crew, then lit on Monahan. "You're in charge here." It was a statement, rather than a question.

Monahan took a step forward. "It's my camp. I'm Doug Monahan."

Rinehart studied him intently, squinting as if to see him better. "Monahan, you're trespassing."

Monahan felt the stretch of tension within him. He had heard about Captain Rinehart. This old man controlled the R Cross, which sprawled haphazardly over a big part of Kiowa County, its boundaries ragged and loose — and uncontested. Once a Texas Ranger, and later an officer in the Confederate army, he had been the first man to move into this county and stay. He had pushed the Indians out. In the years that followed, no one had ever seriously challenged him.

Kiowa County, it said on the map. Around here they called it Rinehart County more often than not.

"Well now," Monahan said. "We have a contract from Gordon Finch to fence his ranch, so I don't see how we could be trespassing."

Rinehart's gaze searched over the men on the ground. "Where is Gordon Finch? Finch, step out here."

Finch moved hesitantly. He came out from behind the chuckbox and stood beside Monahan. His mouth opened, and in his face was a fleeting intention to speak up to this stern old cowman. Then his eyes fell, and his mouth closed.

Rinehart's voice was as hard as flint rock. "I never would've thought you had the nerve, Finch. Now you're through around here. Catch up your horse and git."

Without lifting his eyes to those of the men around him, Gordon Finch walked out to where his horse stood hitched to a stunty mesquite behind the woodpile. He swung into the saddle, shoulders sagging.

"Sell out and leave," Rinehart said to him. The old man didn't speak loudly, but his voice carried the crack of a whip. "I don't want to see you around here again."

Just like that. *Sell out and leave.* And Monahan knew Finch would do it.

Finch rode off without a glance at Monahan. His cowboys followed after him, all but one whose name Monahan remembered was Dundee. Dundee held back a moment, his eyes touching Monahan's and making a silent apology. Dundee's holster was empty. Some R Cross cowboy had gotten himself a six-shooter mighty cheap.

Rinehart's gaze cut back to Monahan. "This isn't Finch's range. It's *mine.* It always was."

Monahan clenched his rough fist. He ought to have guessed, but he hadn't. Finch had tried to run a sandy, and he hadn't had the nerve it took to go through with it.

Monahan said, "He told me it was his, and I had no reason to doubt him."

Rinehart's eyes were cold. He thought Monahan was lying. The captain glanced at a man who sat beside him on a black-legged dun. "All right, Archer!"

Men stepped down from the horses and started throwing loose cedar posts up into a pile. They heaved the red spools of wire up atop the posts. Someone took Paco Sanchez's big coal-oil can and started pouring kerosene.

"Rinehart," Monahan protested, "I tell you I didn't know! Finch lied to me. Everything I've got is tied up here. Finch hasn't paid me a cent."

If Rinehart heard him, he gave no sign of it. He just sat there stiffly on the big gray horse, watching.

"Burn it," he said, looking at the rider he had called Archer.

This was a tall, angular man of about thirty-five, a stiff-backed man who might have been the captain's son, he was so much like him. He had the same aristocratic bearing, the same strong face, the same driving will. He struck a match on the sole of his boot and flipped it onto the posts near the bottom of the pile. The flames licked upward, spreading hungrily, seeking out the kerosene.

Monahan took an angry step forward, then stopped as he felt a gunbarrel poke him in the back. Rinehart's men pitched his crew's bedding and camp gear into the flames.

The one called Archer stood watching the fire, his face grimly silent. It was then that Monahan noticed the man's eyes.

They were black, compelling eyes, framed in heavy, dark brows and long black lashes, eyes that burned with a ruthlessness that seemed even greater than the captain's.

Monahan remembered then. He had heard of this man, too. Archer Spann, his name was. Foreman of the R Cross, and the captain all over again except younger. The captain had never had a son, they said, but he had found Archer Spann, and Spann was as much like him as a son could ever be.

Spann picked up the kerosene can and climbed up into the chuckwagon. He poured the rest of the contents out over the chuckbox and into the wagonbed. Paco Sanchez had held still through all that had happened. Suddenly now he broke loose as he realized that the old Bar M chuckwagon was about to be destroyed.

"No, no," he cried, "don't you burn my wagon!"

He grabbed at Spann's long legs, trying to pull him down. Spann lifted the heavy can and swung it at Paco's head. Stunned, Paco went down on hands and knees.

Spann pitched a match into the kerosene. As the flames spread, he dropped down from the wagon.

Near Paco's hands the water basin had fallen to the ground. He grabbed it, scooped up sand and threw it on the flames. Spann jerked the pan from his twisted hands. It went spinning away. One of the horses, nervous already because of the fire, broke into pitching. In a moment of wild confusion, the riders pulled one way and another, trying to stop the bucking horse.

Raging now at the destruction of his wagon, Paco found his fallen pothook.

"No, Paco!" Monahan shouted and jumped to stop him.

Spann stepped back in sudden alarm as the pothook swung at him. It missed, and Paco never had a chance to swing it again. Spann's gun came up. It roared. Paco jerked under the impact, falling against the burning wagon.

"Paco!" Monahan rushed to the old Mexican, grabbing him and dragging him back from the flames. In desperation he ripped away the cook's heavy black shirt. The old man caught a sharp, sobbing breath. For a moment he struggled to speak, but no words came. His tough old fingers closed on Monahan's hand, telling in their own way what Paco wanted to say. Then they relaxed, and the scarred, twisted hand fell away.

Monahan was on his knees, stunned, just holding Paco's body and not knowing what to do. Then, gently, he eased him down to earth and stood up, trembling in fury.

Spann was watching him, his own face taut. He held the smoking gun, its barrel leveled at Monahan.

Captain Rinehart said, "Put the gun away, Archer."

Monahan leaped at the man. He saw the gunbarrel tilt upward. He grabbed Spann's wrist, forced the gun aside as it roared again. He reached for Spann's throat.

Spann wrenched loose. There was a quick swish, and the gunbarrel struck Monahan behind the ear. He fell solidly, the ground smashing against his face. He lay there tasting sand. He pushed onto his knees, trying to clear his head and find Spann again, but the horsemen seemed to swirl around him. He was conscious of the flames, the crackling heat, the stench of smoke. But he could not see. There was sand in his eyes, and a blinding pain-flash of red.

Rinehart's riders held their nervous horses as still as they could, gripped in sudden shock by the quick explosion of violence, the death of the old Mexican. It had not been part of the plan. Rinehart's riders waited uncertainly, and Monahan waited, too, half expecting the gun to roar again.

"I said put it up," Rinehart spoke in a

quiet but commanding voice.

Spann dropped the six-shooter back into its holster.

Cold reason returned to Monahan then. He blinked hard, shaking his head, trying to clear his sight. He couldn't fight them now. But he wouldn't forget. He'd bide his time and take whatever else they dealt him, for there would be another day. . . .

The bed of the blazing wagon broke. Camp goods spilled through the charring bottom. The heavy chuckbox lurched sideways, hung a moment in the balance, then slid to the ground with a crash of tin plates and cups and cutlery and a shower of hot sparks.

Horses danced excitedly away from the flames. Captain Rinehart held his big gray with a strong, steady hand.

"We didn't come to kill anybody, Monahan," he said evenly. "I didn't mean it to happen. But it doesn't change anything. This is open range. It was that way when I came here, and it will remain so. Now move out, Monahan. Don't stop for anything. Move out, and don't come back!"

He turned his gray horse about then, and pulled away without a backward glance. His cowboys drew aside to let him pass. Then they fell in behind him. Some of them looked back at the blazing ruin of the camp, but Captain Rinehart never did.

Doug Monahan dragged himself to the old Mexican. He gripped the corded brown hand, closing his eyes against the sudden rush of hot tears. Stub Bailey came and laid his hand on Monahan's shoulder.

Monahan said tightly, "I can't remember a time when Paco Sanchez wasn't somewhere around. As far back as I can remember, he's been with me."

Paco had taught him, had guided him, had occasionally used the double of a rope on him when Doug's own father wasn't there and the job needed doing.

"Time has a way of going on, Doug," Stub said quietly. "It takes away the old things we been used to. We can't hold them forever."

Bailey and the others of the fencing crew threw sand on the fires, snuffing them out. Doug couldn't stand up to it, and right now he didn't care.

Presently he looked up to find the fires out. Bailey was digging around under a flat rock just outside of camp. He came back carrying a bottle, wiping the dirt off onto his shirt. He held the bottle out to Doug.

"Take a good stiff one. You need it."

Monahan managed two long swallows and

choked. It was cheap, raw whisky. Bailey took the bottle and turned it up for himself.

"One thing they didn't burn up," he commented, wiping his mouth on his sleeve, his blue eyes watering from the sting. "Bet you didn't even know I had this."

"I knew you had it," Monahan replied. "I just didn't know where."

Bad as the whisky was, it made Monahan feel better. Stub knelt uncomfortably beside him, looking at Paco. One of the men dragged a half-burned blanket out of the fire and covered the body with it.

"We saved some of the stuff," Bailey said. "Cedar ain't easy burned, so most of the posts are still good. Them wooden spools burned quick, though, and the wire's tangled up into an awful mess. Lost the temper, too, I expect. I don't reckon it'll be to where we can salvage much of it."

Monahan stood up painfully to look over the shambles. "Thanks, Stub."

Bailey said, "You better let me fix that place where they hit you. It don't look good."

"It'll be all right." Doug's voice was hollow.

Bailey shrugged. The boss was old enough to take care of himself. "What do we do now?"

"First thing, we better see if we can find a shovel that isn't burned up."

They had to bury Paco without so much as the Scripture, for the only Bible had been in the chuckbox. It hadn't been used much. Sometime, Monahan thought, he would try to find a priest and bring him out here. Right now, a short prayer had to do.

They had just finished filling the grave when Noah Wheeler and his daughter came back, driving three plodding Durham cows. The cows warily skirted the camp, but the two riders came straight in. Their eyes were grim as they read the meaning in the burned-out camp, the cut fence, the new mound of earth where a fire-blackened piece of the chuckbox lid stood as a temporary headboard.

The old farmer solemnly looked over the faces of the men in camp, mentally tallying up. He glanced at the grave and said, "The cook?"

Monahan nodded stiffly. Wheeler slowly climbed out of the saddle. The girl also got down. Her soft voice was tight. "Who did it?"

"Rinehart," Monahan said bitterly.

"The captain?" Noah Wheeler shook his head incredulously. "He's a hard man on occasion, but he's never killed without the need for it."

Monahan said, "Archer Spann did the shooting."

The old farmer nodded grimly. "Cold as ice. He's the man they say will own the R Cross someday." With sorrow, Wheeler said, "I reckon it's my fault. I should have told you it was Rinehart's range, but I figured it was none of my business."

"Wouldn't have mattered," Monahan replied. "It was already too late."

Trudy Wheeler carefully touched the wound on Monahan's head. "That looks bad."

"It'll heal."

Noah Wheeler frowned. "You-all better come with us for tonight. We got plenty of room at home, and plenty to eat."

Monahan shook his head. "The captain's down on us. You take us in, he's liable to bear down on you, too."

"No," said Wheeler, "we've never had any trouble with the captain." He smiled then, but behind the smile was a dead seriousness. "I'm just an old dirt farmer. Nobody bothers me. Now you come along with us and get some rest."

Trudy Wheeler reached far into the overturned water barrel on the ground beside the blackened wagon, and found a little water there. She soaked a handkerchief in it and returned to Monahan. "We're going to clean that wound."

She paid no attention to his objections. Her fingers were quick and sure and gentle. Watching her closely, keenly aware of the nearness of her, Monahan realized that Trudy Wheeler was less a girl than she was a woman, that there was much of beauty and maturity about her that a man might miss the first time he looked.

"Too bad we have nothing to put on this," she said as she finished. A bottle of iodoform had been smashed when the chuckbox fell.

Bailey brought out his bottle again, gazed regretfully at the little bit still in the bottom of it, and handed it to her. "Here."

It burned worse outside than it had inside.

"You-all catch up your horses," Trudy Wheeler said. "You're going over to our place."

Monahan was a little surprised at the firmness of her voice. He had first reckoned her as quiet and meek. Now he had a feeling that there was nothing meek about her.

He gave in because the men had to sleep somewhere, and there was nothing left of the camp. "Just for tonight, then. Tomorrow we'll leave."

■ ■ ■ ■

Doug Monahan half expected to see the usual next-to-starvation look he had found in so many dugout and brush-corral nester outfits, including some of the farms over on Oak Creek. He was surprised. Hard work and careful planning had gone into Noah Wheeler's place, and it showed.

"Got four sections here," Wheeler said proudly. "That is, I'm sort of partners with a bank in Fort Worth, you might say. Most of it's still grazing land. I've got sixty or seventy acres broken out, about all I can farm by myself."

Four sections. If you went by deeded land, that probably made Noah Wheeler about as big an actual landowner as there was in this part of the country right now. That was more than twenty-five hundred acres, if you figured land that way. This wasn't the high-rainfall land of East Texas. Here it took more land to produce as much, and most people figured it in sections instead of by acres.

Monahan wondered if Captain Rinehart owned title to as much as four sections. He probably did; most of the cowmen here-abouts had bought the land where they built their headquarters, and where they could, they bought that around their best water. Control of the water gave control of the land, even though the most of it still belonged to the state, or to schools, or to the railroads which had received it as a grant in earlier times. The ranchers ran their cattle on this land without let because so far there had been little other claim on it. They might own only one section in fee, yet control twenty.

There were some who owned no land at all but simply let their cattle run loose on the open range. By unwritten rule, such land could be used by the first man who claimed it, and any other man who tried to usurp it had better throw a mighty big shadow. Gordon Finch had tried, and he hadn't made it. This unwritten title was so well established by custom that a man might sell his ranch to another without actually owning the land.

Fifteen or twenty good Durham cows were grazing in a green winter oat patch. Monahan noted that there was no fence around it. Wheeler proudly waved his hand toward the cattle.

"That's going to be the end of the Longhorn. I'm building me a nice little herd of Durhams. You won't find any better in a hundred miles. I've already got a few cow-men buying bulls from me, and I'll sell a lot more as my herd grows. A few years from now, they'll have the Longhorn blood pretty well bred out of the country."

The three cows the Wheelers had brought back trotted out into the field toward the others, pausing here and there to grab a bite of green oats.

Monahan frowned. "This is wide-open country. How can you hold your strain pure if you can't keep the native bulls out of here?"

Wheeler said, "That's the biggest trouble we got. We just have to ride our country good every day or two and run the Long-horns out. It's the best we can do. A Long-horn calf shows up from one of our cows, we just have to figure on making beef of it. We can't keep it in the herd."

They skirted past the oatfield. Next to it, lying fallow through the winter, was Whee-ler's hay land, plowed clean and neat, the furrows arrow-straight. This field was circled by two strands of slick wire put up on crooked mesquite posts.

"Will that fence turn a cow back?" Mona-han asked.

Wheeler shook his head. "Not if she wants in very bad. And when the field is green, they want in."

A Durham bull and two cows came plodding back from water.

"There's my bull," Wheeler said. "He's got a pedigree and a name as long as your arm, but I just call him Sancho because he's such a pet."

He was a big roan bull, not so leggy as the Longhorns but deeper-bodied, with flanks coming down farther and a wide, full rump that would carve out a lot of beef.

"The only trouble with him," Wheeler commented, "he can't outfight these native bulls. I almost had to shoot one of Fuller Quinn's the other day to keep him from killing Sancho. But one way of looking at it, old Sancho will win out in the long run. His progeny'll still be around when the Longhorns are gone."

Pride glowed in Wheeler's voice. "It's nice to be able to count your cattle in the thousands like Captain Rinehart, but I'll settle for having better quality."

A scattering of chickens scratched all about the place. Ducks swam leisurely in a large earthen tank. A few hogs rooted around in damp ground in a pen back a healthy distance east of the house.

Noah Wheeler's solid frame house stood near a spring that bubbled a strong, clear stream of water, the beginnings of a small creek which wound down past the fields and out across the grazing land. Both the house and the barn behind it were painted a bright red. Red barn paint was cheap and not hard to get.

"Built that house myself," said Wheeler. "Hauled the lumber down from the railroad right after they built into Stringtown."

It was a good house, a pleasant-looking house, though not a big one. Monahan wondered where the old stockfarmer intended to bed them down.

"There's a lean-to out in the barn," Wheeler said. "Built it for my son, Vern. If we can't find enough bedding for you fellers, we got plenty of hay out there to help stretch it."

"What about your son?" Monahan asked. "Won't we be crowding him?"

Wheeler shook his head. "Farming got too slow for Vern. He's over at the R Cross, working for the captain." His voice held a touch of regret. "Vern's not cut out for a plow, I guess. There's work aplenty here for both of us, but he'd rather cowboy and be on his own. We don't see him much anymore."

Trudy Wheeler smiled. "There's a girl in town, and he's saving every dime he can.

He's afraid if he gets off of that ranch he'll spend some money."

Noah Wheeler rode past the barn and stood up in the stirrups, looking over into a corral. "Wonder if old Roany's had her calf yet?"

Monahan saw a fine Durham cow that was springing heavy, and had made a bag. It was easy to see that the calf was due any day now.

"Roany's my pet," Wheeler said. "Best cow I ever owned, or ever saw, for that matter. She's fixing to have a calf by Sancho, and it'll be the best one in the country when it gets here, I'd bet my boots on that."

Trudy Wheeler smiled. "Dad's been like a kid at Christmas, waiting for that calf."

Noah Wheeler dismounted and opened a corral gate. "Bring your horses on in. We got plenty of feed for them. While you get unsaddled, Trudy and the missus will rustle you up something to eat."

Doug found Mrs. Wheeler a strong, clear-eyed farm woman who talked with her husband's warm enthusiasm for their place and for the country in general. She ran the house in a quiet fashion but with a firm hand. Doug thought he could see where Trudy Wheeler had gotten her deceptively shy manner.

Suddenly Monahan was glad he had come. Sitting here in the front room of their little house, enjoying the company of these good people, he had forgotten his own trouble for a time.

Noah Wheeler said, "You haven't got any business moving out till you get yourself rested a little. Why don't you stay with us a day or two?"

"Just tonight. We'll leave in the morning."

"What do you figure on doing?"

Monahan's face darkened. "I'm not real sure what I'll do later. But first thing, I've got a bill to collect from Gordon Finch."

3

Finch's headquarters lay near the bottom of a long slope, with a big shallow natural lake just below it, lying lazy in the late-winter sun. Spotted cattle of every color watered at its edge, which already was beginning to shrink away from the rank growth of weeds and grass that had sprung up after last summer's rains and now lay dead and brown from the winter frost.

Doug Monahan skirted the lake, Stub Bailey riding beside him. He had sent the rest of the men directly to town to wait for him. In a quick splash of water, cattle scattered as the two horsemen approached. After running a short way, they would turn and look back, ready to run again if it appeared the riders were coming after them.

"Natural location for a ranch headquarters," Stub observed. "Old man named Jenks settled it first. They say Finch cheated him out of it someway or other."

Sitting high on the slope was a big rock house that would be Gordon Finch's. Riding in, Monahan saw corrals that had loose or broken planks and needed repair. A gate sagged and was half patched with wire. An old broken-down wagon stood right where the axle had snapped. No one had bothered to fix it or move it out of the way. Weeds had grown up through the rotting wagonbed.

Monahan rode up to the house, dismounted and strode up the steps. This had been built out of rock hauled in from a breaky stretch of hills a mile or so off yonder up the creek, and Doug was reasonably sure it had been built by Finch's predecessor. It was too good for Finch.

He walked across the lumber-built gallery and knocked on the door. A dog trotted around the corner and began barking at him, but there was no answer from within. Monahan knocked again, trying to see through the unclean oval glass. There was a good chance Finch was inside, avoiding him, but pushing in might give Finch an excuse to put the sheriff on him. Monahan turned and walked back down to the horses. The dog followed him partway, still barking.

Down across the yard was a long frame

building with smoke curling out of a tin chimney.

"We'll try the cookshack," Monahan told Bailey. "One thing we know for sure, he likes to eat."

A man stood in the cookshack door, blocking Monahan's way. Monahan sensed that he had come to the right place.

"Mr. Finch ain't here," growled the ranchhand. He was one of those who had been supposed to help guard the fencing camp.

Monahan eyed him closely. "You sure?"

"I *said* he ain't."

"I heard you," Monahan replied, and made a move toward the door.

The cowboy reached behind him and brought up a shotgun. "Stay where you're at, Monahan."

Monahan heard footsteps behind him. He turned quickly, not wanting to be caught between two of Finch's men. He saw the cowboy named Dundee, who had been with Finch at the fencing camp.

"Don't pay him no mind, Monahan," Dundee said, humor flickering in his brown eyes. "He won't use that shotgun. And Finch is in there, all right, a-hiding from you. Been lookin' back over his shoulder ever since we rode away from your camp."

Monahan stared curiously at Dundee,

then back to the cowboy at the door. "Well," he asked flatly, "what about it?"

The cowboy slowly lowered the shotgun and stood back. Monahan stepped through the door and blinked in the dim light. There behind the bare dinner table sat Finch, a cup of coffee and a whisky bottle in front of him. He scowled, but in his eyes Monahan could see the sick touch of fear.

"What you want, Monahan?"

"I want my pay."

"You didn't finish that fence. I don't owe you nothing."

Monahan stiffened. "Paco Sanchez was worth more to me than all the land and cattle you'll ever own, and you got him killed. But I'll settle for payment for two miles of fence, completed. Twenty-one spools of barbed wire, burned. All the posts I can't salvage. And two wagons. I got that figured down to twenty-four hundred dollars, even money. I'll take a check, right now."

Finch shoved his chair back. "I ain't paying you nothing, Monahan. You took that job, and you didn't finish it."

"Finch, you used me to try to run a bluff you didn't have the guts for yourself. You ran off like a scalded dog and left me and my men to take the whipping for you. You're going to pay me for that."

Finch turned to the man at the door. "Put him out of here, Haskell. If he won't go, use that shotgun."

The man raised the gun but hesitated to move further. Dundee stepped through the door and placed a firm hand on Haskell's arm. "If he wants Monahan run off, let him do it hisself."

Finch reddened. "Dundee, you're fired."

Dundee shrugged. "I was fixin' to leave anyhow. This outfit's washed up."

Bailey appeared in the doorway, prepared to help Monahan if Dundee threw in with Finch. But that wasn't going to happen. Monahan looked at the cowboy, thanking him with his eyes. Then he turned back to Finch. "If you haven't got a blank check, *I* have."

He pulled one out of his shirt pocket and dropped it on the table. "I got it filled out. All you got to do is sign it."

Finch blustered. "You can't get away with this. It's robbery."

Monahan shook his head. "It's payment for a job. Legal. And I got a witness." He glanced at Dundee, and was caught off guard when Finch lunged, fist catching Monahan on the nose and flinging him backward against a cabinet. Tin plates and cups clattered to the floor. A bottle rolled down and smashed.

Then anger gushed through Monahan. He surged back at Finch. His fist caught Finch's jaw a hard blow that jerked the man's head back. Finch staggered a step or two. Fear flickered in his eyes as he stared wildly at Monahan. He had triggered this fight out of desperation, and now suddenly he was afraid, not knowing how to stop it.

Hatred burned in Monahan, but he checked himself. Finch would not fight back now. Do what he might, Monahan later would be ashamed of himself. He gripped Finch's collar and jerked him up close. He heaved him backward into a chair.

"Sign that check, Finch."

Finch signed it while Monahan tried to stop his nosebleed.

Dundee moved a step inside the door. "Just as well write me one too. I got a month's pay comin'."

Never looking up, Finch dug a blank check from his wallet and wrote it out. He turned away then, staring out the greasy cookshack window, sagging in defeat.

Bailey still stood at the door, hand on his gun, ready in case the trouble got bigger than Monahan was.

"Let's go to town, Stub."

Dundee followed them out. "Be all right with you if I tag along? Looks like my business around here is all wound up."

Monahan shrugged. "Suit yourself."

"I got a warbag and a roll over at the bunkhouse and a horse in the corral," Dundee said. "I got no good-byes to say."

Directly he rode back, thin bedroll secured behind the saddle, a warbag of clothing and personal belongings hanging from the saddlehorn atop his rope. He rode a long-legged bay horse that had a strong showing of Thoroughbred. Monahan looked questioningly at the bay.

"Don't worry, he's mine," Dundee said. "Owned him when I came here, and I've had to pay Finch for all the feed he's et."

They edged around the lake, scattering cattle again. Monahan showed some uncertainty about the trail to town, and Dundee pointed it out.

"What'll you do now, Dundee?" Monahan asked after a while.

Dundee shrugged and rolled himself a cigarette. "Never gone hungry yet. What about you?"

"Buy me a new outfit and start over again, more than likely."

Dundee's eyebrows went up. "You mean build more fence?"

"It's a living."

"You're on Rinehart's list now. You build another fence around here and the captain's liable to wrap that bobwire around your neck."

Monahan's voice was grim. "He won't find it easy to do."

It was midafternoon when they reached town. Stub Bailey was looking toward the saloon and licking his lips. But Monahan had his eyes on the bank.

"First thing I got to do is deposit this check before Finch sends in here to stop payment."

Dundee said, "I reckon I can use my money, too."

Bailey pulled his horse aside. "Go ahead, then. You-all know where I'll be at," and he turned in and dismounted at the nearest saloon.

The teller was a small, middle-aged man, bald and friendly looking. He glanced at Monahan's check, and his forehead wrinkled in surprise.

"What's the matter?" Monahan asked, suddenly worried.

The teller shook his head. "Nothing wrong, Mr. Monahan. Just endorse it, will you?"

While Doug scrawled his name across the check with a scratchy bank pen, another man stepped out of a back office. He was a huge old gentleman, weighing perhaps three hundred pounds. Grinning, the teller said, "Albert, come over here, will you? Mr. Monahan, I want you to meet Albert Brown, president of the bank. Albert, you've lost a bet."

Pulling his glasses down from his forehead to his nose, the portly banker read Finch's check and the endorsement. "Well, well," he mused with humor, "I wouldn't have believed it."

The teller explained. "You see, Mr. Monahan, when you first came here, Albert bet me ten dollars Gordon Finch would weasel out of paying you for any fence you might build. After I heard what happened yesterday, I was ready to forfeit to him."

The old banker was smiling. "It was worth losing the bet. I just wish we could collect what Finch owes *us.*" He glanced at Monahan's right hand. Doug was suddenly conscious of the skinned knuckles. Brown chuckled. "Perhaps we could, if we were a little younger and had your method."

The teller grinned. "You could always sit on him, Albert."

"One of these days I'm going to sit on

you," Brown grunted.

Monahan took out enough cash to pay off his men. Then he waited on the boardwalk outside while Dundee cashed his check.

Twin Wells was pretty much an average for a West Texas cowtown, he thought. It had the essentials. From the bank's front walk he could count two mercantile stores, five saloons, a church and a school. Scattered around haphazardly were one good hotel, one cheap one, a big livery barn at the head of the street, and a smaller one at the far end to keep the big one honest. There was a blacksmith shop and a little chili joint.

Dominating the town was the courthouse, an imposing two-story rock building squarely in the center of a large block of fenced-in ground that probably was as big as the rest of the business section put together. In the summertime, cowboys would ride into town and tie their horses along this stake fence in the shade of the big live oaks instead of in the sun at the hitchracks that stood in front of most of the business houses. Behind the courthouse stood a smaller structure, built of the same stone, looking very much like the courthouse except that its windows were barred.

When Dundee came out, Monahan told

him, "I'm going over and talk to the sheriff."

"I'll string along with you, if it's all the same. I'm curious what Luke McKelvie's goin' to say."

"It's up to you."

They strode across the hoof-scarred street, pausing to let a cowboy ride past them and a loaded wagon roll by. The live oaks had held their leaves all winter, and now they were a muddy green, almost ready to fall and give way to the fresh leaves that spring would bring. A thick mulch of old leaves and acorns crunched beneath the men's feet as they passed under the big trees and through the open gate toward the jail.

The sheriff sat at his desk, frowning over a fresh batch of reward dodgers. Luke Mc-Kelvie was fifty or so. He had a lawman look about him but somewhere back yonder he'd been a cowboy before he strayed off into the devious trails of politics, Doug Monahan judged. He still retained a little of the cowboy, but years in town, with easy work and not much heavy riding, had left him a shade soft around the middle, a little broad across the hips.

"I'm Doug Monahan."

The sheriff looked up with tired gray eyes. He stood and extended his hand. "Evening. Figured you'd be in, sooner or later. Sit down. You too, Dundee."

The two men dragged cane-bottomed chairs away from the bare wall.

"You've heard about yesterday?" Monahan asked.

McKelvie nodded. "The captain was in with Spann. They told me."

"You could've come out and investigated."

The sheriff's eyes were steady. "I did. Rode all the way out there, and all I could find was a grave."

Monahan felt a touch of guilt for the way he had spoken. He had taken it for granted that the sheriff had done nothing.

McKelvie said, "You should've waited for me. Not just buried the old man and rid off like that."

"Didn't seem to be much else we could do. We had no food left, or bedding or anything."

The sheriff shrugged. "I don't reckon it matters now anyway."

"One thing matters to me. What're you going to do?"

McKelvie frowned. "What *should* I do?"

"A man was killed out there. We all know who killed him. You do anything about murder around here?"

The sheriff pointed his finger at Monahan. "About murder, yes, but was it murder?

Look at it the way I have to. In the first place, you were trespassing. You had no business out there."

"I took the job in good faith. I didn't know I was trespassing."

"Whether you knew it or not, you were. Take it to court and they'd find the captain was only protecting his property. In the second place, your man had a pothook in his hand, and he could've brained Archer Spann with it. I'll grant you Spann maybe didn't have to kill him. But he did it, and I expect any jury would acquit him on the grounds of self-defense.

"We got to look at it for what it is, Monahan. Whatever he was to you, to folks around here he was just an old Mexican that nobody knew, in a place where he shouldn't have been."

"Is that the way you feel, McKelvie?"

McKelvie's eyes sharpened as Monahan's pent-up anger reached across to him. "No, it isn't. I hate to see any man die. But I've got to be practical. There's no use putting the county to the expense of arrest and trial of a man the jury's bound to turn loose anyhow. There's nothing you or me can do. You'd just best forget it."

Monahan's hands were tight on the edge of the chair. "Just like that! They kill the old

361

man who brought me up and I'm supposed to forget it."

McKelvie leaned forward, his eyes level and serious. "That and a little more. I'm advising you to gather up whatever loose ends you got around here and leave, Monahan. It's my job to keep the peace, and I got an uneasy feeling it won't be peaceful as long as you stay."

"Is that an order, McKelvie?"

The sheriff shook his head. "Just good advice."

Monahan stood up stiffly. "I'm not ready to go yet. Maybe, like you say, there's nothing I can do about the men who killed Paco. But I'll guarantee you this, I'm not leaving till I try." He turned to go.

"Wait a minute, Monahan," the sheriff said. Monahan looked back at him and saw a coldness in McKelvie's face. "I don't blame you for the way you feel. But I'm not going to let you stir up a lot of trouble. First time you step over the line, I'll bring you in."

"We'll see," Monahan replied thinly.

4

Walking back across the dusty street, Doug Monahan managed to get a tight rein on his anger. He asked Dundee, "What about the sheriff?"

Dundee shrugged. "He didn't say anything that wasn't the truth. McKelvie's a pretty good kind of a man. Punched cattle for the captain a long time ago, till the captain got him made sheriff. It was about like staying on the R Cross payroll. But things have changed here lately. New people comin' in, people that don't figure Rinehart's got any claim on them. Been tough on McKelvie sometimes, I expect, bein' sheriff for them and the captain, too. He wants to be fair, and he's havin' a hard time figuring out what fair is."

They stepped up onto the plank sidewalk that fronted the little saloon where Stub Bailey had gone. The small sign said, TEXAS TOWN, CHRISTOPHER HADLEY, PROP. Two men sat on the edge of the porch, whittling and spitting and soaking up the fleeting sunshine. They stared curiously at Monahan. Doug knew the story had gone all over town, probably all over the county.

It was a shotgun-shaped saloon, narrow in front but somehow longer than it had looked outside. Stub Bailey sat at a table toward the back. The rest of the fencing crew was there with him. The proprietor brought two fresh glasses. Bailey poured the two full from a bottle he had sitting in front of him. He hurriedly drank what was left in his own glass and refilled it too.

"I always like an even start with the crowd," he said.

Monahan took a quick swallow of the whisky and grimaced at its fiery passage. He hadn't really wanted it.

For Bailey, it went down smoother. His glass was half empty when he set it back on the table. "You're all the talk around here today, Doug. Some of the captain's cowboys was in here talking about you when I came in. They finally recognized me and shut up. They were betting on how quick you'd be out of the country."

Doug said dryly, "You ought to've taken a little of their money."

The proprietor had been watching Monahan until he figured out for sure who he was. Now he came back smiling, bringing a bottle.

"Welcome, Mr. Monahan," he said. "My name's Chris Hadley. This is my place." He picked up the bottle Stub had been using and put the other one down in its place. "This is on the house. It's a pleasure to serve someone that's had the nerve to stomp the captain's toes."

Monahan eyed him noncommittally. "I'm afraid you got it backwards, friend. He did all the stomping."

"You're still in town, aren't you?" Hadley replied. He was a shortish man, growing heavy now in his late forties, his hair receding to a light stand far back on his head. There was something about him that made him a little out of place as a saloonkeeper. He bore himself with a dignity which hinted of a better background than this.

Presently Doug heard a stir out in front of the saloon. A couple of cowboys pushed through the door and stood looking over the thin scattering of customers. The pair wore woolen coats, unbuttoned now because the day was not unpleasant. They had on chaps and spurs, and one wore leather gloves. They spotted Monahan and moved toward him.

Monahan stiffened, an angry red ridge running along his cheekbone. The tall one in the lead was Archer Spann.

Spann stopped and stared at Monahan, a vague contempt in his black eyes. "Monahan," he said sharply, "the captain's outside. He wants to see you."

Monahan stood up angrily, changed his mind and sat down again. "Tell him if he wants to see me, he knows where I'm at."

Spann said, "When the captain says come, you come."

"*I* don't." Monahan sat there with a deep anger smoldering in him. He was hoping this grim man would make a move toward him, hoping for an excuse to lay his gunbarrel against that hard jaw and watch those black eyes roll back.

Spann shifted his weight uncertainly from one foot to the other. It was plain enough he wasn't used to running up against a situation like this. But he could not miss the dangerous smoulder in the fence-builder's eyes. Suddenly, he turned and walked out again.

The proprietor moved to the front window and looked outside. "It's Captain Rinehart, all right. He's out front there on that big gray horse of his."

Chris Hadley nervously wiped his dry

hands on his apron. "Four years I've had this place, and the captain's never set foot in it. Folks used to ask him permission to do this or do that. I never did. I put this place up, and I never asked him anything. Couple of years, no R Cross cowboy ever came in, either. But they've been starting to drift in. The old man's word doesn't carry as strongly as it used to."

Spann came in first and held the door open. Captain Andrew Rinehart strode in with stiff dignity. He paused a moment, letting his eyes accustom themselves to the room light.

"He's back here, Captain," Spann spoke, waving his hand toward Monahan.

It took the captain a moment to pick Monahan out. Monahan stood up slowly and pushed his chair back. The captain stopped a full pace in front of the table.

"I thought you'd be gone," the old man said.

Monahan's voice was calmly defiant. "I'm still here."

The cowman's piercing eyes had a way of seeing right through a man without revealing much of what went on behind them. "Maybe you're broke," he said. "I understand you've got some barbed wire stored over at Tracey's Mercantile. I'll buy it from you. That'll give you enough money to be on your way."

Monahan said, "I'm not broke. The point is, I'm not running. I'll leave when I get ready, and I'm not ready."

A sharp edge worked into the captain's voice. "I'm trying to be fair about this, Monahan."

"Like you were yesterday?"

"What happened yesterday wasn't all planned. Sometimes things just happen that weren't figured on atall. You'd better forget it."

Forget it. Twice now Monahan had heard that.

"You burned up my wagons, destroyed my supplies and killed a harmless old man. How do you think I could forget that?"

"Sometimes it's best for a man to make himself forget, Monahan."

"I'll bet *you* never did, Captain. I'll bet you never in your life let a man get away with anything."

A tinge of red worked up the old rancher's ears. "Monahan, I was in this country when you were just a little boy. I came out here when everybody else was afraid to. There were Indians here, but I took the country, and I held it." His beard quivered with emotion. "Other people have come in, sure, but only because I let them. It's still my country. It goes by my rules. They've been fair rules, and one way or another, I've seen that they've been kept.

"People may say I've been a hard man. Well, it took a hard man to run the Indians out. It took a hard man to get rid of the cow thieves. Even yet, there's all kinds of land grabbers and leeches, waiting to move in here the minute I soften up. They'd love to see Kiowa County split apart. And you know how barbed wire can split people apart. It's done it other places, and it would do it here. I'll not allow you to come in and stir up dissension. I've told you to leave. I'll not tell you again!"

Doug Monahan had been standing out of his habitual deference for men older than himself. He realized suddenly what he was doing, and he sat down. He said nothing, but the defiance in his eyes gave his answer. The captain stood there stiff-backed, his old fists doubled.

Spann moved up to the captain's side. "I'll take care of this for you, sir."

"No," said the captain, "no saloon brawl." He had too much pride for that. "You're feeling ringy, Monahan, because one of your men was killed. I'll take that into account for now, but don't crowd your luck." He turned on his heel and strode stiffly out the door.

Spann hung back, watching Monahan. "You won't find me as easy to talk down as the old man."

Monahan replied tightly, "And you won't find me as easy to kill as a poor old Mexican with a pothook in his hand."

The saloonkeeper, Chris Hadley, stood at the window, wiping his hands on his apron as he watched the riders pull away. He came back, a little of nervousness still hanging on him.

"Well, Monahan," he said, "you've made the history books. But what are you going to do now?"

"Build fence, if I can. I'm not running away."

Chris Hadley was more than just a barkeeper. He was a man given to quiet contemplation. He said, "Maybe you're the one, Monahan, I don't know. For a long time we've needed somebody to wake people up and make them stand for their rights. The captain was a great man for his time. He came here when it was a raw, wild land. He tamed it and he built it up. But he got it to a point where it suits him, and now he wants it to stay there. In the old countries, he's what you'd call a benevolent despot."

Monahan said, "What's benevolent about him?"

Hadley shrugged. "There are some good things about him, believe it or not. But he's still a despot, and we've outgrown that kind of man, Monahan. We've outgrown him, but were too weak to do anything about it."

Presently two men came in and walked up to the bar. "Hey, Chris," one said, "wasn't that the captain we saw walking out of here?"

Hadley nodded, and the man whistled softly. "We must be comin' to the end of the world."

The other man said, "I saw the captain ridin' out of town like he was on his way to a lynching. A big bunch of R Cross cowboys was with him. I guess they all left."

"All but one," the first man corrected him. "That Wheeler boy stayed in town."

"Wheeler? Vern Wheeler?" Worry crept into Chris Hadley's voice. "Where did he go?"

"Last I seen he was headed in the direction of your house," the man said, grinning slyly.

Chris Hadley lost interest in his customers. He absently wiped the bar, his troubled gaze pinned on the side window of the saloon. His house lay in that direction.

■ ■ ■ ■

Vern wheeler lacked three months of turning twenty-one. He was a large young man, as husky as his father, old Noah Wheeler. He had a squarish, handsome face with bold, honest features, a picture of what his father must have been thirty years before.

He carried a brashness and a recklessness, though, that were strictly his own. He walked right up to the Hadley house and knocked on the door, standing there on the front porch for all to see him.

Paula Hadley opened the door. Her brown eyes lighted with joy at the sight of him. "Vern Wheeler! What are you doing here?"

"What do you think? I came to see you. You going to make me stand out here in the chill all day?"

She hesitated. "Vern, you know Papa. . . ." Then she opened the door wide. "I guess you might as well come on in. They'll all talk, either way."

He walked in and she closed the door, leaning back against it. She studied him with a happy glow in her brown eyes. Paula Hadley was a slender, small girl who looked even tinier beside big Vern Wheeler. She dressed plainly because her father disapproved of anything else. As she was a saloonkeeper's daughter, austerity was a penalty she had to suffer to keep her beyond suspicion. But nothing could hide the quiet beauty of her face, a beauty enhanced by her happiness now as she looked at Vern Wheeler.

"Gosh, Vern, it's been a long time. Can't you come around more often?"

"You know I'm working, Paula. Captain Rinehart's got me and another feller staked out in a line shack way over on the north end of the ranch."

"You weren't in that incident at that fencing camp, were you?"

"No, I didn't even know about it till it was over."

That brought her relief. "Gosh, Vern," she said again, "it's been a long time. Two months."

"Costs money to come to town, Paula. I'm saving mine. You know why."

She nodded. "I know why. Vern, who's with you in the line camp?"

"Fellow named Lefty Jones. I don't expect you know him."

She shook her head. "I'm glad it's not that red-headed Rooster Preech you used to run around with. I was afraid he'd get you in trouble someday."

"The captain wouldn't give Rooster a job."

"And you know why."

Vern Wheeler smiled. "Rooster's all right. Folks just don't understand him, is all."

"*I* understand him. He's too shiftless to do honest work."

Vern Wheeler moved toward her, grinning. "Honey, I didn't come here to talk about him."

He held his hands out, and she reached forward, taking them. At arm's length they looked at each other.

"Gosh, Paula," he said admiringly, "you sure look pretty." He took her into his arms. "Paula," he said, "why don't we just go and tell your dad about us? Tell him we want to get married."

"Vern, you know how Papa feels about things. He's got his heart dead set on sending me off to school. He scrimped and saved for years. It would just about kill him."

"He's bound to know about us, Paula."

"I guess he does, a little. He just doesn't realize how serious it is between us. But give me time, and I'll find some way to tell him."

"Tell him about the money I'm saving. It won't be like you were just marrying some saddle bum. They're still holding more than a year's wages for me out at the R Cross. I haven't taken a thing out of them except a little tobacco money and a few dollars for clothes.

"I got my eye on a piece of land back yonder in the hills. It's got a good spring on it, and good grass. A little longer, Paula, and I'll be able to buy it, and the stock to go on it. You tell your dad you'll be marrying a man who knows how to work and save and make his money count. We'll amount to something one of these days."

"I know we will, Vern. Don't you worry about Papa. Now you'd better go, before the gossips all get started."

"All right, Paula," he said. "But one of these times I'll take you with me."

He kissed her and walked out. She stood on the porch and blew him a kiss as he swung onto his nervous-eyed sorrel bronc. Showing off a little, he jabbed his thumbs into the bronc's neck. The sorrel went pitching off down the street, Vern Wheeler laughing and waving back at Paula.

Chris Hadley came walking up as Vern's bronc eased down into a trot, his back still humped. Hadley stood at his front gate, frowning, watching the young cowboy disappear.

"You're home early, Papa," Paula said in surprise as he walked into the small house. "I don't have supper ready yet."

"Business wasn't much, and I wasn't feeling very good anyway," he replied. He watched the girl worriedly as she put on an apron and moved into the kitchen. He followed her, leaning against the kitchen door.

"Vern Wheeler was here, wasn't he?" he asked.

"He came by to see me."

"You let him in the house?"

She paused. "Papa, we wouldn't do anything we shouldn't. You know that."

"I know, Paula, but some of the neighbors around here don't. You've got to remember, you're a saloonkeeper's daughter. With some people it doesn't matter whether you did anything wrong or not. The only thing they see is that you *could* have."

He walked over to the stove and checked the coffee pot. "Paula, I'm going to send you back where you can be with good people, like your mother's folks were."

Impatience came into her voice. "I can remember them. When I was just a little girl, after Mother died, you took me back to see them. They wouldn't have anything to do with us, not you or me either. They were too good for us, remember, Papa? Your family had lost its money, so we weren't good enough."

"It wasn't you they didn't like, Paula, it

376

was me. They didn't want me to marry your mother. We ran off and got married anyway, and it turned out just the way they said it would. We drifted around from one sorry place to another. I dragged your mother down, just like they said."

"Did she ever complain, Papa?"

"She wasn't the kind who would. But I ruined her life. Now I want to make it up. I want you to have the things she never could have."

"Maybe they're not the things I want."

Chris Hadley studied his daughter intently. "Paula, I know how it is when you're young, but I want you to listen to me. Vern's a good boy, I'll grant you that, but look at him. Look at any of these people. Look at those women over on Oak Creek. Do you think I want you to wind up like them someday, washed out, worn out, all their hope and spirit gone? I'm not going to let it happen." He shook his head. "Paula, I don't want you to see him again, ever."

5

The Oak Creek section had always been considered some of the sorriest rangeland in Postoak County. Its grass was stemmy and lacking in strength. The country had a tendency to go to scrub brush, which didn't leave a lot of room for grass in the first place. In the days when no one had ranged this country but Captain Rinehart, most of his cattle had kept out of the Oak Creek section of their own will. Only a few scattering cows of the bunch-quitter type stayed down there much. There were cattle like that, just as there were that kind of men.

But the section had one thing in its favor, the creek itself. Water was always a big consideration in West Texas, where rainfall came only when it got good and ready and could never be depended upon.

So when the farmers began to move in, they started locating on Oak Creek. At first there was resistance on the part of some of the cowmen. A few of the earliest farmers took the hint and moved out again. But as time went on, it became obvious that the farmers couldn't be squeezed out forever.

Captain Andrew Rinehart circulated the word, and the farmers were allowed to settle along Oak Creek. If there had to be farmers, then it was better that they be concentrated in one place than to have them bringing in the Texas Rangers and scattering all over the county, breaking up the rangeland, the captain said. Besides, there were some advantages to having a few farmers around. Cowmen could buy hay from them, and vegetables and butter and the like. When the farm work wasn't pressing too hard, the ranchers could hire the farmers to do the menial jobs that most of their cowhands scorned doing.

Only one farmer had broken the pattern. Without a word to anybody, without even a tip of the hat to Captain Rinehart, Noah Wheeler had bought land scrip for four sections right in the middle of the best rangeland and moved his family out from East Texas.

There had been some bitter talk about it. Fuller Quinn, angry-faced ranchman on Wagonrim Creek, was in favor of riding over there in force and burning the farmer out before he could get himself fairly settled. "Let that nester squat there and he'll attract others. They'll crowd us right off the grass!"

Actually, Quinn was doing more crowding than anybody. He had built up his herd of Longhorns until it was too big for the range he controlled. He let them spill over into his neighbors' country, let them trample across the planted fields along Oak Creek. The one thing about which he was careful was that his line riders keep them turned well back from Captain Rinehart's country.

Unexpectedly, and without any explanation, Captain Rinehart had vetoed action against Noah Wheeler. "If any other farmers start looking over his way, we can quietly discourage them," he said. "But Wheeler will stay where he is."

So they'd left Wheeler alone, and some of the cowmen had come to like him. Wheeler was no ordinary squatter. He had a far-reaching way of looking beyond things as they were now and seeing how they could be. He had turned some of the cowmen into good customers for the feed he raised. A stockman himself, he had sold many of them on the idea of improving their beef by using better breeds of bulls.

But one thing hadn't changed. The other farmers had stayed on Oak Creek. There, more or less congregated, they could turn back most of the stray cattle which worked in from the open ranges around them. True, when the crops were good, some of Fuller Quinn's cattle always seemed to find their way into the best fields. Nobody ever caught Quinn or his men drifting them in there, and there probably wasn't much a farmer could have done about it if he had. Still, it was a constant source of irritation that a good stand of corn might be ruined in a hurry if the farmer was not eternally vigilant.

So it was that Doug Monahan had received expressions of interest from several Oak Creek farmers even before he had started the ill-fated fencing job for Gordon Finch.

"Slick wire and brush enclosures just won't turn them cattle when they're hungry," complained Foster Lodge. "It's got so I have to chase three or four Quinn heifers out of my oat patch every mornin'. I'd like to try a little of that there bobwire, if the price was right."

"I'll make it right," Monahan had promised. "Just as soon as I finish this job for Finch, I'll be over."

The Finch job had finished abruptly. Now, this sharply cool winter morning, Doug

Monahan was on his way a-horseback toward Oak Creek. Short, burly Stub Bailey rode beside him to point the way.

"That yonder's Lodge's place," Bailey said finally as they splashed their horses across cold Oak Creek. "I expect Lodge is about the best farmer there is along the crick here. But he don't hold a candle to Noah Wheeler, even at that."

Lodge's place was smaller but neat and well kept, even as Noah Wheeler's had been. Grubbed-up brush ringed his fields, giving the whole thing some appearance of a bird's nest. Doug thought that was where the word nester came from. Lodge had a good set of pens for his work and milk stock. It struck Monahan that these pens were patterned after those of Noah Wheeler.

"They all copy Wheeler, don't they?" he said.

"You see a man doing the right kind of a job, you're foolish if you don't model after him some."

Foster Lodge still lived in the original dugout he had carved back into a hillside. A sign of improving times was that he now had a tin covering over the original sod roof. It would turn the water, where the sod never did. There was a fairly new lean-to, built of lumber, probably raised for propriety when the children began to grow up.

Lodge heard the barking of his dogs and met Doug and Stub at the door. "Come in, come in. Too cool to stand around outside. Did all my chores and hustled myself back in here where it's warm."

A cast-iron cook stove threw welcome heat. Dry mesquite stumps and roots were piled in a box behind the stove, along with axe-cut dry mesquite limbs.

Mrs. Lodge, a thin, morose woman who acted as if she resented the company, came out and poured them some coffee. Lodge avoided the sharp cut of her eyes. Doug figured she had him buffaloed. Like too many others, she probably had resented leaving security and the small comforts somewhere farther east to try to build something better out here in a raw new land. He was glad when she retreated into the lean-to room and closed the door.

Doug said, "I came to see if you're still interested in having some fence built. We're not busy now. We could start any time."

Lodge made no sign that he knew what had happened to the Finch job. He hadn't been to town, Doug guessed.

"Well, yes I am," Lodge said. "I've talked with some of my neighbors. We been thinkin' we might all have some fence built and share the cost where we can share a fence."

"It would sure save you a lot of damage from stray cattle."

Lodge frowned. "Right there's the only hitch, Monahan. All of us own a little livestock, too — milk cows, work horses and mules, a few beef critters. Some of the boys don't quite trust this bobwire. If it cuts up some of Fuller Quinn's strays, so much the better. But they're afraid it might cut up our own stock, too."

"It won't," Doug assured him, "not after they get used to it."

"I don't know," Lodge commented doubtfully. "It's mean-lookin' stuff. They're goin' to have to see proof, I'm afraid, before they'll go through with it."

Monahan chewed his lip, thinking darkly. How could he show them proof when there wasn't a barbed wire fence anywhere around? Then he remembered an exhibition he had seen in San Antonio.

"I believe I can prove it to where it'll satisfy all of you," he said. "Would you be willing to gamble a few head of cattle on it?"

Lodge frowned. "Gamble? Well now, I'm not a rich man. I ain't got enough livestock to go gamblin' with them."

"Then *I'll* do the gambling," Doug said.

"I'll guarantee to pay you for any cattle that get crippled or cut up bad."

"What do you figure on doing?"

"I'll pick out a spot someplace on the creek here, where everybody can see it. I'll put up a good-sized barbed wire corral and turn cattle into it. You'll see how quick they learn what the wire's there for." He studied Foster Lodge. "If it proves out all right, and you men are satisfied that it won't hurt your stock, will you contract with me to build the fence?"

Lodge thoughtfully rubbed his jaw. "Personally, I'd go along with it. I think I can speak for the others. You give the boys a good show and you've got yourself a job, Monahan."

Captain Andrew Rinehart swung stiffly down from his big gray horse and stood a moment holding on to the horn, steadying himself. He was bone-tired after a full day in the saddle. This weariness made him angry at himself, for he used to ride all day and half the night without tiring so.

"Need some help, Captain?" Archer Spann had walked up behind him, leading his own horse.

"No, thank you," Rinehart said firmly.

"You're tired. I can unsaddle for you."

With a flare of impatience the captain replied, "I've always saddled and unsaddled my own horses. I see no need to change that now."

He loosened the girth and slid the saddle and blanket off the gray's back, letting them ease to the ground. He patted the horse on the neck. The captain had always loved horses. Especially gray horses. That was all he rode anymore. There was something about a gray horse that gave a man stature.

He pulled the bridle off and watched the horse turn away. The gray walked across the broad corral, nose to the ground. When he found a place that suited him, he dropped down, hind legs first, and rolled in the dust. This was a sight that had always been restful to the captain. Out of ancient habit he counted the rolls. One, two, three. A horse is worth a hundred dollars for every time he rolls over, the old saying went. Three hundred dollars.

I couldn't roll over once anymore, he thought. *I'm not worth much.*

"Anything else that needs doing tonight?" Archer Spann asked.

"Nothing, thank you," the captain said, jerked back to reality. He hoisted his saddle up onto a wooden rack, placing the blanket on top of it to dry the sweat out. He watched

Spann walking away from the barn, and he felt a momentary regret for having spoken so sharply to his foreman.

Spann was quiet and coldly efficient. There was nothing in the way of ranch work that he couldn't do, and do better than anyone else on the payroll. He would get it done quickly and well, with little lost motion, or emotion. Just as the captain himself had done in his younger days. With others, Spann was sometimes harsh, even overbearing. He had little patience with other men's errors, and he seldom made one of his own.

He had an inner, relentless drive that the captain had seen in few men. Occasionally, without warning, Spann could burst into sudden violence, as he had done that day at Monahan's fencing camp.

The captain had instantly regretted that killing. If anybody had needed killing, it had been Gordon Finch, a land-hungry coward who had tried to use someone else to take for him what he lacked the guts to take for himself. Doug Monahan, the captain was convinced now, had been no more than a victim of circumstance. There had been a time, the next day, when the captain would have been willing to make restitution, if it could have been done quietly and honorably.

Now it had gone too far. However innocently Monahan had wandered into this situation, he had now set himself up against Rinehart. From now on, he could only be regarded as an enemy.

Darkness was drawing down over Rinehart's ranch headquarters, and with it came the sharp chill of the late-winter night. Rinehart drew his coat tightly around him. Even the cold bothered him more than it used to. Rheumatism had set up a dull ache in his shoulder, where he had stopped an arrow in a fight with the Comanches way back yonder, while he was a Ranger.

Rinehart wearily climbed the wooden steps to his high front porch. His boots clumped heavily, the spurs jingling sharply in the cold night air. He pushed open the door of the big rock house, and he heard Sarah call, "Is that you, Andrew?"

She always asked that, every time he came in. It had been the same for forty years. With Sarah, it was a manner of greeting rather than an actual question. She had never failed to greet him at the door in the good young years.

Now she was ailing and often had to remain in her bed. Age was catching up with Sarah, too. But she was never too sick to call out to him as he came in. He dreaded the day he would walk into this big old house and not hear that voice.

Automatically he removed his hat. The ranch might be the captain's, but the house was his wife's. He walked into the bedroom and saw her lying there in the gloom.

"You're awfully late, Andrew," she scolded, but her voice was soft with affection.

"It's so dark in here," he said. "Why didn't you have Josefa light the lamp?" He struck a match and lighted the wick, clamping the shining glass chimney back into place.

"Dusk," she said. "It's restful to tired eyes."

She reached out and touched his hand. The captain sat down on the edge of the bed, looking at her. It angered him somehow that he could do nothing for her. He had always been a strong man. All his life, what he had wanted to do, he did. What he wanted to have, he took. When he spoke, men moved. His power had been great.

Yet now he had no power to help this woman he loved. Sometimes she was up and about for two or three weeks at a time. Then she would be down again, weak and helpless as a child. Lately he had begun to consider how life would be without her. It was an empty and terrible thing to contemplate.

"Doctor been out today?" he asked.

She nodded. "He just left some more of those awful pills. I think he uses them to keep his patients sick, so he'll have a steady income."

He was grateful for the good humor he could see in her eyes. Sarah had always been his refuge. When things went wrong, Sarah always seemed to be able to muster a smile from somewhere and make misfortune easier to take.

"I sent for Luke McKelvie," he said. "Has he been here?"

"He came in about sundown. He went down to the cookshack to eat."

Rinehart stood up. "I'll go on down there, then. I need to talk to him."

Sarah reached out and caught his sleeve. "Andrew, I want to ask you about Charley Globe."

"What about Charley?"

"He came up here today and told me he's quitting. Andrew, Charley's been with us ever since we came up to this country. He's one of the few real old-timers."

The captain frowned. "What's eating Charley?"

"It's Archer Spann. Archer's too abrupt with him. Charley feels he's entitled to some extra consideration around here occasionally because he's been with us so long. He's getting old, and he can't always keep up. He doesn't like to be browbeaten by some younger man. And what happened over at that fencing camp the other day didn't set well with Charley, either. Andrew, you've got to do something about Archer Spann."

Rinehart said defensively, "Archer's a good man, Sarah, the best man we ever had. Sure, he's hard. But it takes a hard man, sometimes."

"But you'll talk to him, won't you? And to Charley?"

"I'll talk to him. And I won't let Charley quit."

The cookshack and bunkhouse were combined in one long L-shaped frame building. Captain Rinehart walked up the steps and onto the porch where the washbasins were. He found Luke McKelvie sitting there in the near-darkness, smoking a cigarette.

"Evening, Captain," the sheriff said, standing up.

"Evening." They shook hands.

McKelvie said pleasantly, "The place never changes, Captain. It's just the same as it was when I worked here. Even after all these years, this is the only place that seems like home to me."

"No," the captain agreed, "it doesn't

change. As long as things suit us, there's no reason why they should ever change, is there?"

McKelvie shook his head. "I reckon not." Then he said, "Cook's got a good supper fixed in there. You ought to eat a bite."

Damn it, the captain thought, *they're all trying to take care of me like an old man.* "Supper'll wait. I've got something more important. Have you heard what that fellow Monahan is up to?"

The sheriff nodded. "A little."

"You know he's been keeping some wire down at Tracey's Mercantile. He's taken some of it out, and he's hauled several loads of cedar posts out to Oak Creek. He's putting up some sort of a barbed wire corral."

McKelvie said, "I know. I was out there. He's going to run a bunch of stock into it to show the farmers that bobwire won't kill their animals."

"You know what he's fixing to do, don't you, Luke? He's trying to get those farmers to let him fence their land for them."

"I understand he's already got them sold, if he can show them that the stock won't be hurt."

Already sold! That jarred the captain a little.

"Luke, you've got to stop it."

"Stop it?" McKelvie dropped his cigarette and ground it under his boot. "How?"

"I don't care how. Throw him in jail. Run him out of town. Why should I have to tell you how?"

"Look, Captain, I can't just jail a man or run him out of town because I don't like him, or don't like what he's doing. As long as he's not breaking the law, I can't touch him."

"Luke, you know what that wire can do to this country! It's always been an open range. It's been *our* range. Once a few of the farmers start, some of the ranchers will. In a couple of years they'll have the range cut up into a hundred pieces. We'll be fenced off from half of our water. The cattle won't be able to graze free with the rain and the grass. When the dry spells come, they won't be able to move the way they used to. They'll stay right there and graze it and tromp it into the dust, and there won't be anything left."

McKelvie sat down again. "I don't know how we can stop it. If it's a man's own land, it's his land, and that's all there is to it. There's no legal way."

The captain's voice grew heated. "If we can't stop it legally, then we'll stop it some other way. But stop it we will!"

"If we find a legal way, fine. Otherwise, Captain, you'll have to count me out."

"Luke, are you forgetting who put you in there as sheriff? Are you forgetting who you're working for?"

"I'm not forgetting anything. Sure, you got me put in office a long time ago. You've kept me in, and I'm grateful for it. You've been like a father to me, Captain. Over the years, I've admired you more than any man I ever knew. But there are other people in the county now. I'm working for them, too. Don't make it any harder for me than it already is."

"I counted on you to stand by me, Luke. Sometimes it seems like I haven't got many friends I can rely on anymore."

"I'm your friend, Captain. And as your friend, I'm telling you to not do anything rash. The old days are gone."

McKelvie stood up again and extended his hand. "Good night, Captain."

Curtly Rinehart said, "Good night," and turned away.

The old days are gone, McKelvie had said. Not yet they weren't!

Old age may be beginning to slow me, but it hasn't got me down, the captain thought angrily. *I'm not going to quit while there's any fight left in me. There was a time when nobody ever questioned me. I knew what was good for this country, and I saw that it got done. People recognized that I was right.*

Now I'm slowing down. I can't get around like I used to. My eyesight's getting bad. I can't see all that's going on around me. But I can see enough to know that they're beginning to point their fingers at me and talk. They're coming in all the time now, these new ones, looking enviously on what I have and plotting to steal it away from me.

Damn them, if it hadn't been for me there wouldn't be anything here! I fought for this range, and bled for it and sweated for it. Now they think because I'm getting old that they can take it away from me! But I've still got friends. I've still got men with the old spirit. They'll find out the R Cross is as strong as it ever was. . . .

Archer Spann walked out of the cook-shack.

A hard man, some said about Spann. But he was a man you could depend on when you needed something done.

"Archer," the captain said, "come walk out to the barn with me. We've got some talking to do."

6

The fencing job went off smoothly enough. The ground near Oak Creek was not rocky, so the digging was not too hard work. By themselves Doug Monahan and Stub Bailey set the posts and strung up the red barbed wire. It was a square corral about a hundred feet long on each side, with a wire gate in one corner and short wings just off the gate to help in penning cattle.

Because it was a temporary job, just for exhibition, they hadn't dug the holes as deep as usual, nor done as tight a job of stringing wire. But it was sufficient for the purpose.

"There she is," Doug told Foster Lodge. "Ready to go. The more people we can get out, the better."

He looked toward Lodge's milk pen. "Folks'll always come out if you offer to feed 'em. You got a fat calf we might butcher?"

Lodge frowned. "Well, there's one out there, but I'm not a rich man, Monahan, and I got a family. You know, I can't . . ."

"I figured on buying it from you, Mr. Lodge. *I'll* give the barbecue."

Lodge brightened. "In that case, now, I reckon maybe I could. . . ."

When they got off to one side, Stub Bailey worriedly caught Monahan's arm. "You sure you know what you're doing? That's a wicked-lookin' corral. One bad break and you'll own a bunch of cut-up cattle."

Monahan said, "I don't think so. We'll let them ease in there and get a smell at the fence. Once they know the wire will stick them, they're not apt to hit it very hard."

"I hope you're right. But you're sure givin' a cowbrute credit for an awful lot of sense."

It looked for a while as if the milk-pen calf wasn't going to be enough. Even Foster Lodge was amazed at the size of the crowd which turned out for the exhibition. Every farmer on Oak Creek was there, along with his family. The kids played up and down the creek and among the trees. They hadn't been there long until one of them fell in the icy water, and a farmer had to grab him up and rush him to the Lodges' dugout, where the women gathered to exchange gossip. Mrs. Lodge was an unwilling hostess, but she managed to cover it up fairly well when the rest of the women began arriving.

Even though Doug had hired a couple of out-of-work ranch cooks to prepare the dinner, many of the women had brought along cakes and pies anyway. It was a good thing, because most wagon cooks couldn't have baked a cake, even if they'd wanted to.

A good many people from Twin Wells were on hand, too, for a look at this new curiosity. Albert Brown, the portly old banker, had left the lending institution in the able care of his teller and was at the barbecue. He was shaking hands and exchanging pleasantries with everybody he could get around to. He seemed to be laughing all the time. One banker who could refuse you a loan and make you feel good about it, Monahan thought.

Three or four of the smaller ranchers from up at the head of Oak Creek were there, too, rubbing shoulders with the farmers and townspeople. These were likable men, and Monahan spent what extra time he could find visiting with them. They were like the neighbors he had known in South Texas, before the drought.

Most of the men spent their time down around the corral, feeling of the wire, testing its strength. More than one of them tore his shirt.

"A taste of this," Doug heard one of them say, "oughta ruin the appetite of them Fuller Quinn cows."

"If Quinn had to pay me for all the feed his stock has ruined, he'd be out twistin' rabbits, he'd be so broke," another said.

Sheriff Luke McKelvie rode out about mid-morning. He didn't have much to say, just stood around and watched, and listened. Once he walked up to look the fence over. He shook his head distastefully as he fingered the sharp barbs.

Still siding with the captain, Doug Monahan thought. He wondered if McKelvie had something up his sleeve.

"Monahan," the sheriff asked, "what do you figure on getting out of all this?"

"A living, Sheriff. You make yours keeping the peace. I make mine putting up fences."

McKelvie grinned dryly, and there wasn't much humor in him. "You're making it darned hard for me to keep the peace. There's lots of people around here who don't like your bobwire."

"But there are lots who *do* like it and need it."

McKelvie frowned. "It's your right to build it, I reckon, and I can't stop you. But I'll tell you frankly, Monahan, I don't like the stuff. It's been a pretty good country, just the way it was. Maybe I'm just old-fashioned, but I don't want to see it changed."

"Change is the only thing you can be sure of in this world."

McKelvie hunkered down and watched the farmers examining the corral. "Look at it like a cowman — that's where your main opposition is going to come from. Bobwire, once it gets started, will cut him off from a lot of watering places, and a lot of free range he's always used. It'll cut him off from the trails he's accustomed to following to market.

"Then there's the extra cattle you always find on the open range. They don't belong there, but you got to figure on 'em. Maybe the barber or the saloonkeeper or the mercantile man have twenty or thirty head apiece. A lot of cowboys, too, have a handful of cattle in their own brand. They just turn 'em loose and let 'em run on the free range.

"As the country closes up, those people will find themselves crowded off first one place, then another. They'll double up wherever the range isn't fenced yet, and make it hard on the ranchers who hold out to the last before they give in and fence too.

Eventually it'll freeze the free-grass man plumb out.

"Then, look at it the way the cowboy will. It takes a lot of cowboys to keep a cow outfit running, the country wide open like it is. But you cut this land up into little pieces, it won't take near as many men to work it. A lot of those boys'll be out of a job, and they're smart enough to see that already."

Monahan nodded soberly. "You've got some good points there, Sheriff, but look at it from the other side. As long as the range is wide open, how can a man develop his own land, other people's cattle crowding into his water and onto his grass? A range hog like this Fuller Quinn keeps throwing more cattle on the range all the time and squeezing the other outfits. The rancher can't breed up his own herd much because so many stray bulls are running around loose. Cow thieves can latch onto a man's cattle and carry them off, and he'll never miss 'em till branding time.

"But you put a fence around him, now, and he can do what he pleases. He can build up the best cattle in the country if he's a mind to. He can fence the range hogs out. He can put a crimp in the cow thief because it won't be easy to put stolen cattle across half a dozen fences and not get caught somewhere.

"What I'm getting at, I guess, is that with the fence the country will finally be permanent. It'll produce more and make a living for more people. There'll be more towns, and they'll be bigger ones. Sure, barbed wire is going to hurt some people. But it'll help a lot more of them than it hurts."

McKelvie had rolled a cigarette. He licked the edge of the brown paper and stuck it down, then sat there with it in his fingers. He eyed Monahan keenly.

"We're both putting up some pretty talk, Monahan. Now let's just break down and get honest with each other. I meant all I said, but I reckon the main reason I'm against your wire is because it's going to hurt the captain. You can't understand this, maybe, but he's been a great man in his day.

"And when we come right down to it, you're not really much interested in the people of Kiowa County, or whether they get their land fenced or not. If it hadn't been for what happened in your camp the other day, you'd've probably left here and everything would've been peaceful. But now you're mad, and you got a hate worked up for the captain. You're determined to stomp on him, and nothing else matters much to you."

Monahan shifted uncomfortably. "I'm going through with it, McKelvie. It's too far gone to pull back now, even if I wanted to."

McKelvie nodded. "I knew you would. But I wanted you to know how I stand." He stood up stiffly and started to move away. He paused a moment and turned back around. "There must be an awful emptiness in a man, Monahan, when all that matters to him is revenge."

The barbecue was about done, and Monahan was getting ready to call the crowd to dinner when a young cowboy rode up looking for McKelvie.

"Sheriff," he said when he found him, "there's been a fight down at the T Bars. They sent me to get you."

McKelvie studied the boy, debating whether he ought to go. "What kind of a fight? Anybody hurt?"

"I don't know, Sheriff. I wasn't there. They just sent me to get you."

McKelvie cast a worried glance at the barbed wire corral, then at Monahan. "All right, son," he said then, "let's go."

Monahan ladled out red beans to the crowd. Stub Bailey stood beside him, forking barbecue onto tin plates as the people came by in single file.

"When that banker Brown comes up," Monahan said, "be sure you give him plenty. He's liable to be lending the money for a lot of fence."

After a while the crowd had finished eating.

"They sure didn't leave much of that calf," Bailey remarked ruefully. He had been one of the last to get to eat, and he hadn't found much that was to his liking.

"So much the better," Doug said. "The more there are, the more fence we may get to build."

Once fed, the crowd was getting restless, wanting to see something.

"All right, Stub," Doug said, "it's time to give 'em the show."

The cattle they wanted were scattered in a green oat patch behind Lodge's barn. The two horsemen circled them slowly and eased them down toward the creek. Some were gentle milk stock, but a few showed a strong mixture of wild Longhorn blood. These part-Longhorns were quick to take the lead, stepping long and high and holding their heads up, looking for a booger.

They didn't have much trouble finding it. With women's billowing skirts and the shouting of playing youngsters, the cattle kept shying away from the crowd. Not until the third try did Monahan and Bailey manage to get them to the wings and push them into the corral. Monahan rode through the gate, stepping down to close it from inside.

The cattle pushed on to the far side of the corral and stopped there, nervously smelling of the barbed wire. This was something new to them, and they distrusted it, especially the high-headed Longhorns. Some of them jerked their heads back and pulled away when they touched their noses to the sharp barbs. A couple of the gentler cows licked at the wire until they hit a barb.

Monahan allowed the cattle a few minutes to get used to the enclosure. Then he rode in behind them, slapping his rope against his leg to get them milling. They circled around and around the fence, looking vainly for a way out, but never did they let themselves brush against the wire.

The crowd had worked down to the corral now.

"By George," a farmer exclaimed, "that's not half as bad as it looks. They got onto it in a hurry." He pulled back from the fence and ripped a hole in his coat.

"They learn faster than *you* do," his wife commented.

Deciding the crowd had seen enough to convince them, Monahan stepped down and led his horse through the gate. He left the cattle inside.

Walking up to Foster Lodge and a dozen others who had gathered around him, Monahan asked, "Well, what do you think now?"

Lodge replied with satisfaction, "I reckon you proved what you set out to. And you don't owe for any cattle. We're ready to talk business."

"There'll never be a better time."

Monahan had been so intent in watching the reactions of the bystanders that he hadn't seen anything else. Now he heard a murmur of alarm move through the crowd. He saw a woman point excitedly, and he turned quickly to see what the trouble was.

A group of cowboys, maybe twenty in number, had ridden up to the opposite side of the creek. Now they came spurring across, splashing the cold water high. Gaining the bank, they spread out in a line and moved into a lope, yelling and swinging ropes. A few fired guns into the air.

Women screamed and grabbed up their children. Bigger boys and girls lit out for the protection of the oak timber. Men pulled back in a hard trot away from the corral.

Caught by surprise, not carrying a gun,

Monahan only stood and watched the cowboys coming, the dust boiling up behind their horses. The line split. The riders circled around his corral. Ropes snaked out and tightened over fence posts loosely tamped in the dry dirt. Riders spurred away, their horses straining as they began pulling the fence down.

The cattle inside were running wildly from one end of the pen to the other. Now, seeing the fence go down, they made a panicked break for the opening. Some cleared the wire, but others jumped into it, hanging their legs and threshing desperately as cowboys yelled and pushed them on. Most of them watched as the cowboys finished destruction of the corral badly. Two steers were hopelessly enmeshed, legs tangled in the vicious wire. They lay there, fighting in terror.

Archer Spann rode up, gun drawn. He stared coldly at Monahan and leaned over, firing twice. The steers stopped threshing.

Most of the crowd had retreated to the oak timber and watched as the cowboys finished destruction of the corral. Monahan stood in helpless rage, knowing there was nothing he could do to stop it.

In a few minutes it was over. The corral was down, a hopeless tangle of wire and posts. The cowboys gathered on either side of Archer Spann. One who somehow had fallen into the wire had his woolen shirt ripped half away, and he was holding one arm that appeared to be badly cut. A couple of the others were looking it over. Spann turned his horse so that he faced the crowd in the trees.

"You folks listen to this," he said loudly, "and you'd better remember. The captain says tell you there'll not be any bobwire fences!"

He turned away from the crowd and faced Monahan, who stood alone out there in the open. "As for you, Monahan," he said evenly, "this means you pull out of the country and stay out. The next time, you'll *eat* that wire!"

Monahan's fists were clenched, and his face darkened. "I swear to you, Spann," he said bitterly, "I'll even up with you if it takes me twenty years."

Sheriff Luke McKelvie solemnly looked over the tangled wire and pulled-up posts and the two dead cattle. "I got back out here as quick as I could. I thought there was something suspicious, that boy being sent to fetch me. It was a trick, all right, to get me out of the way."

Monahan shrugged angrily, not knowing whether to believe the sheriff or not. It could have been a put-up job.

"Not much we can do about it now, Sheriff, unless you're willing to arrest the men that did it."

McKelvie caught the doubting edge in Monahan's voice, and it irked him. "I can and I will, if you'll sign the complaints. But even if you get them in jail, there's not much you can do. Under Texas law it's nothing more than a misdemeanor to cut or tear down another man's fence. If I throw them in jail, the captain will bail them out, and the judge will give them the lightest fine he can because he's in debt to the captain."

"Wouldn't hardly pay me then, would it, McKelvie?" Monahan asked with bitterness.

McKelvie shook his head. "Not hardly."

Monahan and Stub Bailey rode back to town with the sheriff.

Monahan said, "I thought of one thing I could get Spann for. It's a felony to shoot a man's cattle, isn't it?"

The sheriff said, "Yes, but they were Foster Lodge's cattle at the time they were shot. Do you think Lodge would prefer charges?"

Monahan grudgingly answered, "No, I don't reckon he would." Disappointment was still heavy on his shoulders. He had come so close to selling those farmers. Then, suddenly, the whole thing had blown up in his face. They had backed away from the project as they would from a loaded shotgun.

"You saw them, Monahan," Foster Lodge had said excitedly, his face half white. "The captain's men and some of Fuller Quinn's, too. We can't fight those big outfits. We don't aim to try."

The sheriff pulled up as they passed the big rock courthouse. "Whatever you decide, let me know. But I think you should forget it and leave town."

"Thanks for the advice," Monahan said angrily, not even looking back at him. He headed across the street for Hadley's saloon. If there had ever been a time he needed a drink, this was it.

Oscar Tracey, the mercantile man, saw him from the front porch of his store and hailed him. Monahan hesitated, not knowing whether he wanted to talk to anybody right now or not. But he reined his horse over to Tracey's.

Tracey, a tall, sickly-thin old man, came down off the porch steps in great agitation. "Come around back with me, Mr. Monahan. I've got something to show you."

Monahan and Stub Bailey followed the old storekeeper around the side of the building and out the back. There, in a smouldering pile of ashes and snarled black wire, lay all that was left of the many spools of barbed wire Doug had stored in the shed back of the mercantile.

"They came in here a while before dinnertime," Tracey said. "They took out your wire and piled it on a bunch of old lumber scraps that was lying there. They poured kerosene on the whole mess and set it afire. They said if I ever had another roll of barbed wire in my place, they'd burn the whole store down."

The storekeeper's voice was high-pitched with apprehension. "I'm sorry, Mr. Monahan. I'd like to do anything I could to help you, but you can see what I'm up against. I'm too old to start over again. I've got to protect what I have. You see that, don't you?"

Monahan nodded gravely. "I see it, all right. I'm obliged for all you've done, and I won't ask you to take any chances for me. Looks like I'm out of the fence-building business around here anyway."

Shoulders slumped, he pulled his horse around and headed across to Hadley's saloon. Bailey caught up with him.

"You mean you're giving in, Doug? You're leaving?"

Doug Monahan shrugged. "I don't see what else I can do." His jaw tightened. "But on my way out, I'm going to hunt down Archer Spann and beat him half to death!"

They walked into Chris Hadley's place and moved toward the back. Hadley brought a bottle and a couple of glasses. In his eyes was a quiet sympathy. The news already had reached town.

"Tough day," he said.

Monahan nodded sourly and took a stiff drink.

Hadley said, "So Captain Rinehart's still the big man on the gray horse." He shook his head regretfully. "It could be a good country for a lot of people, but it'll never amount to much as long as the captain's sitting up there like God, holding it back with his fist. For a little while I thought maybe this would be the time. I thought we'd fight our way out from under."

Noah Wheeler moved through the front door, closing it behind him. He sighted Doug Monahan and came walking back, his big frame blocking off much of the light from the front window.

"Been looking for you, Mr. Monahan."

Monahan stood up and shook the old

412

farmer's hand. "Nice to see you again, Mr. Wheeler." He motioned with his hand, and Wheeler sat down.

"Have a drink with us?"

Wheeler said hesitantly, "Well, I'm not much of a drinking man. . . ."

"Neither am I," Monahan replied morosely, "but this seems to be an occasion for it." Trying to shake his dark mood, he asked, "How is everybody?"

"Fine. Just fine."

"Did your cow ever have that calf you were looking for?"

Instantly he saw that he had touched a nerve. Wheeler's lips tightened. "She had the calf." He fingered the glass, frowning. "Best cow I ever had, old Roany. And Sancho, there's not a better bull in all of West Texas. For months I've waited, wanting to see what that calf was going to turn out like. Well, it got here, all right."

He turned his glass up and finished it. "It wasn't from Sancho atall. It was from one of Fuller Quinn's scrub bulls. Big, long-legged calf, spotted with every color in the rainbow. Just a pure-dee scrub."

The old farmer turned his eyes to Monahan, and Monahan could see keen disappointment in them. "I want to have a good herd, and the only way I can build it is with good calves out of cows like Roany. I'll never get the job done as long as any old stray bull can come across my land. So I want one of your fences, Mr. Monahan!"

Monahan almost choked on his drink. He got it down. "Are you sure you know what you're saying?"

Wheeler nodded. "I'm sure. Three days now I've thought it over. I want you to build me a fence."

"Haven't you heard what happened today out on Oak Creek?"

"I heard."

"And you still want to go on?"

"It's *my* land," Wheeler said stubbornly.

Deep inside, conscience was telling Doug Monahan not to agree. Angered because of that scrub calf, the old man might not fully realize what he was letting himself in for. Conscience said to turn him down.

But Doug Monahan paid no attention to his conscience. Suddenly he felt a wild elation, a soaring of spirit. Out of defeat had come his chance.

"Then, come hell or high water," he declared, "we'll build you that fence!"

7

Doug Monahan walked up to the town's smaller livery stable and found the owner out front, patiently hitching a skittish young sorrel to a two-wheeled horse-breaking gig, a light buggy with long shafts that would keep the animal from kicking it to pieces. Doug watched with interest while the man tied a rope on one of the pony's forefeet, then drew it up through the ring on the hames.

"He starts to run," the liveryman volunteered, "I'll just pick up that forefoot. He can't make much speed on three legs."

Cautiously the man climbed up on the rig, and it looked as if the horse was going to break and run. "Whoa now, be gentle," the man said in a soothing voice.

"You seen Dundee?" Doug asked quickly, for it looked as if the horse was going to run anyway. "They told me he was here."

The liveryman pointed with his chin and

took a tight hold on the reins. "Out back yonder, shoeing his horse." The sorrel moved forward, quickly stretching into a long-reaching trot, looking back nervously at the rig which wheeled along behind. The liveryman had him under full control.

Doug glanced up and grinned at a sign over the door: COWBOY, SPIT ON YOUR MATCH OR EAT IT. A livery stable fire was a thing to dread.

Passing through the dark interior and its musty smell of hay, he found Dundee behind the barn, shoeing his good bay horse in the shade. This was one of those mildly warm Texas winter afternoons when an idle man enjoyed leaning back in a rawhide chair and soaking in the fleeting sunshine, while a man working came to appreciate the shade.

Dundee had shod the hind feet first. Now he lifted the horse's left forefoot and ran his thumb over his preliminary hoof-trimming job. He straddled the foot and held it between his legs, rasping the trim job down to a smooth finish. The horse began to lean on him, and Dundee heaved against him. "Get your weight off of me, you lazy ox."

He glanced up at Doug Monahan. "Gettin' him in shape to travel. Looks like we got to, if we're both goin' to eat much longer. The captain's got the word out he don't want any ranch around here hirin' men who worked for Gordon Finch."

"Got any plans?"

Dundee shrugged and carefully felt of the hoof, noting an uneven place in it. "Never had a plan in my life. I get tired of a place, I just move on and hunt me somethin' else. I'd purt near used this place up anyhow."

Doug squatted on his heels and examined the shoe Dundee was going to put on the horse's hoof. "How'd you like to work for me?"

Dundee stopped the rasp. "Doing what?"

"Building fence."

Dundee smiled indulgently. "You still on that? Somebody'd have to hire you before you could hire me. And who's goin' to, after what happened out there on Oak Crick?"

"Somebody already has."

Dundee straightened. "Who?"

"Noah Wheeler. Nobody knows it yet, and I want it quiet as long as we can keep it that way."

"I won't say anythin'."

"What do you think about that job?"

Dundee dropped the horse's foot and wiped his half-rolled sleeve against his forehead, leaving a streak of sweat-soaked dirt. He dropped the rasp into a box. "I never could get a shovel handle or a crowbar to fit these hands of mine," he said, holding out his right hand and bending the fingers.

"Fit a gun all right, though, don't they?"

Dundee smiled. "They always considered me a fair to middlin' good shot."

"Maybe I'll need that gun hand more than the shovel-handle hand. I never was any great shot, myself."

"It'd take more than just me. You'd have to have several good men, Monahan, if you was to really make it stick."

"That's where you come in, Dundee. I need a good crew. Most of mine left the country. I figured you might know some good men who can work hard and at the same time could handle a fight if one came at them."

A strong flicker of interest was in Dundee's eyes. "I think maybe I could rustle up a few."

Relieved, Monahan said, "It's a deal, then? I've got Stub Bailey left, and maybe one or two more. If you can find me as many as six or seven more, I can use them. What're cowboy wages around here?"

"Vary with the man. Average about thirty dollars a month, and found."

"I'll pay forty. And a little bonus if we get the job done without too much cut wire or other damage from the R Cross."

Dundee grinned with admiration. "You get your mind set on somethin', you just don't quit, do you? I thought they'd quit makin' that kind anymore." He turned back and patted the bay horse on the neck. "Well, old hoss, looks like we may stick around a while and watch the show."

It was a fifty-mile ride to the cedar-cutters' camp, down on the river and out of Kiowa County. That was a long way to haul posts in a wagon. It would have been easier to use mesquite or live oak, but Doug was convinced that cedar would make better, longer-lasting posts.

He reached the camp in time for supper. The night chill was moving in with a raw south wind, and he was glad for the sight of the big side-boarded tent the Blessingame men used for a home. They would set it up in the heart of a cedar thicket and proceed to cut the cedar down from around it. When the posts were all cut and sold, they would simply hunt another thicket.

In the edge of camp, amid a tinder-dry litter of trimmed-off limbs and browning dead cedar leaves, Monahan saw dozens of stacks of cedar posts, some of them no more than three inches across the top, and some of the longest ones a foot or more, stout enough to build an elephant pen.

He could hear a clatter of pots and pans. The noise stopped, and huge old Foley Blessingame ducked through the tent flap, looking to see who was riding up. His big voice boomed, "Git down, Doug, and come on in here. We'll have a bite to eat directly."

Foley Blessingame was crowding sixty, Doug knew for a fact. If he hadn't known, he wouldn't have been able to guess within twenty years. Foley stood six feet four, and his powerful shoulders were axe handle–broad as he stood there, his tangled red beard lifting and falling in the cold wind. The man had arms as thick and hard as the cedar posts he cut for a living.

"You ain't going to like the supper," Foley said, "but it won't be any worse on you than it is on the rest of us. Mules spooked the other day and run over me with a wagonload of posts. Bunged up my chopping arm. I got to do the cooking now till I kin handle an axe ag'in. The kids are out yonder workin'."

From somewhere in the brush echoed the ring of steel axes biting deep into heart-cedar.

"Just bunged up your arm?" Doug asked wonderingly. "Is that all the damage it did?"

"Well, it like to've tore up an awful good

wagon." Blessingame motioned at Doug's horse. "Just skin the saddle off and turn him loose. He'll find our bunch and stay with them. The kids'll put out a little grain directly."

Doug unsaddled and followed the old man through the tent flap. A big woodstove had it much warmer inside, but the place reeked of scorched grease and burned bread.

"Never did care much for cookin'," Blessingame complained. "I'd rather cut fifty trees with a dull ax than stick my hands in a keg of sourdough. I always leave this chore up to the kids. Ain't no job for a growed man anyhow."

"Let me take a turn at it," Doug offered, and the old man stepped aside. "I'd be much obliged."

Paco Sanchez had taught Doug a deal about camp cooking. There wasn't much he could do about old Foley's sourdough now. It was too late for a new batch to rise before supper, so he'd just have to use this. He sliced thick venison steaks off a tarp-wrapped hind quarter hanging from a tree outside. He salted them and flopped them down, one by one, into a keg of flour, until they were well coated. The Blessingames made their living cutting cedar, but Monahan noted with relief that the fuel in the woodbox was all dry mesquite. It was better for cooking.

Old Foley sat on the edge of a cot, grinning. "You missed your callin', boy. You ought to been a wagon cook."

That brought up a memory of Paco Sanchez, and Doug Monahan's face went tight. Blessingame was quick to sense the change.

"One of the kids was in town day or two ago and heard a rumor," he said. "Heard you lost that good old cook you had."

Doug nodded, dipping lard out of a big bucket and dropping it into a skillet. News sure could get around. He told Blessingame the whole story.

The old man nodded gravely. "Looks like a good country for a smart man to stay out of. There's plenty other country needin' fences anyway."

"I'm not staying out of it," Doug told him.

Blessingame's bearded face showed a little of a grin. "I figured that. I said a *smart* man."

When the supper was about done, Blessingame walked outside and gave a great roar. His voice was as strong as his bull shoulders. That yell should have reached to Kiowa County.

In a moment he returned. "Here come the kids."

The "kids" were four huge, brawny men with red hair and red whiskers. The youngest was in his mid-twenties, the oldest probably thirty-five. Every one of them showed the gross stamp of old Foley Blessingame in the breadth of shoulder, the deep boom of voice. Doug had made a point to have flour and dough on his fingers so he wouldn't have to shake hands with them as they came in. Those great ham-sized hands would crush his own like an egg. Even as it was, they pounded him on the back till his breath was gone.

Here was a family known all the way back to East Texas, old Foley Blessingame and his four "kids," Foy, Koy, Ethan and John. Nearly three-quarters of a ton of hard muscle among them, and not an ounce of it fat. Most of the time they stayed out in the country and never bothered anybody. But when they came to town for a little unwinding every two or three months, townspeople took up the sidewalk, locked their doors and hid their daughters.

Widowed fifteen years, old Foley never let his boys outpace him. "Snow on the roof ain't no sign the fire's out inside," he often said.

When the hangovers were done, he always went back to town alone and sober, remorsefully paying for the breakage. "Bunch o' growin' boys," he would explain; "a man can't always hold them down."

None of the boys had married yet. The sight of them, Doug imagined, was enough to stampede a girl anyway. Even if one ever got interested, she was bound to reason, and correctly so, that she would immediately find herself burdened with cooking and washing and scrubbing up after the rest of the family as well as the one she took on.

There wasn't much extra room in the tent, what with five cots and a cookstove. Doug left supper in the pans he had cooked it in, letting the five men file by and take what they wanted. They took plenty.

"Doug's havin' a little trouble convincin' some of the boys over in Kiowa County that he likes his fences to stay up," old Foley told his sons. "I think mebbe we ought to some of us step over there and give the folks a little lecture."

Doug fidgeted uneasily. "Well, that's not exactly what I came over here for. Mainly I need a big order of posts."

"We got 'em," Foley said. "We been choppin' more than we been sellin' here lately."

"I noticed that," Doug replied, "and I've been thinking. Maybe you ought to quit chopping awhile and let the demand catch up with the supply."

"Got to eat someway," said Foley.

"You could work for me, building fence."

Foley frowned. "Sounds like hard work. That's the main reason I quit farmin' back in East Texas, wanted to git away from that hard work."

Doug grinned. There wasn't any harder work in the world than cedar-cutting, and Foley Blessingame knew it better than anyone.

"The way I see it, Foley, you and your boys could have a hundred yards of fence built while most people were still gouging out that first posthole. And when the folks over in Kiowa County see the size of the Blessingame bunch, they're going to study awhile before they do anything to sour your temper."

"Well," Foley conceded, "I've noticed folks gin'rally let us have our way about things. Not that any of my kids ever loses their temper. We're easy to get along with."

"I'll pay you good."

Foley nodded. "I know you would. But I ain't sure about it. Never did cotton to working for the other feller. Always liked to be my own boss, you know what I mean? Never any argument thataway. I worked for a man once when I was jest a button, twenty-five or -six years old. He got to sassin' me one day, and I let my temper git the best of my good judgment. Always did feel sorry for that feller afterwards. I just rode off and never even let him pay me the wages I had comin', I felt so bad about it."

He frowned. "Course, I would've had to wait a week to git it. He was that long comin' to."

Foley got up and began gathering the boys' tin plates, dumping them into a tub. "Say, Doug," he asked pleasantly, "you like to play poker?"

Doug shrugged. "Used to, a little."

Foley commented, "I'd rather play poker than eat, only I can't get these shiftless kids of mine to play anymore."

Doug didn't feel like playing, and he caught the friendly warning in the eyes of the Blessingame boys. But he wanted to keep on Foley's warm side. "I'll play you a game or two, if we don't put much money in it."

"Penny ante's fine. Ethan, you go fetch us some matches to use."

In two hours Foley seldom lost a hand. He had a pile of matches in front of him that could burn off all the grass in three counties. Doug never had seen anybody with such a phenomenal streak of luck.

Even at penny ante, he had lost more than he wanted to.

"Bedtime," Foley yawned at last, raking up the matches and starting to count them out. "Unless you want to keep on and try to win it back."

Doug shook his head. "I can't beat your kind of luck."

Foley walked outside a few minutes, and Ethan Blessingame whispered, "We tried to give you the high sign. It ain't all luck. He cheats!"

Next morning Doug got up and cooked the breakfast. He started a pot of red beans and mixed up a new batch of dough before he left the Blessingame camp. Foley watched admiringly as Doug put the dough together.

"You ought to been a woman," he said. "But on second thought, if you was, you wouldn't be out here. I reckon we'd best leave well-enough alone."

Doug said, "Made up your mind yet about working for me?"

Foley nodded. "Full stomach always weakens my judgment, Doug. We decided we'd take you up on that proposition. Jest one condition."

"What's that?"

"Make sure there's somebody in your outfit can play poker. You play a mighty poor hand, yourself."

From the Blessingame camp Doug rode on to Stringtown, the nearest point on the railroad from Twin Wells. He struck the rails several miles out and followed them in. They still had a little of the new shine to them, and the ties hadn't weathered out badly yet. It hadn't been more than a couple of years since the line had come through.

Stringtown wasn't fancy to look at, but it was all new. The original paint coat still stuck to those frame buildings which had been painted at all. Stringtown had sprung up because of the railroad.

Doug's first stop was the railroad depot, where the telegrapher was tapping out code on the key. "Can you take a message to Fort Worth?" Doug asked.

"If you can write it to where I can read it," the little man said and nodded at some sheets of yellow paper weighted down by a small gear wheel from a locomotive.

Doug wrote the address of a Fort Worth hardware company and asked the price of a hundred spools of No. 9 barbed wire, including freight to Stringtown. He handed the message to the telegrapher. "I'll be back around directly for the answer," he said.

He walked out of the depot building,

thinking he might cross over to a saloon and while away the time where it was warmer. On the platform, he heard the whistle of an approaching train, and he leaned back against the yellow-painted wall to watch it.

It was an eastbound passenger train. It whistled again, coming into town, and began slowing down. A conductor hung precariously off the side of one car as the train's momentum slowed, and he jumped down to the ground, his shoes sliding on the grime-blackened gravel. A Negro porter stepped down and set a wooden platform in place.

Suddenly Doug wished he wasn't standing out in the open this way, for he saw Sheriff Luke McKelvie of Twin Wells, walking up to the train. A sullen young man was handcuffed to him. A tall man in a dark suit stepped off the train, looked around, then moved directly toward the pair. McKelvie shook hands and motioned toward his prisoner, saying something. Taking a key from his pocket, he removed the handcuffs. The other man immediately brought out his own cuffs and locked himself to his new prisoner. The engine whistled a warning. The two boarded the train and disappeared inside.

McKelvie watched until satisfied. Then he

turned and walked toward Doug Monahan, dropping the cuffs in his coat pocket. "Hello, Monahan. Saw you as I came up, but I was too busy to say howdy. Had to transfer a prisoner."

Monahan shook hands with him, wishing he hadn't had the misfortune to run into the Kiowa County sheriff.

"Got my job done, and now I can relax," McKelvie said. "Care to have a drink with me?"

Monahan declined as gracefully as he could. "I got some business to attend to, thanks." He didn't care to have McKelvie pumping him, and he had a notion the sheriff could worm a lot of information out of a man without really seeming to.

"Well," replied McKelvie, "that's too bad. But I think you're showing good judgment, getting out of Twin Wells."

A sharp thrust of stubbornness brought a reply from Monahan before he could stop himself. "I haven't left there for good. I'll be back soon enough."

The sheriff's easy smile faded. "I'm sorry, Monahan." Regret clouded his gray eyes.

Monahan watched the sheriff walk down the street, and he felt like kicking himself. Whatever secret there might have been was out now. McKelvie would probably poke around until he knew just what Monahan was up to, and the report wouldn't be long in getting to Captain Rinehart.

Well, that was the way it went. A man got mad and said things he didn't mean to. There wasn't much he could do about it now except go right on as he had planned. He didn't go across to the saloon, though. Instead, he went back into the depot and sat down on a hard wooden bench, leaning back against the wall and waiting for the answer to his wire. When it came, he sent another message constituting an order for wire and staples to be shipped to him at Stringtown. He promised to send a check immediately. Mailed here, it would be in Fort Worth before they got the order ready to ship.

Handing it to the telegrapher, he asked, "Who's a good freighter around here? I'll want him to haul this shipment out for me."

The telegrapher said, "Try Slim Torrance over at the livery barn. He's got new wagons, and he's a good man. Besides, he's my brother-in-law."

"Reason enough for a recommendation," Doug said.

The livery barn bore the name Spangler & Torrance, and it smelled strongly of dry hay and liniment and oil, horse sweat and manure. A practical combination, Monahan thought, livery barn and freighting outfit. He found Slim Torrance in the rear of the barn, rubbing some evil-smelling concoction on the leg of a lame mule.

"I got a shipment of barbed wire due from Fort Worth in a few days," Doug told the chunky, red-faced freighter. "I'd be much obliged if you'd haul it over into Kiowa County for me."

Torrance nodded. "Freightin's my business. You jest tell me where you want it, and I'll git it over there."

Monahan gave him instructions as to the trail. He added, "It wouldn't be a bad idea if you skirted around town. Folks don't have to know about it for awhile. Wouldn't hurt to cover the load with a tarp, too, so it won't stand out if somebody happens to pass you on the trail."

Torrance frowned. "Wait a minute now. If it's one of them kind of deals, I don't know . . ."

"I'll pay you half of it in advance."

Torrance wrestled with himself a minute, and the money won. "All right, I'll do it."

Writing out the check, Monahan said, "It'll be better for all of us if nothing's said about this till the shipment's delivered. No use setting out bait to catch trouble."

"No use atall," Torrance agreed, carefully folding the check and shoving it deep into the pocket of his denim pants.

"By the way," Monahan said, "I sure could use a wagon cook. Know anybody around here who can cook and needs the job?"

Torrance said, "Got jest the man for you. Come on back in here."

Later, riding out, Monahan saw McKelvie's horse tied down by the depot.

In there now pumping the telegrapher, he thought, more angry at himself than at McKelvie. *He won't leave town till he knows.*

8

Riding in abreast of the Blessingames' three post-laden wagons, Doug found that Stub Bailey and Noah Wheeler had been busy while he was gone.

"Watch out for those stakes yonder," he called back to old Foley Blessingame, on the lead wagon. "They mark where the posts are to be set."

Foley saw them and swung his mules a little to the right so the heavy wheels would pass between two stakes, set a rod apart.

Stub Bailey rode out grinning to meet the wagons. He shook Doug's hand and motioned toward the line of stakes. "Half afraid you wasn't comin' back, Doug. I sure would've hated to drive all them stakes for nothin'." His gaze roved over the Blessingames' wagons, and especially over the Blessingames themselves. "Man alive," he breathed, "they all come out of one family?"

Monahan nodded, and Bailey shook his head. "I'd sure hate to be the woman who had to give birth to that bunch."

Monahan grinned. "Well, they came one at a time, I reckon. They'll haul in all the posts we need, then stay and help us build the fence."

Bailey approved of that. "I'll bet they can make a pick and shovel sing 'Dixie.' "

"The first Rinehart man who gets himself crossways with them may sing a little, too," Doug said.

Big old Noah Wheeler was standing in front of his barn waiting as the three heavy wagons rolled up, their iron rims grinding deep tracks into the shower-dampened earth, crushing the cured brown grass. "Howdy, Doug," he said. "Looks like you've brought the makings."

Doug stepped off his horse and shook the farmer's rough hand. "Ought to be enough posts to get us started. Plenty more where these came from. Wire ought to be here by the time we get enough posts up to commence stringing it."

He hadn't realized how tired the long ride had made him until he sat down a moment on the barn's front step. He was glad to be back here. He felt himself drawn to this pleasant place with its good corrals, its scattering of Durham cattle, its ducks swimming out there on the surface tank, and its chickens scratching around in the yard. He liked the Wheelers' little red frame house with the front porch that would be so good for sitting and rocking in the late summer evenings.

Without wanting to show it, he looked around for Trudy Wheeler and felt vaguely disappointed that he didn't see her anywhere.

"How's the family, Noah?"

"Fine, getting along fine." Wheeler looked toward the house. "Halfway thought they'd come out to look, but I reckon not." He frowned. "Doug, in case they say anything, don't worry yourself too much about it."

"What do you mean?"

"They're not as much in favor of this fence as I thought they'd be. Fact of the matter, they're against it. You know how women are. Or do you? You're not married, are you?"

"No, sir."

"Time you get married, you'll know what I mean. A man ought to go ahead and do what he wants to and not let the women bother him, I guess. Ought to let them know he's the boss. But when the time comes, you hate to do it. A man who's got women-folks has just got to put up with a certain amount of that, I reckon."

Doug had an uneasy moment, afraid Noah Wheeler was leading up to calling the whole thing off. He thought of Captain Rinehart, and of his foreman, Archer Spann, and he felt his heart quicken. Wheeler *couldn't* call it off now, and cheat Monahan out of the satisfaction he'd get from humbling them.

Wheeler put an end to his anxiety. "I thought maybe we'd start down on the southwest corner and work up. That's where the most of the strays come in from, and we'll cut them off first."

There was the immediate problem of getting settled. Best thing to do with the posts was to unload them right where they would be needed.

"Where'll you be putting up, Doug?" Foley Blessingame asked. When Doug showed him the barn, the old cedar cutter said, "If it's all the same to you, we'll just put up our tent when we bring that last load of posts. Me and the kids is used to it, and the barn won't be none too roomy anyhow with this crew you got." Dundee had brought out four men.

Out at the side of the barn, Doug rigged up three posts and stretched a tarp to them from the edge of the roof. This cover would help protect the cook in bad weather. They could set up a stationary chuckbox out here under the tarp. The cook could have his fire just beyond it, where the smoke would lift clear and not drift back underneath.

The cook was Simon Getty, the grunting, red-faced man Doug had picked up in Torrance's livery barn. Monahan had borrowed a horse from Torrance so the cook could ride with him. Torrance was to pick up the animal when he brought the wire. But the cook had barely managed to stay on him to the Blessingames' camp. From there, he had ridden the last wagon.

"Looks like what he needs is a good sweat bath," Foley had commented dryly. "Sweat the alcohol out of his system. Man ain't got no use drinkin' if he can't hold his liquor."

"Looks to me like he's holding too much of it," Monahan had replied.

Getty was a shortish man with a puffed face and a soft paunch. And, it had developed, a short temper. He hadn't been in condition to do the cooking the first night at the Blessingames', but he had done it since. He put up a pretty decent meal, too, if a man didn't mind listening to him complain.

"Damn these outfits that don't give a man

decent pots to cook in," he said ten times with every meal. "I've cooked for a hundred of 'em, and there ain't a one ever give me anythin' I'd cook for a dog in."

Doug took it with a grain of salt, for he had seen few wagon cooks who didn't gripe a little. It put a little extra flavoring in the food, like salt. And, as long as it didn't get to rankling anybody, it gave the rest of the crew something to snicker about — when they got out of earshot.

Stub Bailey came around, and Doug asked him, "Did you go over and see what cooking equipment you could salvage from Paco's camp?"

"I went over, but there wasn't anything left. Somebody beat us to it. Stole ever' Dutch oven, beanpot, knife, fork and spoon there was. Even a couple of wagon wheels that the spokes hadn't burned out of."

Monahan swore under his breath. "I was counting on that stuff. Been borrowing from the Blessingames, and I didn't want to keep on doing it. Took everything we had, did they?"

"One of them poverty nester outfits over on Oak Crick, I figured. Took everything but the posts and burned-up wire. I don't reckon there's anybody fool enough to want that." Bailey added as an afterthought, "By the way, there's plenty of good posts over there, in the ground. They ain't set so hard yet but what we could take a good team of mules and yank them out of the ground one at a time."

Monahan shook his head. "They're Gordon Finch's posts. He paid me cash for them. He can take them up himself, if he wants to."

Out of the corner of his eye, Doug kept watching for Trudy Wheeler to show herself. But so far as he could tell while they were setting up camp, she never did. She was staying in the house.

Late in the afternoon everything was in its place. The Blessingames' wagons had been unloaded and made ready for a return trip after more posts tomorrow. The cook had a fire going just beyond the tarp on the side of the barn, and pots and pans were rattling. It would be a while before supper.

Doug walked to the Wheelers' house, up onto the porch, and knocked on the door. He could hear a stirring inside, and presently Mrs. Wheeler opened the door. Doug took off his hat. This tall, strong, graying woman looked at him with no unfriendliness but with no special welcome.

"Good evening, Mrs. Wheeler."

"Good evening, Mr. Monahan."

"We've gotten everything in order, and I thought I'd come over and pay my respects."

"That's nice of you."

He tried to see around her, but he couldn't spot Trudy Wheeler. He could tell that Wheeler had been right about the women. They weren't strong at all on this fencing business. It showed on Mrs. Wheeler, in her withdrawal from her inborn hospitality. She was vastly different from the last time he had been here.

When it became evident that she wasn't going to invite him in, he said awkwardly, "Well, I guess I better be getting back. Horses got to be fed." A shading of disappointment crept into his voice. "I'll be seeing you again, Mrs. Wheeler."

"Yes," she replied, and he thought her voice softened a little, for she must have caught his disappointment. "I'm sure we'll see each other, Mr. Monahan."

He put his hat back on and walked off the porch, discontent gnawing at him. He hadn't considered this, the opposition from the women. He was at a loss to put a reason to it. Well, what difference did it make to him, anyway? Main thing was to get the fence up.

After all, they weren't *his* women.

■ ■ ■ ■

The Blessingames were up before daylight. By the time the sun broke over the low hills to the east, they had their horses hitched to the three wagons and were ready to go. Doug Monahan stood there watching the breath of the horses rise as steam in the sharp morning air.

"Going to be cold up there on those wagons' seats, till the sun gets up high enough to take the chill off," he told Foley.

The huge old man tolerantly shook his head. "Like a spring day. You South Texas boys don't know what cold weather is. Prob'ly never saw a frost in your life till you come up here."

Doug shivered and smiled. "Well, I know what it is now." He went serious then. "Be careful, Foley. It'd be better if nobody saw you. If anybody asks you, don't tell them where the posts are going. I'd like to get all the wire and posts in before any trouble starts. After that, they can do what they please, and we'll be ready."

Foley flipped the reins and led off with his wagon. From a hundred yards away he turned and yelled back in a voice that would have scared a Longhorn bull out over the corral gate: "Don't you worry none about me and the kids. We'll be as quiet's a mouse!"

The wagons rolled away with a groan of wheels and clanking of chains. Horses snorted in the cold. Doug watched until they were well on their way. Turning then, he saw Trudy Wheeler walking toward the spring, carrying a wooden bucket in each hand.

It was the first time he had seen her since he had returned, except for a glimpse or two of her at a distance as she stepped out on the porch a moment. He stood watching her, admiring her slenderness, her easy way of moving. Then he followed after her.

Entering the rock spring house, she filled the buckets one at a time from the water which bubbled up to flow through the milk-cooling trough and on out into the creek. As she straightened, Doug said, "I'll carry them for you."

Startled, she whirled to face him. "Oh, it's you." Her breath came fast for a moment. "Why don't you make a little noise when you come up behind somebody that way?"

"I was afraid you might walk away and leave me."

She fixed a half-hostile gaze on him, and her voice was cool. "I might have, at that."

He picked up the buckets. "Where to?"

"The washpot. We're fixing to put out a washing today."

He walked along beside her, trying to think of something to say which might offset her coolness, but nothing came to him. She contributed nothing, either, until they reached the big blackened pot behind the house.

"Just pour a little water in there and let me sweep out the pot," she said.

He did, and she swept the water around inside the pot with an old wornout broom, washing away the settled dust. When she swept the last of the water out she said, "I'll handle it from here on, thank you."

He shook his head. "It'll take a lot of water. I'll do it."

He kept toting water until the pot was filled. While he was doing that, Trudy was piling dry mesquite wood underneath and around the pot. She poured a little kerosene around it from a five-gallon can, struck a match and flipped it under the pot. The flame spread slowly, timidly, at first, then grew stronger and bolder with the taste of the wood. In a few minutes it was a crackling blaze.

The warmth of the fire felt good in this chill. But watching it, Doug could not help

444

thinking about another fire a few days ago, and a restless spirit moved in him. "I've been wanting to talk to you ever since I got back. Why've you been avoiding me?"

"Don't you know?"

"No, I don't, except your dad says you don't like the fence."

"The fence itself is all right. It's what we may have to go through because of it that I don't like."

"If there's a fight, I'll be here to handle it."

Her eyes were suddenly flinty. "That's just it, you know there'll be a fight. That's why you're here in the first place. You don't really care whether we have a fence or not. You're just looking for a fight with Captain Rinehart, and by building us a fence you figure on provoking it."

He opened his mouth but she cut him off before he had a chance to reply. A mounting anger colored her face. "There's one thing you can say about the captain — he's no hypocrite. He tells you what he wants and doesn't want, and no mistake about it.

"We all felt sorry for you that first day, Mr. Monahan. We brought you here because you'd been done an awful wrong. I can't say I blame you, even yet, for wanting to get even. But when you take an old man like

Dad and talk him into building a fence so you can provoke trouble and have a chance at getting revenge, you're doing him an awful wrong, too. You're just using Dad and us for bait!"

"Now, that's not the way it is. . . ."

"Isn't it?" Her eyes sparkled. "Then maybe you can tell me what way it is. No, I don't want you telling me anything! I just want you to leave me alone."

She turned her back on him, and he knew there was no use trying to talk any further with her, not today. He could feel the red color warm in his cheeks. Something between anger and hurt swelled in him. He left her and walked back toward the barn.

Stub Bailey came out the barn door and saw Monahan's face. He looked past Doug to the girl, who was cutting up blocks of homemade soap and stirring it in the heating water with a wooden paddle, agitating it a lot more than she needed to.

"Got the lecture, did you?" Stub said. "I could've told you."

Monahan felt like snapping at Stub to shut up, but he managed to withhold that. Still, he couldn't look Bailey in the face.

"I got a little of the same, but I expect she saved the big load for you because you're the boss," Stub said. He paused and gazed seriously at Monahan. "Maybe you ought to take a good look at yourself and do some thinkin' on what she said. She could be ninety percent right."

9

Captain Andrew Rinehart sat in the heavy oak swivel chair at his big roll-top desk, cavernous eyes blinking in disbelief at his foreman Archer Spann.

"Noah Wheeler building a fence? You must be mistaken, Archer."

"No mistake, Captain. Shorty Willis and Jim was scouting that south prairie when they came up on three wagons loaded with fence posts, moving northwest on that old freighter trail. There was a big old man driving the lead wagon, and four others coming along on the other two wagons. Whole bunch was redheaded and looked like a set of giants, Shorty said. Shorty stopped and asked them where they was taking the posts. The old man told him, 'To hell, Sonny, and we'll take you with us if you don't go on about your business.' "

The captain shook his gray head. "Red-headed giants. Sounds like Shorty's been

448

drinking. I've warned those boys. . . ."

Spann protested, "He wasn't drinking, Captain. Jim backed him up. They left the wagons but circled back and trailed them. They went straight to Noah Wheeler's place."

"Did the boys look around any? What did they see?"

"They saw men digging postholes and setting posts. They didn't see any wire, but there were posts scattered along Wheeler's boundary, up next to Fuller Quinn's country."

The captain took a long breath and let it out slowly. Regret sharpened his wind-bitten face. "Noah Wheeler. He's the last one I'd ever have thought would do it."

"The last one?" Spann asked sharply, then softened the edge in his voice. "He was the first one to move into this country and break up land away from Oak Crick. He's never asked you about anything or told you what he was going to do. He's got a head of his own, that nester has, and it's time somebody bumped it for him."

The captain studied Archer Spann silently, his eyes unreadable.

Spann said, "I tried to get you to let me do something about him when he first moved out there and took up land that you'd been using. It would've been easy to chase him back to the crick. Clear out of the country would've been even better." Spann's dark eyebrows knitted, and his black eyes took on an eager light. "It's not too late. When we get through with him, he'll pack up and leave, and he won't look back."

"What would you do, Archer?"

"Burn him out. Tear up whatever fence he's got built. Run cattle into his fields. Show him he's nothing but a farmer after all, no better than the rest of those Oak Crick nesters."

The captain slowly shook his head. "He's more than just a nester, Archer, a great deal more. There won't be any burning him out. And there won't be any R Cross cattle on his fields, either. We'll just ride over there and talk to him."

Spann swallowed hard. "Talk to him?"

The captain nodded. "He'll see our way."

Disappointed, Spann said, "It's a mistake, sir." The captain eyed him sharply, and Spann backed down a little. "I mean, sure, we'll talk to him first, if you'd rather. We can do something else later, if we have to. When do you want to go?"

"In the morning will be all right."

"I'll get a bunch of the boys ready."

The captain sounded impatient. "We don't need a bunch of men! Just you and me. We're going to talk to him, that's all. He'll listen."

Spann nodded in resignation. "I hope so, sir. I hope so."

He walked out, softly closing the captain's office door behind him. Out of the old man's sight, he let the welling anger run its course. He struck his right fist sharply into the palm of his left hand.

He half hoped Wheeler wouldn't listen. Then perhaps Archer Spann could give that contrary old farmer what he'd been asking for ever since he had been out here.

Sarah Rinehart made her way into the captain's office and sat down, breathing a little harder for the effort. She had done better these last few days. She had been walking some outside, and she seemed to be regaining much of her strength. There was color in her face that the captain hadn't seen in months.

Seeing her like this had given him a lift he hadn't felt in a long time. Every cowboy at the headquarters had noticed how much better the captain's spirit had been. At times he would even soften up and laugh with them. It had been a long time since the captain's stern manner had eased so.

"What was the matter with Archer Spann?" Sarah asked. "He walked out of here looking awfully mad."

"Mad?" The captain sounded surprised. "He didn't act mad. A little disappointed, maybe."

"Looked mad to me. What happened?"

Briefly Rinehart told her. Worriedly Sarah asked, "What are you going to do, Andrew?"

"Nothing much. Just go over and talk to Noah."

"And if that doesn't change his mind? What then?"

The captain frowned darkly. That possibility evidently hadn't entered his mind. "It will, Sarah. Don't you worry yourself over it."

Sarah said, "Perhaps if it were just you, I wouldn't worry about it. But Archer Spann worries me. And lately he seems to have a lot of influence over you."

Rinehart stiffened. "I always do what *I* want to, Sarah. No man ever tells me what I ought to do."

"No man ever used to," she said resolutely.

Archer Spann pulled up his horse and pointed out across the rolling gray prairie. "Yonder it is, Captain, just like Shorty said."

Andrew Rinehart felt a sharp stab of

disappointment, seeing the line of firmly set fence posts stretching several hundred feet along Noah Wheeler's boundary line. All the way out from the ranch headquarters the captain had tried to maintain a hope that the boys had been wrong. He had known all the time that it was a vain wish. Yet, seeing the proof now brought a painful letdown.

"Looks like I owe Shorty Willis an apology," the captain conceded quietly. From the corner of his eye he caught the fleeting smile of self-satisfaction that crossed Spann's face before the foreman could suppress it.

It brought a touch of anger to him, for the captain was still a man of pride, a man who hated to be found wrong in any degree, who hated most of all to give another man the satisfaction of having been right.

"I'll do the talking, Archer," the captain said curtly. Spann had the good judgment to nod agreement. "Yes, sir."

From behind them somewhere a horse nickered. Turning in the saddle, the captain saw a rider trailing along at a respectful distance, saddlegun cradled in his arm. Rinehart realized that they probably had been under surveillance for some time. He clenched his fist and had a sudden feeling of being squeezed into a tight corner.

"Not a friendly outfit," Spann observed.

The captain squinted but could not make the man out. "Who is he?"

"Name's Dundee. Used to work for Finch."

"I passed the word around I didn't want anybody hiring any of Finch's hands."

"It looks like he's working *here,*" Spann said pointedly.

Grinding out a harsh word under his breath, the captain touched spurs to his big gray horse, moving across the thick mat of cured grass toward the fencing crew. The men who had been digging holes and tamping in posts dropped their tools and drifted together. The captain could see they were all armed. It was different from the way it had been at Monahan's fencing camp.

He saw a thin wisp of smoke rising, and the sight of a campfire reminded him how cold he was. Riding in closer, he kept watching for Noah Wheeler. His fading eyesight made it hard for him to see faces, but he finally recognized the big farmer's tall frame, moving toward him from a pile of cedar posts.

"Hello, Andrew," Wheeler said.

Spann glanced sharply at the captain, surprised at this farmer's casual use of Rinehart's first name. He had never heard anyone but Mrs. Rinehart herself call the old cowman Andrew.

"Hello, Noah." The captain held back a moment, then reached down and took the big hand that Wheeler offered.

Wheeler said, "Pot of coffee on the fire. Get down, Andrew, and have a cup with me."

The captain waited, and Wheeler said, "You must be cold. A little hot coffee would do you good."

The captain caught the pleasant aroma of the simmering coffee, and he felt a strong yearning for it. He was a-quiver from the morning cold which had worked through to his bones.

He felt the eyes of the men upon him, however, and he hesitated. He had not allowed himself much familiarity with anyone these last years. Men watched him in awe, and part of the reason was that he somehow stood apart from the others, apart from and a little above them. With familiarity, some of this awe would surely vanish. Many a lonely time he would have given half of what he owned to be able to mix with men and be one of them again, the way it had been forty years ago. But with his strict self-discipline he had managed to remain aloof

— aloof and alone. Noah Wheeler held out a cup of hot coffee. "Come on, Andrew, for old times' sake."

And Captain Andrew Rinehart stepped down from his big gray horse and took the farmer's cup. "Thank you, Noah."

Archer Spann watched in wonderment.

The two men stood staring at each other, sipping their coffee. "Been a long time, Andrew," Wheeler said presently, "since we stood around like this and drank coffee together."

The captain nodded gravely. "A long time and a long way off. Things were different then, Noah, and so were we."

Wheeler thoughtfully shook his head. "Not so much. We're a right smart older, but I doubt that we've really changed so much."

"I guess you know why I've come, Noah," said the captain.

Wheeler nodded. "The fence."

"I thought you knew how I felt about fences. I thought everybody knew."

Wheeler nodded. "I know."

"Then why are you doing this?" the captain said sharply.

Wheeler frowned into his cup, studying hard for the right words. "Because I have to, Andrew. I've done a lot with this land in

456

the years I've had it, but I've gone about as far as I can go with it open the way it is. I've got to close it in; then whatever I build can stay."

"Fences will ruin this country, Noah."

"You're wrong, Andrew. They'll change it, but they won't ruin it. You watch, they'll be the making of the country."

"I like it the way it is."

"Andrew, you were one of the first white men to come to this country and stay. You could see the possibilities in it, but you had to make a lot of changes first. Now other people are coming in, and there are a lot of changes *they've* got to make.

"I've got a dream for my place here, Andrew. I know what I want to do and how I've got to do it. But right now I can't raise good crops for stray cattle coming into my fields. I can't breed better cattle as long as scrub bulls keep getting with my cows. If I can't do these things, then from here on out I'm standing still. That's why I've got to have the fence, Andrew."

The captain said, "I can send some of the boys by every two or three days and keep the cattle thrown back, Noah."

Wheeler shook his gray head. "It wouldn't work. Every two or three days wouldn't be enough, and besides, your men have more things to do than help me to farm. If I want to make anything, I'll have to make it for myself."

The captain saw a rider coming up in an easy lope. He squinted, trying to recognize him. The horseman was less than a hundred feet from him before he recognized Doug Monahan.

The captain said, "I should have suspected, Noah. That the man who's building your fence?"

Wheeler nodded and faced around as Monahan reined up beside him. Monahan's eyes were cold. "Any trouble, Noah?"

"No trouble, Doug. We were just talking."

Doug looked at the captain, his face grim. "If you've come threatening, Captain, you'd just as well go home. We're ready for you this time. This fence is going up, and it'll stay up."

The captain stared hard at Monahan, and he felt the young man's eyes hating him. It disturbed him somehow. The captain had never tried to be a popular man. He moved in his own way, in his own time, caring little what anyone else thought. He was becoming increasingly aware of the talk that went on behind his back, but much of it came from people who wore a pleasant smile when they faced him. Not in years had anyone boldly shown him such unmasked enmity as he saw in Doug Monahan's blue eyes.

It brought an immediate response in kind. The captain said, "Monahan, I've given you more chances than I'd give most men."

"I'll make my own chances, Captain, and I'll take them."

Spann, who had not dismounted, edged his horse a little closer. "Say the word, Captain, and I'll put him in his place."

Noah Wheeler took a step forward, placing himself in front of Monahan's horse. "This is my place, Andrew. Doug Monahan is here because I want him here."

The captain's face colored. "He thinks he has a private war with me, Noah. Don't let him drag you into it."

Wheeler replied, "I'm not in any war and I don't want any part of one. I'm just trying to fence my land so I can build this place into what I want it to be, that's all."

Restlessly the captain moved his cup around and around in a circle, sending the remains of the coffee to spinning.

"If it was only you, Noah, I wouldn't care. But if you build a fence, others will. Out of respect for old times, I'm asking you not to do it."

Wheeler solemnly shook his head. "Out of

respect for old times, Andrew, I'm asking you to understand why I *have* to do it."

The captain looked at him with sorrow. "That's your answer?"

Wheeler nodded.

The captain flipped the rest of his coffee out and dropped the cup into the brittle grass. He stepped stiffly back into the saddle. His spurs tinkled as he reined the big gray horse around and headed out again the way he had come. He never looked back.

Archer Spann rode silently beside him, watching the old cowman's face twist with the bitter conflicts that went on in his mind. When at last it seemed that the captain had made his decision, Spann asked, "What was there between you and Noah Wheeler, years ago?"

The captain made no answer, and Spann said, "Whatever it was, he seems to've forgotten about it. He's declared war on you, Captain. When do we hit him?"

The captain frowned, his mind still dwelling on something else, perhaps something far back in time. "Hit him? What do you mean, hit him?"

"Burn him out."

The captain pulled his horse to a stop, and Spann reined up, turned back to face him. He had seldom seen the captain's face clouded so.

"Whatever else we have to do," Rinehart declared, "I don't want to hurt Noah Wheeler. Doug Monahan's the one behind this. He's the one we want to hit. Cut his fences, burn his posts, run off his men. Do what you have to to stop Monahan. But leave Noah Wheeler alone!"

Spann rode along silently a while after that, keeping his thoughts to himself. Finally he asked, "What about Wheeler's boy?"

"Wheeler's boy?"

"Vern Wheeler, the kid we've got with Lefty Jones over in that north line shack."

The captain nodded then. "I'd almost forgotten. Better let him go, Archer. If he's any account he'll want to side with his father. And if he's not any account, we don't want him anyway."

Archer Spann smiled a little then, and the pleasure of anticipation shone in his dark eyes. He doubled his fist.

"I'll go over there as quick as I can."

He was waiting in the line shack when Vern Wheeler and Lefty Jones rode in from the morning's work to cook themselves some dinner. He had been there an hour, resting in the warm comfort of the little bachelor stove, and had made no move to fix anything to eat. He would let them do that.

Husky young Vern Wheeler shook hands with him, showing him the deference of a well-brought-up youngster to the older man he works for. Lefty Jones, fifteen years older than Vern, nodded and gave Spann a civil howdy but didn't shake his hand. It was plain enough that he didn't think much of the foreman, yet he wouldn't go so far as to be insubordinate. Jones' glance flicked to the stove, then to the coffee pot which still sat cold and empty on the cabinet top. Range etiquette demanded that Spann fix coffee for the chilled incoming riders, if he didn't do anything else.

Jones went about the business of fixing dinner, saying nothing. The way he saw it, if there was any talking to be done, it was Spann's part to do it. Vern Wheeler, younger and more eager, tried to be polite by drawing Spann out, asking him questions about the rest of the ranch. Spann gave him short answers, when he answered at all. He waited until dinner was over before he sprang it.

"I came over to tell you you're through here, kid. Your dad double-crossed the captain."

Vern Wheeler stiffened, almost dropping the dirty dishes he was carrying to the cabinet. In a strained voice he demanded, "What're you talking about?"

"He's putting up a fence, a bobwire fence. And after the captain all but begged him not to."

Lefty Jones snickered at the thought of the captain begging anything.

Shaken, Vern put the dishes down on the cabinet and turned back to face Spann. "My dad wouldn't do anything he didn't have the right to."

"In this country the captain tells people what they've got a right to do. He said no bobwire fences. Your old man's building one anyway."

"And you're firing me for it?"

"You're his son. If we can't trust him, we can't trust you."

Face darkening, Vern Wheeler took a threatening step toward Archer Spann. "Watch what you say about my dad!"

Spann stood up, bracing himself. "Noah Wheeler's nothing but another dirt farmer who's let himself step over the line, kid, and before we're through, he'll know it."

Lightning flashed in Vern Wheeler's eyes, but the youngster held himself down.

Spann pulled a small roll of green bills out of his pocket. "It's been three weeks since last payday. I've got you twenty-one dollars counted out here. Take it and git."

Vern Wheeler stared incredulously at the money. "Twenty-one dollars?" He hurled the bills to the floor. "I've got a year's wages coming to me! You've been holding them."

"Back wages? You're crazy, kid. This is all we owe you."

Vern's face drained. "You're a liar, Spann. You've got it. You've been holding it, saving it for me so I could get married. Now I want my money, Spann."

Spann's hand dropped to the butt of the six-gun on his hip. "I told you, boy, you've got all that's coming to you. Now pack up and git!"

Vern's voice rippled with fury. "Not without my money, Spann. You give me my money."

He lunged at the foreman. Spann's hand came up, the gun in it. Lefty Jones grabbed Spann's arm and wrenched. A blast rocked the line shack, and sugar spilled in a white stream from a can on a raw-pine shelf. Spann swung his arm back. The gun struck Jones in the face and sent him sprawling.

Vern Wheeler got hold of Spann's arm, trying to twist it, to get his hand on the gun. Spann strained, cursing as he attempted to throw off the heavy weight of this husky farm boy. He wrenched savagely and tore his arm free. He swung, hard. The gun glanced off Vern Wheeler's head, staggering him.

Spann saw his chance then. He lifted his knee to the boy's groin. Wheeler gasped and stiffened. Spann lifted the gun and brought it down again. Vern Wheeler dropped like a sack of grain, a red welt rising angrily on the side of his head.

The boy struggled to regain his feet. Spann stood heaving, trying for breath. When Vern had almost managed to steady himself, Spann swung the gun again. This time Vern Wheeler wouldn't get up, not for a while.

Lefty Jones sat on the floor, rubbing his hand across his bleeding mouth, still half dazed.

"You pack up too, Lefty," Spann said. "You're done. You had no business poking in there. It was between me and the kid."

Jones was coming around. He blinked a few times, finally managing to focus his gaze on Spann. "That boy wasn't lyin'. You owe him that money, and you're stealin' it from him."

"I owe him nothing, Lefty."

"Three hundred dollars. It's all he talks about. The captain wouldn't steal it from him. That leaves you."

Archer Spann grabbed Lefty Jones by the collar and jerked him to his feet. Jones stood awkwardly off balance, his hand moving to take Spann's fist from his collar. Then he stopped, feeling the fury that rippled in Spann's face, seeing murder in Spann's eyes.

Jones swallowed and looked down. Fear touched him with a death-cold hand.

"All right, Spann, mebbe I was wrong."

"Ride, Lefty." Spann's voice crackled. "Don't even go by town. Don't stop riding for a week." The voice dropped almost to a whisper, but it stung. "If I ever see you again, I'll kill you!"

He gave Jones a shove, and the man fell back against a table, turning it over with a crash. The cowboy got up, silently gathered his scattered belongings and rolled them in his blankets. With a quick glance down at Vern Wheeler, then up at Spann, he walked out the door and off the porch.

Spann already had heard the hoofbeats trailing away before Vern Wheeler began to stir. Spann gathered up the remaining clothes and personal effects he found around the line shack. He rolled them in Vern Wheeler's bed. As Vern pushed himself to his knees, Spann pitched the roll at him. He drew the gun again and stood there holding it, letting Vern get a good look at it.

"I could kill you and swear you made me do it, Wheeler, but I won't. You just go on and keep your mouth shut about that money. Mark it up to experience and your old man's fence."

Vern Wheeler got shakily to his feet. He touched a hand to his face and felt the stickiness of blood. He stared blankly at his hand, and the red smear that was on it. His eyes lifted to Spann. They were glazed by pain, but they held a writhing hatred.

"I'll go, but don't you forget me. I'll be back, and one way or another, I'll get my money."

Spann watched him go, then reached in his pocket and touched the roll of greenbacks there. He felt like cursing himself, now that it was over. He had brought the money with the intention of paying young Wheeler. He didn't know what had changed his mind. Some grasping impulse had driven him into a spur-of-the-moment decision, and once it was made, he could not back down. He realized now that it probably had been a mistake. He pulled his hand away from the money as if it had been hot. What was three hundred dollars to the man who might someday control the R Cross?

Archer Spann had been on his own most

of his life. As a boy he had known much of hunger and desperation, and it hadn't been many years since a dollar bill looked as big as a saddle blanket to him. The memory of those grim times still haunted him, still put a cold touch of fear in the pit of his stomach when he thought of them.

That, he realized, was what had prompted him to keep the money. In a man who yearned to be big, this was a deeply ingrained streak of littleness that he despised but could not purge from his soul.

10

The bitter anger grew in Vern Wheeler as he started the long ride home. At nightfall he stopped and made a dry and hungry camp beneath a wind-breaking cutbank, no food or coffee to warm him. He wrapped in his blanket and kept a small fire going through the night, more miserable here than he would be in the saddle. But a thin blanket of clouds hid the stars from sight. He knew he might get lost in the darkness and ride many unnecessary miles.

Before daybreak he was up and traveling again, the cold having driven through to the bone. His head throbbed dully from the pistol-whipping. His stomach was tight and painful from hunger. The bitterness grew rather than subsided. He rode in a swirling, blinding anger.

Sight of the fencing crew at work slowed him but little. He paused for just a moment, making note of the fact that there was one, just as Spann had said. He felt a sharp resentment of the fence. This was what had brought his trouble.

Unseen, a rider came up on his left side, saddlegun across his lap. "Who're you?" the man demanded.

Vern Wheeler glared at him. "None of your damned business!"

He started to ride on, but the man touched spurs to his horse and pulled up directly in front of him. The saddlegun lifted now, not quite pointing at Vern but resting in a position from which it could instantly come into play.

The man eyed him levelly. "I don't mean to be rough, kid. I just asked you who you are. I'll even go halfway with you and tell you my name. It's Dundee. Now, what's yours?" The voice was pleasant but firm. That gun wasn't to be argued with.

"I'm Vern Wheeler." It was a grudging answer.

The saddlegun lowered. Dundee said, "I ought to've seen that for myself. But it would've saved us both some trouble if you'd just said so to start with."

"To hell with you!" Vern said angrily and rode past him.

The encounter served to fan his anger. By the time he reached the farmhouse his hand was a-tremble on the reins.

Trudy Wheeler saw him and set down the basket of dry laundry she was carrying in from the clothesline. She moved toward him in an easy walk at first, then quickened her pace as she got close enough to see his face.

"Vern, what's happened to you?"

Vern Wheeler swung down from the horse and stood weakly for a moment, holding onto the saddle, for the strength had been worn out of him.

Trudy caught hold of his shoulders. "Who beat you?"

"Archer Spann. He pistol-whipped me. Robbed me of the pay I had coming. And all because of that infernal fence out yonder. What's the matter with Dad, anyway?"

Trudy Wheeler bit her lip. "Tie the horse and come on into the house, Vern. You're cold, and I expect you're hungry."

She took him in the warm house, got the heavy coat off of him and sat him down in front of the big wood stove. She poured coffee into a big tin cup and placed it in his hands. He held it there, enjoying the warmth until it worked through the cold skin and became burning hot.

Vern started to sip it but found it scalding. He blew it gently, watching his sister. "I asked you about the fence." His black mood showed in the way he moved, the way he looked at her.

Just then their mother came in, and the answer was delayed. He had to repeat the whole story for Mrs. Wheeler. The retelling of it did little to cool his anger. Trudy already had some biscuits pressed out and rising.

When Vern once more asked about the fence, Mrs. Wheeler parried the question. "He's hungry, Trudy. Put those biscuits in the oven. Let's fry him some beef."

Vern ate hungrily, letting the question ride while he satisfied the insistent grumbling of his stomach. But when he was finished, he pressed for an answer.

"Vern," said Mrs. Wheeler, "you need to go and rest. Forget about it all for a while."

Vern looked at Trudy, and she said, "Have you heard of a man named Doug Monahan?"

"The fellow who was building a fence for Gordon Finch? Yeah, I heard about him. I wasn't in on any of it, though. I was off in a line camp."

Trudy said, "Well, he's the one building the fence."

"Is he out of his head? He knows what happened the first time. It'll happen to him again."

472

Trudy shook her head. "Not to *him,* Vern. To *us.*"

Face clouding, Vern Wheeler set down his coffee. He rubbed his head, feeling the painful swelling where the pistol had struck him. "It started with me."

Trudy said with bitter feeling, "He's looking for a way to get even with the R Cross. He caught Dad on his weak side and talked him into letting him fence the place. He knows Captain Rinehart won't let it go by without trying to stop it. He's set us up like a target, and he's got rough men hired out there, waiting for a fight. He doesn't care what happens to us, just so he gets his chance at the captain."

Mrs. Wheeler said sharply, "Hush, Trudy. You're making it worse than it really is."

"I'm not. It couldn't *be* worse."

Vern clenched his fist. "And for this Monahan I lose my job, and all the money I've saved for a solid year. I lose the place I aimed to buy, and I might even lose my girl. I'd like to see this Monahan. I'd like him to get a taste of what I got yesterday."

Trudy Wheeler was looking out the window. "You won't have to wait long. He's riding up with Dad."

"Trudy!" Mrs. Wheeler cried.

Vern Wheeler stood up, shoving his chair

back abruptly. He moved to the window for a good look at Doug Monahan.

"No better time to do it than right now," he said.

Mrs. Wheeler said, "Wait a minute, Vern. There's no call for trouble, and you're not in any condition . . ."

She was talking to empty space, for Vern Wheeler had gone out the door.

She turned back on Trudy, her eyes flashing anger. "Don't you know what you've done? You sent him out there spoiling for a fight, and he'll be beaten again. In his condition, that's all that can happen. You've done to Vern what you're blaming Doug Monahan for doing to us."

Trudy flushed guiltily as her mother's words went home to her. She moved to the door, wishing for some way to stop what she had started, and knowing there was nothing she could do.

Doug Monahan and Noah Wheeler rode up to the house together and stepped out of their saddles. The old farmer's gaze swept to the porch and caught his son, standing there.

"Vern! Dundee said he ran into you. What're you doing home?"

Vern's gaze was not on his father but on Doug instead. "Ask Monahan."

Doug stopped short, seeing fire in the young man's eyes and at a loss to understand it.

"Because of you, Monahan," Vern Wheeler said, "I was beaten up and robbed of my wages and thrown off of my job. You've put my family in line for even worse than that. But I'm going to stop you."

He stepped down off the porch, his fists tight, his angry eyes on Doug. He towered tall above Monahan.

Noah Wheeler said, "Hold on, Vern."

"Stay out of this, Dad."

Monahan took a step backward. "Wait a minute, Vern. I don't understand what this is all about, but we can work it out someway."

He could see the swollen red streaks where the gun had struck. He could see the exhaustion in Vern Wheeler's face. But Vern kept coming. He looped a hard swing. Monahan leaned and caught the jar of it on his shoulder.

"You wanted a fight," Vern shouted. "Now you got one."

"Vern, I don't want to fight you." The boy went on swinging. Doug put up his hands to ward off the blows. "Vern, listen to me. . . ."

He had to keep backing up. Vern hit him a

hard blow on the side of the face and it jarred him, set his ears to ringing. He caught a right fist with his arm, then felt half the breath gust out of him as Vern's left came in under his ribs.

"Fight!" Vern shouted. "Come on and fight!"

Doug kept his arms in close to his body, trying to anticipate where Vern would hit him. "Vern, I'm not going to fight you!"

Vern was breathing hard, exhaustion catching up with him. He kept swinging until the strength was all gone from him, until he could barely stand. His father stepped in and grabbed his arms.

"Vern, stop it!" He shook his son. "Vern, I don't know what touched you off, but you're wrong, dead wrong. Now go back in that house and sit down. You've got nothing to blame Doug Monahan for. You ought to be thankful he didn't knock your head off. He could have."

Breathing heavily, Vern pointed his finger at Monahan. "Another time. I'll do it another time."

"Come on," Noah Wheeler said curtly, turning Vern around and leading him back toward the house. Mrs. Wheeler came down the steps and helped.

Trudy Wheeler stood on the porch, her

stricken gaze following her brother first, then drifting back to Monahan.

Noah Wheeler paused at the door. "Trudy, come on in the house. I got something to say, and I want you to hear it."

There was a bench out in the yard. Doug Monahan slumped on it, his hand over his ribs where Vern had struck him hard. He struggled to regain the breath that had been knocked out of him. A thin trickle of blood worked down from a small cut above his eye. His battered hat lay on the ground. Either he or Vern had stepped on it.

Hesitantly Trudy Wheeler came down off the porch and moved out beside Monahan. He watched her silently, pain in his eyes.

"I'm sorry," she said haltingly. "I'm afraid I caused this. I wanted it awhile ago, but now I'm ashamed."

"It's all right. I expect I know why you did it."

"You could have hurt him bad, if you'd wanted to."

"It looked like he'd been hurt enough already."

"Thanks," she said softly, "for not hurting him anymore."

Noah Wheeler called her again. Trudy glanced once more at Monahan, then went into the house.

■ ■ ■ ■

Paula Hadley took it better than Vern
Wheeler had hoped.

Soberly staring at his big hands, trying to
keep down the lump of disappointment in
his throat, he said, "I reckon we'll have to
put off getting married. I can't buy that land
till I find some way to get my money."

They sat together on the sofa in the front
room of the Hadley house. Paula took his
big hand in her little one. She lifted it to
her lips and kissed the bruised knuckles.
Tears glistened in her brown eyes.

"I don't care about the land, Vern. You're
all that matters."

"I'm not going to marry you broke, Paula.
When we get married, I want it to be open
and proud, and your dad approving of it."

She gripped his hand tightly. "It isn't fair,
one stubborn old man like the captain, ruining things for us this way. We're just little
people, we couldn't hurt him. What does he
want to hurt us for?"

"I don't know."

"Keeping your money that way — three
hundred dollars can't mean much to him."

"Maybe that's it. It don't mean much to
him, and he can't realize how much it

means to somebody else."

Paula said, "Or he doesn't care. He's too used to running everything to suit himself. Somebody needs to show him that we don't belong to him. Nobody belongs to him."

Vern's face was troubled. "Maybe that's it. I was so mad, I didn't realize it at first. I've watched the R Cross push other people ever since I've been here. None of it ever touched me but now I've had a dose of it myself, and I can see it for what it is."

Understanding came into his face. "They pushed Monahan, and he's fighting them back the only way he can. He's about the first one that ever did."

"What about your father, Vern? Doesn't he realize what he's getting into?"

Vern nodded soberly. "He sits still most of the time and don't say much, but he sees everything. Maybe he just figured it was time folks declared their independence."

Paula leaned her head against Vern's broad shoulder. "That doesn't make it any easier on us."

"Maybe it wasn't meant to be easy. The things that count don't always come easy, Paula."

"What're you going to do, Vern?"

"Go help them, I guess. I'll find some way to get my money back, maybe. And even if I don't, maybe I can help whittle that bunch down to size."

Heading down the track-ribboned dirt street for the road out of town, Vern heard a youthful voice call his name. "Vern Wheeler, hold up there!"

He pulled his horse around and spotted his old friend Rooster Preech stepping off the boardwalk in front of a saloon and striding out into the sun to meet him. A broad grin cut across Rooster's red, freckled face. He always had looked as friendly as a collie dog. Uncut red hair bristled out over his ears and curled into a tangled mess on the back of his neck, just above the collar. A short, uneven thicket of rusty whiskers covered his face, too, some of them still soft and fine, some stiffening with the arrival of manhood.

"Don't be in such an all-fired hurry, Vern. Come on, let's have us a drink together."

Vern glanced toward the saloon, his eyebrows raised. "You reckon they'd let us have it?"

"Sure, I got the barkeep thinkin' I'm twenty-five."

Vern doubted that. He figured the barkeep just didn't care. He swung down from the horse and slapped Rooster on the shoulder. "With all that cover on your face, he

480

couldn't tell but what you was sixty. You been out in the brush lately?"

Rooster waited while Vern tied his horse, then held the door open for Vern to get in ahead of him. "I was. Cattle been keeping me busy."

"Who you working for?"

Rooster was a moment in answering that. "Well, myself, I guess you'd say."

"You haven't got any cattle."

Rooster laughed. "I stay busy."

The bartender looked questioningly at Vern Wheeler. Self-consciously, Vern said, "I'll take whatever Rooster does."

"Bourbon," said Rooster. The bartender left them a quarter-filled bottle and two glasses, and Rooster watched over his shoulder till the man was gone out of hearing. "I happened to run into Lefty Jones yesterday. He was leavin' the country in kind of a hurry."

Vern's interest quickened. "I been wondering about him. He sure got away from that line camp fast. I never even saw him leave."

"From what he told me, Archer Spann didn't give him much choice."

Vern frowned darkly. "That figures."

"Lefty told me what happened to you. Pretty raw deal about your money, son." Rooster had a habit of calling Vern "son," even though they were the same age. It was his way of showing he'd been around more and knew more of the world and its ways.

An eagerness was in Rooster's voice as he leaned forward. "You want to get even with 'em, don't you?"

When Vern did not reply, Rooster said, "Sure, you do! And you'd like to git your money back while you're at it, wouldn't you?"

Vern looked up sharply. "What're you driving at, Rooster?"

Rooster nodded at Vern's glass. "Drink up." Vern cautiously tasted it and flinched. Little as Vern knew about whisky, he could classify this in a hurry. "I like my women and my whisky cheap and plentiful," Rooster used to say, even when he was too young to have much savvy about either one.

Vern set the glass down still nearly full. "Get to the point, Rooster."

Rooster grinned like a fisherman seeing a fish well on the hook. "Workin' that line camp, you oughta know that country up on the north end of the R Cross mighty well."

"Like the back of my hand."

"You know where the best grazin' is and where the cattle is gen'rally at. You could find 'em in the dark, and you'd know the best way to push 'em outa there in a hurry."

Sensing the rest of it, Vern drew back, a vague disappointment bringing pain to him. But he knew there was no reason for surprise. He'd known Rooster Preech a long time, had liked him and ridden with him. But he had always sensed that Rooster would wind up riding the back trails with a fast horse and a quick loop, worth more money in jail than out.

"Rooster, I'm not going to steal any R Cross cattle."

"Nobody said anything about stealin'! But if you was to decide to take enough cattle to get your three hundred dollars back, I know where there's a man who'll take 'em off your hands and not ever worry hisself about the brand on 'em. It wouldn't really be stealin'. It'd jest be gittin' back what they stole from you."

For a moment Vern was tempted. Why shouldn't he do it? They had taken his money with no compunctions at all.

"It's dangerous, Rooster. There's been men got their necks stretched out real long for getting caught with R Cross cattle."

"They got caught. We won't. You know that country to where we'd always have a way of gittin' out."

Vern studied him speculatively. "Rooster, what would you be getting out of this, if we just took three hundred dollars' worth of cattle?"

Rooster smiled and looked back over his shoulder to make sure the barkeep was still out of earshot. "Now, you wouldn't want them to git off scot-free, would you? I thought we might jest take along a few extry head. Sort of exemplary payment, they call it in court. Enough to justify me and another feller or two I know for helpin' you. You wouldn't have to have them extry cattle on your conscience. As far as you're concerned, you'd only be takin' enough for your three hundred dollars. The rest'd be jest between me and them other fellers."

Vern stood up, shaking his head. "Thanks for the drink, Rooster." Most of it remained in the glass. "But I reckon not. I want to fight the R Cross, but that's not how I figure on doing it."

Rooster shrugged, disappointed but still smiling. "Well, you can't say I didn't try, son. It's still a good offer, and any time you change your mind, jest holler."

Chris Hadley closed his saloon at dusk and walked home, content to let the other places have the night business. A man with a teenage daughter couldn't leave her alone all the time. He moved along with head down, barely nodding to the people he met on the street, for his mind was on other things.

He hung up his hat and coat and stood before the wood heater, warming in its pleasant glow. His daughter said, "Good evening, Papa. I'll have supper ready in a little."

Worry creasing his high forehead, Chris Hadley said, "Paula, come here and sit down. I want to talk to you."

She came, but she didn't sit, for she had supper cooking on the stove.

Hadley said, "Vern Wheeler was in town today. He came here, didn't he?"

"Yes, Papa, he did."

A grimness came to Chris Hadley's face. "What for?"

Paula was a moment in answering. Her face tightened with decision. "I guess you know, Papa, without having to ask, but I'll tell you. He asked me to wait for him. And I told him I would."

Chris Hadley sat down wearily and exhaled a long breath.

He rubbed his hand over his face without looking up at Paula. "I knew we'd stayed here too long. I ought to've sold out and moved a year ago. Paula, I'll not let you do it."

"I love him, Papa. I'm going to marry him."

Hadley said, "Paula, for years I've saved so I could send you back where you belong, give you the kind of life you were born for. I'm not going to let you throw it away on Vern Wheeler or anybody like him."

"I don't know anything about any other kind of life, and I don't care. I just know I love Vern Wheeler, and I'm going to marry him."

Angered, he said, "Paula, you never gave me any trouble when you were growing up. No man could have had a better daughter. I never thought you'd ever defy me this way."

Her lips trembled, but her brown eyes were firm. "I never thought I'd have to."

"I'll remind you, Paula, you're under age! I can stop you from marrying. I'll send you away somewhere to school until you forget this foolishness."

She brought her hands up over her breasts and clenched a small fist over the locket her mother had left her. "It's your right, Papa, but I'll tell you this: I won't forget. As soon as I'm of age, I'll come back, and I'll marry Vern Wheeler!"

11

Doug Monahan was worried. The barbed wire hadn't arrived. The work had gone on without trouble. Occasionally a rider would show up on the high rise out yonder and sit awhile in the gray grass, watching. Eventually Dundee would drift his way, and the man would get back on his horse and fade out of sight.

The line of set posts was a long one now, stretching well over a mile already and waiting for the wire.

"Stub," Monahan said, "something's wrong. That wire ought to've been here a week ago. I wish you'd take a horse and ride over to Stringtown. See what's the matter."

Stub returned bringing the kind of report Doug had expected.

"That wire's sittin' over there in the depot gatherin' dust. They won't anybody haul it."

Angrily Doug said, "What about that

freighter, Slim Torrance? I paid him half of the freight in advance."

Stub Bailey dug a wrinkled, sweat-stained check out of his shirt pocket. "He sent it back to you. Here."

Doug swore under his breath while Stub explained. "Sheriff McKelvie seen you over there that day and knew there was somethin' up. He hung around till he found out what it was, and he went to see this Torrance. Now, it seems like Torrance did something or other over here one time that wasn't strictly according to the statutes. He never did say just what. Anyhow, the sheriff told him if he brought a spool of that wire into this county, or even had it sent, he'd yank him up by the scruff of the neck and throw him in the jailhouse over at Twin Wells."

Stub added, "So that's the reason we ain't had any wire. And not apt to get any unless we go fetch it ourselves."

Doug Monahan drew his lips in tight and smashed his fist into his hand. "Then we'll go get it ourselves. And we'll haul it right through the main street of Twin Wells!"

Stub frowned. "That's askin' for trouble."

Angrily Doug replied, "We already got trouble. That's just telling them we can take care of it."

He left Stub Bailey to oversee the post-setting job, Dundee to continue his watch. He took the five Blessingames and three wagons. And, because he wanted to go, Vern Wheeler.

Vern had come back from town with his anger at last expired. He had apologized and asked to be allowed to help. A husky boy, he had made a good hand ever since, digging holes, tamping posts, throwing in where the hottest and the hardest work was. Some deep-seated determination seemed to be driving him. He was setting a strong pace for the rest of the men to follow.

They left as soon as darkness had lifted enough that they could see the wagon trail. Doug and Vern rode horseback, the Blessingames on the wagons. The morning was uneventful, but about midafternoon a rider broke over a hilltop and spotted them. He sat there a while, watching, then pulled back and disappeared over the hill.

By the time the wagons groaned into Stringtown the second day, Monahan was positive they were being followed. Several times he had glimpsed a rider far behind them. The man never got any closer or dropped any farther back. Now, as they loaded their wagons at the depot, he saw a man sitting his horse across the dusty street, watching. When the rider turned away, Monahan caught a glimpse of the R Cross on its hip, stamped with the small horse iron. He looked questioningly at Vern Wheeler.

"Name's Bodie," Vern said. "Kind of a straw boss for Archer Spann sometimes. If Spann has got any friends atall, I reckon Bodie's one of them."

Starting back, Doug knew within reason that they would find a reception committee somewhere on the trail. He wished they had Dundee and the other men with them. But he couldn't afford to leave the Wheeler place without protection.

"We'll just have to face up to it ourselves," he told the men. "Seven of us, and burdened down with loaded wagons."

Foley Blessingame spat disdainfully, leaving a string of brown tobacco juice in the dust. "Don't you worry none, Doug. You got *thirteen* men, the way I see it. Them four kids of mine will count for two men apiece, and I'll count for three."

"Thirteen's an unlucky number, Foley," Doug pointed out.

"For whoever tries to tamper with us."

They rode watchfully, guns never far from reach, but nothing happened the first day. In camp that night, two men were on guard all the time, and others were never deeply asleep.

Nothing came that night, and home was not too far away. As they broke camp, Vern Wheeler pulled up beside Monahan.

"Doug, I been thinking where I'd go to stop a string of wagons, if I was Archer Spann and wanted to. It just occurred to me that Drinkman's Gap would be the best place on the whole trail to do it."

Doug remembered the gap, although he hadn't known what it was called. It was a place where the trail passed through a line of small rocky hills too rough to go around in a wagon. It was nothing like a mountain pass, but it did provide a place where a few men, well-positioned in the mouth of the gap, might halt a string of wagons. Horses could move freely enough up the hillsides, but a loaded wagon could move only through the pass.

"If they're of a mind to stop us," Vern said darkly, "I reckon they could do it. We couldn't move these wagons off the road, and they'll likely block it with men."

"Then," replied Doug, "if we can't get the wagons off the road, we'll just have to get the men off of it."

The gap came into sight at mid-morning. Doug rode out in front of the wagons for a look-see. Sure enough, men waited down there, sitting on the ground, smoking, holding their horses. He counted nine, perhaps ten. At sight of him they stood up. Most of them swung leisurely into their saddles.

They didn't move after him. They plainly preferred to meet him on their own ground. They couldn't have chosen a better place.

Doug rode back to the wagons. He saw Vern Wheeler checking his six-shooter. "I don't want you using that, Vern. Not to shoot anybody, anyway."

"They're blocking the trail. How else we going to get through?"

"We'll get through, and we shouldn't have to shoot anybody."

He dismounted by Foley's wagon. He lifted down a heavy spool of wire and eased it to the grass. "Hand me that pair of wire cutters in there, Foley."

This wire was a different brand from the one he had used before. This one did not have the coat of red paint. Pulling up one end of the wire, Doug held it out to Vern. "Here, take ahold." Then he pushed the spool along on the ground, unrolling a piece which he judged to be about twice as long as the gap was wide. He snipped the wire off, then doubled it back. While Vern held the two cut ends, Doug twisted the wire.

"Double thickness," he said, "will be strong and a lot easier to handle than just one strand."

He coiled the doubled wire, lifted the rest of the spool back into the wagon and remounted his horse. "All right, let's go. We'll take it slow at first. Let them think they're going to stop us. Then, when I give the signal, let those mules have everything you've got."

He motioned Vern to ride beside him. They moved out twenty or thirty paces ahead of the wagons. They held their horses in a walk, so the wagons could keep up with them. Slowly they drew closer to the gap, where the R Cross waited. Most of the men were a-horseback, but a couple stood afoot, holding their horses.

"That's Spann, isn't it?" he asked Vern.

Vern nodded, and his blue eyes were hard. "That's him." His fingers flexed, and Doug knew the boy itched to get his hands on Spann.

"Take it easy," Doug said. "We're not aiming to kill anybody, no matter how bad he may need it."

They rode closer. The men in the gap were at ease, confident that all they had to do was wait, and the wagons would fall into their laps like ripe apples out of a tree.

"It's time now," Doug said. He handed Vern one end of the doubled wire. "Take a wrap on your saddlehorn and pull yonder-way with it. Then spur for all you're worth."

Vern nodded, face taut. He comprehended for the first time what Doug Monahan planned to do.

When they had the wire stretched out tightly between them, Doug looked back over his shoulder and gave Foley Blessingame the nod. Then he yelled and spurred his horse. He heard old Foley's voice rise behind him like the angry squall of a panther. He heard the rattle of chains, the sudden clatter of the mules' hoofs on the hard ground as the lead wagon jerked forward.

For a few seconds there was confusion among the riders at the gap. They stared in consternation. Then they saw the barbed wire, stretched between the two horsemen, coming straight at them.

There is something about barbed wire that strikes dread in those who know it. A man stretching fence always has his nerves keened by realization that the wire may snap and lash at him with its sharp and wicked barbs. A man running a horse alongside a fence, chasing down a runaway cow, knows the fear of falling, of hurtling helplessly into the ripping wire.

These men saw the wire coming, and it loosed a sudden panic among them that guns might not have done. They spurred up the hillsides, out of the way.

Archer Spann stood afoot in the middle of the gap, shouting at them, cursing, so angry he did not realize his own situation. Seeing it then, he tried to swing into the saddle and run. But the excitement had carried to his horse. The animal reared, jerking the reins from his hands. It loped up the gap, head high in panic. It stepped on one of the dragging reins and nearly threw itself to the ground. The horse turned aside from the trail then and started up the hill.

Spann stood rooted to the spot, watching helplessly as the wire flashed toward him between Monahan and Vern Wheeler, the wagons hurtling along behind. He started to run, saw he couldn't make it, then dropped to the ground as the wire sang over his head. Heart pounding, he heard the hammering of the mules' hoofs and the rumble of the heavy-laden wheels. Desperately he rolled over in the dust, got to his knees and scrambled out of the way.

The wagons rolled past him, leaving him choking in the cloud of dust that the heavy iron rims had raised from the hard ground. He got to his feet and watched the wagons pulling away. He ripped off his hat and hurled it to the ground, cursing and stomping.

Slowly his men worked back down from the hillsides and gathered around him.

"Washerwomen!" he shouted. "I ought to fire every blessed one of you!"

"Archer," offered the one called Bodie, "we could still catch them."

"And do what?" Spann demanded. "You had them right here, the best place on the whole road, and you scattered like a bunch of quail."

The men sat red-faced, smarting under the tongue-lashing he gave them.

Bodie finally put in, "You don't know what that bobwire can do, Archer."

"I know what it'll do to this country if they ever put it up," he exploded. "About half of you hombres'll be riding the chuckline."

One of the men left the group — gladly — and caught Spann's horse. By the time he brought him back, Spann had cooled a little.

"The R Cross has always meant something in this country," Spann said, calmer now. "It's not something that people laugh at. But they'll laugh when they know what happened here."

His face twisted as he looked down the gap to the dust of the wagons. His knuckles went white, the way he clenched the leather reins. More than anything else, more even than the idea of Noah Wheeler's fence, he hated the thought of ridicule.

"They won't laugh long," he gritted. "Not very long."

Doug Monahan moved out to one side to drop the twisted wire out of the way, then eased up, letting the wagons go past him. He loped along behind them, looking over his shoulder for reassurance. Then he touched spurs to the horse again and pulled up beside the wagons, one by one.

"Slow them down now. They're not coming after us."

The Blessingames sawed on the lines, gradually bringing the heavy wagons to a stop. The ground was softer here, and dustier. Doug pinched his eyes shut as the dust from the wheels drifted past him. He sneezed once and turned his face away.

Foley Blessingame was laughing and slapping his knee with a hand as big as a Percheron's hoof. "Did you see that feller's face jest before he hit the ground? You never saw a madder man in your whole life!"

"That," Doug told him, "was Archer

Spann."

Foley's eyebrows lifted. "So that was him. Well, we give him a nice remembrance, I do believe."

Vern Wheeler was grinning, but it was a bitter, vengeful sort of grin. "I wish we could've rimfired him with that wire. It wouldn't have been any more than he deserved."

"It would have killed him," Doug pointed out.

Vern said flatly, "There's not much wrong with that."

The Blessingame boys were off, patting their mules, talking gently to them and calming them down.

Foley Blessingame said, "Well, Doug, you still aim to take these wagons right through town?"

Doug's jaw had a firm set to it. "Right through the big middle!"

Their arrival in Twin Wells could not have attracted more attention if they had brought a brass band. People came out and stood in front of houses and stores to watch them pass. Dogs trotted along, barking at the mules, and kids ran beside the heavy wagons. Some people smiled, some frowned with disapproval. Many just watched silently, withholding judgment or, if they had made it, hiding it.

Paula Hadley stood in front of her picket fence. Vern Wheeler pulled his horse over toward her. He reached down and gripped her hand a moment, and the look that passed between them said all there was to say.

Doug Monahan caught this, and he smiled. He had heard a little, and he knew now that there was even more to it than he had heard.

Sheriff Luke McKelvie strode out from under the heavy old live oaks in the courthouse square. There was something of resignation in his crow-tracked eyes as Doug Monahan pulled over beside him.

"Still not taking any advice, are you, Monahan?"

Doug shook his head. "Not yours, McKelvie."

"I was afraid you wouldn't. But I thought a little discouragement or two along the line might make you listen to it, anyway."

Resentfully Doug said, "We wouldn't have had to go after this wire if you hadn't thrown a scare into my freighter. Why did you do it?"

"Like I said, I hoped a little discouragement would slow you down till you had time to do some thinking."

"I'm not breaking any law, McKelvie. What business is it of yours?"

"I'm a peace officer, Monahan. It's been a peaceful country, in the main. I do what I can to keep it that way."

"The only thing I can't understand is why the captain didn't send somebody over to destroy the wire in the Stringtown depot."

McKelvie shrugged. "Mainly, I guess, because he didn't know it was there."

Surprised, Monahan demanded, "You didn't tell him?"

McKelvie shook his head. "Like I said, keeping the peace is my job."

12

With the wire on hand, the fencing job began to show some real progress. Doug and his crew started by burying a big rock "dead-man" anchor for the corner posts, then bound the wire securely around these posts and started stringing it from the corner. The wooden spools were built with a hollow center. Two men would shove a crowbar through it. Then, one on either end of the bar, they would walk up the fence-line, the wire unrolling itself as they went.

They had no regular fence-stretching equipment. Instead, they would block up the axle of a wagon, secure the wire to a stick wedged between the spokes, and turn the wheel by hand, drawing the wire taut against the posts. They drove sharp staples into the hard cedar posts, fastening the wire solidly in place.

This was a faster job than setting the posts, so Monahan left most of the crew on the digging and tamping job, trying to keep ahead of the wire stringers. With the winter lull in his own field chores, Noah Wheeler spent most of his time with Monahan's crew, helping at the work and joying in the strong fence that shaped in his hands.

The crew worked well together, broken in to the hard labor now. Foley Blessingame and his four sons kept the men in good humor with rowdy jokes and rough horseplay that stopped only a fraction short of broken arms and legs. Old Foley was an everlasting wonder to Doug — how any man that old could do so much hard work. He would wear a young man into the ground and then do the work for both of them.

Then at night, under lanternlight in the barn, he would play poker with anyone who still had the courage to sit in against him. Almost everybody in the crew except Stub Bailey had tried him, and to a man they had lost.

Every once in a while Foley would make a try for Stub: "Why'n't you come on and play me a game? You can git your fun and eddication at the same time."

But Stub always turned him down with a grin. "I never was much of a hand at poker. You better stick to the experts."

502

Some of the crew who had considered themselves as experts were reappraising themselves after a set-to with old Foley. That he cheated was common knowledge. Just how he did it was a mystery. At penny ante it wasn't too expensive, and the men started choosing up to see who would play against him each night while the others watched, trying to catch him in a trick. They never did.

The only misfit in the bunch was Simon Getty, the cook. His cooking was decent enough the first few days, but he finally got the "rings," as the cowboys called it. He grumbled and carried on about everything and everybody. Foley Blessingame and those "kids" of his ate more than ten men decently ought to. That Dundee thought he could ride into camp any old time he felt like it and eat. Didn't he know that dinner was ready at twelve o'clock, and not at one or two or three? That saddlegun he toted around didn't make him any privileged character.

And those men Dundee had brought out — some of them didn't know enough to wash their hands before they shoved them into a man's Dutch ovens. That Stub Bailey, sneaking a bottle out of his bedroll these cold mornings and lacing his coffee on the quiet. Doug figured the cook's main objection here was that Stub hadn't offered him any of it.

And Doug Monahan himself — why couldn't he buy a man something decent to cook in? A man couldn't cook for a pack of pot hounds with the equipment this outfit furnished him.

Doug took it quietly. He knew a cowcamp cook's temper served to keep the rest of the crew in its proper place. But sometimes a man could overdo a thing, even if he was right.

Simon Getty made his big mistake one cold morning as the Blessingames came up under the tarp for breakfast. Faces flushed from the raw chill, they approached the chuckbox with a raging hunger. They found Simon Getty ringier than usual. He must have been cold too.

"Damn you, Foley Blessingame, stop kicking sand into the ovens. Lift up them big feet before I take a singletree to you."

Normally Foley would have retreated, for few men ever tampered with the cook. His revenge would be certain and hard to swallow. But this time Foley stood his ground, his mouth setting in a hard line. The cook had jumped him just one time too many.

Getty growled, "Five growed men without

504

no better manners than a heathen Comanche Indian! The whole bunch of you swarm around them ovens like a passel of razorback hogs. Pity you don't fall in that crick and drown."

Foley's bearded face changed color a couple of times. He said abruptly, "Speakin' of fallin' in the creek, I don't recollect as I've seen you take a bath since you been out here. Right now would be as good a time as I know of."

Before Getty could draw away, Foley had him by the shoulders, his huge hands holding the cook as helpless as a baby calf. A couple of Foley's sons grabbed the cook's legs, and they packed him down to the creekbank like a sack of bran. Without ceremony, they heaved him in.

The first two times the cook crawled out cursing. They pitched him back. The third time he got out on the opposite side, so busy shivering and moaning and coughing up water that he couldn't say much. Presently Getty circled clear around the spring and came back on the other side, blue with cold. He went directly into the barn, took off his wet clothes and crawled into his blankets. He lay there sulling like a possum.

The news brought no cheer to Doug Monahan, even though it didn't surprise him much. "Well, Foley," he said, "since you ran off the cook, it's up to you to finish the breakfast."

He knew he would have to send Getty back to Stringtown. What would he do for a cook now?

Trudy Wheeler gave him the answer. "What were you paying him?"

"Forty dollars a month."

"And furnishing the food?"

"Yes."

"Pay me that and I'll take the job."

Doug didn't know if she was serious or not. "Thought you didn't like this fencing project."

She shrugged. "You're not going to stop it, and men have to eat. If you're paying, I'd just as well get some of that money as see someone else take it."

Doug was pleased. A woman's cooking would go over a lot better with these men than that of a camp cook, no matter how good he was.

"You wouldn't like cooking out in the open like this," he pointed out.

"I'd cook in the house, on the big wood-stove."

Doug felt relief. Trudy Wheeler was softening. He had thought he saw it after Vern Wheeler had come home fighting. Now he was sure.

"Then you're hired," Doug said. He extended his hand, and she took it. "You can start right now, and fix dinner."

Captain Andrew Rinehart paced the scarred pine floor of his office with the slowed step of an old man. An uneasiness creased his weathered face as he looked at Sheriff Luke McKelvie.

"What else is new in town?"

It wasn't the question he wanted to ask, McKelvie knew that. The captain would bide his time, but he would get around to that question eventually if the answer didn't come of its own accord.

"Not a great deal," the sheriff said, dropping cigarette ashes into a chip-edged old saucer. The captain never had ash trays around. Too strong-willed to indulge himself in life's smaller pleasures, the captain made no allowances for those who did.

McKelvie said, "Gordon Finch has left. Dumped the ranch, livestock and all, right into the bank's lap. Just rode off and left it."

The captain nodded in satisfaction. "It's what I told him to do."

"Albert Brown's wringing his hands. He says he's a banker, not a rancher. He don't know what to do about it."

The captain frowned. "Funny he hasn't come to me. I'd buy it, he ought to know that."

McKelvie stared reflectively at the captain. A thought came to him, but he kept silent about it.

The captain evidently sensed McKelvie's thought anyway. His frown deepened. "You think maybe he don't want to sell to me?"

The sheriff shrugged, not wanting to make a definite answer. "I wouldn't know, Captain. I haven't talked to him about it myself."

The captain paced some more, pausing to look out the window. "They're talking in town, aren't they?"

McKelvie said, "They're talking."

The captain shoved his hands deeply into his pockets. His voice was defiant. "Let them talk, then. It's *my* town. I built it. I don't care what they say."

But by the dark worry in the old man's face, the way the gray head was bowed, McKelvie could tell that Rinehart *did* care. He had been the patriarch, the bell-wether, much too long to stop caring now.

McKelvie said, "It was just a little place in the old days, Captain. Everybody in town worked for you or owed you something. But it's not that little anymore. There are lots of people in it who don't believe they owe you a thing. They think they can get along without you."

Rinehart gave him an angry, raking glance. "Who are you working for, Luke, them or me?"

Not attempting to answer, McKelvie switched his gaze to Archer Spann, standing gravely by the door, out of the path of the captain's restless pacing.

"They're talking about you, too, Archer," the sheriff said. He caught the quick resentment in Spann's narrowed eyes.

"What're they saying?" Spann demanded.

"Laughing, mostly, about that incident over at Drinkman's Gap."

Spann colored. Mouth hardening, he sat down stiffly in a straight chair covered with a stretched, dried steer hide, the red hair still on it. Spann seemed to submerge in his own dark thoughts, losing himself from the other two men. It was almost as if he had left the room.

The captain said, "The ranchers are all with us, that's what counts."

"Are they?" asked McKelvie. "I heard Archer made the rounds, trying to work up all the opposition he could against the fence. I heard some of them turned away from him."

Stubbornly the captain said, "They'll come in with us when they realize what this fence will do to the country."

McKelvie considered awhile before he made any comment. "I've spent a lot of time asking myself what that fence means to the country. It could bring some good things, Captain."

Captain Rinehart stared incredulously. "Luke," and there was shock in his voice, "are *you* turning against me?"

The sheriff looked at Rinehart. "I'm not against you, Captain. I'll never fight you," he said in a hurt voice.

The captain walked back to the window and stared out awhile, a growing tension in the ceaseless flexing of his nervous, rope-scarred hands. "What's that story they're telling about the Wheeler boy, and three hundred dollars?"

McKelvie replied, "All I know is what I hear. You better ask Archer."

Spann glanced up sharply at mention of his name. "It's a lie. It's just something they made up to swing people against us. You know I took the cash out to that boy. You counted it off to me yourself, Captain."

The captain said, "He's right, Luke. I counted it out. The R Cross doesn't steal from its men."

McKelvie kept his eyes on Archer Spann. "No, the R Cross wouldn't."

Tiring, the captain sat down at his desk. He was silent awhile, his mind running back to other times and other places. He opened a drawer and took out a small object. He gazed at it a moment, then extended it to McKelvie.

"Ever see that, Luke?"

"Arrowhead, isn't it?"

The captain nodded. "I caught it on the Pecos, a long time ago. Packed it around in my shoulder twelve or fifteen years. Maybe I was still carrying it when you were on the ranch here, I don't remember. It finally worked close to the surface, and I had it taken out at Fort Worth."

There was a strange gentleness to the captain's voice as he talked of the olden times.

"Quite a souvenir," McKelvie commented.

The captain took it back and gazed at it with something akin to reverence. For a while, then, he forgot the worry of the present. He talked of things that had happened in those early days, of a time when he was in his element. Of a time of open range and freedom and plenty of opportunity for the man who had guts enough to try the impossible and make it work. A time when he had youth and vitality and a driving ambition.

It had been years since McKelvie had heard the captain talk like this, and he knew it for what it was. Sensing that time was inevitably closing in upon him, sensing the trouble that already had begun and could no longer be stopped until it had run its course, the old cowman was taking momentary refuge in the past.

"Those were the real times, Luke," the captain said. "They're gone now. There's a new breed of men in the country, men that don't know what we went through in the old days. They want to tear down all we built. Can you blame me, Luke, for wanting to keep it the way it used to be?"

McKelvie shook his head. "I can't blame you, Captain. But I will tell you this: you can't stop them. You'd just as well go out there and try to stop the river. You may slow the thing down, you may destroy some people. But in the end, Captain, they'll get you. They'll destroy *you.*"

The captain stared unbelievingly, his face drained a shade lighter. Finally he pushed wearily to his feet, as if he carried a huge weight on his shoulders. His heavy-browed eyes were more sad than angry. His voice was pinched with hurt.

"I reckon you'd better go, Luke. If that's

the way you feel, I don't want you around here anymore."

Luke McKelvie blinked back a burning in his eyes. The old cowman had been like a father to him. Now McKelvie yearned to go to him and put his arm around the old man's shoulders and help him see it through. But he realized that the way was hopelessly blocked, that it had been blocked from the beginning by stubborn pride and an old man's deep-etched memories of a time when he had been king.

"Captain," McKelvie said, "think hard before you do anything."

"Go, Luke. Just go."

Luke McKelvie picked up his hat and walked out of the room without looking back. He moved with his head down, the hatbrim crushed in his strong, unfeeling hand.

Sarah Rinehart was waiting for him at the front door. Seeing the look in his eyes, she knew. "You quarreled?"

McKelvie nodded. "I'm sorry, Sarah, I did the best I could. I knew it was going to happen, though, sooner or later."

"I know," she said. She brought a handkerchief out of her old lace sleeve. "What're we going to do with him, Luke?"

"I don't know, Sarah. He's getting set for

a big fall. About all we can do is wait and try to help him up again."

Sarah said, "A lot of it's Archer Spann. Oh, I know Andrew barks at him sometimes, to remind him who's boss. But he's getting old, and he thinks he sees something of himself in Archer. He lets Archer influence him more than any man ever has before."

Luke McKelvie took Sarah Rinehart's thin hand. He could feel more strength in the old fingers than had been there in a long time. "I'm glad to see you looking better, Sarah. You've got to take care of yourself for his sake. One day soon, he's going to need you. You've got to be here."

She said, "I'll be here, Luke."

In the office Archer Spann stood at the window, watching Luke McKelvie mount his horse. "They've bought him off, Captain. He's sold out."

Captain Rinehart sat heavily in his big office chair, his hands hanging limply. Weariness settled in his eyes, and he closed them. He rubbed a hand over his forehead, wondering why Providence had chosen to set Luke McKelvie against him. He knew his friends were dwindling in number day by day, but Luke McKelvie was one he had counted on.

He knew Spann was wrong about McKelvie. Luke would never sell out. He just looked at the thing differently, that was all. But whatever the reason, he was in the enemy's camp now. And that camp was growing.

Spann said, "Time's getting short, Captain. The farther they go with that fence, the harder it's going to be to stop them."

Rinehart was only half listening. He was thinking of other days, of happier days when Luke McKelvie had been an R Cross cowboy, one of the best the captain had ever known. Losing him now was almost like losing a son.

Times like this, Rinehart wished he *had* had a son. Everything else he had wanted in life had been provided him. But this he had always been denied. Once Luke McKelvie had come close to filling the need. Of late, it was Archer Spann.

"What about it, Captain?" Spann pressed with a trace of impatience.

"I've told you, you can do whatever you want to about that fence and about Monahan."

"We need to go farther than that. You don't stop a snake by cutting its tail off. We need to hit Noah Wheeler, too. Hit him with all we've got, and we'll stop this thing for good."

The captain shook his head. "No, Archer, I've told you that, too. We're leaving Noah Wheeler alone."

Spann rubbed his hands nervously behind his back as he looked out the window again. "Do you mind telling me, Captain, what it is about Noah Wheeler that makes him so special? What's the hold he's got over you?"

The captain frowned and stared at his rough old hands. "It goes back a long, long way. We were in the war together, Archer. Maybe you don't see him as much except a quiet old farmer, but I know differently. I can remember.

"We were both in Hood's Texas Brigade. I had a commission — still got it put away in an old trunk somewhere — and Noah Wheeler was one of my sergeants. We went through some hard times together — Gaines Mill, Second Manassas." He smiled faintly, calling up memories. "We had a marching song then, called 'The Old Gray Mare Came Tearing Out of the Wilderness.' I'll never forget Noah singing that song as the men went marching down the road.

"Then we came to Antietam. You never saw a hungrier, dirtier bunch of men in your life. They put us up against Hooker and his federals, and it was murder. It looked like the Yanks had us whipped when Hood

516

ordered us to charge. Up through the cornfield we went. It was the nearest thing to hell there'll ever be on earth, the bullets whistling like hornets, the shells screaming in. But we kept on going.

"I caught a bullet in my leg and went down right under a Yankee gun. They had me. I was looking death in the face, and there wasn't any way out. But Noah Wheeler came and stood over me and put that gun out of service while the bullets ripped by him like hail. Noah Wheeler brought me out of that battle alive, Archer.

"That's why I'm not going to hit him. I owe him my life."

13

Dundee was getting impatient. "I'm beginnin' to think I never will be able to get in a lick," he complained to Doug Monahan as they sat on the edge of the Wheeler porch, eating supper. "Two miles of fence already strung up and they're not makin' a move against it. All I do is wear out my saddle lookin' at the scenery."

Doug gulped a big swallow of black coffee. "We ought to take that as a blessing. Or maybe you just like fighting a lot more than I do."

Dundee shrugged. "I wouldn't exactly say I like it. It's only that I seem to thrive on trouble. Always did, even when I was a kid. Others could go fishin'. Me, I always had to go get in a fight. Things got too quiet, I got restless, started looking for something to muddy up the waters a little bit. I generally managed to find it."

Doug said, "Maybe you were born a few

years too late. You ought to've been in the army, fighting Indians."

Dundee shook his head, smiling. "About the time the fightin' started, I'd've been in the guardhouse for hittin' an officer. I never did cotton to takin' orders."

"You've taken them from me."

"If I hadn't liked 'em, I wouldn't have took 'em."

They were the last ones to eat. Since Trudy had taken over the cooking job, the men came up to the house for their meals, filling their plates from food piled high on the kitchen table. They usually sat on the porch outside to eat it, for the house would be uncomfortably cramped with that many men sitting around on the floor.

Stub Bailey was finishing up, rubbing his stomach in satisfaction. He had been back to the table the second time. Watching Stub, Dundee said, "That girl's cookin's goin' to cost you a heap extra, Doug. One thing about Simon Getty, he wouldn't make a man overstuff himself." He smiled then. "Of course, I reckon there's more to it than just the cookin'. Most of 'em go back the second time just to take another look at that girl."

Dundee's eyes touched Doug Monahan's for a moment with a hint of shared secrets. Doug knew Dundee was including him, too.

Dundee had a way of standing off and shrewdly sizing people up, and he wasn't often wrong.

Funny the way it was with Trudy. After all she had said earlier about the fence, she had loosened up and become friendly and easy-mannered to the men of the fencing crew. There wasn't one of them now who wouldn't have charged hell with a bucket of water if she had asked him to. Maybe she had belatedly caught some of her father's enthusiasm about the fence.

Dundee finished first and walked off toward the barn. Doug sat on the porch, eating the last of a big slice of gingerbread. Trudy walked out onto the porch with a large pan in her hands. Leaning over Doug, she dropped another piece of gingerbread into his plate.

"Whoa now," he said, "I've had enough."

"There's too much to throw away and not enough to keep," she told him firmly. "Eat it." She ran her kitchen in the ironclad manner of a wagon cook, and she made the men like it.

Doug smiled, remembering how wrong his first impression of her had been. That day she had ridden into his fencing camp with her father, he had her figured as a quiet, shy little country girl who would never speak above a whisper. He had missed by about a mile and a half. There was something of steel about Trudy Wheeler. It might be hidden most of the time, but stress would bring it out.

Doug knew he was thinking too much about her. It wasn't that he wanted to. But whenever she was anywhere in view, he found himself watching her, hoping she didn't notice.

Doug Monahan had never been in love in his life, and he didn't want to be in love now. There was too much else to worry about.

He couldn't tell for sure what was wrong that night. An uneasiness came over him as darkness settled down, a prescience he had felt at other times, one he had learned to respect. He watched the men crawl into their blankets in the barn, but he didn't go to bed himself.

"What's the matter, Doug?" Stub Bailey asked.

"I don't rightly know. Just got a queer feeling."

"So've I, but it was just that third slice of gingerbread. It'll be all right in the morning."

Doug went outside and walked restlessly

in front of the barn. He smoked half a cigarette, then flipped it away. It didn't taste right.

It was dark outside, except for the brittle winter starlight. He didn't like it, and he wished the moon would rise. Then he remembered it was time for the new moon.

Restlessness still needling him, he saddled his horse and rode down the steadily lengthening fenceline. His horse nickered, and another answered from nearby in the darkness. Doug kept his hand on his gun until he assured himself that the other horseman was one of the two guards he had constantly riding the fence.

"Who is it?" a stern voice demanded. Doug heard a hammer click.

"Me, Doug." He rode up slowly. He had to get close before the man could be sure of him in the darkness. The rider relaxed then and slipped the gun back into its holster.

"Just checking up, Milt," Doug said. "See or hear anything?"

"Nope, quiet as a church. Just like it's been every night."

"How long since you've seen Wallace?"

"Passed him ten minutes ago. He was ridin' along on the other side. He'll make a *vuelta* and be back directly. Somethin' wrong?"

"Nothing I can put my finger on. Just a feeling."

He found the other guard presently and got the same sort of answers. Doug was almost ready to concede that it *was* too much gingerbread and go back to the barn. But, to satisfy himself, he decided to make a short swing of a mile or so out in the direction of the R Cross headquarters.

The horse picked them up first. How a horse could unerringly find others of its kind in pitch darkness had always been something of a mystery to Doug. His mount perked up its ears and turned its head a little. Doug stood in the stirrups, looking and listening. He could hear and see nothing. He swung out of the saddle to get away from the constant creak of leather and stood off at the reins' full length from the horse.

He began to hear it then, the muffled thud of hoofs in the dry grass, a fragile tinkle of spurs and bit-chains in the crisp night air.

They were coming.

He swung back into the saddle and spurred into a long trot, hoping the sound would not carry to the oncoming riders as their own had come to him. The sharp breeze was in his favor. He hurriedly found his two guards.

"Riders on their way," he said. "Wallace,

you ride back to the barn and pick up the rest of the crew. Milt, you and I'll go down to the end of the fence."

They struck an easy lope down the fenceline. Doug wished for good moonlight, but he knew there would be little of it. They wouldn't see their enemy until the men got close. But that worked both ways. The fencing crew wouldn't be easily seen, either.

He wondered why he hadn't thought of the new moon before. The R Cross probably had checked the almanac to be sure of coming in the dark of the moon. With a little thought, Monahan would have known they'd come on a night like this, if they were coming at all.

At the end of the fence were stacked the spools of wire and most of the cedar posts which hadn't been used yet. Down here the R Cross riders could do more damage in ten minutes than they could elsewhere in half the night, laboriously snipping away at the finished fence.

Saddlegun in his lap, Doug sat his horse quietly and waited, the blood pounding in his temples. Maybe Dundee would get his satisfaction tonight.

He heard a faint hum in the fence. Somewhere above, someone had cut a strand and eased the tension of the wire.

Doug's hand tightened on the gun. All that hard work, and they were setting in to destroy it! Listening hard, hearing the sharp gnash of cutting edge against cutting edge as the steel cutters bit through the wire, he felt growing in him the same anger that he had known the day Paco Sanchez had died.

But this time there was a difference. This time he was not helpless.

The horses were coming down the fence. Doug stepped out of the saddle, squatting low in the brittle grass so he could see the riders against the skyline. The sky was almost as black as the ground, and he could make out only the blurry outlines of the men as they reached the corner posts. He tied the ends of his split reins together and looped them over his arm.

"Here's the end of it," a man said in a low voice. "Them spools have got to be here someplace. Fetch up them kerosene cans." There were three riders, maybe four; it was hard to tell. That others were still busy up-fence, Doug was certain.

He lifted the muzzle of the saddlegun just enough so the slug would clear the men's heads, and squeezed off the shot.

His horse jerked back, almost throwing Doug to the ground. A couple of the raiders' horses squealed in panic. The wire stretched and sang as a horse hit the fence. Doug flinched at the sound. He heard the solid clank of a small kerosene can hitting the ground as some rider turned loose of everything and concentrated on staying in the saddle.

Doug moved so the men could not pinpoint him by the flash of the gun. For a moment or so there was confusion among the riders. Their horses danced excitedly, and Doug thought he heard a man hit the ground. Hoofs clattered as a horse broke in terror out across the prairie. One man afoot, Doug thought.

Somebody fired in Doug's direction, but it was a wild shot, more an angry gesture than an earnest attempt to hit him. The riders backed off.

He could hear men cutting the fence farther up. And there was a louder noise. The top strand of wire sang loudly. Staples sprang out of the posts.

"What're they doin' up there?" Milt asked worriedly.

"Tied on with a rope, I think. Trying to jerk down as much wire as they can in a hurry."

"Shouldn't we go stop 'em?"

"No," Doug replied, "we got to guard these stacks till the rest of the bunch gets here."

He fired again in the direction of the fence cutters. Someone shouted. He knew he was hitting close to home.

Then came the sharp rattle of gunfire farther up the fence. His own crew was coming now. They were shooting wild, trying to scare the raiders back from the fence. The guns moved nearer as the fencing crew strung out. Doug and Milt joined in, firing into the blackness until their gunbarrels were too hot to touch.

"Doug," a voice shouted, "where you at?" It was Dundee's.

"Here, at the corner."

He heard the roll of hoofbeats from across the fence. The raiders were retreating in hasty confusion. The wild, indiscriminate fire from the strong fencing crew was hard to face. There was no cover anywhere along the fenceline, no protection from the bullets that came whining by in the black.

The R Cross men were not gunfighters, and they were not getting gunfighter pay. They were drawing wages as cowboys, twenty-five to thirty-five dollars a month, depending on what they were worth for solid cow work, done a-horseback. No frills, no fancy stuff. They might be good men, top cowhands, but most of them probably had never been shot at in their lives, and they found this first time hard to take. So they were leaving.

It was the smart thing to do, Doug conceded. In their place, he would have done it himself.

Dundee came loping up. The fencing crew was strung out behind him. "We got 'em on the run," he shouted. "We could maybe catch up and give 'em somethin' to really remember us by."

"No," Doug said, "it's too dark. They'll remember us, all right."

Dundee was shaking with the excitement of a high-strung Thoroughbred horse which has just finished its race and still wants to run. For a moment he acted as if he'd go along anyway. "I say we ought to go after 'em!"

"No," Doug replied firmly, "if we push it any farther, somebody's liable to get killed. We ran them off, that's all I aimed to do."

Dundee accepted the decision with reluctance and shoved his gun back into the holster. "They've done us some damage. We oughtn't to just let it go like that. They get the idea we're an easy mark, they'll be slippin' back in here every night, cuttin' wire and makin' a nuisance."

"We're not just letting it go by," Doug told him, although he wasn't sure yet just what he was going to do about it.

Then Foley Blessingame brought him his answer. "Lookee here what me and the kids found," he said jubilantly. He pushed in close enough so Doug could see a man afoot at the end of a rope. "Feller lost his horse out yonder," Foley explained.

"Who are you?" Doug demanded.

The cowboy gave him a go-to-hell look.

Young Vern Wheeler came to see who it was. "Howdy, Shorty," he said. The R Cross man softened a little at the sight of Vern. "Howdy, Vern."

Vern said, "He's Shorty Willis. We worked together some while I was on the R Cross. Let's go easy on him. He's a pretty good feller."

"We don't aim to hurt him, Vern," Doug promised, "unless he gives us a reason to. Right now I'd just like to get a little information out of him."

"I got nothin' to tell you," Shorty said.

Doug glanced quizzically at Foley Blessingame. "Reckon he'd change his mind if you dunked him in that icy creek?"

Foley grinned. "You mean like we done that grouchy cook? I expect it'd loosen up his tongue a little. It sure made the cook talk."

The cowboy looked pleadingly at Vern

Wheeler. Vern said, "You better tell 'em what they want to know, Shorty. They'll make you talk sooner or later. You'd just as well do it now and save yourself a soaking. That's mighty cold water."

Shorty Willis shrugged. "I ain't paid to do no swimmin'. What do you want to know?"

"Who-all was on the raid, and how many?" Doug asked.

"Big part of the R Cross cowboys, all that Archer Spann could round up without havin' to drag 'em in from the line camps. He got some of Fuller Quinn's bunch in on it, too. Quinn's been itchin' to do somethin' about this fence, only he ain't had the nerve to try it by hisself."

"Were Quinn and Spann both out here?"

"Yep. Spann was givin' the orders, though. He allus does. It's a funny thing to me, Quinn bein' a ranch owner and all. When Spann's around, Quinn lets him give all the orders, and Spann don't even own a good horse, much less a ranch. Somethin' about him that naturally makes a man sit up and take notice, I reckon."

"What was his plan?"

"He figured on cuttin' and rippin' out all the wire you'd strung. We was goin' to burn all the posts and wire you had stacked up out here. Cripple you good, he said, and you'd quit."

Doug said, "It didn't get very far, though, did it?"

Willis shook his head. "The dark had us boogered some to begin with. Spann said there'd be nothin' to it, that you'd fold up like a wet rag. But it's a creepy feelin', movin' into somethin' like this and not bein' able to see what's ahead. You-all could've been settin' up an ambush for all we knew. And when the guns opened up and them slugs started whinin' around, it was too much. A few of the boys started pullin' back, and then all of us was scatterin' like a bunch of quail. Archer Spann was fit to tie, but he couldn't stop it."

The cowboy rubbed his hip. It evidently was sore. "One of them wild bullets got my horse. Spilled him right on top of me. I hollered for somebody to pick me up, but everybody was so excited I guess they didn't hear me. Nobody except" — he nodded his head at the Blessingames — "them big oxes there."

Foley Blessingame grinned. "I always taughts my boys to give a man his money's worth."

Doug asked Willis, "Were you going to meet again somewhere after the job was through?"

Willis nodded. "Spann didn't seem to have any doubt we'd do the job up right. He said if we got scattered to meet at the Lodd line camp. He left some whisky there and said when we got back ever'body could celebrate." Willis grimaced. "Some celebration!"

Vern said, "I thought it was against R Cross rules to have whisky on the place."

"What the old man don't find out about won't hurt him any." Willis shook his head. "Funny about Spann. Never touches a drop hisself. He's as straitlaced as the old man. But he'll buy it for somebody else if it suits his purpose, and that's somethin' the captain never would do."

It would be a different kind of a whisky party than Spann had anticipated, Doug figured. They'd be drinking to quiet their nerves and drown the ignominy of the rout.

"Let's mount up," Doug told the men. "We're going to drop over to that line camp and join the party."

14

The fencing crew sat their horses in a live oak motte above the line camp and looked down through darkness at the dim outline of a little frame house. This had been built as some small rancher's home, before the captain had bought him out. Or run him out.

"I don't hear any celebratin'," Stub Bailey commented dryly. "I thought they were really goin' to hang one on." There was no light in the window.

Doug Monahan smiled, but it was a grim one. "Wasn't much to celebrate. I imagine they tanked up and hit their soogans. How many horses down there in the corral, Dundee?"

Dundee had just come back from a short exploration afoot. "Ten, maybe twelve. I don't figure the men all stayed. Some of 'em likely just wanted to go home and hide their heads."

Doug nodded in satisfaction. Ten or twelve men would be all he wanted to try to handle anyway.

"Cold up here," he said evenly. "Let's go down where the fire is."

They moved down out of the motte and across the open stretch of tromped-out ground in front of the corrals. Doug's ears were keened for any noise down there which would indicate they had been seen. But he doubted there would be any. Whoever was in that house now would likely be too groggy to see or hear anything.

Nearing the house, he made a motion with his arm, and the men fanned out into a line. He could barely see the men on the ends, it was so dark. He stepped out of the saddle and motioned Dundee and Stub Bailey and Foley Blessingame to come with him. Vern Wheeler dismounted and held their horses. Doug drew his gun and moved carefully to the creaky front porch.

Quietly he pushed the door open and stepped inside, quick to get out of the doorway. Dundee and Bailey followed suit. Foley Blessingame was a little slow, standing there and blocking the door until Doug caught his arm and gave a gentle tug.

The place smelled like a distillery.

Doug gripped the gun tightly, listening

and watching for movement. Someone turned over and groaned beneath blankets on the wooden floor. Doug leveled the gun on him and held it there until the man began to snore.

His eyes adjusted to the darkness, and he made out a kitchen table in a far end of the room. On it sat a lamp. "Cover me," he whispered, and moved slowly toward the table, careful not to step on any of the sleeping men. Lifting the glass chimney, he struck a match on his boot and lighted the wick. He slipped the chimney back in place.

Someone halfway across the room rose up on one elbow and rubbed his eyes. "Put out that damned light," he said irritably, blinking. He stiffened then as it penetrated his brain that the man at the lamp didn't belong here.

The lamp was smoking. Gun in his right hand, Doug trimmed the wick with his left. "Just take it easy," he said. "Keep your hands where I can see them."

The light and the sound of the voices stirred some of the other men. But Doug's fencing crew was coming in the door. As each man woke up, his sleepy eyes beheld someone standing in front of him, holding a gun in his face.

"You boys just get up quiet and peaceful,"

Doug said evenly.

Dundee and Vern Wheeler made a round of the room, picking up guns wherever they found them.

It took a while for the full meaning to soak in on some of the men, and it wasn't hard to tell why. Several empty whisky bottles lay scattered about the room. One sat overturned on the table, a big stain around it where the whisky had spilled out unnoticed.

"Looks like you boys were having you a little party," Doug said. "Well, I kind of like parties myself. I got another one planned for you." He motioned with the gun. "Get your clothes on, all of you."

The men fumbled around, trying to pull on their clothes. Two cowboys got their boots mixed up, and each of them wound up wearing one of the other man's, along with one of his own.

To the one that looked the clearest-headed, Doug said, "Where's Archer Spann? Thought he'd be here with you."

The cowboy started to shake his head but stopped abruptly. It hurt. "He was so mad he didn't even stop. Just kept on ridin'."

Doug turned to Vern Wheeler. "They all R Cross?"

Vern nodded. "Most of them. Those four aren't. They're some of Fuller Quinn's bunch." He squinted, looking in a corner. "By George, that's Fuller Quinn himself."

It was indeed Fuller Quinn the range hog, the man who was always crowding his cattle onto somebody else's grass. He glared belligerently, his red-veined eyes glassy with drunkenness. He reminded Doug of Gordon Finch.

Doug had hoped for Archer Spann, but he would take Fuller Quinn as a substitute. He had always disliked range hogs. Today, Doug thought, he'd make Quinn put out sweat for the free pasturage he had stolen from Noah Wheeler in the past.

Dundee was poking around, looking over the R Cross guns. Suddenly he spoke up happily, "Well now, look what I found." He held up a .45 and rubbed his hand over it fondly. "Looks just exactly like one somebody took off of me that day the R Cross raided Monahan's fencin' camp. Same scratches, same feel. Even got the same initials carved on it."

His eyes sharply searched over the men. "Anybody claim it?"

Nobody answered. Nobody would have dared to. At length Dundee said, "Well, if it don't belong to anybody, I reckon I'll just keep it," and triumphantly shoved it into his waistband.

A remnant of warm coals still smouldered in the woodstove. Doug punched them up and put in a little kindling to rebuild the blaze. Slowly he fed dry mesquite into this until he had a good fire going. He set the coffee pot on, then turned to see what he could cook. He was hungry from the long, busy night, and he was sure the rest of the men were, too. Finding a side of bacon, he sliced it. He found a keg of sourdough and filled a big biscuit pan.

When breakfast was ready, he let the R Cross and Quinn men eat right along with his own crew. "You boys that were on those bottles so hard last night better take a little extra of this coffee," he said. "You got a catawampus of a day coming up."

A pink promise of dawn had begun to streak the eastern sky when he herded the men out of the house and made them saddle their horses. Made frisky by the chill, one bronc pitched out of the corral. Stub Bailey had to help the rider up off of the ground. Back across the dry prairie they rode, toward the Noah Wheeler place.

For some of them, it became torture. Two or three had to stop. Doug held up the ride until they finished being sick. Some of the rest were whitefaced and not far from the stopping point themselves, but Doug kept

538

pushing them.

For a long time Fuller Quinn could do little more than groan. He was halfway to the Wheeler place before he finally found his voice. "This is kidnappin'! I'll have you throwed in jail and left there till you rot!"

Doug said caustically, "Why, it's just the good old cow country institution of neighbor help. You came over and helped us last night, and now you're going to help us again today."

In the dark, Doug hadn't been able to see how bad the damage was. Now, riding up to it in the full light of morning, he felt the anger build again. They had wrecked about a mile of fence. In places the wire was pulled down but could be put up again. In others it was cut in so many places as to be useless.

"Made a pretty bad mess of it, didn't they?" Stub Bailey said.

Nodding grimly, Doug turned back to the sobered R Cross and Quinn cowboys. "You fellers can get down now and unsaddle. You're so good at cutting fence, we'll see how you are at patching it up again."

Vern Wheeler took the horses and turned them loose in the grain patch. Doug scattered the raiders, delegating his crew to supervise them. The first thing they had to do was pull down all the short pieces of cut wire for discard. The longer stretches that could be salvaged were spliced together.

By noon they had the splicing done and a good part of the wire restrung. Up and down the fenceline lay scattered pieces of wicked wire, cut too short to be worth anything. Left lying on the ground, they would always be a hazard to livestock.

Fuller Quinn groaned and complained, cursed and threatened all morning. So did a tall, sour-faced cowboy named Sparks, who was with him. After dinner Doug handed Quinn a shovel and Sparks a pick.

"You two are going to bury all that wasted wire. I want a hole four feet deep, big enough to take care of the job. Get after it."

Quinn swore and shook his fists, but in the end there was nothing for him to do but take the shovel and go. Doug left the rest of the men on the wire-stringing job. It was much easier, but most of them were suffering from the night before. They sweated and groaned, and occasionally one fell sick.

Doug no longer pushed them. When he saw a man who seemed to be getting too much of it, he called him out and had him sit down. These weren't bad men. Most of them were cowboys, men of his own kind. What they had done here was not so much out of malice as from the fact that they had been ordered to do it. True, they probably had not registered much objection. They might have enjoyed the idea of ripping out the fence, but they would not have attempted it except under orders. Doug doubted that they would enjoy it so much the next time.

By supper most of the damage was patched up. Even most of the R Cross cowboys seemed to take some interest as the job went along and they saw a good tight fence shaping under their own blistered hands. Once they gave up the idea of rebellion, they pitched in and worked hard. They labored and sweated the whisky out of their systems.

A while before sundown, Doug sent Vern after the men's horses. He signaled the men in. "That's enough. You've done more than I ever thought you would." He smiled now, for the anger was gone. Weariness lay heavy on his shoulders.

"Before you start back, Trudy Wheeler's got you a good hot supper fixed. I don't believe in working a man and not feeding him."

Some of the cowboys grinned. Fuller Quinn didn't. He was swelled up like a toad. So was Sparks, the tall rider who had helped him bury the wire. Doug had made them dig the hole big enough to bury an elephant in. He had made them throw all the wasted wire in the bottom and cover the hole up again.

The way Trudy Wheeler treated the men, a casual visitor would never have suspected that they had come to destroy. Like Monahan, she seemed to feel that they had served their sentence. She smiled and talked and saw that their plates were full. The cowboys watched her covertly, admiring her.

"Vern," said weary Shorty Willis, "if I'd knowed you had a sister like that, I'd've been over here workin' for your old man instead of over yonder with the captain."

After supper, Doug stood on the porch with Noah Wheeler and watched the cowboys ride away.

"Well," he said, "I don't expect I made any friends in that crowd. But Trudy did."

Tired, sleepy, Doug was glad the day was over. Another hour and he wouldn't have made it. All the way out to the barn, he thought of old Foley Blessingame, crowding sixty. This was hard enough on a young man. Pity touched him. The old man was probably already in his blankets, asleep.

Pushing the door open, Doug heard a loud voice. It was Foley's. The cedar-cutter had a small table pushed out in the middle of the dirt floor and sat there shuffling the cards. He was bright-eyed and rarin' to go.

"How about it, Bailey? You worked up the nerve yet to try me a game?"

Archer Spann stood in the back of the Twin Wells mercantile, watching distrustfully while storekeeper Oscar Tracey stacked the goods listed on the R Cross bill. He kept glancing at the duplicate list, making sure Tracey didn't cheat on the count. He never had, as far as Spann knew, but the foreman believed it didn't pay to trust anybody.

Up in the front of the cluttered store, a couple of women customers were stealing glances at Spann, and he knew they were whispering about him. He tightened his fist and tried to keep from looking at them. He had felt that whispering ever since he had been in town. More than that, he had sensed people laughing. They kept a solemn face when they were near him, but he could see the laughter hidden in their eyes.

It was the Wheeler fencing job that had done it. Never before had people laughed at Archer Spann. Some hadn't liked him — some had even hated him — but that hadn't bothered Spann. Let them hate him, for all he cared.

But not laugh at him.

First it had been that fiasco at Drinkman's Gap, and now it was the rout over on Wheeler's fenceline. Twice Archer Spann had tried to stop Doug Monahan, and each time the whole thing had blown up in his face. He didn't know what he would do next. But *this* he knew, next time it would have a different ending.

He felt needles pricking him as a man walked through the front door and closed it against the cold. Noah Wheeler!

For a moment Spann considered going out the back way so he wouldn't have to face Wheeler. He had developed a gnawing hatred for the old farmer. He didn't even want to look at him. But Spann knew that to walk out the back would be taken for a retreat. There had been too many retreats already.

Steeling himself, he shoved the duplicate supply list in his pocket and started to the front. He heard Wheeler say, "I got a list of goods here I need to take back to the farm today, Oscar."

Tracey replied, "Be with you directly, Noah."

Wheeler turned and Archer Spann walked toward him. The R Cross foreman stopped and glared at the farmer. He felt his hatred well up like something indigestible. Here was the real root of the trouble, he thought darkly. Monahan was the most obvious cause, but had it not been for Wheeler, Monahan would not have been able to stay. Even yet, were Wheeler to fold, Monahan could go no farther.

The captain could believe what he wanted to and say what he wanted to about Noah Wheeler, but to Archer Spann he was nothing but a plain dirt farmer too big for his britches.

Spann turned angrily on Oscar Tracey. "Oscar," he said, "the R Cross has bought a lot of supplies from you in the past. If you want to keep getting that trade, you better stop selling to its enemies."

To his surprise, Oscar Tracey never wavered. "It's your right, Mr. Spann, to buy from whoever you please. And it's mine to sell to whoever I please."

Spann rocked back on his heels. A month ago, there wasn't a man in town who would have said that. And Oscar Tracey, this thin, gray old storekeeper who looked ready to blow away if a strong wind hit him, was the last man Spann would ever have expected it from.

Spann stamped out the front door and into the raw chill of the open street. He stopped then and wondered where to go to kill time. He didn't drink because whisky too often got in a man's way, and he didn't like to idle in saloons where men sat around lazily instead of going out to hustle, to make money. There was nothing about this rough little prairie town that he liked. He had always hated it. He hated it even more now that he could feel its laughter.

Someday, he thought grimly, I'll be running the R Cross, and then I'll snub them up short of the post. There won't be any old man going soft and saying hold off. They'll do what *I* tell them, by God!

He half turned and glanced at the window of the store. Spann doubled his fist. Here Wheeler was, right in his grasp, and there wasn't a thing he could do about it. Captain Rinehart had tied his hands. If only . . .

Spann felt a sudden elation. Why hadn't he thought of it already? Sure, the captain had tied his hands, but he had no say-so over anybody else. Not over Fuller Quinn, for instance. And Spann had seen Quinn ride up to the Eagle Saloon down the street an hour ago.

Spann pushed the saloon door shut behind him and stood looking. He spotted Quinn slouched in a chair at a back table. With him was a tall, hook-nosed cowboy —

Sparks, his name was. They had emptied the better part of a bottle of whisky just since they had been sitting there.

The bartender stared in surprise at Archer Spann. The R Cross foreman was seldom seen in a place like this. "What could I get you, Mr. Spann?"

"Nothing," Spann said curtly. Then, because he was cold, he said, "If you got coffee, I'll take that."

He walked back to Quinn's table. Quinn looked up at him belligerently, for some harsh recriminations had passed between them after that affair out at Wheeler's place. Finally Quinn said, "Sit down, if it suits yuh."

Spann nodded toward the bottle. "Hitting that pretty hard, aren't you?"

"Don't see it's any of your business," Quinn responded sharply. As if in defiance, he looked Spann straight in the eye and poured his glass full again.

Spann could see that Quinn was already far gone. He got a look at the palm of the man's hand, lying slack on the table. It was blistered and sore. "That hand looks bad."

"Yours'd be too if you'd spent the whole day with Monahan's gun pokin' you in the face, and you workin' with a pick and shovel like me and Sparks done."

Sparks sat sullenly, feeding on some deep anger and paying little attention to anybody. The barman brought Spann's coffee. Spann sat and blew it awhile, then sipped it as he sized up Fuller Quinn. Quinn might just be mad enough and drunk enough to do it.

"Why don't you do something about it?" Spann asked.

"Like what?"

"Noah Wheeler's over at Tracey's mercantile. Was I you, I'd take it out of his hide."

Quinn glared suspiciously. "The R Cross got a worse dose of it than we got. Why don't *you* do it?"

"The captain says no. Seems he and Wheeler were friends once a long time ago, and he won't let me touch the old devil."

"And you want me to do it?"

Spann shrugged. "It don't make any difference to me. All I said was, you got a good chance, if you're a mind to."

Quinn took another long drink. His eyes watered, and he blinked hard to clear his sight. With one eye squinted almost shut, he rasped, "Tryin' to get somebody else to do the dirty work for yuh!"

Spann said, "It wasn't me that had to dig that hole and bury all that wire. If you got the guts to, you can give Wheeler what he deserves. If you're scared, you can let him go. It don't matter a damn to me."

Fuller Quinn straightened, his face getting redder. "I'm not scared of you or Wheeler or Monahan or anybody else, Spann! I'll do as I please, and you can go to hell for all I care!"

Spann forced himself to keep a tight rein. He had planted the seed, and maybe the whisky would germinate it. There would be plenty of time to make Fuller Quinn eat those words. Spann would not forget them. He stood up and shoved his chair back under the table.

"Take care of those hands, Fuller. I'll see you around."

After Spann's wagon was loaded, he stalled a while and watched for Noah Wheeler to leave the store. Wheeler's wagon rolled off down the street and out onto the trail that led toward his farm. Presently Fuller Quinn and Sparks swayed out of the saloon. With some difficulty they managed to get on their horses. Quinn pointed, and the two headed out in the same direction Noah Wheeler had taken.

Nodding in satisfaction, Spann said to the cowboy who had come with him to drive the team, "Roll 'em. I've seen all I want to."

It was dark when Sheriff Luke McKelvie

came in driving Noah Wheeler's wagon. Noah was slumped on the spring seat beside him, and McKelvie's horse was tied on behind. Men who had been sitting on the porch, eating supper, put their plates down and hurried out to the wagon.

"Easy with him," McKelvie cautioned as Doug Monahan reached for the old farmer. "He's pretty bad beat up."

Noah Wheeler's square face was swollen and bruised and angry red in places where rough knuckles had broken the skin. A white bandage was bound around his head. His clothes were dirt-streaked and torn.

"Easy, Noah," Doug breathed, "just relax and let your weight come on me."

Stub Bailey was helping him, and Foley Blessingame and a couple of the Blessingame boys. The others were crowding around anxiously, ready to make a grab if Wheeler should start to fall.

The commotion caught the attention of the two women in the house. They came running as Wheeler got his feet to the ground. The men moved aside for them. Mrs. Wheeler's face went white, and she swayed for just a moment. Then she was in complete control.

"Bring him into the house," she said. "Whatever's to be done, we can do it better in there."

Luke McKelvie climbed down from the wagon and followed them toward the porch. "Mostly what he needs now is rest, Mrs. Wheeler. The doctor said no bones are broke."

Noah Wheeler protested weakly that he was all right, but they carried him to his bed, pulled off his boots and laid him across it anyway.

Doug turned to the sheriff. "What happened?"

"He left town with the goods he bought at Stacey's. About a mile or so out, Fuller Quinn and that cowboy they call Sparks caught up with him. They were drunk and mad. They roped him off of the wagon and drug him around some, then beat him up."

Doug Monahan felt ice in his stomach.

The sheriff went on, "A kid was out hunting a stray horse and happened up on them. They cussed him out and rode off. The kid got him back up in the wagon and brought him to town."

Doug sat down heavily. He hadn't expected revenge to come this way, not against a helpless old man.

"It's my fault," he said dully. "They were mad at me because I drug them over here and made them work all day. They couldn't get to me, so they took it out on him."

McKelvie said, "It's a wonder they didn't kill him. Drunk like they were, and dragging him around on a rope, they could've done it easy enough, even if they didn't mean to."

Doug sat there dumbly, head bowed, cold chills running up and down his body as he considered what might have happened. He put his head in his hand while Mrs. Wheeler and Trudy got the torn clothes off of Noah Wheeler and pulled the covers up over him.

He only half heard McKelvie saying, "If you don't mind, I'll stay here tonight. Then I'll go over to Quinn's tomorrow and arrest him. He's going to pay for this."

Trudy was saying, "Of course, we'll be glad to put you up, Sheriff."

Suddenly Doug arose. "Noah," he said bluntly, "I'm going to quit!"

All activity stopped. Everybody turned to stare at him. "I'm going to quit," he repeated. "All this is my fault. I brought it on you. I kept telling myself it wouldn't happen this way, that we could protect you, but I know now we can't. We can't watch every minute, every day. I never would've thought they'd waylay you away from home like this, or I'd have sent somebody with you. If it happened once, it can happen again."

He had never seen Noah Wheeler actually angry before, but now he did. Lying in the bed, his face bruised and beaten, the old farmer said loudly, "Doug, I'm not going to let you quit. I was the one that wanted this fence."

Doug shook his head. "No, it was me. I wanted to build a fence somewhere — anywhere — and rub the captain's nose in it. Trudy was right, all I was interested in was revenge. I didn't consider the trouble I'd be getting other people in. I didn't let myself consider it."

Noah Wheeler said, "If you'll just remember, you didn't come to me about building that fence. I was the one that went to you. *I* suggested it, you didn't."

"But I knew what was bound to come. Deep down, I knew it, and I should've told you."

"Do you think I'm a fool, Doug? Don't you think I knew it, too? I did, and I thought about it a heap, and I was still willing to take the risk."

He motioned with his hand. "Doug, come here and sit down." Doug sat on the edge of the bed. Wheeler said, "I got to thinking about that fence the day the captain raided you. I commenced to seeing how much this country needed fences like that, the little

553

men especially. It was the only real hope they had of staying, of building something good. I'd thought I'd let some of the others start first, and I'd see how they looked. But the captain stopped them.

"I've always thought a lot of the captain. Away back yonder we . . . but that's another story, and I'll tell you someday. The point is, as much as I thought of the captain, I knew he was wrong. I knew that no man has got a right to stand in the middle of the road and block everybody else. Somebody had to stand up to the captain and show him that, and I figured it was up to me to be the one."

Monahan had always admired this forthright old farmer, but never so much as now. Wheeler had been thinking beyond his beloved Durham cows — old Roany and Sancho and the rest — and the crops in the fields. Those had been his avowed purposes, but he had been thinking way beyond them.

Trudy Wheeler said sternly, "I was opposed to that fence when it started, but now I'm going to stand by my father. If he wants that fence, he's going to get it. And if you try to ride away from here, Doug Monahan, I'll — I'll shoot you, that's what!"

The heavy weight of conscience lifted from Doug's shoulders. He managed a thin smile. "I reckon you can leave that shotgun in the corner. I'm not going anywhere."

Much relieved, he walked out onto the porch. It was dark now, and the first stars were beginning to wink. Luke McKelvie followed him out. The men of the fencing crew were standing around, waiting.

"Noah's all right," Doug told them. "About all they did was make him good and mad."

The men relaxed, but they still just stood there. Finally it was Stub Bailey who broke it up.

"Foley Blessingame," he said, "ever since you been here you been trying to get me into a poker game. All right then, tonight I'll take you on."

The rest of the crew followed along to watch. Doug shook his head sadly. "Stub's fixing to get himself trimmed," he told the sheriff.

They sat a while on the porch, smoking. Presently Doug said, "You remember one day, Sheriff, you told me there must be an awful emptiness in a man when all that matters to him is revenge?"

McKelvie nodded. Doug said, "You were right. It came home to me when you brought Noah in. I was ready to shuck the whole business. Revenge is a bitter thing when it's your friends who have to pay the price for it."

Young Vern Wheeler came out onto the porch behind them and stood leaning on a post, his face tight with anger.

Doug said, "I'm just glad it wasn't the R Cross that was responsible for this today."

McKelvie frowned and looked back at the boy. "I hate to tell you this, but you'll hear it anyway, sooner or later. Archer Spann was in the Eagle, talking to Quinn and Sparks a while before they went out and followed Noah. The whole town knows it now. They figure Spann egged them on."

Doug Monahan's jaw tightened. "What do *you* think, McKelvie?"

McKelvie took a long, worried drag at his cigarette. "I know Archer Spann. I reckon they're right."

Fury rippled in Vern Wheeler's face. "Archer Spann." Abruptly he said, "Doug, I've got to quit you."

Surprised, Doug said, "What're you going to do?"

"I can't tell you that."

"Vern, you're feeling mad. Don't let it make you do something rash."

"It's nothing rash. I've been thinking about it for quite a while. Only now I'm going to do it." Vern turned and walked back into the house.

When McKelvie was gone, Trudy came out onto the porch. "Let's go for a walk, Doug. I want to talk to you."

They walked along in the moonlight, out to the springhouse and down the creek. The cold began to touch them both. Trudy put her arm in Doug's and walked close beside him.

"Doug," she said, "I didn't mean all I said a while ago. I wouldn't have shot you."

He nodded, smiling. "I guess I wouldn't really have left, either. It would be hard for me to leave here anymore."

"Why?"

"Don't you know why, Trudy?"

He stopped and turned her to face him. She said nothing, but the look in her eyes told him she knew.

He said, "I didn't mean it to happen. I've told myself I couldn't afford to get interested in a woman until I had something of my own again, till I had something I could offer her. But these things happen to a man, and I guess there's nothing he can do about it."

She whispered, "Nothing at all." She tipped her chin up, and her fingers tightened on his arm.

Then he pulled her into his arms and

kissed her. . . .

When he walked into the barn, he heard the rattle of wooden matches on the small table. Stub Bailey had a big pile of them, and he was raking them in to count them. Stub held his mouth straight, but his eyes were laughing.

"Sure you won't try another hand, Foley?"

The whole crew stood around grinning. Old Foley Blessingame sat bleakly staring at the matches. Disbelief was in his red-bearded face. "What for? You done got it all."

Foley stood up, a shaken man, and walked out the door. He beckoned Doug to follow him. For a while Foley just stood there silently in the cold night air, trying to regain his wits. Finally he said:

"Doug, I know how much you like Stub Bailey, and it hurts me to say anything against a friend of yours. But you know what? I do believe that boy cheats!"

15

Captain Rinehart was angrier than Archer Spann had seen him in a long time. He paced the floor of his office, cursing as the captain was seldom heard to do, and through it all he laced the name of Fuller Quinn.

"That fool," Rinehart thundered, "that pig-headed fool! I'm sorry for the day I ever told him he could stay up there on Wagon-rim Creek."

He turned on Spann and Spann hoped the captain could not see the sweat breaking out in his face.

"You know what they're saying in town, Archer? They're saying the R Cross was responsible for it. They're saying you promoted it."

"They're after us now, Captain. They'll say anything."

"You were in town that morning. Did you see Quinn?"

"Yes, sir, I saw him. I tried to talk to him, but I found him drunk, and I left."

"You didn't say anything to him about Noah Wheeler?"

Spann felt the sweat trickle down his face. A little of it stung his eyes, but he dared not even blink while this fiery old man studied him so closely. "No, sir, I did not."

A worry was digging at him. He thought he knew Fuller Quinn. He thought Quinn would sull and say nothing. But he could be wrong, Quinn might start talking. What then? What if Quinn said Spann had browbeaten him into going after Wheeler?

Spann cared little what anyone else thought, but he had to keep the captain's confidence. It would be his word against Quinn's. He had always managed to make the captain believe him in the past. Could he do it again? For the first time, Spann was really beginning to worry.

Cautiously Spann asked, "What else do you hear, Captain? What're they doing out at Wheeler's?"

"They're going on with the fence."

Spann sagged a little. He had hoped the beating might stop the fencing project. He decided to take a gamble. "Captain, I'd like to say something. I know how you feel about Noah Wheeler, and I can understand why.

But maybe Quinn had the right idea, in a way."

He knew he was on thin ice by the way the captain's eyes narrowed. The old man's eyes seemed to be boring into Spann. "How so?" the captain demanded.

"Monahan won't scare, we've found that out. The only way to stop him will be to cripple or kill him. But if we can stop Wheeler, we don't have to worry about Monahan."

"Noah Wheeler doesn't scare, either. I've known that since the war days. I just told you he's going ahead with his fence."

"He'd stop quick enough if we hit him the way I've said all along. Burn him out. Run off his cattle. You don't kill a snake by cutting its tail off. One quick, hard thrust, right to the head. That's how we can stop this fence."

The captain turned away. He wasn't even considering it, Spann saw. "Look, Captain, that war was a long time ago. Things are different now. He's fighting you, and you don't owe him anything. He's not your friend anymore, he's made that as plain as he can. You let him by and you'd just as well take down the sign."

Captain Rinehart sat down with his brow furrowed. For a while he just sat there with his eyes closed and tugged at his gray beard, the way he always did when he was worrying out a dark problem.

Spann felt the warming of sudden encouragement. Maybe Rinehart was beginning to see it his way. Maybe now he would cut this rope that had kept one of Spann's hands tied behind his back.

But finally Rinehart shook his head. "Not yet, Archer, not yet. Maybe we'll have to do it in the end, but . . ." his face was thin-drawn and brooding ". . . I want to wait a little longer — see what's going to happen."

Impatience prodding him, Spann tromped down to the barn to see how Charley Globe was coming along with his horse. He wasn't worth much anymore except in shoeing a horse occasionally or in raking the yard. If it were up to Spann, he would have put Charley off the place. No use having an old relic like him hanging around long after his usefulness was done.

Charley was putting the last shoe on Spann's dun. He could tell somehow that Charley knew he'd had a hard conference with the captain.

"Well," Charley said, "what's the captain say? We going to run Noah Wheeler out the country?"

It was none of Charley's business, but

Spann said, "We decided to wait a while."

Charley snickered. "*We* did? I'd like to've heard that."

Spann felt color squeezing into his face.

Charley Globe said, "What'd he say about you eggin' that Fuller Quinn on to beat up a helpless old farmer?"

Spann's hand shot out and grabbed Globe's frazzled collar. He jerked Charley so hard that the old man dropped the hammer. "That's a lie!"

The old cowboy was shaken, but he wasn't scared. "If I was younger, Spann, I'd'a knocked you in the head with that hammer. But I'm old enough now to have better sense. I know you ain't worth it. I'll still be here when you're gone."

Spann let go of Globe's collar and stepped back. "You better shut up, Charley, or I'll forget how old you are."

Charley Globe leaned against Spann's dun horse. He was angry now. "You know, Spann, I've spent a lot of time tryin' to figure you out, and I reckon I got you pegged. By rights you ought to be a big man. You don't drink or gamble or waste time with the women, like most men do. You never make a mistake when it comes to cow work. There was a time I thought you ought to be as big a man someday as the captain is. But you never will, Spann, and you know why?

"You got a mean, selfish streak in you a mile wide, Spann. Inside you, you're rotten. You're tryin' to pattern yourself after the captain, but you'll never fit the cloth. There's nothin' big about you. Deep down you're little and greedy, like when you took that Wheeler boy's money. No, don't deny it. I know you done it, and most other people know it, too. You're little and greedy and mean."

Archer Spann stood stiffly, wondering why he took this. He could break this old man in two with his bare hands. But what was the use?

Angrily he replied, "You say I'm mean; well, maybe I am. I never had anything in my life I didn't fight for, even when I was a kid. Maybe you'd be mean too if you had a drunken bum of a father that beat you and made you work, then took what you earned and drank it up and left you with an empty belly. I lived for just one thing, and that was to get big enough to whip him. One night I did it. I beat him with my fists till he went down, and then I took a club to him. I found out later that I hadn't killed him, but I always wished I had.

"I swore I'd amount to something some-

564

day, and by God I will! I learned a long time ago that a man's got to watch out for himself, that nobody else cares. The captain's got no son to leave all this to. I'm taking the place of that son, Charley, and some day all this will be mine. It's a mean world, and you got to be mean to get anything out of it. No dirt farmer like Noah Wheeler and no grubby fence builder like Doug Monahan is ever going to stop me!"

Charley Globe said solemnly, "Then you got some fightin' to do, Spann. And you know somethin'? I don't think you'll make it. I think when the showdown comes and you're up agin the taw line, you'll fold. Alongside that meanness, you got a yellow streak in you, Spann. And some day the captain's goin' to see it."

Vern Wheeler slapped his coiled rope against his leather chaps and yelled hoarsely at the cattle strung out before him. Dust burned his eyes and grated at his throat. Far ahead of him he saw a tough, sun-darkened rider turn in the saddle and wave impatiently at him. He couldn't hear the words. The bawling of the cattle wiped away all other sound like the roar of springtime thunder. But Vern could see the whisker-fringed mouth, and he knew well enough what the man was shouting.

"Hurry up! Bring up them drags!"

It had been a fast, hard drive, risky as walking the edge of a sharp-hewn cliff, and there was plenty more of it ahead.

Young calves in the bunch had dropped back to the drags. They shambled along with heads down, tongues protruding.

"*Hyah,* babies!" Vern shouted at them, slapping his chaps. The sharp noise picked some of them up a moment or two, but not for long. They were hopelessly worn out.

The big rider spurred back in a long trot. He was a begrimed, bewhiskered man in a greasy black hat and filthy blue wool coat. "Button," he shouted in a coarse voice, "how many times I got to tell you? Let them calves drop out if they can't keep up."

"They'll starve back there," Vern protested.

"It's none of our lookout," the man said, and jerked his horse around again. "Keep them cattle moving."

Vern nodded angrily and pulled around a couple of limping baby calves. He knew what would happen to them without their mothers. They would dogie, and most of them would die. Those few which learned to rustle for themselves on the dry grass would be forever stunted by the ordeal.

Still, Vern knew the dusty, harsh-voiced old cow thief was right. They must keep moving, and moving fast, for these bawling cows bore the R Cross brand on their left hips, the R Cross swallowfork in their right ears. And they were still on R Cross range.

Restlessly Vern's eyes searched the skyline for sign of riders. He'd had a bad feeling about this thing ever since it had started. Rooster had agreed to help him take and sell enough cattle to make up the three hundred dollars he had coming. Vern had sworn he would buy his little piece of land and put up a fence around it and kill the first man who touched a hand to one strand of the wire.

But Rooster had brought three hardened old cow thieves along with him. And instead of taking a small bunch, they cut deep and greedily took out several hundred head. Now they were driving fast for the nearest boundary of the R Cross range, driving for the brush country that would swallow up this herd in a maze of mesquite and catclaw and whitebrush. Vern had wanted to pull out of it, but it had been too late.

The one called Bronc had drawn his six-shooter and leveled it carelessly at Vern's heart. "It's gonna take all five of us to push these cattle outa here. Don't you git any idees 'bout quittin' us, boy."

Rooster Preech was helping Vern bring up the drags. He worked his horse over beside Vern's. Dust lay like powder on his face. "Don't you pay much mind to Bronc. He talks mean, but he's a pretty good old boy."

Vern scowled. He knew better than that. The time he'd spent with Rooster's three outlaws had convinced him of one thing: there was mighty little good about any of them. They were greedy and dirty and coarse and mean. Not one of them had any inclination to try to make an honest living. Vern was convinced that any one of them, and Bronc especially, would shoot his own brother if there was a good profit in it.

Vern had known at the outset that he was making a mistake. He didn't belong here. It had looked like a good idea at first, but he wished now he had never hunted up Rooster, that he had never heard of Bronc and these other two.

Rooster said, "You're sure makin' a bust, Vern, not takin' but three hundred dollars. Your share of this bunch oughta be worth two or three times that much."

Stubbornly Vern shook his head. "The R Cross owes me three hundred dollars. That's all I set out to get, and it's all I'm going to take."

Rooster shrugged. "Suit yourself, it's just that much more for the rest of us. Sure beats diggin' postholes, don't it?"

Vern glanced sharply at Rooster. They'd been friends for years, but Vern could see that Rooster was getting to be just like these three cow thieves who rode swing and point. Though still a brash kid, he was talking like them, acting like them. He was picking up their cautious habits, their free and easy way of looking at the law and at the rights of other people. When the three old rustlers bragged of slick thefts and fast deals they had pulled in the past, Rooster had one or two of his own to tell about. Granted that they were mostly lies, there was enough of truth in them to prove one thing. Rooster belonged to the back-trail bunch now.

Vern could see now that it had been in the cards all the time. He hadn't recognized the signs because they had been boyhood friends, and he hadn't realized things would ever change. Rooster's mother was dead, and his father paid little attention to him.

Rooster had swept out saloons sometimes to get something to eat. A time or two he was caught taking money out of the drawer behind the bar, and the barkeep had peeled the hide off of him. Later, it was bigger things. Luke McKelvie had tried to talk to him, but by the time it came to that, Rooster had little use for anyone who wore a badge.

He had been left to his own devices. When at last he came to that big fork in the road, lacking any sound guidance, he took the wrong one. It was as simple as that. Watching him now, Vern doubted that there would ever be any turning back for Rooster. He had already gone too far down that road.

Now Vern Wheeler was on the same road, and he wondered what he would do if he found himself trapped on it, unable to turn back.

He was going to try hard not to be. When they finished this drive, he was going to take his three hundred dollars and run like a scared rabbit. Never again in his life would he lay a hand on an animal that didn't belong to him, not even if, as he had told himself over and over, he was only taking that which was due him anyway.

Once more Bronc came riding back. "You two think we got a tea party here? Spread out and drive these cattle, or I'll take and pistol-whip the both of you when we git where we're goin'."

Rooster jerked his horse away and started yelling at the cattle. Vern let a couple more tired calves drop out. He wondered how many had fallen back since they had started.

Thirty or forty. That many calves left to die or go dogied.

An old cow kept turning, bawling for one of the calves that had stayed behind. The calf tried hard to follow, but his tired, spindly legs barely carried him anymore. Twice Vern choused the cow back into the bunch. The third time she tried to break out, he made sure Bronc wasn't watching, and let her go.

One calf saved, anyway.

He looked back with a glow of self-satisfaction to see the cow smelling the calf in the worried way that only a cow can, and the tired calf butting his head against her bag, getting the milk that meant life to him.

Then it was that he saw the riders. Two of them broke out over a rise and hauled up, watching the cattle. Vern jerked his horse to a stop and sat frozen. They were so close to him that he could have hit them with a rock. He recognized them both. They were R Cross men he had worked with. And he knew they recognized him.

Bronc saw them, too. He came riding back fast, leaning down to pull a saddlegun out of its scabbard. The R Cross cowboys saw him coming. One of them started to pull away, but the other held his ground. Pulling out his six-shooter, he fired a long shot that kicked up dust thirty feet from Bronc. The cowboy swung the gun back on Vern. Vern sat stiffly, paralyzed with horror as he realized the cowboy was going to shoot him.

He saw the flame, and he felt the sudden jar that struck his shoulder with the weight of a sledge. It carried him halfway around and lifted him far out of the saddle. For a second or two he tried desperately to regain his balance. Then he saw the ground coming up. He hit it hard and tasted dirt.

He was only half conscious of his horse plunging in terror, his hoofs barely missing him, and he realized dully that he had somehow held onto the reins. He let go. The horse jerked free and ran.

In sudden terror the cattle in the drag turned back and ran, too. The clatter of their hoofs broke past Vern. He lay helpless, waiting to be trampled, and somehow he cared little if it happened. The wounded shoulder had him twisting in agony.

But he wasn't trampled. In a moment Rooster rode up, bringing Vern's horse. He jumped down and knelt beside Vern.

Somewhere over the rise, the shooting continued.

"You all right, boy?" Rooster asked. "Think you can ride?"

Clenching his teeth against the pain, Vern

said, "I don't know. . . ."

"You got to, boy. The fat's really in the fire now."

Rooster helped Vern to sit up. Vern's head reeled. He brought his right hand up to the left shoulder and felt the wound warm and sticky to the touch. The very bone seemed to be afire.

Vern fell over on his face and was sick. Rooster stuck by him, holding him. Presently Bronc and the other two outlaws came back over the rise.

"They got away," Bronc declared, cursing. "Hell of a help you two was." He jerked his head angrily toward the scattering cattle. "Git out there and git them cattle throwed together. We really got to push 'em now."

Rooster hesitated. "Vern's hit. He can't take no fast pace."

"Then he'll hafta stay here. He oughtn't to've got hisself shot."

When Rooster still held back, Bronc drew his gun. "I said move."

Rooster glanced apologetically at Vern. "Sorry, boy," he said, and mounted his horse.

For a while Vern sat there unable to move. The other riders drifted away from him and he was alone, sitting in a patch of brittle grass miles and miles from help. He looked up at his horse, which stood calmly now. If he could only get on him . . . But he knew he lacked the strength. He felt the blood still flowing slowly out between his fingers. Holding his handkerchief over the wound, he had gotten the blood clotted and stopped most of the flow. But a little of it still trickled, slowly draining the life and the hope from him.

He didn't know how long it was before Rooster came. His friend rode up in an easy lope, slowing down before he got there so he wouldn't cause Vern's horse to jerk away. Rooster jumped to the ground and looked back over his shoulder.

"Whether you think you can do it or not, boy, you got to get on that horse. Old Bronc'll be along lookin' for us directly, and we better not be here."

With Rooster's help, Vern managed to get into the saddle. He would have fallen off again if Rooster hadn't been there to hold him on.

Rooster said, "Bronc'll be back huntin' me soon's he finds out I slipped away. But there's a crick down yonder a ways, and plenty of brush. Maybe we can hide in there. He can't spend much time lookin'."

Rooster holding him, they rode to the creek. Rooster took time to dip up water in his hat and let Vern gulp it down. Then they made their way into a thick tangle of mesquite and catclaw. Vern stayed in the saddle, slumped low over the horn. Rooster stepped to the ground and kept watch. Presently he saw Bronc top out over the hill. Rooster drew the horses deeper into the brush and stood holding his hands over their noses so they wouldn't nicker to Bronc's horse. For a little while they could hear Bronc riding up and down the creek, cursing and calling Rooster's name. Bronc knew they were in there somewhere. Then, because of the urgency of moving the cattle, he gave up and disappeared out over the hill.

Rooster led the horses into the open. He took another look at Vern's wound. "You're fixin' to get in a bad way, boy, if we don't get you some help. Hang on, I'm takin' you home."

Painfully Vern shook his head. "No, not home, Rooster. I don't want to bring the R Cross down on them."

"You've probably done that anyhow. But have it the way you want it. I think I know another place we can go."

Vern nodded dully. "Let's get started, then."

16

Captain Andrew Rinehart stopped his gray horse in the thick dust left by the running cattle. Somewhere above him he could hear gunshots, and he knew his cowboys had run down the two thieves who had tried to break out over the hill. The third thief lay here on the ground, facedown, his fingers frozen with the last convulsive movement that had made them dig into the dry earth. A greasy black hat lay on the grass, and drying blood was edged out from under the blue wool coat.

A cowboy stood over him, gun in his hand. The cowboy's face was white, his hands a-tremble.

"Take it easy, Shorty," the captain said calmly. "It's always hard, the first time."

Shorty Willis tried twice and the third time managed to get his gun back into the holster. He licked his dry lips and wiped the cold sweat from his forehead onto his sleeve.

"It happened so fast," he said. "All of a sudden there he was shootin' at me, and I shot back. Just once."

"Don't let it start eating at you, Shorty, or you'll carry it with you a long time," the captain said. "Just remember this, he was a cow thief and he was trying to kill you. You did right."

The captain motioned with his chin. "Looks like he's got a real good gun, Shorty. It's yours by rights, if you want it."

Shorty drew back, shaking his head. He mounted his horse and turned away from the body which lay there in the dry grass.

The rest of the cowboys came riding over the hill. The captain nodded in satisfaction as he saw that they had the other two thieves with them, hands tied to the swells of their saddles. They were foolish, he thought, to have kept trying to get away with the cattle after being discovered. Too greedy to let go, apparently.

"Good work, Archer," the captain said to Archer Spann.

Spann explained, "They ran off down there a ways and decided to give up. That one yonder" — he indicated the dead man — "was the only tough one."

He looked speculatively at the pair. "There's a creek over that hill. And some cottonwood trees."

The captain said, "No, I think this time we'll take them in, Archer."

"You wouldn't have in the old days."

"The old days are gone," the captain replied. Then he was suddenly uncomfortable, for he realized that this was the same thing McKelvie had said to him, and Monahan.

"How about Vern Wheeler?" Spann demanded.

The captain frowned. He turned to one of the cowboys. "Mixon, are you sure it was the Wheeler kid?"

Mixon nodded confidently. "I was as close as from here to that bush yonder. It was him all right. And I winged him. I saw him fall. That redheaded Preech kid was along, too. There was five of them, and we only got three here."

The captain said, more to himself than to anyone, "I wonder where they could've gone."

"We all know where they went," Spann declared. "They hightailed it back to the Wheeler place. Don't you see it, Captain? All the time you've been thinking Noah Wheeler was your friend, he's been stealing from us. Why do you think he sent the kid over to work on the R Cross? It wasn't any case of a hungry nester butchering one stray steer. They were moving them out wholesale. No telling how many they got while that kid was at the north line camp."

The captain said, "Archer, Noah Wheeler wouldn't steal from me," but his voice was beginning to lack conviction.

Spann argued, "You're remembering how he used to be in the war, Captain. But that's been a long time ago, and men change. He's used your friendship and dealt you a bad hand all along. I've tried to tell you, and now you can see it for yourself."

The captain's head was bowed. He was tugging at his gray beard, and a tinge of red showed along his cheekbone. Spann could tell that he was wavering.

"Now," Spann said, "maybe you'll let us do what I've been trying to get you to do all along. We can put a stop to Noah Wheeler and that fence once and for all, if you'll just give me the go-ahead."

Rinehart still hesitated.

Spann said, "Captain, it's your choice, but you've got to make it now. It's either you or Wheeler. Which one is it going to be?"

Captain Rinehart closed his eyes a moment. Then he stiffened. He raised his chin, and he was the same iron-hard old soldier he had always been. He had made his decision.

"We'll do it your way, Archer."

Sarah Rinehart was horrified. She stood stiffly in the doorway, watching the captain strap his old cartridge belt around his waist and fill it with shiny brass cartridges that winked with the light.

"Andrew, you're making a terrible mistake!"

He never looked up at her. "The mistake I made was in waiting."

She folded her thin arms. A strength showed in her determined face that hadn't been there in a long time. "If it hadn't been for Noah Wheeler, you wouldn't be here today. He's been your friend. Are you forgetting that?"

"He's forgotten it, I haven't."

"Perhaps Mixon was right about the Wheeler boy. It doesn't prove that his father had anything to do with it."

"Everything adds up, Sarah." Impatience grew in his voice.

"Archer Spann has told you it does. To me, it doesn't. I don't believe it. I won't ever believe it unless I hear it from Noah Wheeler himself."

"You can stop arguing with me, Sarah.

My mind's made up."

There was ice in her voice. "Then so is mine, Andrew. You're making a mistake today that's going to wreck you. If I can't stop you, then I don't want to be here to see it."

Rinehart stopped and stared incredulously at her. "What do you mean?"

"This isn't the place it used to be, Andrew. Once it was a happy place, and I loved it. But it's changed. *You've* changed. And do you know when it started? When Archer Spann came. You think you run this ranch, Andrew, but you don't, not anymore. Spann does. He makes you think they're all your ideas, but he plants them and sees that they grow.

"He's ruining you, Andrew. In fighting Wheeler and those small men with their fence, you're riding a dead horse. If you raid Noah Wheeler, the whole world will fall in around you because you're wrong — dead wrong!

"I've thought a lot lately about leaving. I've thought I might go to Fort Worth, where I wouldn't have to hear about Archer Spann, and wouldn't have to watch you wreck the R Cross because of him."

The captain's voice was dull with shock. "Sarah, the trip would be too much for you.

You might never make it."

Firmly she said, "I can try. If you leave here today, I'll get Charley Globe to drive me to town. When I've rested up, I'll take the stage to Stringtown and catch the train. It's up to you, Andrew."

For a long time he stood there staring at her, not knowing whether to believe her or not. He could hear the thud of hoofs outside as the men gathered from the line camps. Spann had even sent for Fuller Quinn's men.

The captain motioned toward the window. "You see all that, Sarah? It's too late now for me to stop it, even if I wanted to. And I don't want to. We're going through with it."

Sarah Rinehart's lips tightened. For a moment her eyes misted, then she drew herself up and blinked them clear. "Very well, Andrew."

She stood stiffly, listening to him stamp out of the house. When he was gone, the stiffness went out of her. She sat wearily in her favorite rocking chair and listened to the sound of horses and men in the big yard below.

As the horsemen left, she called to the Mexican woman who cared for her. "Josefa," she said, "go see if Charley Globe went with them. If he didn't, tell him I want to see him."

Not far from the Wheeler place, Spann raised his hand and drew up. He turned and looked back over his men. Sixteen of them. It wasn't as many as he had figured on. He'd been sure of Fuller Quinn, and Quinn had let him down.

Scowling darkly, Quinn had said, "The first time you suckered me in, I spent all the next day with a shovel in my hands. The second time, they throwed my tail in the hoosegow. This time you can go to hell."

Nor was Quinn his only disappointment. Something was chewing on the captain. Spann had been able to see that ever since they had left the headquarters ranch. Something between the captain and his wife, Spann knew. The captain had been visibly shaken as he had walked out of the house.

Spann wondered why a strong man like the captain ever let a woman influence him as Sarah Rinehart did. That was the trouble with women, as Spann saw it. They were always interfering in man's business, trying to run things that were better left up to a man.

"Bodie," Spann said, "I want you to take four men and hit that fence. Don't get close enough to get hurt. Hunt out some cover and snipe at them. Draw them all away from the house and the barns. When it's clear there, the rest of us will charge down from the other end and set everything afire."

"What about the fence?" Bodie asked. "We'll never be able to touch it if we draw that bunch down on us."

"You won't have to. If we can stop Noah Wheeler — burn him out — we'll automatically stop the fence."

Bodie nodded, satisfied. Spann pulled a watch out of his pocket. "You got a watch?" he asked. When Bodie said yes, Spann told him, "Give us an hour to make a wide circle. Then go on in." He told off the four men who were to go with Bodie. "Don't get close enough to get hurt," he warned them again. "If you have to retreat some, fine. Main thing is to draw them away from the headquarters till we've had time to do our job."

He pulled away then, and his men started their circle.

They reached their point in a little less than an hour and drew up there to wait. Most of the men smoked quietly. They were nervous, and he could tell that some of them didn't like it.

Shorty Willis was the main one. "We're

makin' a mistake, Spann. Them's good people down there."

"If you don't want to go with us, Shorty, then ride out. But you're through in this country. You'll never get another job anywhere around here."

Shorty ignored Spann. He pulled his horse up beside the captain, who had been riding along silently on his big gray, his gaunt old face creased with worries of his own. "Captain, you know this is wrong. Even if Vern *was* helpin' steal them cattle, he mebbe thought he had a good reason."

The captain peered intently at Shorty. "What do you mean?"

"You've heard the story about that three hundred dollars, ain't you? Spann says it's a lie, but Vern told me about it that day Monahan had us fixin' the fence. He talked like a man tellin' the truth."

Spann felt a momentary surge of panic. The captain was listening to Shorty. Damn that boy and his three hundred dollars! They'd brought Spann nothing but trouble.

"Shorty," Spann blurted, "there's no truth in it! You're fired!"

The captain raised his hand. "I'll do the firing. Just what was it the Wheeler boy said?"

Shorty started telling it, and Spann felt

his mouth go dry. He could see that the captain was wavering. The old man didn't want to go through with this thing, that was apparent. Now he was looking desperately for some reason to call it off.

The shooting started. The crisp crackle of guns rolled in from the distance. Spann shouted, "Everybody in the saddle!"

The tension went out of him with a long sigh. Shorty Willis wouldn't get a chance to finish that story now. With luck, maybe he never would.

Spann put his horse up over the top of the hill, so he could see the farmhouse and the barn and the yard, the fields and the grazing cattle. The gunfire was coming clearer and sharper now. More guns had entered into it. His riders gathering around him, Spann watched two men spur away from the barn down below and lope out along the fenceline. He watched and saw no more activity at the house.

The captain said, "Archer, just a minute . . ."

He was going to call it off, Spann realized. "Let's go!" he shouted, and spurred down the hill.

Trudy Wheeler stood on the front porch, squinting her blue eyes and wishing she could see what was going on down there where the shooting was. Her father and one of the Blessingame boys had been at the barn repairing a wagon when the shooting started. Although still stiff and sore from the beating, Noah Wheeler had thrown a saddle on a horse and loped down to make a hand. That left no one here but Trudy and her mother.

Some new noise made her spin around. She saw the horsemen loping down the long slope toward the house. Instantly she comprehended the R Cross strategy.

"Mother," she cried, "they're raiding us!"

Mrs. Wheeler ran to the front door and looked out. For one short moment she stood with hands pressed against her paling cheeks. Then she shouted, "The shotgun. We've still got the shotgun in the house." She whirled and ran back for it. She brought it out, and with it a handful of shells.

Trudy took the gun from her hands. "Here. I always was the best shot."

Chickens flew away squawking, and ducks waddled hurriedly across the tankdam and out into the water as the riders reached the haystacks. They milled around, some of the men getting down. In a moment thin smoke began to curl. Red flames burst out of the stacks, and smoke suddenly swelled thick and gray.

Her heart drumming with excitement, her face heating with anger, Trudy had to fight against the temptation to run out and try to stop them. She knew it would be useless. She could not save the haystacks. She could not save the barn, if they decided to set it afire. All she could do was stay here and try to keep them away from the house.

Sure enough, the next move was the barn. Trudy spotted Archer Spann, and she leveled the shotgun at him. The heavy recoil jarred her shoulder. The range was too great for strong effect, but through the angry wreath of powder smoke she saw Spann's horse kick up. The well-spent pellets had stung him.

Spann rode his horse right through the open barn door, and a couple of men followed him. Hay was stacked inside the barn too. In a moment smoke was rolling out the door and squeezing between the red planks in the siding. From the barn, Spann pulled over to the nearby chicken house. Not even that was he going to spare.

A couple of Monahan's horses ran crazily about in a pen next to the barn, panicked by the fire and the choking smoke. One of the R Cross cowboys mercifully opened the gate and let them out. Spann raised his six-shooter and leveled it as they came by. He fired twice, and both horses went down, threshing.

Trudy felt rage swell helplessly within her, forcing hot tears to her eyes. She saw the R Cross cowboy who had opened the gate staring in disbelief. Then the cowboy shouted something at Spann and shook his fist. Spann paid him no heed. The R Cross foreman turned back to other pens where some of Noah Wheeler's good Durham cattle had been eating hay. He stopped at the fence and fired over it.

Trudy cried, "Oh, no, he's killing the cattle!"

Horror-stricken, she realized that she had seen her father's favorite, old Roany, walk into that pen with her half-Longhorn calf not twenty minutes ago.

Most of the R Cross cowboys had stopped and were watching Spann in shocked fascination. Turned loose to destroy at will, he was suddenly a man burning in fury, loosing all the pent-up hatred he had nursed for a world which had once treated him harshly, releasing that pressure of bitterness in an unreasoning spasm of destruction.

Old Roany made a break through the gate, her long-legged calf well in the lead. Spann was delayed a moment, reloading. Then he jerked his horse around and came spurring.

Trudy gripped the shotgun and jumped off the porch. She ran to meet Spann, screaming at him as she ran. He was paying little heed. She saw him level the six-shooter at the cow, and she pulled off a quick shot at him. She realized instantly that she had missed.

The thunder of the big gun brought Spann up short. Black with fury, he reined his horse at Trudy. She stood in the middle of the yard, struggling to get another shell into the shotgun. He leveled the pistol at her, but some remnant of reason made him lift it again. He spurred harder. In her haste Trudy got the shell jammed halfway in the chamber. She looked up, her eyes widening in alarm as she saw that Spann was going to run her down.

She tried to step aside, and the horse tried to miss her. But Spann held the animal with an iron hand and spurred him savagely. The horse's shoulder struck Trudy a blow that sent her spinning. Then the panicked horse was over her, trying desperately to miss her with his hoofs. But one foot struck Trudy in the small of the back. The breath gusted out of her. A blinding pain knifed through her. Another hoof struck her before Spann's horse got away.

She lay helpless, fighting for breath. A sickening darkness reached for her, trying to pull her down. She was conscious of Archer Spann stepping off beside her. She groped for the shotgun, got it in her hands.

Spann slapped her and grabbed the shotgun, smashing it on the ground. She tried to push to her knees, and he slapped her once more.

"Touch her again and I'll kill you, Spann!"

Spann jerked his head up in surprise. Shorty Willis stood in front of him, a gun in his hand and death in his eyes. Spann took a step forward, then stopped abruptly. He saw that Shorty meant it.

Cursing him, Spann whirled and remounted his horse. He took a few seconds to look around him. The haystacks were alive with fire. Smoke billowed from the blazing barn, flames licking up through the shingled roof. He swung his hand in an arc and shouted at the other R Cross men.

"Come on. There's more to be done!"

To his astonishment they all stared at him as if he were some wild animal. He shouted again, and they made no move. He looked around sharply and saw Shorty Willis kneeling beside the Wheeler girl.

Realization struck like a mule kicking him in the belly. They had rebelled. It had not been without warning. He could remember the hesitancy, the reluctance many of the men had shown. He could remember how some like Shorty Willis had tried to argue with him.

He cursed them, and they sat on their horses and stared at him. He jerked around and spurred toward the Wheeler house. From down the fenceline he could see dust rising. Monahan was coming with his crew. This had to be finished in a hurry.

Mrs. Wheeler was running across the yard toward her daughter. Spann jumped off his horse and ran into the house. Just inside the kitchen he spotted a kerosene lamp. He smashed it against the wall, splashing kerosene over the wallpaper and spilling it down onto the floor. He hurried into the next room, found another lamp and hurled it down. He struck a match, dropping it. As the flames crackled and spread, he retreated into the kitchen and tossed another match.

Outside the house again, Spann saw the dust moving closer. They would never make it in time now, he thought with a thrill of triumph. Try what they would, there would be nothing left here but ashes. Smoke drifted all around the place, panicking the horses, choking the men. Spann swung onto his head fighting mount. He saw the roan

Durham cow and her leggy calf, the ones he had tried to shoot when that crazy woman opened up on him with the shotgun. He loped after them, fired once and saw the cow go down. The calf was running like a jackrabbit. Spann started to follow, then decided to let it go.

He looked back. To his amazement, many of the R Cross men remained in the Wheeler yard. Some of them were running afoot toward the house.

He blinked hard, not believing what he saw. *They were going to put the fire out.*

He sat there numbly watching, realizing that the rebellion had been complete. Victory had been in his grasp, and suddenly his own men were snatching it out of his hands.

Soberness slowly came to him then. His heart still hammered from excitement. His mouth was so dry his tongue stuck to the roof of it. He watched most of the R Cross men start drifting back toward the hill where the captain had waited and watched the whole thing.

Spann turned and moved that way too. As he approached the men, he felt them watching. He looked, and he saw no loyalty in their eyes — only fear or contempt and, in some of them, hatred.

He glanced at the captain. For a fleeting

moment he saw bitter disillusionment and heartbreak in that gaunt old face. Then the captain turned away from him, his shoulders slumped. The captain touched spurs gently to his big horse and moved down the other side of the hill.

In that moment, Archer Spann knew he was done.

Trudy was not the only one needing a doctor. One of the fencing crew had been wounded in the skirmish with Bodie's decoy force. One of Bodie's men had taken a bullet in the leg and had been left there by the others. So Stub Bailey headed for town.

When the smoke had been cleared from the house, Monahan gently picked up Trudy and carried her in. He winced at the sharp odor of charred wood. He placed her on her bed and stood beside her, holding her hand, not knowing what else to do.

Shorty Willis of the R Cross had stayed with the girl. "I think she's got some broken ribs," he said quietly. "Spann ran his horse over her."

Mrs. Wheeler pointed to the door. "You men get on out of here. This is a woman's job."

Doug moved out of the room, Willis with him. He stood with hands shoved deep into his pockets. He stared blankly at the blackened wall. R Cross men had beaten out the flames before they could spread far or eat deeply. New wallpaper would hide the black. As to the floor, fresh paint and some kind of rug would cover the damage.

Noah Wheeler found old Roany lying on her side, kicking in agony, a bullet in her stomach.

He reached out to Dundee, and Dundee silently handed him a pistol. Wheeler raised it, held it a moment, then let it down, shaking his head. "Here, Dundee. You do it." He handed the pistol back.

Dundee waited until Wheeler had walked away. Noah Wheeler flinched at the shot.

In the house, Doug clenched his fists and blinked at the burning in his eyes. To Noah Wheeler he said, "I should've known it would come to this. I ought never to've started that fence."

Noah Wheeler rubbed his hand across his smoke-blackened face. "I told you before, Doug, it's not your fault. I wanted the fence. It's my fault this happened." His face was grave. "But it's not going to whip us. We'll build it back better than it ever was."

Shorty Willis said, "It's Spann's fault. It would've happened sooner or later, fence or no fence. Spann kept pushin' the captain. I think he believed the captain would leave the R Cross to him someday. He always did want to drive you farmers out, and he had his eye on some of the little cow outfits, too. The fence was just a startin' place. Gave him an excuse he hadn't had before. Then, when your son got caught with them R Cross cattle . . ."

Noah Wheeler's head jerked. "Vern? What cattle?"

Willis frowned. "You didn't know?" He stared at Noah Wheeler, satisfying himself that the old man really didn't know. Then he told it.

Noah was pale and shaken. "How bad was he wounded?"

Willis shook his head. "I wasn't there. All I know is, they said it knocked him outa the saddle."

Noah Wheeler stood up shakily and walked out of the house, head down. Willis looked after him worriedly. "Monahan, is there anything we can do for him?"

Doug said grimly, "Not unless you know where we can find that boy."

The doctor came just before dark. He stayed a long time in the room with Trudy. When he came out he said, "She'll be all right, but it'll take a while. She's got some cracked ribs and some very bad bruises. I don't think she'll stir out of that bed for a good many days."

Shorty Willis sighed in relief. "She's a brave little woman."

Doug Monahan walked into her room. Mrs. Wheeler smiled at him and left, closing the door behind her. Doug stood by Trudy's bed. Trudy raised her hand, and Doug took it.

"Doctor says you'll be all right, Trudy."

Pale, she nodded. Doug said, "I've been waiting outside there the whole time. I couldn't make myself leave the house."

Trudy smiled weakly. "I knew you were there, Doug, and I liked it. I want you to keep on staying there. I want to know that you're somewhere close around."

"I'll be around, Trudy, I promise you that. Only one thing. I'll be gone awhile tomorrow. But I'll get back as soon as I can."

He saw the worry cloud up in her eyes. "The R Cross?"

He nodded, and she said, "I wish you wouldn't. It was foolish, me running out after Spann that way. I don't want you to do something just as foolish because of me."

Doug didn't want to argue with her. He said simply, "I'll get back soon as I can." Impulsively he leaned over and kissed her. He started to straighten, but she reached up and caught him and pulled him down to her again. He felt the wetness of her tears against her cheek.

"Go then, if you have to," she whispered. "Only be careful, and come back to me."

17

Doug hadn't intended to take anyone with him, but the whole fencing crew was up in the darkness long before dawn. The fire in the barn had destroyed all their bedding and personal belongings, so they had slept on the floor in the house, the wood heater aglow to keep them warm.

"It's my fight," Doug had said with stubbornness.

"It's ours," Dundee replied solemnly. "No use arguin', we're goin' too."

Doug had given in reluctantly. "All right, you can go along to make sure it stays fair. But otherwise, keep out of it."

As he rode in the raw chill, his mind dwelt on Trudy. Again and again he pictured Spann forcing his horse to run over her. A throbbing anger built in him.

He had never been to the R Cross before, but he headed instinctively for the long L-shaped bunkhouse. Seeing no movement, he reined up and shouted. "Spann, come out here!" Steam rose from his lips in the frosty air as the words came.

He could hear movement in the building, a clinking of tin, a scuffle of boots.

"Spann, come on out here or I'll go in there and drag you out!"

An R Cross cowboy came out the door, a crooked grin on his face. He gave Monahan a careful appraisal, then said, "He'll be out directly."

Up at the big house on the slope, Captain Rinehart walked out onto his high front porch. Seeing the riders in front of the bunkhouse, he moved slowly down the steps and limped stiffly toward the stamping, nose-rolling horses. Other cowboys came out of the bunkhouse and stood in front of it, watching the door. Then came Archer Spann, moving slowly, his feet dragging a little. His clothes were rumpled. His face was haggard and unshaven, his eyes red from loss of sleep. Doug Monahan sensed that something had happened here yesterday after the raid, and that Spann had had a hard time of it.

He looked into Spann's sullen eyes, and his own rising anger came to the boiling point. He stepped out of the saddle and handed the reins to Dundee.

Spann demanded, "What do you want, Monahan?" His voice was hoarse.

"I've come to settle with you for what happened at Wheeler's. And I'm going to settle for Paco Sanchez, too."

"I shot the Mexican in self-defense, you know that."

"A court might have to accept that, but I don't. You just wanted to kill somebody. Paco gave you an excuse, and you did it."

Archer Spann's eyes glowed, but he said nothing.

Doug gritted, "It's not just a poor old Mexican with a pothook in his hand, or an old man on a wagon, or a girl standing out in the middle of an open yard. It's me, and I got a gun on my hip. I'm going to kill you with it, Spann."

The men along the bunkhouse wall began spreading out, giving room. The riders moved from behind Doug. Archer Spann stood watching Doug Monahan, his square jaw twitching.

Doug's voice cut like the popper on a bullwhip. "I'll give you a chance, Spann, a chance you never gave Paco Sanchez. You got a gun on. I'll give you first grab. Go on, reach!"

Spann just stood there.

Doug moved a step toward him. "Reach,

Spann. Damn you, reach!"

Spann's hand shook, but he made no move toward the gun.

"You're a coward, Spann. You're tough when you got somebody helpless, but now look at you, standing there shaking like a cur dog. Damn you, reach for that gun!"

Spann's hand inched downward, then jerked away as Doug's own hand darted. Doug stopped his gun halfway out of the holster. Spann would never draw. Doug swallowed the bitter gall of disappointment. In his rage he burned to cut Spann down. But he could see the fear curdling in Spann's reddened eyes. He knew he could not shoot the man in cold blood.

Doug closed the gap. He reached down and grabbed the gun out of Spann's holster. He hurled it away, then slapped Spann's face with the back of his hand as hard as he could swing.

"If you won't shoot it out with me, then I'll beat it out of your hide!"

His right fist came up and sent Spann flying back against the bunkhouse wall. For a moment Spann cowered there. Then his own bitterness and hatred welled up. He waded into Monahan, fists swinging.

They grappled there in the rising dust like two fury-driven stallions, swinging, driving, choking, rolling over and over in the dust and getting back to their feet and driving against one another again. Doug Monahan could taste the salty bite of blood on his lips, and his left eye was afire from an ugly cut above it. His knees were weakening. Each blow of his fists struck a bolt of pain through his bruised and bleeding knuckles. But none of it mattered now. Nothing mattered except this roaring anger that drove him.

For Archer Spann, it was a losing battle almost from the start. He had burned up much of his anger, much of his hatred, in the blazing raid on the Wheeler place yesterday, and there was little left for him to draw on. There had been little sleep for him last night, because he had felt the showdown coming, and he had known somehow that he was going to lose. He had lost the captain already, and the R Cross cowboys.

So Archer Spann fought, but dragging him down was the bitter knowledge that no matter what happened here, he had already lost.

At last Spann went down to stay, but Doug Monahan was not through with him. He dragged the man to his feet and struck him a smashing blow to the ribs. When Spann crashed to the ground, Doug grasped his collar and pulled him up again. This time he drove his fist into Spann's jaw. Spann rolled over against the bunkhouse and lay there in a crumpled heap.

Heaving, Doug took a step toward him and bent down to pull him up a third time. But Dundee gripped Doug's arm.

"That's enough, man! The next one might kill him, and you don't want that on your hands. You've made him pay."

Doug leaned with one hand against the bunkhouse for support. He fought for breath. Sweat rolled down his face, mixed with blood and dirt. His mouth was dry, and his tongue seemed swollen. His lips were puffed, bruised and broken. His hat was gone somewhere. He rubbed his sleeve over his forehead and his face and stood up straight, looking at the solemn faces of the men around him, his own fencing crew and the R Cross alike.

He saw Captain Rinehart standing at the edge of the group. The captain was looking down blankly upon his battered foreman, Archer Spann.

Doug tried once to speak but found his tongue too dry. The second time, he managed it. "Take a look at him now, Captain." His voice was weak, but it crackled with the last embers of his anger. "That's not just Spann lying there, it's you, too. After this, there won't anybody be afraid of you again. You're whipped."

There was no emotion in the captain's face. It was as if he already had been whipped, as if he no longer cared.

Doug Monahan heard the dull thud of hoofs. He turned stiffly and saw Sheriff Luke McKelvie riding up. The sheriff stepped to the ground, walked over to Spann, then glanced up worriedly at Doug.

"He's not dead, is he?"

Doug shook his head. "He's not dead. But he's finished." McKelvie breathed a long sigh of relief. "For a minute I was afraid . . ." He looked up at the R Cross men. "You better take him inside. He needs some attention, looks like."

Not one of them moved toward Spann. McKelvie nodded then, seeing how it was. Spann stirred a little, and McKelvie knelt beside him. "Archer, can you hear me?"

Spann nodded weakly.

McKelvie said, "I got a warrant here for you. But I'd rather have you out of the country than in my jail. Soon as you're able to get up, you saddle your horse and go. Don't stop anywhere in this county, and you'd be better off if you kept right on riding to New Mexico. I ever catch you here again, I'll lock you up. You hear me?"

Spann nodded again.

McKelvie turned away from him and toward the captain. "I'm sorry, Captain. I've got to put you under arrest."

The captain blinked. "What did you say, Luke?"

"I said I've got to put you under arrest. I've got the warrant here in my pocket."

The captain suddenly looked tired. His gaunt old face was drawn and haggard, and his eyes had lost their luster. Tonelessly he said, "I thought you were never going to fight me, Luke."

McKelvie answered solemnly, "It don't look like there's much fight left, does it, Captain?"

The captain slowly shook his head. "No, Luke, it surely doesn't."

Luke McKelvie placed his hand on the old man's shoulder. "I wish it didn't have to be this way, Captain. I tried to tell you, but . . ." He bit his lip. "Take all the time you want to tell Sarah. I'm not in any hurry."

The captain spoke almost in a whisper. "Sarah's not here. She's gone." He was a broken, spiritless old man. "I've got nothing to go to the house for. Have somebody saddle my horse, and I'll be ready to go."

■ ■ ■ ■

The Wheeler place was a sad sight to come home to. The outbuildings lay in ashes, charred timbers standing like the ribs of a skeleton. The haystacks that represented a year of work for Noah Wheeler were only piles of black dust, lifting and spreading and falling with each gust of dry wind. Here and there dead cattle lay with stiffened legs in the air. Fine Durhams they had been, Noah Wheeler's pride.

Doug Monahan looked upon these things and felt a sharp pain touch him, for this place had become home to him. But the anger and the hatred were gone now. They had worked out of him in the fight with Archer Spann. He was purged of them, and now there was only the cold sense of regret, the knowledge that it had all been without cause, without reason.

He was surprised at all the people he saw there. Two or three buggies and buckboards and a couple of wagons stood in front of the house. Several saddled horses stood hitched wherever their riders had found something to tie them to.

He realized these were neighbors and townspeople. Some wandered around, looking tight-lipped at the destruction. Several were piling up wreckage, clearing the littered ground. Two men with sleeves rolled up were making temporary repairs to a damaged corral so it would hold livestock. A couple were dragging dead cattle off to get them away from the house. Doug noticed that the two dead horses were gone.

He found the house half full of people, bustling about. Women were peeling charred paper from the wall. Two men were scraping black from the floor. The kitchen was crowded with food the visitors had brought. Women stood stolidly in Mrs. Wheeler's way and cooked while she protested vainly that she was perfectly able to do it for herself.

Banker Albert Brown sat in a corner with Noah Wheeler, figuring up what it was going to cost to rebuild everything. "Don't you worry about the financing, Noah. Folks aren't going to forget that you took the whipping for all of them."

Noah was only half listening, his mind miles away. At sight of Doug Monahan he stood up quickly. "Doug, did you see or hear anything of Vern?"

Reluctantly Doug shook his head. "I'm sorry, Noah."

He peeked in Trudy's room but found her asleep. Quietly he closed the door.

He looked at all the people, and he felt an uplift of spirit. It was real neighbor help, the kind he had known in South Texas. When a man faltered, his neighbors helped pull him to his feet. When one man faced trouble, his neighbors sided in and faced it with him.

Doug could see something more in this: a declaration of independence from the rule of the R Cross. In this show of respect and support for Noah Wheeler, they demonstrated that from here on out they would do as they pleased.

After a while Noah walked out of the house. Big Albert Brown came over and placed his hand on Doug's shoulder. "Would you like to listen to a proposition?"

Doug said, "If it's a good one."

"I'll let you decide that." The banker peered intently at Doug. "I like you, Monahan. I have, right from the first. Fact of the matter, I even went so far as to do some checking on you. Wrote a letter to the bank back where you came from. They said you're a good cowman."

"It's all my family has ever done."

"They said you'd be ranching yet except for drought and low prices both hitting you at the same time. That's a combination nobody can beat."

Doug shook his head. "I know *I* couldn't."

"Well, Gordon Finch left the country. Left his ranch and cattle and everything in our hands. Now, I may not be very smart, but I do know one thing, I need to stick to banking. I'm no cowman. I've been wanting to find somebody who could take over that Finch outfit and get us our money back out of it. Then it would be his, and he could do anything with it that he was big enough to."

Doug's breath left him. "You're offering it to me?"

"You come by the bank and look over the books. See what you'll be up against. Then, if you want it, it's yours."

Trudy waked up. Doug found her sitting up in bed. Her eyes widened in dismay at sight of his battered face. "Doug, you're hurt."

He shook his head. "No, I feel fine, Trudy. After all this, I feel fine."

"What happened over there, Doug?"

Solemnly he said, "I'll tell you sometime. Not now. But I can promise you this, it's over. The R Cross won't fight you again."

She reached out and took his hand. "I'm glad. I only wish now we knew what happened to Vern. He could be dead somewhere, for all we know. We don't even know where to start looking."

Doug touched his hand to her cheek and wiped away a tear that started there. "Maybe something will turn up, Trudy."

It did. Chris Hadley, the saloonkeeper, rode up to the Wheeler place and dismounted. Walking inside, he signaled Noah Wheeler and Doug with a quick jerk of his balding head. "May I see you, right now? It's important."

The three of them walked away from the house, out toward the grim pile of ashes that had been Noah Wheeler's barn. Hadley said, "Noah, it's your son. He's hurt, and my daughter's gone to him. I think you'll want to go, too."

Wheeler caught Chris Hadley's hand. "Is he . . . how bad is he hurt?"

"He'll live. Badly wounded, though. That wild, redheaded Preech boy came to my house after midnight. He'd taken Vern to an old deserted shack a couple of miles from town. He was afraid to fetch the doctor, so he came to get Paula.

"I'm a pretty good gunshot man. In my trade, I've treated quite a few. We got your boy fixed up all right. I left Paula and Preech with him and came on out here."

He paused, frowning. "The boy's badly disturbed, Noah. He doesn't know whether he ought to run or give up. I think you'd

611

better go to him."

Noah Wheeler was already on his way to catch a horse. He stopped and turned. "Doug, I know you're tired, but I'd like to have you go with me."

Doug wondered how he could make another long ride without sleep, but he said, "Sure, Noah."

As they rode, Chris Hadley told them, "I tried every way I knew to break it up. I told Paula I'd rather be dead than see her go through the kind of life her mother had. I even threatened to send her off to school. But watching her out there, helping take care of that boy, I could tell I was barking into the wind. You can't live your kids' lives for them. They're in love with each other, and there's nothing I can do about it. I'm not going to fight it anymore."

Rooster Preech sat on the front step of the shack, whittling on an old weathered piece of pine. He stood up, dropped his hand to his gun and kept it there until he recognized the men.

"He's inside yonder," Rooster said nervously.

The shack was an old one some small rancher had built and hadn't managed to stay in. The country had whipped him, as it whipped many of those who tried to fight it instead of taking it for what it was and learning to live with it. Now the shack was leaning, its windows broken out. But it stood, and it broke the cold wind.

Noah Wheeler pushed open the front door, which dragged heavily on the buckling pine floor. His son lay on a blanket-covered cot in the corner. Paula Hadley sat on the cot beside him, holding his hand.

An old wood heater was glowing. Doug thought it was a wonder that its rusting chimney hadn't set the shack afire.

Noah Wheeler stood just inside the door a long moment, looking across the little room. He took three long strides then and knelt by Vern. He placed his big hand on the youngster's arm, and his shoulders began to heave.

About that time something got in Doug's eyes — out of that leaky flue, he thought — and he walked outside for fresh air and a long smoke. But he could hear Vern Wheeler's voice.

"Dad," Vern was saying. "Paula and I have talked it out. There's just one thing we can figure. I'm going to Sheriff McKelvie and give myself up. I don't want to run. If I start it now, I'll be running the rest of my life, and Paula with me. Whatever it is I have to do, I want to do it now and get it over with, so we can have a chance."

Doug glanced in the door. He could see the pretty girl still sitting there, keeping Vern's hand clasped tightly in her own, her soft brown eyes never leaving the young man's face.

Noah Wheeler was nodding gravely. "I'm glad, Son. It's the right thing. Sure, I know it's going to be hard. Time seems mighty precious when you're young, and you hate to give any of it up. But it's the right thing."

Rooster Preech was whittling faster, his freckled face twisting with the run of his thoughts. When Noah Wheeler came out, Rooster looked up at him and Doug.

"You fellers fixin' to go pretty soon?"

Noah nodded. "I expect. It's not too far to town, and I think Vern can make the ride."

Rooster was having a hard time gathering up the words. Nervously he gouged holes in the gray pine siding with the sharp point of his knife. "I know it's the right thing for Vern, but with me it's different. I was wonderin' if you fellers would mind too much me jest saddlin' up and ridin' off. I might get me a few hours' start on the sheriff. That'd be all I need."

Doug thought he could understand. He

judged this Rooster Preech to be the kind who would always be in trouble. Likely they'd give him a tougher sentence than Vern Wheeler would get. No matter whether he rode away now or not, he would probably soon be in somebody's jail, somewhere.

Noah Wheeler said, "You're free to do what you want to, Rooster. I just want you to know we appreciate what you did for Vern."

Rooster shrugged. "No more than he would've done for me, and mebbe not near as much. I better step in and say good-bye to him, then. I don't expect I'll ever be back around here ag'in."

And in a few minutes Rooster Preech was gone with a jingle of spurs, a smiling flash of teeth and the wave of a greasy hat above his tangled red hair.

18

Captain Andrew Rinehart sat in the tiny six-by-six cell, staring miserably at the rock wall just as he had stared ever since he had been brought in here. Seated in a cell next to the one occupied by the two cattle rustlers he himself had sent in, he hadn't spoken a word and had hardly moved.

Sheriff Luke McKelvie watched him covertly from his chair at the roll-top desk. What he saw in the captain's desolate face was what he had seen in the eyes of a wild horse that had been caught and thrown and tied, a captive thing waiting with broken heart for death to bring once again the freedom it had lost.

McKelvie stood up and paced restlessly across the floor, pausing to look out the door. He turned away from it, and couldn't remember a thing he had seen out there.

"Captain," he said, and his voice almost pleaded, "isn't there something I can bring you — coffee maybe, or something to eat?"

The captain slowly shook his head, not even looking up. "Nothing, Luke, thank you." McKelvie could hardly hear the voice.

McKelvie said, "If it's cold in there, Captain, you can come out here by the stove."

The captain gave no sign that he had heard. McKelvie turned away, a tightness in his throat.

"Captain," he said, "I'd give anything in the world if —"

He broke off. Blinking rapidly, he looked down at the star pinned to his vest. He studied it awhile. Then, abruptly, he unpinned it and hurled it to the floor.

The captain looked up at him then, and his voice was firm. "Put it back on, Luke."

Luke McKelvie shook his head. "Captain, I've done some hard jobs in my time, but this . . ."

"Put it on, Luke. There's not another man in the county can wear it half as well as you."

McKelvie stared unbelievingly. "How can you say that, after what I've done to you?"

Rinehart shook his head. His voice was soft again. "I did this to myself, Luke."

"Archer Spann was the one who brought it on."

"I didn't have to listen to him, Luke —

but I listened. I knew almost from the first that I was wrong about Noah Wheeler. But I'd been mad there for a little while, and I'd told Archer yes. Then I had too much pride to back down. Pride's a treacherous thing. It can be the making of a man, or the breaking of him.

"I guess the main trouble was that I'd lost confidence in myself. You don't know how hard it is to find yourself an old man and lose confidence. You find people aren't listening to you anymore. You can't do the things you used to do, you can't ride like in the old days, you can't even see good. Things you do turn out wrong, and you get to wondering if you ever can do anything right again.

"That's the way it was with me, Luke. Then Archer Spann came along. He was a real hand, never made a mistake. I'd look at him and I'd see myself the way I used to be. I got to leaning on him, letting him make up my mind for me. I guess you could say I was letting him be the captain."

McKelvie said, "Archer Spann never saw the day he was fit to wipe the dust off your boots."

"I shut my eyes to the bad things till it was too late. You tried to tell me, and so did Sarah. But I wouldn't listen because when you spoke against Archer Spann, it was like you were speaking against me."

The captain went silent for a time then. Presently he said, "Luke, there *is* a favor I'd ask of you."

"Anything you want."

"I wish you'd find out if Sarah is still in town. I wish you'd tell her I'd like to see her."

"I'll go after her, Captain."

A woman's voice spoke from the doorway. "Never mind, Luke. I'm here."

Sarah Rinehart walked slowly toward the cell. Luke McKelvie hurried to help her, but she waved him away. She was a tired old woman, but she had the Rinehart pride. "I'm all right." The sheriff stepped to the cell and swung the door open. It never had been locked. Sarah walked inside, and McKelvie dragged a couple of chairs up close to the stove.

"Out here," he said gently. "That cell is no place for a lady."

The captain said, "Hello, Sarah," then dropped his head and stared at the floor. Sarah Rinehart took his hands and led him out of the cell, to the chairs McKelvie had set up. "It's all right, Andrew. I know what you want to say."

"I was wrong, Sarah."

"And so was I, Andrew. I should have known I could never leave here. I never got farther than the hotel. Then I was ready to go back to the ranch where I belong. When this is over, we'll go back together. We'll pick up whatever is left and make it good."

"What can we do, Sarah?" the captain asked miserably. "We're old. Time has gone off and left us."

"Time never goes off and leaves anyone," she replied evenly, "unless he is standing still."

Sight of the captain sitting in the tiny cell, a helpless, bewildered old man, brought tears to the eyes of Noah Wheeler. The big farmer motioned Luke McKelvie to one side.

"Luke, that's no place for a man like the captain."

Luke McKelvie looked surprised. "Noah, you know why it has to be. You're the one who's suffered."

Noah Wheeler shook his head. "Sure, he's made a mistake, Luke, but look at all the big things he's done, too. The country still owes him too much to let him sit here in jail."

Doug Monahan stared at Noah Wheeler, wondering how the old farmer could so readily forgive. But then he looked at

Captain Rinehart, and he thought he could understand. He had never believed the captain could be shattered like this, so thoroughly humbled. Looking at him, Doug realized that he no longer hated the captain, either. All the anger, all the bitterness somehow had drained out of him, and now he felt only pity.

Noah Wheeler pleaded, "Let him go, Luke. For me, let him go."

McKelvie's eyes were grateful. "I reckon if that's the way you feel, Noah, there's no use me holding him. If you won't press charges, there's not much case."

"No charges, Luke."

McKelvie walked across the room and opened the cell door. "You hear that, Captain? Noah won't prosecute. You're free to go."

The captain arose stiffly, hardly believing. Noah Wheeler moved forward, meeting him halfway, his hand outstretched. "We used to be friends, Andrew. As far as I'm concerned, we never stopped."

The captain took Noah Wheeler's hand, but he made no reply. He couldn't.

The front door opened. A breath of chill wind came with the shadow that fell across the room. Luke McKelvie stared in surprise at the pale young man with the bandaged shoulder, and the girl who stood beside him.

"I've come to give myself up," Vern said. "For stealing Captain Rinehart's cattle."

The captain swallowed hard, studying the boy and looking at Noah Wheeler. "Son," he said, "I've lost no cattle."

Vern replied, "You would have, if we'd got away with it."

Luke McKelvie put in, "Why did you do it, Vern?"

"To get my three hundred dollars, the money the R Cross owed me."

McKelvie said, "It was Spann that took your money."

The captain frowned. "What were you going to do with the money, Vern, your three hundred dollars?"

"Buy some land with it. A start for me and Paula."

The captain nodded. "I started like you once, and I didn't have three hundred dollars. The R Cross will pay you what it owes you. As for cow theft, I don't know what you're talking about. There weren't but three cow thieves. Two of them are in that cell yonder, and the other is dead."

After that, there wasn't much to be said. They all stood around looking at each other. Paula Hadley was crying into a handkerchief, and Doug Monahan was afraid someone else was going to start.

Luke McKelvie said with studied curtness, "Well, if we got all our business attended to, I wish you-all would clear out of here and let me get my paperwork done. I'm a week behind on the mail."

As they went out, Doug heard the captain say, "Noah, you remember that old marching song we used to sing, 'The Old Gray Mare Came Tearing Out of the Wilderness'?"

Noah nodded, smiling. The captain said, "I've fogotten some of the words. I'd like you to freshen up my memory on them sometime."

"I'd be tickled, Andrew."

Doug Monahan held back as the others left. "McKelvie, I want to apologize for the things I've thought and said about you. You're a pretty good Indian."

McKelvie passed it off with a shrug of his shoulders. "I still don't like your infernal bobwire fences, but I reckon they're here to stay. You're apt to have enough fence-building now to keep you busy a long time. I expect even the captain will come to it by and by, in self-defense."

Monahan nodded. "It's no life's work, Sheriff, but it's a living. Maybe it'll put me back on my feet and into the cow business again."

McKelvie said pointedly, "This is as good a cow country as you're ever apt to find."

Monahan said, "That's the way I see it, Sheriff."

Noah Wheeler got back to the farm long before Monahan did. Doug rode up and found a lot of neighbors still milling around, cleaning up the debris. One of the Oak Creek farmers had even brought a milk cow, a hungry calf trotting along behind her, grabbing a drop or two of milk every time the cow stopped for a moment.

Doug found Trudy sitting up in a big rocking chair in the front room. Her face was swollen, and it had several spots bruised blue. But some of the healthy color had returned. Doug took her chin in his hand.

"How you feeling?"

"Better. How about you?"

"I'm fixing to get me a blanket and crawl up in that corner yonder and sleep for a week."

Trudy said, "Dad's already given us all the good news."

Doug smiled. "Maybe not all of it." He reached in his coat pocket and withdrew a bundle of papers. "I stopped by the bank and had a long talk with Albert Brown about the Gordon Finch place. It's not the Finch place anymore."

Trudy's eyes widened. "You mean you . . ."

Doug nodded, grinning. "I'm going to have to build many a mile of fence to help pay for it, but it's mine." He gripped her hand. "Or it can be *ours,* Trudy, if you'll have it that way."

"Ours." She tested the word fondly. She reached up and caught his chin and pulled him down to kiss her.

"Yes, Doug, I think I'd like that a lot."

ABOUT THE AUTHOR

Elmer Kelton (1926–2009) was the seven-time Spur Award-winning author of more than forty novels, including *The Way of the Coyote* and *The Smiling Country,* and the recipient of the Owen Wister Lifetime Achievement award. In addition to his novels, Kelton worked as an agricultural journalist for forty-two years, and served in the infantry in World War II. He passed away in 2009.